BONE RATTLE

Also by Marc Cameron

The Arliss Cutter Series
COLD SNAP
(on sale May 2022!)
STONE CROSS
OPEN CARRY

The Jericho Quinn Series
ACTIVE MEASURES
THE TRIPLE FRONTIER
DEAD DROP
FIELD OF FIRE
BRUTE FORCE
DAY ZERO
TIME OF ATTACK
STATE OF EMERGENCY
ACT OF TERROR
NATIONAL SECURITY

The Jack Ryan Series
TOM CLANCY: POWER AND EMPIRE
TOM CLANCY: OATH OF OFFICE
TOM CLANCY: CODE OF HONOR
TOM CLANCY: SHADOW OF A DRAGON
TOM CLANCY: CHAIN OF COMMAND

BONE RATTLE

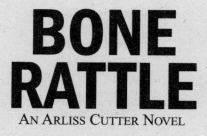

An Arliss Cutter Novel

MARC CAMERON

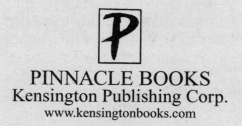

PINNACLE BOOKS
Kensington Publishing Corp.
www.kensingtonbooks.com

PINNACLE BOOKS are published by

Kensington Publishing Corp.
119 West 40th Street
New York, NY 10018

ISBN: 978-0-7860-4763-5

First Kensington hardcover printing: May 2021
First Pinnacle paperback printing: April 2022

10 9 8 7 6 5 4 3 2 1

Printed in the United States of America

Electronic edition:

ISBN: 978-0-7860-4765-9 (e-book)

To my brothers and sisters of the
United States Marshals Service
America's Star

Koa aere a rauuru te noo nei a mata.
Only the drones are left. The warriors have gone to work.
—COOK ISLAND MAORI PROVERB

PROLOGUE

Alaska

A single bone—or even a bone shard—wouldn't just slow work down. It would stop everything.

Dead.

The snort and belch of the backhoe rattling along the mountain made Merculief feel less isolated than he actually was.

There were thirty-seven men working at this mine, including the guy driving the backhoe and the laborer leaning on a shovel next to Merculief. That was way too many witnesses for anything sketchy to happen—other than having to endure a few elbows and junior-high-level taunts in the chow trailer. They wouldn't have hired him if they didn't want him around. Would they?

Merculief turned up the volume on his phone, letting "No One Knows" by Queens of the Stone Age pour through his earbuds. He tried to forget about the hatred, reminded himself that he could be working in an office, and kept his eyes peeled for bones.

Remote didn't begin to describe the Valkyrie mine. He

wasn't just at the end of some dirt road or at the top of a mountain.

Roughly thirty miles south of Juneau by boat, the excavation pro ject leading to the mine adit known as Valkyrie #3 cut along the side of the mossy-green mountain, tucked deep in a glacial valley inside Port Snettisham, a T-shaped inlet of pristine waters off Stephens Passage.

Everything here looked near vertical to Merculief, or at the very least, too steep for a road. But there had been a road, once upon a time, back in the glory days after Auke Chief Kowee guided Joe Juneau and Richard Harris to gold at Quartz Gulch. Avalanche chutes had washed a good portion of it away. Berry bushes bristled between the remaining timbers, hidden beneath the muck. The narrow ledge was rarely much wider than the backhoe tracks at any point, and much of that had been sheared off by heavy snow. Persistent rain turned the rock and freshly dug earth into soup, forcing the Native archeologist and the skinny laborer slouching next to him to be constantly on the move or risk sliding down the hillside into the raging creek that rushed along the valley floor. The mountain on the far side of the narrow valley rose steeply, absent the ugly excavation scar. Snow-fields still perched higher up, shielded from the rays of the sun by the perpetual shadow of steep angles. Towering cedar and spruce, jagged boulders—it all felt close enough to touch.

Rain pattered on the hood of Merculief's Helly Hansen jacket. He would have heard the *pop, pop, pop* of the droplets but for Queens of the Stone Age blaring in his earbuds. A steady wind blew down from the icefields above, making the raindrops sting his face if he looked in the wrong direction. Alaskans knew that cotton killed in the cold and damp. Merculief preferred layered wool and a waterproof rain suit. Southeast weather scoffed at "water resistant." An oilcloth ball cap and tall rubber XTRATUF boots—often called "Juneau sneakers"—kept him relatively dry during the long hours he spent standing over the dig.

The big 953 Caterpillar track crawler belched and clanked, working steadily along the mountain. Its massive steel bucket swung back and forth overhead, chewing steadily through blueberry brush, moss, and a layer of deep brown earth. Almost black with age and tannin from the surrounding vegetation, a series of logs were arranged side by side on the ground, close together, like the walls of an old fort that had fallen over.

It was sad, in a way, to see the old corduroy road torn up. A piece of history—gone. But it was not a piece of that history Merculief was paid to care about. He breathed in the chilly, ionized scent of wet dirt and decaying wood. The rough-cut logs had been laid down over a century before, during the heyday of gold mining in the region. They formed a road to keep the wagons and ore carts out of the ever-present muck. Had there been no old road, the bosses would never have gotten the permits to build a new one. The Tongass National Forest was designated roadless. Period. Fortunately for old man Grimsson, the Valkyrie's owner, he'd located this easement to the old mine adit. That meant he wasn't building a new road. He was merely improving one that had been constructed in 1904 to carry ore out of the mine a half mile farther up the valley. Those miners had tunneled in two hundred yards and quit, not knowing they were a scant eleven feet from a rich vein of gold bearing quartz. Harold Grimsson had found it, and now he wanted to punch a hole through to the vein—but first he had to rebuild the road.

Core samples projected an ounce of gold for every six barrels of ore they hauled out of the mountain. In the mining world, that was a whole lot of gold. They were almost there. It had been the natural place to build a road in the early nineteen hundreds, when few cared about rolling roughshod over sacred Native sites. Unfortunately for Valkyrie #3, these last three hundred yards folded back and forth in a series of cliffs and crags, the perfect spot for a burial ground.

The twenty-eight-year-old archeologist focused on bones— and his music—when he should have been worried about the heavy backhoe bucket swinging back and forth on the boom over his head. Dean Schimmel, a laborer in tattered Frogg Toggs raingear that looked like he'd found them wadded up in the trunk of an abandoned car, perched on a crumbling hummock of mossy earth a few feet up the valley. As ever, he leaned on a shovel, looking as spindly as the shovel's handle, and extremely glum. He was supposed to act as safety. To keep an eye on Merculief, make sure he didn't get himself brained by the swinging backhoe bucket, but Dean Schimmel was just as likely to stare at a passing raven or puff on his cigarette and watch a shuffling porcupine. He was probably a decent enough guy, though he put far too much stock in what Dallas Childers had to say.

That guy was bad news. Merculief could feel it.

Childers, the scowling dude behind the controls of the bright yellow beast, was supposed to stay to the existing road. Instead, he used it as a vague guideline, taking bites of moist earth and rock the size of La-Z-Boy recliners out of the mountain at every other turn. Merculief didn't try to stop him. Violations of US Forest Service regulations weren't his problem—unless they involved old bones or Native settlements.

The mine had a strict no-gun policy, but Childers said he'd seen a brown bear a couple of weeks back, so the foreman let him carry his big Glock on a chest rig over his

Carhartt overalls. He practiced with it too, every day, out on the old tailings by the ocean. He used oil cans for targets and always made sure someone else was watching so they could see how good he was. He was fast, which was part of being good, Merculief thought. There were no more bear sightings, but Childers just kept right on carrying his Glock. No one ever told him not to. Had it been anybody else, Merculief might have felt safer, but when he thought it over, he was a lot more concerned about Childers and his Glock than any brown bear.

The bulk of the crew was working down at the main operation, through the thick forest, a quarter of a mile away, most of them deep underground. It would be all too easy for Childers to murder him and bury him with the backhoe. Forget finding any bones. Childers just flat hated Indians.

A mixture of Tlingit, Portuguese, and Russian, Isaac Merculief had grown up in Petersburg, a hundred and sixty miles to the south. He knew how to dress for Southeast Alaska weather—mist, rain, fog, snow, wind, or any combination thereof. Extra layers could be shed on the rare but spectacularly beautiful sunny days—but cold and wet was always just around the corner, waiting to slap you in the face. Merculief didn't mind. The endless rain kept everything an unimaginable green.

The archeologist pulled the collar of the fleece jacket inside his raincoat tighter around his neck, eyes moving from the teeth of the heavy bucket to Dallas Childers's sheep-killing-dog look. It was in Merculief's nature to try to say something friendly, a joke to cut the tension, but the backhoe's engine isolated the three men and left them each cloistered away in their own world, free to despise or pity the other.

Merculief had just looked away, resting his eyes for a

moment from the monotonous back-and-forth movement of the backhoe's boom, when he heard the telltale rattle of the diesel engine revving a little more than usual. Childers had uncovered something and was attempting to swing the bucket back over the top of it.

It was too late. Merculief leaped forward, scrambling in the soupy dirt, nearly falling in front of the backhoe. He shouted, frantically waving his arms, for Childers to stop. A strong hand grabbed the collar of his raincoat and yanked him backward. He heard spewed curses, muffled, but angry, as Schimmel dragged him away.

Childers killed the engine, letting the silence creep in to join the raging hiss of the river below. Everyone at the mine knew he'd been a sniper in the Marine Corps. Isaac thought he still looked at everyone like he was seeing them through the crosshairs of a scope. He slumped in his seat without leaving the cab for almost half a minute, eyes locked forward as if he was trying to figure out his next move.

Isaac hardly noticed the man's gloom. The miners might not be happy, but this was a real find. He could tell that at first glance. The backhoe had stripped away a large table of stone above the ledge, exposing long, cream-colored leg bones. Human leg bones. The remaining earth had fallen free quickly as the bucket had swung sideways, revealing most of an entire skeleton, situated on a decaying wooden frame. Protected for decades by rock and thick vegetation, the grave was now suddenly exposed to wind and rain. Isaac found himself giddy by the time he climbed down in the roadbed and leaned in to get a better look. Three copper bracelets encircled the wrist bones of the left arm. The remnants of a leather apron lay across the skeleton's lap, adorned with deer hooves and bits of shell. A rattle about the size of a drinking gourd lay next to the tiny bones that had once been the dead person's hand, as if he or she had been holding it at the time of burial. It looked to be made of bone and boiled horn—like nothing Merculief had ever seen.

Schimmel moved into the dig, shoulder to shoulder with Merculief, shovel still clutched in his hand. He backpedaled when he saw the skull, mumbling a hasty prayer. Merculief would have laughed had he not been so excited. Schimmel was always talking about haunted mines and Tommy knockers, the ghosts of dead miners who tapped on the adit walls.

Childers remained behind the controls of the backhoe, slouching, talking on his radio.

Merculief threw back the hood of his raincoat and squatted down to get a closer look at the gravesite without touching anything. "Deer-hoof apron, bracelets, Raven rattle . . . I bet you this was a shaman."

"Like a witch doctor?" Schimmel whispered.

"Probably more like the guy who hunted witches," Merculief said.

"A witch hunter?" Schimmel stammered. "That would be a good guy, right?"

"I'd say so."

Schimmel's slack-jawed gaze was glued to the bones. "No shit? The Indians around here really had witches and witch hunters?"

"The oral traditions say so," Merculief said. "The way I understand it. The people who lived here believed witches wielded a force that made people sick. Shamans like this guy would have figured out who was the witch and then healed the sick person."

"There's witches in the Bible," Schimmel muttered, always trying to remain relevant. "Did you know that?"

"I did," Merculief said, giving this goofy dude a side-eye,

then leaning forward to take a photo of the rattle with his phone.

Merculief could hear Dallas Childers talking on the radio but couldn't make out the words over the sound of the river. The bosses had to be pissed. They were probably trying to figure out a way around this. There wasn't one.

This find was beyond incredible.

"This rattle is different," Merculief said, grabbing a jutting stone in the muck to support himself so he could lean in and get a closer look.

The rattle was roughly a foot long and five or six inches at its widest point. The image of a human figure in a raven mask was faintly visible on the horn body.

"All the rattles I've seen have been carved from cedar or other kinds of wood—and newer, otherwise they'd have rotted away. This one looks to be very old. I think it's made of Dall sheep horn, boiled so they could form it."

Schimmel grunted. "So?"

"Dall sheep were sacred to the Tlingit," Merculief said. "Lots of taboos surrounded their hunting." He put a hand on Schimmel's shoulder, squeezing him in excitement. "I've got so much work to do, so many questions. I'm not even sure they had Dall sheep in this area at the time this was made. This grave could help identify ancient trade routes between coastal and inland peoples—"

"Is it worth anything?"

"The rattle?"

Schimmel nodded, chin on his hands, hands on his shovel. "Yeah."

"I'd say it is," Merculief said, hovering over the bones like a mother bird protecting her nest. "A wooden Raven rattle about this same size sold for over half a million bucks last year."

Schimmel stood up now. "Half a million? Dollars?"

"Yep." Merculief stood. He was unwilling to molest the site any more. He had Tlingit blood in his veins, but not the cultural expertise to know what needed to be done to take care of the site. "I need to make a call."

Childers was still busy on the radio, but he looked up to listen to what Merculief was saying now.

"Sorry to stop you, guys," the archeologist said. "We need to get someone in here who can tell us if special ceremonies are needed."

"What do you mean, ceremonies?" Schimmel asked.

Merculief gave an emphatic nod. "If I'm right and these bones belong to an actual Tlingit shaman, there will need to be some prayers, that sort of thing." Childers relayed everything over the radio, stopping short when Merculief said, "We may have to reroute the road."

Childers lowered the radio a hair and glared. "We can't reroute the road."

Merculief, enthralled in his new find, failed to notice the darker mood shift.

Instead, he babbled on. "True, I suppose. Tlingit customarily buried their shaman in out-of-the-way places, but there is a lot we don't know. There could be other burial sites all around here. I don't know how much land is considered sacred around a shaman's tomb. These are questions for a cultural expert. Not me. They'd have to make that call."

Childers raised the radio to his lips again, listened for a while, and then held up a hand.

"Mr. Dollarhyde agrees."

"Wait. Mr. Dollarhyde is here?" Merculief had expected to deal with Auclair, the mine foreman, not Harold Grimsson's creepy fixer and right-hand man.

Childers gave a smug nod. He was more relaxed now that

his de facto boss was on the scene. "He says to tell you good catch. This is a hell of a find, he says."

"He's not mad?"

"No," Childers said, stone-faced. It was almost like he was reading from a script. "According to Mr. Dollarhyde, your bones could put Valkyrie Mine on the map. Might even help with public relations for all our other projects. He wants you to grab a few photos, and then he'll take you back into Juneau in the fast boat."

This was certainly not the way Merculief thought it would play out.

"No," he said. "I should stay with the dig."

Childers lowered his eyes, peering down from the seat of his backhoe. "You want me to get on the radio and tell Mr. Dollarhyde you said no? See how that works out for you. Personally, he says I'm going in the fast boat back to Juneau, I'm getting my ass in the fast boat back to Juneau. Sounds like he wants to do a press release with you about your discovery."

Merculief took a half step back, shaking his head. "It's a little early for press—"

"He's the boss," Schimmel grunted.

"No, Dollarhyde works for the boss," Merculief said.

"So that makes him our boss," Childers said.

A man wearing dark green rain gear came around the trees on a growling four-wheeler below. Auclair, the grizzled mine foreman, bounced up the rough roadbed, dodging rocks the size of basketballs. The rain was beginning to pick up, and Merculief was relieved to see that he'd brought some tarps.

"Dollarhydesaidbringthese." The foreman habitually blurted out everything he wanted to say at once, like he didn't want to spend the effort to space his words. "Coverthesite. Keepitdry."

Merculief exhaled sharply through his mouth, tension leaving on the cloud of vapor. Maybe the boss *was* on board with this.

Dean Schimmel wasn't against work, so long as the bulk of that work meant he was leaning on his shovel and watching other people. Childers was pissed, he could tell, and that always made him a little nervous. It took fifteen minutes for the four men to help construct a makeshift tent over the shaman's grave using tarps and heavy rocks. The fool archeologist ran his mouth the entire time, like he'd just found the Crystal Skull or some shit and not a bunch of dried-up bones. All of them were soaked and covered with mud by the time they got the rain directed away from the gravesite. Finally, Auclair put the babbling archeologist on the back of his four-wheeler and carried him down to Dollarhyde and the waiting fast boat.

Childers and Schimmel stood in the ankle-deep mud, hoods pulled up around their faces for a while, and smoked. Childers didn't feel like talking to Schimmel, and Schimmel never knew what to say unless someone else started the conversation, so they stared at the hole they'd dug and listened to the stream rush down from the glaciers.

Ten minutes after he finished his second cigarette, Dallas Childers threw back the hood of his raincoat. He grabbed the bar on the side of his backhoe and hauled himself into the cab with a grunt.

Schimmel, still leaning with both hands on the shovel handle, looked up, trying to make sense of what was going on.

"What are you doin'?"

"We got a road to build," Childers said. Settling into his seat, he snatched up a thermos and unscrewed the top to get a warmup from the coffee—and the other Kentucky goodness he had mixed in there.

"What about the bones?"

"What bones?" Childers said. "I don't see any bones."

"And the archeologist?"

Childers chuckled at that. "What archeologist? Auclair is taking him to the south dock to meet Mr. Dollarhyde. Nobody's gonna see him get on that boat."

Schimmel gave a slow nod as the understanding crept in like a tickle on his brain.

Mr. Dollarhyde would shoot Merculief, or maybe hit him with a rock. You could never tell with that guy. He might even tie an anchor around the kid's feet and dump him over alive—that dude was always licking his lips and smiling that sadistic smile. Schimmel didn't want to know the details. Not knowing meant he could tell himself he wasn't a witness to a murder. He wouldn't have minded killing the dumbass kid himself. But witnessing a killing made you a loose end, and Schimmel sure as hell didn't want to be a loose end with lip-licking Dollarhyde sneaking around tying things up for Mr. Grimsson.

Schimmel stepped back as the backhoe's diesel engine rattled to life. This shit was about to get real. It was better to stay in the dark about the details.

"Get your ass outta that dig!" Childers yelled. He bent over to fiddle with his backhoe controls.

Schimmel stooped quickly and lifted the edge of the tarp, scooping up the bone rattle while Childers was busy, and shoving it in the pocket of his Frogg Toggs. He glanced sideways, holding his breath, bracing himself for the shit storm that would fall on him if Childers saw him try to walk off with evidence that the burial site existed. Tension always made him feel like he had to pee.

Childers sat up straight in his seat again. "I told you to get out of the dig!" No mention of the rattle. Childers was so deaf from the rumble of diesel engines and gunfire over the years that Schimmel was sure he hadn't heard a thing the archeologist kid had said about how much the bone rattle was worth.

Schimmel scrambled out of the roadbed, dragging the blue tarps with him so there would be no trace when Childers put the skeleton and creepy deer-hoof apron back where it belonged, deep in the dirt. His hand dropped into the pocket of his rain coat, fingers wrapping around the handle of the bone rattle. It felt exceptionally heavy, especially with Childers frowning down at him, with the big gun strapped across his chest. Half a million bucks was a lot of money. Worth the risk, Schimmel told himself. Still, you couldn't spend a dollar if you were dead. He could sell it at a discount to someone who knew how much it was worth. But he didn't know anyone who had more than a couple hundred bucks besides Mr. Grimsson or Mr. Dollarhyde, and he sure as hell wasn't telling them. No, he'd have to figure something out. But he had time.

He wondered if the rattle might be cursed. It could be. There were curses in the Bible. Bad ones, and witches too. Maybe. He wasn't really sure about the witches. Schimmel lit another cigarette and ran a finger along the bumps and ridges of the carved horn inside his pocket. Maybe Isaac Merculief had eaten all the bone rattle's bad luck. Knowing

Mr. Dollarhyde, the kid was already taking a saltwater snooze by now.

He adjusted his earmuffs and then leaned on his shovel to formulate a plan. If everything worked out just right, he'd make some good money, and it probably wouldn't get him killed.

DAY ONE

CHAPTER 1

Anchorage

Supervisory Deputy U. S. Marshal Arliss Cutter's grandfather had warned him early on: *If they're cornered, just about anybody on earth would jam a pencil into your eye.*

That was Cutter's job—cornering people.

On paper, Jarome Pringle was just number 3 on a list of wanted criminals the Alaska Fugitive Task Force had focused on for the week—nothing special. Not dangerous. But then, Jarome Pringle had never been cornered.

Cutter took his grandfather's teachings to heart—and passed them on to the deputies he trained, the deputies he kicked doors with.

Like today.

Whenever possible, Cutter liked to hunt his fugitives in the tiny sliver of time when dogs and dopers overlapped their sleeps. It was the safest, if not the most convenient time to hit a house for a fugitive.

It lowered the odds that anyone on his team would get a pencil in the eye.

It was still dark, but that rarely helped you tell time in Alaska. In this case, it was early, a little after five a.m. It was still cold enough for a coat, but getting warmer every day, warm enough that the gray mountains of snow—fifteen, twenty feet high—that had been piled up in virtually every Anchorage parking lot and neighborhood cul-de-sac would weep rivulets of dirty water into the streets as soon as the sun came up in a couple of hours.

With any luck, the task force would be done by then, and making ops plans for the next fugitive.

Fugitive work—often simply called "enforcement"—was the sexy side of the Marshals Service. Everybody had to hook and haul prisoners at some point in his or her career. Deputy US marshals—DUSMs—sat in court and listened to attorneys drone on for so long they probably could pass the bar. They took mug shots, rolled fingerprints, conducted strip searches (lift and turn please), met the airlift with van loads of bad guys—but nobody came aboard for all that. You got a job with the Marshals Service because you wanted to work enforcement.

You wanted to hunt.

A good chief deputy spread the wealth. Jill Phillips was one of the best. She made sure every POD—plain old deputy—in the District of Alaska, even the ones who'd just graduated from Marshals Basic at the Federal Law Enforcement Training Center, had a warrant or two of their own to work.

PODs divided their time between court, judicial protection, asset forfeiture, hurricane aftermath, guarding dignitaries with State at the United Nations General Assembly—pretty much anything the Attorney General decided he or she wanted the Marshals Service to do. Deputies assigned to the Alaska Fugitive Task Force rarely had to dilute their schedule with collateral duties. They hunted. Every day—and many nights. They cornered the name on the paper, took him or her to jail, and then moved on to the next warrant in the stack, all the while trying not to get shot or stabbed by some bad guy's baby mama.

Cutter mulled over his grandfather's wisdom as he drove through the backstreets of midtown Anchorage in the gunmetal chill of the predawn darkness. Gravel popped under the tires of his government-issue SUV. It was a Ford Escape—surely a joke from USMS fleet management in DC.

His partner, Deputy Lola Teariki, a Polynesian of Cook Island Maori descent, sat in the passenger seat. She was not a particularly large woman—but her personality sprawled across the inside of the vehicle and took up a lot of space. Still a ways from thirty, she had four years on with the Service. Thick ebony hair piled high on her head in a tight bun, still glistening from the shower after her zero-dark-thirty workout. She and Cutter were dressed alike—navy blue long-sleeve shirts, khaki Vertx pants, and olive drab load-bearing ballistic vests with a five-pointed circle-star badge and POLICE: US MARSHAL embroidered in white across the back.

Gazing out the passenger window, she brooded over something. She'd speak up soon. She always did. Even half-formed ideas seemed too much of a burden for Lola to carry around. She had to get them off her chest. That usually meant telling it all to Cutter, letting him in on what she'd figured out with the certitude that came from her two-point-something decades on the planet. . . . He didn't mind. She was a good kid. A little blabby, but her heart was in the right place—and she'd sure proved herself. Fit, smart, and hit on by pretty much every male officer or agent who met her, she was tough as an old boot, ready to jump in and go to town when more fragile souls might shy away. She could bat her lashes innocently one minute, then intimidate the hell out of some bad guy when she rolled her eyes and scrunched her nose the next. She called it "going Polynesian-princess to Maori-warrior face."

For now, whatever notion that was taking shape inside her head was still in its early stages, so she was quiet, allowing Cutter to ponder on his grandfather while he drove the last two blocks to the meeting.

For as long as Arliss had known him, the old man, called Grumpy by most, lived by a certain creed. He called these doctrines his Grumpy Man-Rules, and passed them on to the grandsons he'd raised. Arliss's brother, Ethan, had gone on to become an engineer. A noble profession to be sure, but a mystery to Grumpy. The old man had been an officer with Florida Marine Patrol. He chased poachers, rescued idiots, patrolled in his airboat to enforce the law on the water—and there was a lot of water in Florida. Arliss had followed, but on the federal side of the business, which riled the old man at first. Still, Grumpy saved back a few of his axioms that had special meaning to someone who carried a badge, even if it was for the feds, who he generally felt were as useless as tits on a boar hog.

Well over a decade in the US Marshals—not to mention Cutter's time with the 75th Rangers—had borne out the old man's wisdom in spades.

Cutter made a left.

Lola kept quiet, still forming her notion.

Jarome Pringle's warrant file said he was harmless, but Cutter knew better. There was no such thing as harmless, not in this line of work.

Cutter mulled over the possible outcomes, letting the chilly wind through his open window hit him in the face, bracing him awake.

Spring in Alaska wasn't all kite flying and daffodils. Breakup, they called it. As in the ice on the rivers was breaking up. Breakup in the city meant mud and dust and more mud. He found himself glad that temps had dropped into the high twenties overnight, frosting the grass and freezing the mud while they worked this warrant.

Some sourdoughs joked that there were only two seasons—winter and July. A native of Florida and lover of all things to do with the sea and beach, Cutter found the Great Land pleasant—mostly. He loved the fall, enjoyed the summers, found new things to learn in the austerity and bitter winters of the Interior. But breakup . . . there wasn't much to like about slop and slush and windshields that you could never get clean.

The light was good, though. By mid-May the sun would rise in Utqiagvik—or Barrow—and wouldn't dip below the horizon again for eighty-four days. Anchorage wasn't as drastic. Here, they gained something like five minutes a day until they had about twenty hours of light.

Cutter was the supervisory deputy over enforcement in Alaska, which meant he ran the task force. He chose which paper the teams worked, approved the operational plans, and kicked the biggest ones up to the chief for her check before anyone kicked a door. Safety for all members of the task force fell to him. It didn't matter if they were deputies like Lola Teariki, officers detailed from Anchorage Police Department, Alaska State Troopers, or other feds from DHS or ATF. Cutter led from the front—which often meant getting out of the way and letting his guys do their job— another thing Grumpy had taught him.

A thick head of perpetually mussed blond hair put Cutter at little over six-three. He steered clear of weights for the most part, staying in shape with running, push-ups, pull-ups, and swimming—plus a little work on the heavy bag every couple of days. With a fighting weight of two and a quarter, he was only just able to wedge himself behind the wheel of the midsize Ford SUV when he wore all his tactical gear. In his early forties, Cutter had yet to hit the metabolic wall that caused so many of his peers to turn into Deputy Donuts instead of the lean machines they'd been out of Marshals Service Basic.

He was lucky in that regard. The rest of his life—

"We need a new name, Cutter," Lola said, shattering the silence. The weight of her idea had grown too heavy for her to bear alone. Her father's Kiwi accent sharpened Teariki's vowels and chased away her Rs when she was tired, turning "Cutter" into *Cuttah*.

They were too close to the meeting point to get into a long conversation, which is why he humored her. "A new name for what?"

Lola yawned, big, like a lioness. "For the Alaska Fugitive Task Force. AFTF is stuffed as far as acronyms go. It doesn't mean anything."

"It's too early for this, Lola," Cutter said, driving over a bump of old snow as he took a corner.

"Hear me out, boss." Teariki patted the console between them. "A good acronym says something about what it stands for—like the FIST operations the Marshals Service used to do back in the day. Fugitive Investigative Strike Team. Now that's got verve."

Cutter shrugged. "How about the FALCON roundups."

Lola scoffed, making a buzzer sound. "Lame! Federal and Local Cops . . . I don't even remember. On Nightshift . . . ? No, also stuffed. The acronym should at least make sense." She folded her arms over the front of her ballistic vest and stared out the windshield at the darkness. "I'll keep thinking on it."

"You do that," Cutter said, making another turn down a dark street toward the rally point, where his team would link up with two uniformed Anchorage police officers.

The smell of new birch and cottonwood buds on the cold air pinched his nose as he drove. There were other odors too, coming through the open window, less pleasant. Anchorage was a city of over 60,000 dogs. Which was all well and good. Cutter liked dogs. But not every owner was responsible, and that many pups left behind a lot of little melting land mines as the snows receded.

Another reason not to like breakup.

One of those sixty thousand dogs woofed somewhere down the block, grumbling at the chill.

Another SUV was already parked along the road ahead, along with two marked APD cruisers.

Cutter pulled in behind the SUV, two blocks east of Jarome Pringle's residence.

It was time to not get stabbed in the eye.

CHAPTER 2

Apart from being a tall, fat white guy who spoke with a distinctive Jamaican patois, Jarome Pringle seemed an unremarkable fugitive. The task force had dealt with him before. He'd been no problem—but in that instance, they'd snatched him out of a vehicle on a traffic stop. This time, they were going into his house, or more accurately, his new girlfriend's house.

Cutter had chosen the edge of this vacant lot for a quick briefing. It was near an Anchorage green belt of birch and spruce trees that ran along Chester Creek, but far enough away that no one at Pringle's could hear vehicle doors shutting in the predawn darkness. Cutter killed the headlights and reached between the center console and his seat for his Battle Board.

The dome light remained off when he opened the door—anything else was a recipe for getting shot.

Lola arched her back, stretching, hands pressed flat on the Ford's headliner in another long, feline yawn.

"You got the warrant file?"

"Got it," Cutter said.

He held up the multi-cam Battle Board—essentially a ballistic nylon folder with a clear Plexiglas face, under which he'd slipped a map of the neighborhood and a hand-sketched floorplan of the house.

He'd marked up the map and floorplan with a grease pencil to aid in the briefing he was about to give the two Anchorage police officers who were there to help with the early-morning arrest. He'd gone over everything with Lola and the other two participating members of the task force the evening before.

The DEA had arrested Pringle for possession of heroin the month before. They had some intel that he was trying to establish a foothold for a Jamaican posse in Anchorage, but he'd been holding only a couple of grams at the time—not enough to prove intent to sell. His defense attorney had convinced the judge that he was only holding the drugs for his troubled girlfriend—merely a good man, doing the right thing to help curb the terrible opiate epidemic. The magistrate hadn't exactly believed that theory, but was troubled by the small amount of heroin if Pringle was supposed to be such a player, and allowed him out on bond. He'd promptly gotten arrested again for the DUI. The state judge allowed him out on his own recognizance as soon as he was sober enough to stagger, but the incident had triggered a federal supervised release violation.

Pringle was no rocket scientist, but he was probably bright enough to realize an arrest warrant was trickling down to some guys somewhere with guns and badges. Cutter wanted at least a couple of those badges and guns to be APD. The uniforms gave clarity in these hazy morning hours.

Sean Blodgett, a stocky stub of a deputy with a map of scars visible through his buzz cut, sauntered up beside Cutter. He took another quick look at the Battle Board on the hood of the SUV and gave a knowing nod. A bit of a shit magnet, Blodgett couldn't seem to get out of his own way. He ended up with some sort of sprain, scrape, or contusion at least once a month. Still, he was tough as a bull, spending nearly as much time in the gym as Lola. Other deputies in the office had taken to calling him BAF—for Big-Armed Fed—but Cutter had always thought he looked a little like a T. rex with his arms sticking out of the oversize ballistic vest.

Nancy Alvarez, Blodgett's partner on the task force, wore the same vest, but she wore it better, more naturally. A hell of a man hunter, she was on loan from Anchorage PD—and often acted as liaison, smoothing the way for Cutter when they needed to steal a couple of uniforms to hit a house but didn't want to call in SWAT.

The responding officers—a black female named Brooks and a tall kid named Slavich, who looked like he should have been playing for the NBA, gravitated toward Alvarez. She carried special deputy US marshal credentials, but at heart, she was one of them.

Cutter opened the Battle Board and took out four copies of Pringle's last booking photo. A cold wind rattled out of the birch forest to the northwest, making him thankful for the vest and long-sleeve shirt. He'd have been scuba diving this time of year if he were back in Florida.

Cutter went over the layout of the house and the suspected occupants. "Should be just him and his girlfriend. No kids that we're aware of."

"This Pringle guy a fighter?" Officer Brooks asked. She studied the booking photo under the glare of the streetlight, making a couple of notes in a little pad.

"Not exactly," Cutter said, forcing a half smile for the sake of the two officers. He'd inherited his grandfather's tendency toward a mean mug, but he didn't want all the young troops on patrol thinking the boss of the fugitive task force walked around looking pissed off at the world. He tapped his copy of the photo with his index finger. Pringle was a heavy man, well over three hundred pounds, with a fountain of dreadlocks sprouting off a head that looked the size of a basketball. "He's what my granddad would have called a butterbean—like a regular bean, only bigger. He's got more mass than meanness, but that much mass can hurt you, even if he's just trying to get away."

"We popped him last year at his baby mama's house," Lola said. "He tried to hide his fat ass under a pile of dirty clothes. He had a pet tarantula, though . . . or at least he did . . . kind of freaked me out, to be honest."

"Kill it with fire," Blodgett observed, sounding and looking dead serious.

Cutter put a hand flat on the hood of his SUV, the movement pulling everyone's attention toward him in the scant light. "It goes without saying, but spiders do not constitute a deadly force scenario. Not even big, hairy ones."

"Still," Alvarez said. "Don't hesitate to Tase the SOB if he doesn't comply with your orders. And, for Pete's sake, don't stop in front of him once he starts moving."

"Copy," both officers said at once.

"Small favor," Cutter said, addressing the two uniforms. "Deputy Blodgett is covering the rear of the residence. Would one of you mind helping him out?"

Slavich scratched the top of his head and yawned. It was nearing the end of his ten-hour shift. "I'll go."

"Outstanding." Cutter nodded at Alvarez, who was to explain the tactics. "Nancy."

"We'll try not to kick the door," she said. "Pringle's girlfriend is good for dozens of vehicle burglaries, and thieves are paranoid as hell about anybody stealing the stuff that they stole from someone else. The Silverado parked out front looks to have a working alarm. I'll try to get in it, set it off. She'll come to the door to see who's trying to take her shit. . . ."

She outlined the rest of her plan, rocking back and forth to keep her feet warm.

"Okay," Cutter said, knowing how quickly briefings could devolve. "Last condo on the end of four. Dirty white siding with black trim." He jabbed at the map again to get it set in everyone's mind. "Wooden planter on the right side of the porch."

Much like the "time out" that surgeons did before an operation to make sure they were cutting the right bits off the right patient, Cutter liked to remind everyone of the physical location of their target one last time before they moved. Booting the wrong door could prove every bit as dire as taking the wrong kidney.

"Weapons?" Officer Brooks asked. She was bright-eyed, fit, smaller than Lola, with hardly enough room on her waist for her Glock, extra magazines, Taser, pepper spray, radio, and handcuffs.

"There was a handgun in the drawer during the last arrest," Lola said. "It was stolen, so we took that one, but I'd assume he's replaced it—if only to keep from getting robbed by other heroin dealers."

Brooks nodded slowly, as if she expected as much.

Sean Blodgett's face screwed into an angry grimace. "And maybe a spider," he said.

CHAPTER 3

Cutter tapped the Colt Python revolver at his side—his grandfather's service weapon. The USMS regulation Glock rested over his right kidney. He moved quickly down the street with Lola and Officer Brooks on his heels. They stopped in a line at the edge of the driveway, fifteen feet from the front door, using the shadows of a fat blue spruce for concealment. Cutter took a deep breath of the chilly air, centering his thoughts. There was a certain smell to working a warrant. Brighter, more alive. Grumpy always said if you didn't smell it, you were in the wrong business. Cutter had been creeping up on bad guys for nearly twenty years if he counted his military time. Mud hut, remote cabin, or residential neighborhood—it never got old.

Pistols out and stacked single file, they were close enough to hear one another breathing. Officer Brooks, who brought up the rear, gave Lola a firm tap on the side of the thigh with her nondominant hand. She was good to go. Lola repeated the gesture to Cutter, who did the same to Alvarez, who trotted off without another word.

From this point on, things would unfold at lightning speed.

Officer Brooks and Lola peeled off the line as soon as

Alvarez reached the car, padding softly up the concrete steps to take up positions on the porch on either side of the doorjamb—out of the fatal funnel.

Cutter covered Nancy, watching the windows above while she approached the truck.

Another dog barked. This one closer. Each tiny noise sounded exponentially louder than it really was. The zip of spruce boughs against a ballistic nylon vest surely woke everyone in the neighborhood. Lola's stifled cough echoed all the way down the street.

It was getting light enough to see Alvarez clearly as she lifted the door handle on Pringle's blue Silverado, using the body of the vehicle for cover. She put her hip into the truck, rocking it. Headlights flashed and the horn blared. That part of her mission complete, Alvarez trotted up the steps and parked herself behind Lola.

Now Cutter could move. He reached the porch in four quick strides, skipping all but one step to fall in behind the others at the same moment the door yawned open.

Pringle's girlfriend stepped out wearing nothing but a terrycloth robe and a very large pair of panties. She was a corpulent woman, and the robe, meant for someone much smaller, did little to hide everything that wasn't covered by the undies. One hand shielding her eyes from the flashing headlights, the other held a cell phone. As Alvarez had pointed out, it was astounding how quickly felons called in help when someone tried to steal what they'd stolen from someone else.

Officer Brooks identified herself and motioned the woman the rest of the way out with a flick of her hand. Lola and Alvarez covered the open door with their handguns.

Cutter bumped Lola so she could take a step inside and

cover the entry. The stairway to the second floor was eight feet across the small foyer. Back to the door, Cutter took note of the coat closet to his right—there was always a closet—and the open hall leading to the rear of the house. He covered the landing above with his Colt, while Alvarez covered the interior hall. The heat inside the house was turned up full blast, and the moldering odor of dirty socks and sour dishes hit them full in the face.

It smelled like a felony warrant.

Officer Brooks turned the heavy woman so she could cuff her before the shock of seeing cops at the door wore off.

The ratchet sound of the handcuffs brought the woman out of her stupor. "Why you doin' this? Am I under arrest?"

"Depends," Alvarez said, her voice calm but firm.

"You gonna let me tie my robe?"

"Just face the wall and you'll be fine," Alvarez said over her shoulder, standing just inside the door. "Which room is Jarome in?"

"He's not here," the girlfriend said.

"That's a good way to be under arrest," Alvarez said. "We know he's here. If you hide him, you go to jail for hindering."

"Why you ask me that shit if you already know?"

"I asked what room he's in," Alvarez reminded her.

The woman gave an insolent shrug. "I'm freezing my ass off out here on the porch. How am I supposed to know where he is?"

"Got a long gun leaning against the wall at the top of the steps," Lola piped.

"Who else is here?" Brooks asked.

"Just us," the woman said.

Alvarez shook her head. "Us?"

"Me and Jarome."

Cutter pointed to the left, motioning for Lola to come with him and clear the bottom floor while Nancy Alvarez watched the stairway. He didn't like huddling at the door for too long.

At that moment, Jarome Pringle stumbled around the corner from the direction of the kitchen. Dreadlocks stuck skyward from a hard night's sleep. Belly rolls all but obscured his leopard-print Speedo. He didn't appear to see Cutter until he made it well into the foyer. He tried to spin and run up the stairs but didn't have the dexterity or speed.

"Jarome!" Cutter barked. "Stop! US Marshals!" Unwilling to let him get to the gun, Cutter sprang forward, catching Pringle by the hairy shoulder before he made the second step. The big man roared, furious at having his castle invaded so early in the morning.

Cutter was not a small man, but Pringle had him by at least a hundred pounds and, teetering on the stairs above him, nearly a foot of height. Prudently, Cutter took a step back, knowing from experience what Lola was about to do. The vast majority of fights Cutter had been in over the course of his law enforcement career hadn't really been fights at all, but someone trying to get away while Cutter attempted to stop them. The trouble was, Pringle was running toward a gun.

It was dangerous to deploy a Taser on someone on the stairs, but more dangerous still to let them get to a firearm. Cutter saw the red laser dots settle, one between Pringle's hairy shoulder blades, the other in the geographic center of his buttocks.

"Jarome Pring—" Lola said. He started to run again. "Tase, Tase, Tase!" Lola barked.

There was an audible snap as the nitrogen canisters popped the plastic gates off the front of the cartridge, propelling twin barbed darts on gossamer wires, angling slightly to give a greater coverage, meaning more muscles for the electrical current to disrupt. The barbs followed the red laser dots. Pringle went rigid, the banister post at the base of the stairs arresting his fall and sending him sideways onto the landing. Onlookers might think Cutter stuck out his boot to give Pringle a kick, but in reality, he was making sure the man's head didn't smack the tile floor as he fell.

"Hands!" Lola snapped. She was the one holding the Taser, so she gave the commands.

Pringle moaned. He'd knocked a tooth out on the pillar at the bottom of the stairs and it lay on the ground beside his face.

"You bitch . . ."

"More where that came from," Lola said. "Hands behind your back."

Teetering on his belly, the outlaw complied, hesitantly lifting his flabby arms so she didn't shock him again.

Cutter was closer, so he moved in to apply the handcuffs. Pringle's back was as wide as a barn door, and Cutter had to use two linked sets in order to pull both wrists close enough together.

A heavy clunk thudded from somewhere on the upper floor at the same moment the radio on Cutter's belt squawked. He ratcheted on the cuffs and drew his Colt.

Sean Blodgett's voice poured into the room. "White female and white male looking out the top-floor window, boss. Might be Shiloh Watts. Pretty sure the male is Corbin McGrone. Both are 10-99."

10-99 meant the warrant gods were smiling. Bycatch, or scooping up unintended targets when rounding up a fugitive, was common enough. Like fell in with like—and fugitives running from the law tended to do their running in groups.

Another thud came from upstairs, then a woman's scream—long and piercing.

"Bronnnnncooooo!" It was a cry of anger, not ecstasy.

Lola mouthed the name. "Bronco?"

"That's what it sounded like," Cutter said.

"Go ahead," Alvarez whispered. "I've got this one."

Pringle's body effectively dammed the bottom of the steps, forcing Lola and Cutter both to jump over top of him.

Few things compelled Arliss Cutter to run faster than a scream. He forced himself to move methodically but quickly. Colt Python moving in concert with his eyes as he took each step, he brought the second floor into view bit by bit. Lola stayed two steps back, giving herself room to maneuver if things went south.

The woman wailed again, long and trailing—desperate.

The condo wasn't big, allowing Cutter and Lola to clear the single bathroom and another empty bedroom quickly before slowing outside the room with the screaming woman. It was the only door left, so Corbin McGrone—or someone who looked like him—had to be inside. He glanced at Lola just long enough to make sure they were both on the same sheet of music. A quick nod told him she intended to buttonhook to the right around the doorframe while he went left. McGrone was a wiry tweaker who'd run track at Dimond High School. In addition to being fast, he was known to have a propensity to fight that Cutter had read about but never experienced firsthand.

There was no good position of cover in a thin-walled condo, so Cutter rolled in without announcing, preferring not to get shot through the Sheetrock.

He expected to find Watts and McGrone, but instead found a woman he didn't recognize sitting on the edge of a rumpled bed in a pair of gym shorts and a stained white wife-beater shirt. She clutched her greasy red bangs and rocked back and forth, sobbing hysterically. Shiloh Watts was a head taller and had short bottleblond hair. Neither she nor Corbin McGrone were anywhere to be found.

"Hands!" Cutter barked as Lola did a quick peek through the open closet doorway.

The woman raised her hands, but ratcheted up her screaming as soon as she saw the marshals. She spewed saliva with every curse, ordering them out of her room.

If she was a victim, she wasn't looking for help from law enforcement.

The bedroom was cramped and hot, heaped with dirty laundry and old Chinese takeout boxes. A cloying barnyard stench, ten times worse than downstairs, hung heavy in the stifling space, made worse by the piercing screams. There were few places to hide. The window was closed, which left under the bed and inside a heavy oak armoire against the wall. A pile of clothing and coat hangers lay on the floor in front of the armoire. One or even both of them had to be in there. It would be tight, but Cutter had seen full-grown men contort themselves to hide under bathroom sinks.

Cutter pointed toward the bed while he covered the armoire. He wasn't just clearing a room; he was instilling in Lola the correct way to clear a room.

The redhead continued her spit-slinging tirade, glaring at Cutter as if she wanted him to catch fire. Lola kicked a leather boot that was on the floor, sending it sliding under the bed. She stooped at the same moment, getting a quick look. She shook her head.

"Where are they?" Cutter asked, still aimed in on the armoire.

"I'm not telling you shit!" the redhead screeched.

"Hey," Lola said, her voice pointed. "Who's Bronco?"

"Get out of my house!"

Cutter reached for the armoire door with his off hand.

The redhead sprang from the bed in a rage, rushing to intercept Cutter. She had something in her hand, not a gun, but something a shade larger than her fist. . . .

Cutter realized just before the searing pain hit his cheek that she'd tossed the contents of a clear plastic box at his head. The case held not a tarantula, but a small brown scorpion. It was hardly much larger than a quarter. Most of that must have been made up of stinger, considering the acid-like burning sensation between Cutter's eye and the corner of his mouth. He slapped his own face out of instinct, getting stung in the hand for his trouble. The hapless scorpion fell on the floor, and Cutter's boot ended its short reign of terror.

Lola caught the screaming woman by the hair as she ran at Cutter, squatting slightly to lower her center. It had the same effect as clotheslining a runner. The redhead's feet outran her body. Lola held on until just the right moment to let the woman fall flat on her back, knocking the wind out of her sails and mercifully silencing her screams.

"Bronnncoooohhhh," she croaked—the air escaping a slashed tire.

"Stay down!" Lola hissed. She sidestepped to cover Cutter. "What was it? I didn't see a spider. You okay?" Her head moved as if on a swivel, searching the room, while the muzzle of her pistol covered the armoire.

Cutter nodded at the crushed scorpion on the floor. "Got me a good one," he said, then flung open the armoire door.

Worse than empty, instead of Watts and McGrone, they found a four-foot hole cut out of the back of the armoire and completely through the wall into the next condo.

"Sneaky bastards," Lola whispered. "They made a Habitrail."

Cutter jerked the radio out of his pocket while Lola rolled the redhead onto her belly. She laughed maniacally as Lola zipped a pair of nylon restraints around her wrists.

"Watts and McGrone have gone through the wall," he said. "They're in the adjacent condo."

Sean Blodgett answered, "The wall?"

"Affirmative," Cutter said. "Watch the windows. Nancy, if able, you or Brooks keep an eye on the front. The name Bronco ring a bell with anybody?"

Blodgett spoke again. "Billy Gorman. He goes by Bronco. Five-nine, a buck eighty. Used to fight in the AFC octagon until he started running with McGrone."

"Copy," Cutter said. "Nancy. Let's get some more PD folks here and set up a perimeter before we—"

The radio bonked, garbling Cutter's message as one of the other units attempted to talk over him.

Officer Slavich broke squelch as soon as Cutter released the transmit key. Blodgett could be heard shouting in the background. "Three just bailed out the back," Slavich said, breathless, moving. "Gorman took out Blodgett's knee, so I'm going after him. McGrone and Watts are running north, about to disappear into the woods."

Officer Brooks appeared at the bedroom door, announcing herself so she didn't get shot.

"Stay with her," Cutter said, nodding toward the redhead before starting for the stairs.

Lola followed tight on his heels. Almost giddy with the joy of a foot pursuit, she chuckled as they bounded down the stairs. Cold air hit them in the face as they burst out the back door—and ran toward the dark line of trees.

CHAPTER 4

Anchorage PD patrol officer Joe Bill Brackett's primary field training officer once told him that every cop who stayed on the job for more than a few months would have at least one call that stuck with them. The haunting, he called it.

Joe Brackett's haunting came the first day he was by himself on patrol. He was on his own—that is, absent a field training officer critiquing his every move, for a grand total of two hours.

He'd heard Brooks and Slavich dispatched to link up with Nancy Alvarez not far from Chester Creek—that meant the Marshals task force was hitting a house. Brackett loved working fugitives. He would have killed to help with a call like that.

Instead, he got an 11-38. A mental subject.

Brooks and Slavich got to arrest a wanted felon while Brackett had to deal with a crazy out on Point Woronzof. He'd probably have the opportunity to talk to some homeless guy who muttered about how aliens were scanning his brainwaves. Brooks and Slavich might get to boot a door.

Lucky bastards.

Brackett glanced down at the open laptop connected to

the mobile data terminal in his patrol car. His designator turned red, joining the column of officers who were attached to calls. Officers who were free were in yellow. A long column of green designators indicated day shift, who were at this moment sitting in fallout at the new HQ downtown. It was a few minutes before seven in the morning, and they would hit the street shortly, providing overlap staffing with midshift. The sun would be up for real an hour after that. Brackett cracked his passenger window to jolt himself awake. The chilly odor of birch and melting snow was like the ozone smell after a rain, only more biting. He couldn't help but smile.

Even an 11-38 was better than his last two jobs, peddling supplements at GNC or loading money into ATMs. He'd wanted to be a cop since he was a little kid, and now here he was—on his own, the Alpha unit in his area. His city.

In truth, this was to have been Brackett's last day of field training, but Chip Robertson, his FTO for the first and final phases of his eighteen weeks of training, had pronounced him "ready enough" and cut him loose to patrol on his own for the last few hours of the shift.

Brackett turned on Northern Lights heading past Earthquake Park toward Cook Inlet and his waiting 11-38. Mental subjects could be tricky, but Officer Robertson had taught him well. He had this. Elated at his newfound freedom one moment, his heart sank when he heard who his backup was going to be.

Officer Fluke's designator blinked to red on the MDT.

Reed Fluke . . . The one guy on the department Brackett would like to smack with a brick.

In many ways, the field training process was meant to be a gutcheck, a way to see if would-be recruits were ready for this law enforcement job. The first four weeks were overwhelming—nothing was like they taught at the academy. Robertson was stern, but fair, making the time bearable. Fluke, Brackett's second-phase FTO, was a pudgy nine-year veteran who seemed more interested in getting Brackett to quit than teaching him anything. Every night for the entire month, Fluke ordered Brackett to drive to the McDonald's on Muldoon and pick up an application. It was clear, he said, that Brackett was never going to make it as a police officer. The senior officer had chalked it up to training—all in good fun—but Brackett imagined slashing the dipshit's tires or, better yet, knocking out a couple of teeth. Fluke also happened to be on midshift, which meant that Brackett now had to work with the guy.

He groaned, rolled up his window, and shook off the momentary pity party as he turned right, into the Point Woronzof parking lot. Notoriously slow to respond to calls, Fluke was over five minutes away if he drove the speed limit. Brackett hoped to take care of everything before he even arrived.

Brackett slowed, scanning the area for his 11-38. The headlights of his patrol car played across two Subarus in the otherwise deserted lot. Two women, both of whom looked to be in their late twenties or early thirties—older than Brackett anyway—stood next to the hood of a green Outback. One wore blue sweats. Her face flushed, arms folded tightly across her chest, she rocked forward and back. Yep. An 11-38 all right. The other woman was also dressed in running clothes. She looked normal enough from the get-go, had an arm around the one in blue, attempting to console her. Brackett parked so he got some overflow from his headlights but he didn't blind the ladies.

"It's horrible," the woman in blue said as soon as Brackett approached. It was the sort of blurted admission that a kid gave when caught red-handed at something. She continued to rock, eyes dazed and unfocused.

Brackett took a half step closer. He could see both women's hands. No weapons. Still, weapons had a way of materializing out of nowhere. Maybe he should wait for backup . . . except that backup was Fluke, and gaining Fluke was like losing two good officers.

The second woman wore a wool beanie against the chill. She was tall, a few years older, and calm enough that Brackett assumed she hadn't seen the same thing the other one had. She nodded to the rocking woman.

"She was here when I drove up. I could tell something was wrong, but she wouldn't tell me what until just a second ago."

"Can I get your name?" Brackett asked the woman in the hat.

"Liz," she said. "Elizabeth Rains. She told me her name is Toni. I'm sorry I didn't let them know when I called nine-one-one . . . but she hadn't told me yet—"

The rocking woman became more animated. "Don't you understand?" She stared a thousand yards away into the darkness. "This is . . . awful . . . the worst . . ." She spoke in a half whisper, as if to lure Brackett in closer.

Liz Rains gave a visible shiver. She shot a look over her shoulder, toward the bluff and the trail Brackett knew led down to the lonesome gravel beach forty feet below.

Brackett raised a hand, keeping his voice firm but calm. Fear was contagious, and these ladies were scaring the shit out of him. He needed to get a grip on himself and the situation.

"What is it?" he asked. "What did you see?"

Toni shook her head, continuing to rock.

"A body," Liz said. "I didn't go down, but she says it's a girl."

"A dead girl?" Brackett said.

"Very dead girl," Toni gasped, as if suddenly relieved that the burden of her find was now transferred to the authorities.

Brackett used the mic clipped to his vest to apprise dispatch of this new development and get an ambulance on the way, just in case. "And you're certain she's dead?"

Toni's head snapped up and she began to laugh hysterically. "Oh yeah."

"Show me," Brackett said, trying to shake off the chill that ran down his spine. He pointed toward the shadow at the far corner of the parking lot that was the trailhead.

Toni hugged herself tighter and stared at him. "Not in a million years."

A massive commercial airliner roared overhead, lifting off from Anchorage International directly across the road. It looked close enough to touch.

Brackett looked toward the parking lot entrance, surprisingly enough, wishing Fluke would roll up. He was plenty brave when it came to shootouts and fights, but he didn't relish the idea of going down the trail all by himself. "A girl, you say?"

"I . . . I think," Toni said. "I mean, there's not much left of her." Sergeant Hopper pulled into the parking lot just ahead of Fluke.

Hopper was a squat man, thick at the shoulders, big armed, but big legged to match, not like so many guys who focused on biceps and forgot leg day. Originally from Texas, he'd retained his thick accent and a dark, drooping mustache that completely obscured his mouth. It was outside policy, but was such a part of him none of the brass said anything about it.

Fluke sauntered over behind the sergeant, waddling ever so slightly, like he had bad knees.

Brackett groaned, ready to hang back and play rookie now that two senior officers were on scene. He gave the sergeant what he knew, which wasn't much, and turned to find what else he could learn from Liz and Toni.

"You're with me, Brackett," Hopper said, hooking a thumb over his shoulder toward the bluff. "You were first on scene. Fluke, you stand by here."

The senior officer sputtered. "Come on, Sarge . . ."

"We all want action, Reed," Hopper said in his all-knowing Texas drawl. "But somebody has to hold the horses . . . or hang back with the witnesses."

Brackett avoided his old FTO's glare and followed the sergeant to the trailhead. The Alaska sun was still sluggish this time of year, and the morning twilight was just reflecting off the few chunks of muddy pad ice in the chocolate-colored water below. Mount Susitna lay across the Cook Inlet to the west, like a sleeping lady cloaked in white. She'd be covered in snow for at least another month.

The path down was essentially a cutbank carved along the side of the bluff for fifty yards at a steep angle until it reached the beach. Brackett felt the stiff wind off the ocean as soon as he stepped to the edge. Patches of filthy snow adorned the side of the trail beneath the budding poplar trees. It had rained hard the day before and water dripped and oozed down the path. The officers stayed to the side, using their flashlights to be sure they didn't obliterate any obvious tracks with their own boots. The wind gave way to the sound of breaking surf. A raven *ker-lucked* in the trees to the right. Of course there would be ravens here, Brackett thought. They were scavengers, and this looked like a place you might find something to scavenge.

Sergeant Hopper's voice shook Brackett from his thoughts as they walked.

"Probably wondering why I left Fluke up there instead of you."

"Not really," Brackett lied.

Hopper looked sideways in the scant light, rubbing a bit of moisture off the tip of his nose with the back of his Mechanix glove. "I guess the bigger question is why a guy with one year of experience nine times in a row is a field training officer at all."

Brackett found himself glad for the shadows. "If I'm honest," he said, "I have to admit that has crossed my mind."

"You were with him for a month," Hopper said.

"Correct."

"How far are you on the search warrant?"

Brackett blanched. Had he forgotten something important? "Search warrant?"

Hopper chuckled. "For the bodies in Fluke's basement. You should be on line J of the probable cause affidavit after a single week with that guy. He is one weird motor scooter."

Brackett gave a nervous smile, relieved, and more than a little flattered to be let inside the sergeant's inner musings this early in his career.

Hopper stopped at the bottom of the hill, where gravel path became gravel beach. He turned his back to the ocean and the gray lump that had to be the body, as if he wanted to take just a second longer to steel himself before going forward.

"I'll deny every word of this if you repeat me, but the thing is, I'm not in charge of training. And anyway, I guess a smart person can learn some little something from pretty near everyone, even if it's what not to do in a given situation."

"Yes, sir," Brackett said, because Sergeant Hopper seemed like the kind of guy who wanted a two-sided conversation.

"Okay then," Hopper said, ready to move on. He turned to play his flashlight slowly across the beach. Brackett caught his breath when the powerful beam stopped on a gray-white lump lodged at the edge of the gravel in the glistening mud thirty feet above the incoming surf.

The two men approached slowly, staying above the line of flotsam that signified the last high-water mark. Hopper raised his hand when they were still five feet uphill from the torso, signifying it was time to stop.

"Tell me what you see," he said, holding his light steady.

Brackett took a breath, happy there was no smell to go along with the image of butchery and rot before him. "Head's gone," he said. "Both legs cut off at mid-calf. Arms missing below the elbows. No clothing but for a bra . . ."

"That looks like a bra to you?" Hopper asked, moving the beam around the lump of flesh. For the first time, Brackett realized it was moving, alive with creatures that had ridden in with it from the water.

"Maybe a rolled T-shirt," Brackett said, gulping, wondering if this was a test. "Hard to say. I think . . ." He swallowed again. "I believe it's a female."

He closed his eyes for a short mental break. The bright beams of their flashlights revealed tens of thousands of tiny creatures. Collectively known to fishermen as sand fleas, they'd taken up residence in their newfound food source. Saltwater had pickled the tattered flesh, leaving bits of white bone to contrast starkly against the shiny brown mud.

"You think maybe a boat motor did this?" Brackett mused, half to himself.

Sergeant Hopper took his phone out of his vest pocket and held it to his ear. "No," he said, giving a sigh of the inevitable. "I'm pretty certain this was done with an axe."

Mutilated bodies tended to activate the ass-magnet in every officer on shift, drawing in the curious like flies—and sand fleas. It was raining cops by the time the sun peeked over the Chugach Mountains to the east. The mud and gravel surrounding the body was protected by the bluff, leaving it in chilly shadow for another several hours.

Sergeant Hopper sent everyone from shift back to work except for Sandra Jackson, the roving officer assigned as uniformed investigator for this particular shift. The tide was rolling in and he wanted her to grab some photos in case it took the Crime Scene Unit too long to arrive. Assigned to regular patrol areas most nights, UIs got an extra week of training and an expensive camera to document crime scenes for detectives in cases that didn't warrant calling out a full-time technician.

The waves lapped at the mud just ten feet from the body now, but the bank was relatively flat, which meant the water wouldn't have to rise much to cover it completely. Officer Jackson kicked around the beach until she found a suitable piece of driftwood and then drove it into the gravel like a stake, five feet below the torso.

"Do me a favor, Brackett," she said. "Keep an eye on that stick. Let me know when the tide gets to it. I don't want to move the body before the crime scene guys get here, but we may have no choice."

"Copy that," Brackett said, and planted himself on a spot in the gravel overlooking the corpse. A previous tide had surely deposited the torso here, but they had to investigate the slim chance, however small, that there was other evidence around the body.

Jackson took photos from every angle and then went to talk to the sergeant, who stood down the beach trying to get better cell reception.

Though just three years ahead of Brackett, Sandra Jackson was known as sort of rabbi to younger officers. Some of the more senior guys called her Ma because of the way she mother-henned the newbies. She didn't seem to mind. Easy to talk to, Jackson often took recruits aside to give them pointers during training. These moments of "rescue" made her a go-to person for anyone who had questions but didn't want to incur the wrath and judgment of their FTO. Brackett suspected the training officers were all in on it too, but he didn't care. Officer Jackson was smart, and Brackett found himself relieved that she and the sergeant were there to do the thinking until detectives arrived.

His relief was short-lived when he heard a crunch of gravel behind him and looked up to see Fluke sauntering down the trail from the parking lot in the silver-gray light.

"I get to help you babysit the corpse," Fluke said. His eyes locked on the torso as he came to a stop beside Brackett. "Shit. I'd say she was faceup if she had a face . . ."

Hopper was right. This guy was a weirdo.

"She's been in the water a while," Fluke said, pronouncing his judgment of the circumstance just seconds after coming on scene.

"Maybe," Brackett said.

Fluke sneered, looking at his watch. "I see how it is. You've been cut loose for what, fifteen minutes, and now you're an expert on body decomp?"

Brackett sighed, giving a soft chuckle. If this idiot had taught him anything, it was how to manage upward. It did zero good to argue. "Yeah," he said. "It's hard to tell in the water. Big tides and pad ice banging the body around and whatnot. My dad and I used to drop shrimp pots in Prince William Sound. Sand fleas could reduce a couple of fat herring to bones in a single six-hour tide." He nodded toward the torso. "And she's crawling with them."

"True. But . . ." Fluke grinned as if he were fanning a royal flush on the table. He pulled up a photo on his phone and held it toward Brackett. "And this is a hell of a *but*. If you'd take the time to read the intel reports Homicide sends out, you'd know that a foot, believed to be female, washed up near Bootlegger's Cove four days ago. Said foot was still in good shape, which means it hadn't been in the water more than a few hours. And if you remembered your orientation, you'd know that Bootlegger's Cove is not far from here. *Ipso facto*, this body and its foot have been in the water about four days."

Brackett took Fluke's phone to get a better look. He zoomed in. "Unless this torso and that foot don't go together. . . ."

Fluke snatched his phone back and scoffed. "What are you envisioning here? Some guy dumping a wheelbarrow load of assorted body parts into Cook Inlet? I taught you better than that. It's a rookie mistake to look for mysteries when the answers are right in front of your eyes."

Sergeant Hopper stepped forward, putting a hand on Fluke's shoulder. It was getting light enough for Brackett to see his conspiratorial wink. "Since you're so diligent about reading intel reports, Officer Fluke, you also know that a girl named Felicia Meyer reported her older sister, Dee, missing shortly after we found the foot—and that it has been positively identified. Dee Meyer had no tattoos on her legs." Hopper nodded toward the body. Even exposure to saltwater sand fleas hadn't erased the tribal tattoo encircling the stump of the torso's calf.

"Ink," Fluke said.

"*Ipso facto*," Hopper said, demonstrating that he heard all and saw all. "Somebody is throwing parts of assorted bodies into Cook Inlet. We'll leave it up to the detectives to see if he's using a wheelbarrow."

"Actually," Fluke said. "There—"

A breathless voice broke squelch on the radio, causing all four officers to pause. It was Nancy Alvarez, assigned to the Alaska Fugitive Task Force.

"Marshals 5," Alvarez said, panting, voice jostled. "10-28 with three wanted felons."

"Foot pursuit," Brackett said, translating the ten-code out of habit, as if his FTO wanted to be sure he knew what it was.

The dispatcher spoke next, advising all officers to clear the channel for Marshals 5.

"We've got this," Sergeant Hopper said, looking at his watch, then nodding at Fluke. "Day shift is coming on so they'll be sending Bravo units, but head that way and see if they need you to help set up a perimeter in the meantime."

Fluke puffed up like he was going to argue.

"I don't mind going," Brackett said. A foot pursuit sounded great after standing around a hacked-up torso.

"You're primary on this call," Hopper said. "And besides, it's a little early in your career to get your brain all gunked up with the way the feds do things."

CHAPTER 5

Cutter and Lola hit the first floor at a run, crashing through the back door. First, they scanned the area behind the condo for Deputy Blodgett, to be certain he was all right, and then looked for any sign of the fleeing fugitives.

Cutter found Blodgett leaning against the back wall of the condo, one leg drawn up under him like a gimpy horse, as if he couldn't put weight on it. The deputy waved them off, pointing to the line of trees across the open, park-like area behind the building.

"Slavich went after Shiloh Watts!" he yelled. "The two males went that way!"

Cutter heard Nancy put out the call over the radio for more officers, setting up a perimeter. Lola fell in beside him as they ran. She glanced up when one of the K9 units who'd been doing paperwork at the station attached himself to the call.

"That's Blitz," she said as she ran. Her panting breaths punctuated her words. "That dog . . . scares the crap outta me. We'll have to pull off when he shows up . . ."

"Yep," Cutter said, preferring not to waste his breath. "Eyes up while I watch the tracks."

"Copy," Lola said. She was half a foot shorter than Cutter's six-three, but long legged and in good enough shape to match him stride for stride.

It was all too easy to become fixated during a foot pursuit and forget that the person on the run might just decide to wait around the corner and hit you in the face with a rock—or blow your brains out if he or she happened to have a gun. Cutter wanted Lola's mind on what was ahead, not a Belgian Malinois that was still ten minutes away.

This would all be over in ten minutes—one way or another.

The frost on the grass grew heavier as they neared the cold sink of the depression that contained Chester Creek. Slippery, but easy tracking. Two sets of prints, both large, darted left as soon as they reached the tree line. The long strides between each track told Cutter the men were still running. A deep divot in the leafy muck and two handprints showed where one of the runners had stumbled. He'd hit a knee, caught himself, and scrambled to his feet. Muted morning light filtered through gnarled, bone-like branches of white birch. The gurgling water looked like quicksilver in a stream of fog.

The nights were still cold enough to coat the rocks along the bank with a thin layer of ice. In a matter of weeks, snow in the high country would begin to melt. The water would rise and the creek would widen, but for now, it flowed and eddied lazily around and between snot-slick rocks.

The strides began to grow smaller and the tracks zigged and zagged, cutting through the trees as if looking for the best route. Lola shot a glance at Cutter when both sets of footprints ended at the water's edge. The creek was no more than eight or nine feet across, just wide enough to make it un-jumpable without getting wet in the numbingly cold water.

Lola skidded to a stop in the half-frozen duff, scanning the snow-covered bank on the far side. A jogging trail ran along the water, beyond that, the backyard of a faded cedar house, a tall wood fence, and a rusted swing set were visible through the trees.

"I don't see any tracks," Lola said. Her voice was concerned, but controlled. She'd already caught her breath. "So they didn't cross."

Cutter stooped quickly to pick up a fist-size rock, then tossed it into the crystal-clear water where the tracks disappeared.

"This way," he said, turning to trot downstream, cutting in and out of the brush without explanation. Lola was learning to track. This would be a good lesson, but explaining would come later. He wanted to press the runners, force them to stay on the move. Cutter and Lola were loaded with tactical gear, but wore heavy boots and warm, loose clothing meant for rough work. From the looks of the sign, one of the men had fled wearing shower shoes. The other wore a pair of sneakers with wallowing, flopping tracks that said they probably weren't even tied. Cutter doubted either of the fugitives even had time to grab a jacket. Good. Exertion and adrenaline would warm them for a time, but exhaustion would kick in soon. Cutter would let fatigue and cold do the heavy lifting when he caught up with them.

Runners—good guys and bad—almost always had to make a choice between quick or quiet. Fortunately, sloshing and floundering through calf-deep water was much louder than trotting along the frosty duff on the bank.

Cutter heard the two outlaws before they came into view—a series of barked shouts, heavy splashing, the snap of breaking branches. He shot a glance to his left, watched Lola hurdle a rotten birch log like a doe. He gestured forward with a knife hand to make sure she'd heard it too. She gave him a thumbs-up.

Neither drew their pistols—running with a gun in your hand was a recipe for disaster. Both did, however, habitually drop an elbow to make certain their weapons were still in the holsters where they'd left them.

Clipped shouts, angry, then frightened, then angry again, sifted through the tangle of brush above the noise of gurgling water. A low growl, long and feral, slowed Cutter a half step. It was the sound of a cornered animal.

He raised his hand, signaling Lola to slow, straining to hear details and decipher what was going on.

Lola matched his pace.

A sudden scream clipped into a yelp, spurring Cutter forward. Five quick strides through the brush and he realized his fears. McGrone and Gorman had run headlong into a teenage couple out on a chilly morning ride on fat-tired bikes. Both wore orange West High Eagles sweatshirts. The boy, probably sixteen or seventeen, was on the ground, a knee bent oddly behind him. Bronco Gorman already straddled this one's bike. The outlaw's gray cotton sweats were sodden to mid-thigh from splashing his way down Chester Creek. He wore no shirt, and he had to clutch his wet sweats to keep them from falling off.

He was closer to Lola. Cutter left him to her.

The female cyclist was engaged in a brutal tug-of-war with Corbin McGrone over her bike. Blood streamed from her nose and a gash over her left eye. Blond hair stuck out in all directions, giving her a crazed look. A wool hat lay on the gravel beside her bike tire. McGrone clutched the handlebars with one hand while he cuffed her hard across the temple with the other. He was a head taller, but the determined young woman dug in like she'd been hit before. She let loose another growl, chilling, like the one Cutter had heard as he came through the brush. The sound of it at once impressed and infuriated him.

McGrone hit her again.

The young woman reeled from the blow, momentarily letting go of the bike. McGrone put a foot on a pedal, believing he could now make his escape. The young woman wasn't having it. She yowled, grabbing the bike and giving it a furious yank. It squirted out from between them in the process, putting it out of McGrone's reach, but robbing her of that small amount of protection.

Still thirty feet away, Cutter sprang out of the brush and bounded across the creek. Geysers of water erupted around his boots with every step.

"US Marshals! On the ground!"

McGrone snaked an arm around the girl's neck, drawing her to his heaving chest. He backpedaled on the slick ground, spinning, attempting to use her as a shield.

"I'll break her neck!" he screamed, his voice climbing an octave. "Stay back. I swear, I'll do it!"

The girl cowered, looking incredibly small and frail in the big man's arms.

Sirens wailed in the distance. Cutter heard a dog bark upstream. The canine team was close, but not nearly close enough.

Cutter was vaguely aware that Lola had Bronco Gorman facedown in the slush and mud. He'd worked with her long enough now that he trusted her to stomp her own snakes.

McGrone tried to step back again when Cutter was still fifteen feet out. He was a tall man, wiry, cornered. Fighting like a coward, putting the girl out front, worked against him. Even now, he believed Cutter would stop and negotiate.

That wasn't going to happen.

Cutter dropped his shoulder, juking as if he were going to the right.

McGrone roared. "I said stay back!" He dragged the girl across the muck, attempting to keep her between himself and Cutter.

Seeing help on the way, she began to kick and squirm, clawing at the man's groin and raking her shoes against his shins. She'd gotten her bearings now, and sank her teeth into McGrone's forearm as he turned. One leg jerked reflexively upward at the pain, and the momentum from the girl's weight carried him in a stumbling, half pirouette.

Yowling curses, he continued to issue orders, believing he was in charge because he had a hostage.

Cutter crashed in just as the girl slid down to the middle of McGrone's chest, presenting the side of the outlaw's head as a clear target for a sickening elbow.

McGrone staggered but didn't fall—and he kept a grip on his hostage. Cutter let his elbow slide by after it slammed against McGrone's jaw, then reversed course to catch the outlaw again in almost the same spot on the backswing. The strike was less than textbook. It jarred the nerves in Cutter's elbow like an electric shock, but he was rewarded with the crunch of breaking teeth.

The girl bit McGrone again, then threw her head backward to hit him square in the nose.

Stunned as he was, he gave her shoulders a stiff shake to try to intimidate her into calming down.

"I said st—"

Past talking, Cutter grabbed a handful of McGrone's hair and used the outlaw's own momentum to jerk him straight into a hard uppercut over an unprotected kidney. Cutter aimed through rather than at his target. The punch died there, expending all its sickening energy into the frazzled outlaw. Cutter held tight with his left hand and hit the man again and again with his right.

"Okay, okay, okay," McGrone whimpered, growing heavy in Cutter's grasp. He shoved the girl away as if she were the root of all his troubles. His voice was hollow, like he was about to throw up. "I gi—"

The girl stumbled, pitching forward, planting both hands on the ground to arrest her fall. She yelped from the shock and pain. The sadness of it made Cutter give McGrone another smack, driving the man to his knees.

"I said . . . I give . . . up . . ." The outlaw's voice quavered, breaking into tears.

"On the ground!" Cutter barked. He released his grip so the man face-planted into the mud and snow. "Let's see those hands."

Lola had Bronco Gorman cuffed and sitting cross-legged against a birch tree at the water's edge. The dark-blue uniforms of three Anchorage police officers ghosted through the birch trees.

Cutter stooped, ratcheting on the cuffs—none too gently.

"Why . . . ?" McGrone whispered. "Why didn't you just talk? I mighta really hurt her."

"It's a little harder to break somebody's neck than you think," Cutter said.

McGrone winced. "Well, you sure as shit make a good go of it." He turned his head so his cheek pressed against the mud. Tears of pain and anger ran down his battered face. His eyes fluttered. "I . . . wasn't really gonna break her neck. I thought you would negotiate."

Lola laughed so hard she snorted.

"He's not much of a hostage negotiator," she said. "More of a hostage liberator."

The APD officers came through the trees and helped get the prisoners to their feet.

Lola adjusted the holster on her belt, head tilted to listen to the radio in her pocket. "They have Shiloh Watts in custody. Evidently the K9 got her. Stupid woman. Blitz is a hound from hell."

One of the APD officers glanced at her.

She gave him a sheepish grin. "I mean, he's a great dog—for an eater of souls."

"Know what you mean," the officer said.

Once she was sure the officers had eyes on the two prisoners, Lola studied the creek a moment, then glanced at Cutter with a wary eye.

"The tracks stopped at the bank," she said. "I didn't see any sign in the water, and we couldn't hear them at first. How did you know they went downstream and not upstream?"

Cutter calmed a notch once he saw the cyclist McGrone had smacked was giving her statement to one of the APD officers. She was shaken, but physically okay. A fourth officer was tending to the boyfriend's leg. He gave Cutter a thumbs-up and told him EMTs were on the way.

"Come on," Cutter said. "My feet are soaked anyhow. I'll show you." He found a fallen branch and used it to scratch a rough X in the half-frozen mud along the bank. "Let's say this is where they went in." He stepped into the crystalline water, gasping a little as the frigid creek filled his already sodden boots. "Now, watch what happens when I walk upstream."

He took a few purposeful steps on the slick rocks, knocking loose a winter's worth of silt and debris. Bits and pieces flowed behind him, moving through the current directly in front of Lola.

"Ah," she said, catching on immediately. "No floaty gunk washing by means they weren't upstream to knock it loose. So, they had to have run downstream."

Cutter stepped onto the bank, stopping to let the water drain out of his boots. "Exactly," he said. "No floaty gunk."

McGrone stared at the ground in glum defeat. "I had to have Daniel Boone trailin' my ass. . . ."

Cutter looked at the spot where his elbow had burst the flesh over McGrone's cheekbone.

"Are you grinning?" Lola asked, wide eyed.

"What do you mean?" Cutter moved his top lip, feeling the burn again where the scorpion had stung him.

"It's swelling a little," Lola said, reaching to touch the spot with her index finger. He brushed her hand away.

"Knock it off."

"Okay, okay," she said. "I was just checking your injury. That's what partners do."

"I'm not injured."

"A scorpion sting's an injury," Lola said. "And anyway, it makes you look like you're grinning." She gave a shuddering chuckle. "And that is just friggin' weird."

CHAPTER 6

Anchorage PD K9 Blitz deserved the credit for nabbing Shiloh Watts—who was apparently high enough she didn't have enough sense to not turn and challenge seventy-eight pounds of dedicated Malinois. The original warrant had been for Pringle, but Cutter was fine to book three more felons into Anchorage Jail on Third Avenue. Bycatch. Nancy Alvarez had arrested Pringle's stripper girlfriend for hindering, but she was likely out on bond by the time Cutter and the others made it back to the federal building.

Cutter got a call from the chief ten minutes after he sat down at his desk and started his report.

Her office was around the corner from the task force, past the Federal Protective Service contract guards at the main Seventh Avenue entrance. A set of court security officers in blue blazers performed secondary screening for everyone going upstairs to federal court. Behind their counter and X-ray machine, a set of glass doors led to the main offices of the US Marshals, District of Alaska. Most of the PODs—the backbone of the Service—were there, along with the operational supervisor and the presidentially appointed US Marshal. Never much of a garrison soldier,

Cutter stayed away from this side of the building as much as possible.

He liked the chief, though, and didn't mind at all when she called with her summoning phrase, even with the ominous tone that meant something was up.

"Come see me," she said. "Bring Lola."

Lola was her customary bouncy self as they walked, brimming with the energy of an excited puppy. "Maybe this is about that headless torso APD found this morning," she said. "I'll bet they're putting together a task force to find the killer and the chief wants us to be on it." She elbowed Cutter in the ribs, earning a solemn side-eye. Her bubbliness subsided but didn't go away completely. "Wouldn't that be cool, though?"

"We have plenty of work in our own swim lanes," Cutter said.

"Still," Lola said. "It would be pretty great to catch a serial killer."

"I'd be careful about using that phrase before APD does," Cutter warned. "Anyway, not our job. We'll leave the whodone-it stuff to APD. They figure out a suspect and we'll help hunt him down if they ask."

"I know," Lola said. "But you're constantly pushing the boundaries. If you have any theories about the killer, do me a favor and tell me, okay?"

"I won't," Cutter said, nodding to the two court security officers as he walked by. Both were retired APD. He held open the glass door to the Marshals Service suite so Lola could go ahead of him.

"You won't tell me?"

"I won't have a theory," Cutter said.

Chief Jill Phillips's office was down the hall to the right, past the administrative officer and the marshal's office. It was directly across from the men's restroom—something she noticed at least once a week the day after Deputy Glen Little's wife made Mexican food for dinner.

She looked up from her desk when she saw them coming down the hall, and motioned them in.

"How's Sean?" Phillips asked, motioning for them both to take a seat in her two lavender paisley side chairs.

"He's home," Lola said. "Probably got one of those orthopedic ice machines strapped on his leg."

"Figures," the chief said. "He gets hurt so much I imagine he has all kinds of braces, crutches, and ice machines floating around his garage."

Phillips looked at Cutter. "Are you smiling?"

"Told you," Lola said. "It's weird."

"Outlaw's pet scorpion," Cutter said. "I'll be fine."

"You say so," Phillips said. She pushed her chair back and swiveled to face them. It was performance evaluation time, and stacks of personnel files covered almost every inch of real estate on the desk. The chief was a practical woman who wore practical clothes. Her mouse-brown hair was just off the collar, short enough she didn't have to fool with it much after a shower. A healthy splash of freckles covered a smallish nose. She had the look of a pioneer woman who'd been sun kissed, but not yet sun damaged by a life under tough conditions. Cutter thought her attractive, but chose not to say so out loud since she was his boss. She'd gained a tiny bit of weight since her baby was born the year before. He didn't mention that either.

Chief Phillips scanned the folders on her desk until she found the one she was looking for and then leaned back in her chair to peruse it. Her bourbon-smooth Kentucky accent came through loud and clear when she spoke. "I swear,

Sean Blodgett is like a bumper on a pool table. He just lets the bandits bounce off him so you can arrest them."

"He works hard," Cutter said. "Gets a lot of bad guys off the street."

Lola Teariki nodded in agreement.

Phillips eyed them both over the top of the folder and then pitched it on the desk. Her gaze settled on Lola.

"Well," Phillips said, "you can blame Sean's mishap for the rest of this."

Lola sighed. "So I guess this isn't about an ad hoc task force to find a serial killer."

"What are you talking about?" Cutter gave her a quick thumbnail.

"Afraid not," Phillips said, almost parroting what Cutter had said not three minutes before. "They identify a suspect and we'll help if they want us to. Until then, I'm sending you to work a trial in Juneau."

"The Hernandez brothers . . ." Lola said, her voice glum. "Isn't that trial already staffed up? Somebody get sick or something?"

"Nobody's sick," the chief said. "One of the jurors reported that she was followed home last night. Scott says the judge is leaning toward sequestering the jury."

Scott Keen was the Judicial Security Inspector, the specialist who saw to it that judges were protected and security aspects of larger trials went smoothly.

"Sequestered?" Lola said, almost, but not quite, whining. "Do we even do that anymore? I mean, I've heard horror stories—babysitting jurors, censoring their media, listening in on their phone calls . . ." She looked over at Cutter. "Hey, what do we do about cell phones?"

Phillips rubbed her eyes and groaned. "The short answer is, we follow the judge's order. The practical answer is that

I have a call in to headquarters. I want to know what other districts are doing in this situation."

"You'll be fine," Cutter said to Lola, knowing where the chief was going next before she even spoke the words.

"And so will you, Big Iron," Phillips said. She was jealous of the fact that he carried his grandfather's Colt Python and gave him grief about it every chance she got. "If Judge Forsberg does this, we'll have to run two shifts just for the jury. Scott's got his hands full with witnesses and looking after the judge's safety."

"A new threat?" Cutter asked.

"Not new," Phillips said. "But the Hernandez brothers are gang bangers of the first order. Mid-level soldiers, to be sure, but they're connected to some evil bastards further up the cartel chain. Kidnappings, trafficking, assassinations— their people are good for all kinds of bad behavior. Scott's running a portal to portal on the judge, driving her to work, screening her mail, that sort of thing."

"Are there even enough hotels in Juneau to hide a jury?" Lola asked.

"Not hiding," Phillips said. "Sequestering. There's a lot of groundwork to get done, so I want you on the early flight tomorrow."

"Well, shit," Lola said, hanging her head. Phillips shot a quick glance at Cutter. "What?"

"Nothing," Lola said. "I just . . . I mean, I was starting to mentor this girl out at My House this week. You know, that drop-in shelter for homeless youth in Wasilla. Poor kid's got no family, no nothing. She was on the street until a couple of weeks ago. Now she's working as a barista. We're supposed to have dinner tomorrow night, talk about her future."

"That is a laudable thing, Lola," Phillips said. "And if I

didn't need my best people in Juneau, I'd send someone else."

"Understood." Lola brightened a shade at the compliment. "If there's nothing else, I'll go let her know I need a rain check." She bounced a fist on Cutter's shoulder. "I'll set up the flights, boss."

"Take your friend to dinner tonight," he said.

Lola cocked her head, a wide smile blossoming across her face. "Good idea. That's why you make the big money."

"Pull the door to on your way out," Phillips said.

Lola shot Cutter a you're-in-trouble-now look and did as she was told.

"You are teaching her well," Phillips said after her office door clicked shut.

Cutter snorted. "She teaches me, Chief. I know she can get on a body's nerves, but she's a bright kid. One of the brightest I've ever worked with."

"I'm sure," Phillips said. "But she's usually such a ruthless self-promoter, always pushing for more training and assignments to further her career beyond her peers."

"Somebody's got to speak up for her in this outfit," Cutter said. "I mean, no offense to you. You're a hell of a mentor, but the Marshals Service tends to reward ruthless self-promoters."

Phillips scoffed at that. "Big Iron, the world rewards ruthless self-promoters. The Service hasn't got a corner on that market. But that doesn't make it right. Let's take you, for instance."

"Let's not," Cutter said.

"I haven't seen your paperwork for one of the GS 14 supervisor slots."

The Marshals Service had just bumped all journeyman deputies up a pay grade, putting them on equal footing with criminal investigators from other federal agencies. As newly minted GS 13s, every journeyman deputy was now the same grade as inspectors and line supervisors. Former mid-level managers who had competed and won their respective promotions had to reapply for one of a limited number of GS 14 spots in each district if they wanted to remain in management.

Cutter cared little about being a boss. He'd only applied for his 13 to get the supervisor's spot in Alaska and help his sister-in-law after his brother's death.

"You know me, Chief," he said. "All I want to do is arrest bad guys."

"I hear you," Phillips said.

"All right then." Cutter started to get up, eager to put an end to the conversation.

"Keep your seat." Phillips put a hand flat on her desk, not quite pounding, but definitely making a point. "You know how you took up for Sean a minute ago when I called his propensity to get injured into question? And you consistently downplay your role in Teariki's progression." She gave a long sigh. "That's the kind of leadership I want to see in this district. Scott Keen's a good enough guy, but he's all about programs, not people. The promotion is virtually automatic, but you have to do the paperwork. You won't be able to promote to chief if you don't get your 14."

"The absolute last thing I ever want to do is be a chief. Again, I mean no offense, but I have more paperwork than I want right now. You're on the phone with HQ every day. Half the people there think I'm crazy, the other half just think I'm a thug."

"You're a hell of a lot of things, Arliss," Phillips said. "But a thug is not one of them."

"Shows how much you know."

"Do you beat the shit out of people on occasion?" Phillips shrugged. "Maybe. Is that amount of force some-times necessary? Most certainly." She leaned forward, using her elbows to nudge a few of the file folders out of the way so she could rest on the desk.

Cutter was rarely desperate about anything, but he was desperate to get out of this conversation.

"Too much politics."

"You're not wrong about that," Phillips said. "The Mar-shals Service would be the perfect job if not for prisoners and politics. But here's the deal, Big Iron. You need to put in for the slot, even if it's only for self-preservation. If you don't get promoted, that means someone else will be calling the shots. You could find yourself a GS 13 POD in opera-tions because you make the guy in charge feel small. Some-times the world as you know it shifts. When it does, you have to move too, just to stay where you are. I know you don't want to promote, but I think you'd like that a hell of a lot more than hooking and hauling prisoners and pulling court duty every day."

"I'll think about it."

Her eyes narrowed, like she was focusing on the front sight of her pistol. "Think about it while you're filling out the paperwork."

"Yes, ma'am." He got to his feet, stifling the urge to groan. She didn't tell him to sit again so he turned toward the door. "I'm going to cut Lola loose so she can go home and pack. We had an early start this morning."

"You go home too," Phillips said. "I'm sorry about the last-minute trip to Juneau. I know you had some leave planned to help out your sister-in-law during spring break."

Cutter started to answer, but Phillips raised her hand, shak-ing a finger at him as if she'd just thought up an outstanding idea. "You know what? You should take them with you. We're bringing in some out-of-district deputies on special assignment. You'll be working a regular shift by the weekend. I'm also hearing there's a chance the Hernandez brothers will plead out. If that happens, you can take a couple of days leave. Stay down there and enjoy Southeast Alaska with your family."

Cutter stared at the floor, thinking through the ramifications of a family vacation. It sounded good, but . . . "I think Mim's got something going at her church this week."

"Good people always have something going at church," the chief said. "And they almost always have someone to step in for them if plans change. Ask her. Maybe this is one of those times when someone can cover for her. It'll do you both good."

"I'm not sure I understand what you're getting at."

"Well." Phillips sighed, giving a slow shake of her head. "At the risk of overstepping by a mile—I'll bet Mim does."

CHAPTER 7

Harold Grimsson kept a large oil painting of his late wife hanging above the fireplace. It was a beautiful piece, full of light—just as Marisa had been before he drowned her in the bathtub.

Few people visited him on his private island, South of Juneau, but he made certain those who did saw the painting.

The owner of Valkyrie Mine Holdings sank deeper into the soft leather of his overstuffed chair. An orange glow from the stone hearth reflected off the rich mahogany walls, making even the trashy spy novels in the floor-to-ceiling bookcases look like classics. Flickering firelight added dark shadows to the hollows under Grimsson's deep-set eyes. He was a large man, with broad, if slightly stooped shoulders. A healthy layer of fat around his belly made suspenders more useful than a belt to hold up the faded jeans that he kept tucked into a pair of rubber boots. At six feet four, he could pull off a little extra weight. The twinkle in his blue eyes did little to conceal a flint-hard look that said he was happy to bury an axe in your forehead if you didn't get the hell out of his way. A prominent brow bisected thick black curls and a matching beard, giving him the appearance of Popeye's nemesis, Bluto. A villainous silver streak ran up the center of his chin like a skunk. Marisa had found his cruel look charming—until she realized the truth of it.

Grimsson studied the two Alaska state senators seated across from him. Their chairs were slightly lower to the ground than his, making them sit slightly knees up. Grimsson could stand with ease, while they would have to wallow to get to their feet. Ephraim Dollarhyde, seated to Grimsson's right, had seen through the trick on their first meeting, two years before. He was smart, maybe too smart. The furnishings, the lighting, the Viking axes on the wall, they were all meant to keep everyone off balance—everyone but Dollarhyde anyway.

The painting was at once a reminder not to trust anything that beautiful—and a not-so-subtle message to those who worked for Harold Grimsson that he was not above killing a creature he dearly loved.

Her paramour had come forward after her death, revealing that Grimsson had motive. Internet warriors went insane, offering countless conspiracy theories as to why he'd never been arrested. They'd all watched episodes of *CSI* and rested assured that some tidbit of a clue would turn up to put the killer in jail. It hadn't. Grimsson had been too careful. He cooperated with law enforcement, grieved like a widowed husband was expected to grieve, blew up when they told him of his wife's adultery. Police were trained to look for behaviors that were out of the norm. Grimsson's performance was flawless in its normality.

Time ticked by, the news cycled, and winter came and went. The police made no headway, and Internet warriors found other things to rail against. Grimsson donated money to schools and museums. He was careful never to act as if he'd put his wife's death behind him, mentioning her at every public appearance. Most of those who suspected him at first began to see him as a poor guy who'd lost his spouse. The few who still thought him guilty surely saw him as all the more intimidating. If they were right, he'd gotten away with murder.

He raised his tumbler of Glenfiddich toward the senators in a halfhearted toast and stifled a chuckle. That painting scared these dumb bastards shitless. They didn't realize that drowning his wife wasn't the worst thing he'd ever done. It was, though, perhaps the smartest plan he'd ever come up with.

Grimsson had been extremely careful with his approach so she didn't put up a fight. She was already in the tub when he came in, the water lapping at her magnificent collarbones. She'd sat up, half rising the way a guilty wife would do when she thinks her husband might have found out about her lover. Grimsson kept his face passive, even as he'd slammed her head backward against the edge of the tub. The blow had caused a small contusion, no larger than a quarter, behind her right ear. It hadn't knocked her out. Grimsson knew from experience that it was more difficult to knock someone out than Hollywood depicted. It stunned her, though, allowing him to hold her under without much fuss. She'd clawed at him, of course, and thrashed some, but the tub was slick and any bruising was easily explained away by the initial fall that had caused the injury to her head. He'd worn long sleeves—so there would be none of his flesh under her fingernails.

She'd gone limp much faster than he'd supposed she would. He suspected she might be acting. She'd always been so good at that. He held her under for another full minute— watching the gossamer trickle of blood wash away from the wound on her head while the faucet ran wide open at the foot of the tub. Grimsson had simply walked away and flown to Anchorage for business that evening. Marisa's body had lain submerged under an open faucet for two days. The bathroom floor flooded, destroying any clues the authorities might have found. She liked her baths extra hot, meaning she'd steeped there until the housekeeper came in. The medical examiner found it impossible to pin down the time of death.

Grimsson swore that his wife was alive when he left. No one could prove otherwise, no matter what their gut told them to believe.

The senators swirled their glasses ever so slightly, tinkling the ice. They wanted Grimsson to suggest they have a little more of his eighteen-year-old Glenfiddich. He would give it to them, of course. In time. The girls would be here soon and they would take the nervous edge off these two, stop them from fretting like a couple of old women. Girls, flown up from Seattle so they didn't know faces. That always did the trick.

Grimsson finally grew tired of the incessant sound of rattling ice and got up to get more whiskey.

Politicians were a squirmy lot, and keeping one in your pocket meant constant oiling with good booze and submissive women.

Grimsson filled the senators' glasses himself. Not because he was a particularly good host, these buffoons would be too free and easy with his Glenfiddich if he let them pour their own. Dollarhyde always stuck with ginger ale—and though this meant he didn't drink up all Grimsson's good whiskey, it was just another off-putting thing that made it difficult to trust him completely. Setting the bottle down on the oaken bar behind him, Grimsson sank down in the chair and took a black briar pipe from the pocket of his wool shirt.

He'd taken up smoking a pipe shortly after his wife's death. His attorney said it made him look more avuncular, whatever the hell that meant. In any case, the process of cleaning and repacking the bowl took his mind off having to work with idiots like Senator Loop.

The soapy man looked as if he might sunburn if he got too near a lightbulb. He pushed a wispy lock of blond hair off his forehead and stared into his glass. At length, Grimsson shot a quick glance at Senator Fawsey, who gave an almost imperceptible nod.

Fawsey, a politician from Juneau, had the dark features and rugged good looks of a model from a sporting goods catalog. He was easily the more grounded of Grimsson's two pets, with a good head for money and practicality—which meant he was willing to do practically anything that was necessary to make money. It was good to have a steady man on the payroll, but it also meant Grimsson had to fork over more money to him, a factoid both men kept from soapy Senator Loop.

Fawsey took a contemplative sip of his whiskey, closed his eyes to savor it, and then heaved the deep sigh of someone who was about to say something of great import.

"Harold," he began. "I've gotta tell you, everyone worries about how much these Hernandez brothers can be tied back to you."

By everyone, Fawsey meant he and Loop.

Grimsson filled his pipe with tobacco from a leather pouch. He used his thumb to pack it down and then pointed at the other man with the stem. "Don't you worry about the Hernandez brothers."

"Ah, but that's the problem," Fawsey said. "We have to worry. Dirt from your hands gets on our hands. We are tied to you. And if you are suddenly connected to two heroin smugglers, then we are connected to two heroin smugglers by association."

"They can't be linked to me."

Fawsey drained his glass quickly, as if he thought Grimsson might take it away for disagreeing. "There are two assistant US attorneys prosecuting this case. One's a dinosaur, doing his duty, but not going out of his way. Ah, but the other guy, he's young, ambitious, trying to make a name for himself. Are you saying that no matter how deep this ambitious guy digs, he won't discover that you were the one bankrolling the Hernandez brothers?"

"He does seem awfully determined," Loop said.

"I'm telling you that there's nothing to worry about," Grimsson said. "There are things underway that—"

Loop's hand shot up, as if to ward off a blow. "If you say not to worry, then that's enough for me." It was clear from the hollow tone that the man didn't believe his own words. He wanted something to be done, but was terrified of finding out the details. Neither senator wanted to know anything about how the sausage was being made.

"And the new mine road?" Fawsey asked, trying to change the subject.

Butane lighter in one hand, Grimsson clicked the pipe against his teeth with the other, pondering the fate of the Native kid who'd made such an issue of finding the Native burial site. Dollarhyde had offered to pay him—a lot, but the idiot kid remained devoted to his science right up to the moment he realized he was going in the water. By then it had been far too late to bargain. When Dollarhyde decided to dump you overboard, no amount of pleading kept you in the boat.

The senators would both shit themselves if they knew that little detail. Grimsson contemplated telling them, just to watch Fawsey's head explode. Instead, he sighed, and grunted around his pipe.

"We're good as far as the road is concerned. Should get the main bed cut in by late tomorrow. I'll have equipment at the mine by—"

The whine of a boat motor cut him off.

Dollarhyde stood easily, even from his low chair.

"That'll be your entertainment, sir," he said, heading for the door.

Even the gloomy Senator Loop brightened at that. He downed the rest of his drink, but continued to clutch the empty glass like a security blanket. Fawsey hung his head, slightly embarrassed by the boat's arrival. He'd lost his wife the year before and used the company of these women as his drug of choice.

Dallas Childers came in first, shaking the rain off his jacket and stomping his boots in the entryway. He was one of Grimsson's heavy equipment operators at the Valkyrie mine, but Dollarhyde borrowed him often for more sensitive work. Schimmel, Childers's sidekick, brought up the rear, keeping the girls bunched tight between them as if they might scurry off like mice. The boat they'd come in on had an enclosed cabin, but it was raining hard enough to soak the little group on the short walk from the dock to the front door. The girls' hair was plastered to their exhausted faces.

"Rough seas?" Grimsson said, eyeing a fragile-looking blond waif. She swayed on her feet and was awfully green around the gills. Loop would choose this one. Grimsson was certain of it.

"Rain's coming down in buckets," Childers said. "But the waves weren't too bad, sir. Rhonda here just has a little case of the jitters. I offered to take her back to the plane, but she said she needs the money."

"Is that right?" Grimsson asked, tilting the young woman's quivering chin up with the crook of his index finger. "Rhonda, is it?"

She nodded, licking her lips like a nervous animal.

"Do you want to stay? No one is forcing you to be here."

"No . . . I mean, yeah . . ." Her tiny body trembled like a birch leaf in the breeze. Dark half-moons, part smeared mascara, part malnutrition, puffed her eyes. "I mean, I'll stay."

Grimsson smiled, almost smirking. "There's booze and a few other items you might be interested in through that door." He looked at the senators. "Why don't you men entertain these ladies for a few minutes. I have some things to discuss with Mr. Dollarhyde."

Childers and Schimmel led the way into the great room. The four women, all of them prostitutes from Seattle flown up specifically for this evening, followed obediently. They no doubt hoped the "other items" their host mentioned was something a little stronger than alcohol to help take the edge off. They would not be disappointed. Senators Loop and Fawsey brought up the rear. Seattle was only some nine hundred miles away by air. Grimsson doubted the girls even knew they were in Alaska, let alone recognized anyone here. Still, his private plane was stocked like a pharmacy, so they were already beyond caring by the time they arrived.

"I need an honest assessment," he said, as the door was shut.

Dollarhyde sat down again and picked up his ginger ale. He held the glass and sighed. "Honestly, sir, it's not good. We need to take some drastic action to settle things down."

"Meaning it'll get worse before it gets better?"

"In a word," Dollarhyde said.

Grimsson groaned, long and low, animalistic. "Gone are

the days when you can dump someone into the Stephens Passage and be done with it."

Dollarhyde peered up, no doubt thinking how he had recently done just that.

"I hear you, sir," he said, a little too smugly for Grimsson's taste. "But the Hernandez trial has the potential to go south in a hurry."

"I don't want it to go south," Grimsson said. "I want it to go away. I have certain financial obligations, and those idiots got an extremely large investment impounded by the federal government." He jabbed at the air with his pipe again. "That creates a problem for me. I don't need to tell you, but I'm losing money every day that I'm not taking gold out of that new adit. Nothing, and I mean nothing, can happen to delay that road, you understand me? I'll take care of any investigation later, or even a corruption trial if it comes to that, but I need cash flow. There's enough gold in that mine to provide a hell of a lot of goodwill in the way of jobs." Pipe in his teeth, he nodded toward the back room and the sounds of strained female laughter. "And the things money buys, buy me my politicians."

"I can slow down the trial," Dollarhyde said. "Taint the jury or whatever, but to be honest, that only gives the US attorney more time to run at the brothers with a plea deal. Sooner or later, they're going to see it is in their best interest to cooperate. I'm already hearing whisperings."

"I was under the impression those shitballs wouldn't be a problem much longer. Neither of them knows me, but they know people who know me. If either one starts naming names . . . So how about you tell me why they're still breathing?"

Dollarhyde gave a little shrug. "Lemon Creek Correctional

is relatively small. That cuts down on the pool of inmates who might be willing to do a hit."

Grimsson gripped both armrests of his chair and looked hard at Dollarhyde. "I pay you to solve problems like this. Solve it."

Dollarhyde swirled the ice in his ginger ale and stared into it, like it was something potent enough to offer advice.

Grimsson let his head fall sideways. His wife's golden-green eyes stared at him from above the mantel. For some reason, seeing her face there, so vibrant and alive, soothed him, focused his thoughts.

"I want this fixed," he said at length. "Understand?"

"I do." Dollarhyde set his ginger ale on the side table and rose, as if he was getting straight to work. "I'm glad to fix what you need fixed, but in order to do that, things will get bloody."

Grimsson thought of the dead archeologist, dumped in the sea because he was more attached to a bunch of ancient bones than his own. "It's already bloody."

Dollarhyde gave a chilling smile, a dog finally let off the leash to yield to its more basic natures.

"Well, bloodier then," he said. "We'll hit them tomorrow in their weakest spot—between Lemon Creek and the federal courthouse. It's just a couple of marshals and a sedan."

CHAPTER 8

Anchorage

Mim Cutter sat at her kitchen table and tried to hide a satisfied smile from a prickly teenage daughter who sat across from her doing homework. Something was brooding between the twins, but Mim was used to that. Eight-year-old boys fought as hard as they played. Matthew, the younger, and outwardly the tougher of the two, could break into tears at any moment. For now, Arliss had them both happy, and Mim would take all the happiness she could get, thank you very much.

Constance was a different story. She was fifteen and wasn't content unless everyone around her was just as grouchy as she was. The poor kid had a right to be sad, they all did. Mim had basically curled up and gone catatonic after Ethan was killed. Thankfully, people from the church had brought over food for two solid weeks. Otherwise, the kids might have starved. You never really snapped out of losing a spouse—but Mim had gotten numb to the pain. A little. Arliss helped. A lot. Right now, with the sound of the twins' laughter mixing with the celery and black pepper odor of caribou stew on the stove, she just couldn't bring herself to be glum—even if it did piss off her daughter.

Suddenly chilled, Mim reached behind her for the cardigan she'd draped over the back of her chair. It was a ratty thing of natural wool, with frayed sleeves and an oblong hole the size of a hen's egg where the bottom button should have been. As a rule, Mim changed out of her scrubs as soon as she got home from work—too many animalcules floating around the hospital that she didn't want to bring home to her kids. Today, ten minutes before the end of her shift, her last patient was an off-duty police officer who'd nearly severed his thumb with a new hunting knife. She'd been standing directly in the line of fire when he took away the wad of paper towels he'd used as a makeshift bandage, and got a healthy squirt of arterial blood in the chest for her trouble. That put her in a fresh pair of clean lavender scrubs before she walked out the door—perfect for sitting at her laptop and facing the bills. Dirty-blond hair was pulled back in a no-fuss mom-ponytail. Peaches-and-cream complexion flushed, her heart warmed as she watched her brother-in-law try to teach twin eight-year-olds how to cook biscuits.

A white dish towel thrown cavalierly over his shoulder, Arliss explained how his grandfather, Grumpy, had made the perfect biscuit—taking care not to manhandle the dough. Folding it into layers and cutting it square so there wouldn't be any wasted pieces that had to be reworked. Mim's boys had the attention span of a couple of squirming puppies. She'd written off getting anything close to the flaky biscuits she'd known Grumpy Cutter to bake. But, as Arliss often told her, cooking together wasn't about making perfect food, it was about making better boys. If he only knew what that kind of talk did to a mother's heart.

There was noise in the house again. The oppressive despair from her husband's death hadn't gone away, not completely, but Arliss helped chase it into the corners. The boys fought and laughed, and fought some more, like eight-year-olds were wont to do. They loved having their uncle Arliss around. For a man who rarely smiled, he sure made everyone laugh.

Mim hid behind the security of the laptop screen. Constance glared at her, horrifically loud music buzzing out of her earbuds like melting brain matter. Her lips pursed in a perpetually sickened, are-you-kidding-me sneer. If Mim hadn't mandated she stay in the common areas of the house until after dinner, the kid would have stayed in her room and survived on nothing but Cheetos and Diet Coke.

A glance at the spreadsheet on her computer smacked Mim out of her momentary bliss. Budgeting sucked the life out her. Ethan had had good life insurance through his engineering firm, but the heartless bastards were tying up the payout in court, saying the explosion that killed him was his fault. Arliss paid rent—way too much for the cramped bedroom. He offered more, reasoning that she was feeding him, but she reminded him he bought most of the groceries—and cooked them too, like he was doing now.

Matthew, the younger of the twins, opened the fridge. His head leaned back in an honest hoot of laughter that showed his teeth, then darkened suddenly as if he'd just recalled some reason to be angry with his twin brother. Matthew not only looked like Arliss, he also possessed his uncle's tendency toward an impressive mean-mug. Michael, the older twin by mere minutes, stood on a chair at the counter grating a knob of frozen butter into a chilled bowl of flour. He was the darker of the two, and less emotional—like his father. He said something under his breath that

Mim couldn't hear. Whatever it was, it set Matthew off and he slammed the fridge door with his foot. Stumbling in the process, he dropped the entire quart of buttermilk onto the floor.

He froze, straddling the puddle, blue eyes wide, chin quivering.

"I wrecked everything!"

Michael stopped grating his frozen butter on the down-stroke. Even Constance's withering side-eye warmed for a split second.

Mim held her breath. Everyone in the house was always a half a blink from breaking into tears. For some reason, buttermilk had been hard to find at any of the stores around Anchorage. It was essential to Grumpy's biscuit recipe. Cutter barked at people all day long. He was surely tense from work. It was only natural and certainly understandable if he snapped.

Instead, the man who never bumbled anything did a half turn and knocked a cup of flour off the counter with his elbow. He gave an easy chuckle, as if he spilled flour on top of buttermilk puddles every day, and tossed the towel from his shoulder over the mess. Matthew's hesitant sniffle turned into giggles—until he opened the fridge and scanned the inside. "But . . . we're out of buttermilk."

"*Au contraire, mon frère,*" Arliss said, grabbing the regular milk from the fridge. "We'll make some up before we wipe our wreck off the floor. All it takes is a little milk and a couple of teaspoons of vinegar."

"That sounds gross," Michael said, grating the butter again.

"That stew smells delicious," Mim said.

Cutter adjusted Michael's grip so he didn't grate his

fingers off. "We have Chief Phillips to thank for the caribou."

"Speaking of caribou," Mim said, "I found Ethan's hunting knife in the chest of drawers the other day. He called it his M. A.K.—multianimal knife. He took that shop on Fifth Avenue a piece of fossilized mammoth tooth that he'd found and they used it to make the handle. I think he'd want you to start using it when you're out in the bush."

Michael looked up from his grater. "I love that knife store. Uncle Arliss has taken us there before."

"I'm sure he has." Mim smiled at her son and then focused on Arliss again. "Are you sure the chief's okay with this Juneau trip?"

"It was her idea," Cutter said. His eyes narrowed. "Funny thing, though. She referred to you as Mim, like you guys know each other. Am I missing something?"

"Nope." Mim did her best to fake ignorance. She had in fact confided her worries about Arliss's dark moods to the chief.

Arliss studied her for a long moment and then shrugged. He interrogated people for a living, so she doubted he was fooled. He was just too much of a gentleman to press her.

"We'll just get in your way," Mim said, hoping he'd argue with her.

"Not at all." He looked up from helping Michael cut in the grated butter. "I'm only there in case Judge Forsberg sequesters the jury."

"What's sequesters?" Matthew asked.

"When we keep people in a hotel so they won't hear any wrong information. We help them stay safe and get them back and forth to the courthouse so they—"

"So," Constance cut him off. "Basically a glorified bus driver."

"Kind of," Cutter said, nodding thoughtfully. He knew better than letting a teenage girl offend him. "Really it's not even that cool. I'm like the guy who makes sure the glorified bus drivers have what they need to do their jobs."

"I say we go, Mom," Matthew piped.

"Me too!" Michael said.

"You took spring break off to be home with the kids while they're out of school," Cutter said. "I have plenty of air miles and I found a four-bedroom Vrbo that's only twenty dollars a day over my hotel allowance. That's a hundred bucks for a five-day vacation. Sounds like a good deal to me. Make the government work for us for a change." The normally stone-faced Arliss Cutter was beginning to sound giddy. "Come on," he said. "We could go for some hikes, get out and see the glacier, roast s'mores on the beach—"

Michael's head snapped up. "We're going to a beach?"

Constance gave her little brother another dyspeptic sneer. "Not like a warm Florida beach, nimrod. He's talking about a rocky Alaska beach littered with stinking kelp and dead things."

"Wait," Matthew said. "Will it have that kind of kelp that's like a bullwhip? Because that would be so fun."

"Whatever," Constance said. "You guys have a grand old time. I'm not going."

Michael stared at her, dumbfounded, looking for all the world like his father. "You can't stay home all by yourself."

"He's kind of right, you know," Mim said.

Constance bowed her head so her bangs hung over her eyes, glaring. "You already said I could spend a couple of nights at Audrey's."

"I guess I did," Mim admitted.

Her face flushed as she watched Arliss cajole the boys into working together as they rolled, folded, and then cut the dough into buttered squares. It had been a long day and her mouth was beginning to water, even with Constance's sour attitude.

"I guess we'll go to Juneau then," she said, just as Arliss slid the baking sheet into the oven.

Constance shook her head, hiding again behind the sullen bangs. The boys crowed happily, until Michael pushed in too close. Matthew jerked away, finally letting loose with the full-throated cry he'd been holding back all afternoon.

"Come on, bud," Arliss said, assuming he was still upset about the spill. "It's just buttermilk."

"I'm not mad about that," Matthew sobbed.

"What then?" Mim prodded.

Matthew stood rooted in place, eyes flitting back and forth between his mom and his brother. Finally, he turned to Arliss, choking back his tears. "There's a girl in our class. She was my friend first, but Michael came up and was all, 'Hi' and 'Those are cool Sketchers,' telling her jokes and stuff. Now she likes him more."

Cutter looked quickly away, but Mim caught the sadness in his eyes.

"Wish I could help you, bud," he whispered. "But sometimes . . . it just bees that way." He took a quick breath, obviously steadying himself. "Anyway, stew is done, biscuits are in the oven. I'm going to get some of my gear ready." He rubbed the top of Matthew's head, mussing his blond hair. "I think you boys should clean the flour off your snouts before dinner."

* * *

Mim tapped the table with the flat of her hand as soon as Arliss and the boys left the kitchen.

Constance looked up, earbuds dangling.

"Turn your music off," Mim said.

"I can hear you fine."

"Turn it off or lose your phone."

Constance complied, but with the kind of disgusted groan that would have made a less trusting mother lock her bedroom door at night.

"I'm getting really tired of walking on eggshells around you," Mim said, exhaustion settling all the way to her bones. "You're not alone in your misery, you know. It's been an awful couple of years for all of us."

Stoney silence.

"Your uncle is a guest in this house," Mim said. "He helps us in more ways than you know."

"I'm sure he does," Constance said. "But maybe we don't need that much help."

"But we do," Mim said. "He pays rent. He helps with the boys. He—"

"Whatever," Constance said, gathering up her notebook and papers. "I need to wash my face before dinner." She stood, looking down the hall, then back at Mim. "I've decided I am going to Juneau with the family."

"Why?" Mim scoffed. "So you can make everybody else miserable and show Arliss how much you hate him?"

"Holy shit, Mom," Constance whispered. "I can't believe you don't see it. I don't hate Uncle Arliss."

"Then spill it. What is your problem?"

"I'd much rather stay home and go to the mall with Audrey, but I'm not . . ."

"You're not what?"

"I don't know," Constance said, her chin beginning to

quiver, starting to break down. "It just . . . it just seems like you're forgetting Dad."

"Constance!" Mim found it difficult to breathe. "Come with us to Juneau or stay with your friends. But know this, I am allowed a few moments of happiness. That doesn't mean I'm forgetting. I will never forget your dad."

"You gave away his knife, Mom," Constance said, the emotional walls coming up again, spiked with broken glass.

"What should I do? Leave it to rot in the sock drawer? You know what? I've changed my mind. You should stay home."

"I'd much rather do that," Constance said.

"They why the sudden flip-flop? You're giving me whiplash."

"You already know."

Mim threw her head back to stare at the ceiling. Exasperated. "What does that even mean?"

"Make me go if you have to," Constance said. "Or make me stay home. I could not possibly care any less than I already do."

This wasn't all hormones. Something was going on here. Maybe a little distance would do them both some good. "Stay home then."

Constance hung her head, hiding behind the horrible bangs that hung down like flaps on either side of her face. "Whatever."

CHAPTER 9

Juneau

"There is another problem," Dollarhyde said, "beyond the Hernandez brothers."

Grimsson gave an exasperated nod. There was always something. "And what would that be?"

"That reporter from the public radio station has been digging around."

"She's the one that was supposed to do that feel-good piece about the mine a few months ago."

"That's the one," Dollarhyde said.

"Well, it didn't make me feel good."

"I hear you," Dollarhyde said. "Whatever she found while doing that report has her asking even more questions now. Sooner or later she's going to ask the right questions to the right people and be able to connect the dots. My contact at the station says she has a source who can damage you."

Grimsson nearly bit the stem off the pipe. "A source? You're telling me someone from my organization is selling me out to the media? I want to know who this son of a bitch is! I want them standing in front of me on this island, pissing down their legs. And I want it now! You read me?"

"I understand, sir," Dollarhyde said, his voice calm as ever. "We're watching the reporter now. I'll have her phone cloned shortly, then we'll know who she's calling and who's calling her."

"I want that snitch dead," Grimsson said, stabbing the air with the pipe. "Whoever he is, and I want that reporter lady dead."

"I can make that happen," Dollarhyde said. "At least with the source. But every death brings more law enforcement. There may be another way with the reporter."

"Another way?" Grimsson said, still seething.

"Yes, sir," Dollarhyde said, taking a drink of his ginger ale. The sleeve of his leather jacket came up, revealing a gold Rolex Submariner. Grimsson despised ostentatious watches—or any sort of jewelry on men for that matter. Rings and watches were a good way to get your hand ripped off in machinery. But then, Dollarhyde dealt in another side of the business.

"Her husband?" Grimsson asked.

"He died a few months ago." Dollarhyde drained his glass and set it down beside his chair. "But she has a little boy."

"You are one conniving, mean-ass son of a bitch. You know that?"

"So I've been told, sir," Dollarhyde said.

Grimsson tapped the pipe against his front teeth in thought. "A little boy . . . That could work."

DAY TWO

CHAPTER 10

Anchorage

The twins dragged their own suitcases from the rear of the minivan when Cutter dropped them off on the departure level at Ted Stevens Anchorage International Airport. He would leave the van in long-term parking and then walk back to the terminal.

"Want me to take your bag in so you don't have to lug it?" Mim asked Cutter as she pulled her own suitcase to the sidewalk in the dim, early-morning haze.

Maui Jim sunglasses propped up on top of his head for later, Cutter craned his head around to look out the open hatch from the driver's seat. He gave her a conspiratorial wink. "There's some stuff in that bag that might get you in trouble in an airport."

"Ah," she said. "Of course."

She shut the door and watched Arliss drive away in her Toyota, fighting the urge to wave since she'd see him again in ten minutes. The twins were already charging full speed toward the double doors to "look at the stuffed polar bear inside." Mim extended the handle on her hard-sided case and trudged toward the terminal. The shell of the old suitcase was completely covered in a hodgepodge of stickers from Maui, New York, London, and dozens of other places she'd been or wanted to go. Miami Dolphins football, pink ribbons for breast cancer awareness, a sunset over Manasota Key, where she'd first met Ethan and Arliss—and dozens of other causes covered every square inch of the case. Some areas were two stickers deep.

Now, exotic travel meant helping with a school field trip to the Iditarod Museum near Wasilla, north of Anchorage. Until today, she hadn't flown anywhere since she and Ethan took a trip to Maui the year before he died.

Juneau wasn't exactly Maui, but it was somewhere different from the monotony of her everyday life.

She was still thinking about Constance's little outburst when she walked inside the terminal and found Chief Deputy Jill Phillips standing by one of the Alaska Airlines' ticket kiosks.

Looking at once practical and stylish in a light tan Arc'teryx rain shell and Zamberlan mountain boots, Phillips chatted amiably with a guy with a salt-and-pepper goatee. Mim didn't recognize him, but suspected he was a deputy because of his tan Royal Robbins style khaki slacks and a loose-fitting button-up shirt he kept untucked to cover a sidearm. Arliss called it a shoot-me-first uniform, since it was pretty much ubiquitous to plainclothes law enforcement on all levels. Usually provided by the department or agency, it was free, durable, and tacticool. Arliss dressed that way for work because he didn't mind being identified as part of the task force, but off duty, or when he wanted to, as he called it, "go in slick," he stuck with jeans and an untucked mechanic's shirt. If it was cold, he wore wool long johns under the shirt.

Phillips scanned the terminal as she chatted with the deputy, the way Arliss did when he was out in public. She smiled when she saw Mim, then raised her chin slightly, the universal gesture for hey. The guy in the shoot-me-first getup handed her some keys and then excused himself with a polite nod.

Mim caught a glimpse of the handgun on Phillips's belt as she approached. She wondered what it must be like for an attractive woman who was not exceptionally large in stature to wrestle with felons and, probably worse, lead a district jam-packed with gun-toting type A deputy marshals.

"I guess Arliss is parking your rig?" Phillips asked, hands resting easily in the pockets of her "Dead Bird" jacket.

"Yes, ma'am," Mim said. "He'll be here in a minute."

"That's okay," the chief said. "I'm happy to talk to you. This Juneau thing happened on the same day we hired a guy to change out all the winter tires. Government contracts are so complicated I don't even want to try and reschedule. I'm here to help ferry vehicles back to the garage."

Mim nodded. "Arliss dropped his SUV off this morning. We picked him up."

Phillips gave a little nod, as if the last thing she wanted to think about was shuttling cars. "That helps. Glad you decided to make this trip." Her eyes narrowed a little, the way Mim suspected they would during an interrogation. "I can't promise anything, but the Marshals Service does hundreds of trials like this every year. Arliss is helping me supervise things until I get some more deputies up from other districts, but he should have some free time."

"I'm sure it'll be fun," Mim said, as if trying to convince herself. Her mom instinct kicked in and she did a quick head-check for the twins, finding them leaning over the railing to peer down at the stuffed musk oxen on the floor below.

"I'm thinking Arliss could use a little break," Phillips chuckled. "Lola wears him out with all her cheerful zippiness."

"She's so great," Mim chuckled.

Phillips's smile faded. "How is he?"

"Good," Mim said. "I mean, he seems good."

As far as either woman knew, Arliss was still unaware that a former member of his Army Ranger unit had spilled the beans about the horrific events from their last mission in Afghanistan—the murder of a small child that they had witnessed but had been unable to prevent. It wasn't their fault, but the guilt of the killing weighed heavy on every member of the team—chiefly on Arliss, the man who'd been in charge. Though he'd never been one to suffer a bully, the little girl's senseless death had, in large part, formed Cutter into a man who would not abide bad behavior toward a weaker human being—for a single second, no matter the consequences.

Phillips shook her head, deep in her own thoughts.

Mim found herself mesmerized by the amazingly beautiful splash of freckles over the woman's nose.

"He seems the same to me," the chief said. "Though, I guess that's to be expected. Just because we know what happened to him doesn't make him all better."

"I hope it helps us understand him," Mim said.

"Me too," Phillips said. "Sometimes, he just seems so . . ."

"What?" Mim prodded, surprised at her own directness.

"I can't put my finger on it," Phillips said. "I was going

to say 'sad,' but I'm not sure that covers it. Maybe numb is the right word."

"Hollow?"

"Could be that," Phillips said.

"You know he's been married four times, right?"

Phillips gave a tired chuckle. "I guess that would hollow out the best of us."

"You got that right," Mim said. "The first three were oddballs. Girls with problems Arliss thought he could fix. He couldn't, of course, because they didn't want to be fixed. His last wife was different, though. She was sweet. Passed away from breast cancer a couple of years ago. I think her death nearly killed him."

"I've seen her photo in his office," Phillips said. "She looks . . ."

"I know." Mim gave a resigned sigh. "Like me?"

"Sorry," Phillips said. "You must get that a lot."

"Arliss likes to pretend it wasn't so," Mim said, "but I do have to admit he has a type. Barbara was a good soul. I think they could have been really happy—but in the end, she turned out to be another person he was helpless to save."

"You know," Phillips said. "Men like Arliss . . . strike that . . . *people* like Arliss don't come along very often. In some ways, I look at him and think, 'I can tell where I stand with this guy,' and then later I realize there's this whole undercurrent going on behind that grouchy demeanor that I just cannot get a read on."

"I know," Mim said, laughing out loud. "His grandfather was the same way."

"Wish I could have known Grumpy Cutter," Phillips said.

"You know Arliss," Mim said. "So you kind of do."

"Anyway," Phillips sighed. "I should get back. I am glad you decided to go to Juneau."

Cutter came up the escalator just then, pulling two roller bags. Lola Teariki, thick black hair piled in a frizzy bun, was a couple of steps behind him. Cutter caught Mim's eye, stone faced.

"See that?" the chief whispered. "He would have smiled at you if I hadn't been here."

"You think?"

"Look, Mim," Phillips said. "It's absolutely none of my business, but I'd like to think that Arliss and I would be good friends were it not for the whole boss, subordinate thing. You two have been dealt some shitty hands lately. Don't worry about what you believe other people are thinking. Arliss doesn't talk much, but he and I have worked together enough that I can put two and two together. A woman can see things in a guy's face, you know. You've known each other since you were sixteen, so I imagine you can see it too."

Mim nodded.

"You deserve to be happy—even if it's with your brother-in-law." Mim almost snorted. "The thing is," she said, almost to herself, "the me I am now sure ain't the same person he had a crush on back in Manasota Key." She shook her head. "I imagine he's past all that."

"Maybe so." Phillips gave a little shrug, unconvinced. "I'm telling you this woman-to-woman, not chief to deputy's sister-in-law. That guy is . . ."

"What?" Mim prodded, slightly dizzy to hear someone else speak of her and Arliss in the same sentence.

"Let me put it like this," Phillips said. "After your husband died, prayers and faith—your religion—saw you through the toughest times. . . ."

"That's right," Mim whispered.

"Well, my dear." Phillips put a hand on Mim's shoulder. "You have your church, but *you* are Arliss Cutter's religion—and I think you have been for a very long time."

Cutter's preferred seat—other than when he was lucky enough to be upgraded to first class—was 8C, an aisle, toward the front, on the left side of the airplane. This gave him a little room for his knees, put his gun hand on the outside, and kept the Colt from digging into another passenger's ribs. The aisle location also allowed Cutter to get up quickly if the need arose during the flight. Federal Air Marshals—a completely different agency than manhunting US Marshals—handled law enforcement incidents aboard aircraft, but they didn't have people aboard every flight. Crews knew who was armed and where they were seated, and usually weren't shy about asking for help if a passenger got out of hand. Post 9/11, everyone seemed happy for the extra layer of security. In addition to Cutter and Lola, this flight carried two other deputies from the ops side of the Marshals Service in Anchorage, a special agent with National Marine Fisheries, an Alaska State Trooper major, and two US Forest Service LEOs. There were so many gun-toters on board that Cutter almost wished someone would try something.

Mim sat across the aisle in 8D, wanting to keep a tight rein on the twins. She'd reasoned that if they absent-mindedly kicked the seats ahead of them and that passenger got angry and said anything, then Arliss would have to beat that person down. . . . It was funny the way her mind worked. True, but still funny.

Two Filipino women had the window and middle seats

beside Cutter. Both were blessedly small in stature, so he didn't have to jockey for a place to put his shoulders, as often happened with him on commercial aircraft.

Lola Teariki sat directly behind him, always close by to perform her self-appointed duties as his Jiminy Cricket. Cutter didn't want to break it to her, but he already had a huge conscience. That's why he was always on the verge of slapping some jackass who was in need of a slapping.

He thumbed through a copy of the *Economist* as the jet lumbered down the runway, pausing on an article about breast cancer and hair dye. He closed his eyes and thought of his fourth wife. *The charm*, she called herself, as in fourth time was the charm. Barbara hadn't ever dyed her hair—so it hadn't been that. . . .

Cutter's stomach fell away as they lifted off. The twins squealed a little. Mim hushed them. The landing gear clunked as it folded inward. The twins squealed again, but quieter this time.

Cutter looked out the window, past his two seatmates, and watched Anchorage fall away as the plane climbed out to the north. They made a slow arc, passing back over the south end of the runway. The craggy mountains behind Anchorage were still blanketed with snow. Some of it was old, and cracked, and beginning to sluff off, but from the air, it looked smooth as marshmallow cream. Patches of ice still floated in the shadowed ponds and streams. Dark trees speckled the river bottoms that ran along each valley floor. Lola must have been looking out the window as well, because she kicked the back of his seat as the wing passed almost directly over Point Woronzof, the place where the torso had washed ashore. Some areas across Cook Inlet— Point MacKenzie, Knik Goose Bay Road—were plenty developed, though still awfully remote. But the oxbow lakes and swamps above the Susitna River mudflats were nothing but old duck-hunting shacks and the odd cabin tucked in among scrubby trees. Any of it would be a great place for a killer—but then, Cutter had known more than a few of those who'd hidden in cities like Dallas, Detroit, or Denver. A soundproof basement and disinterested neighbors provided all the isolation anyone needed. But somewhere down there, in the bowels of Anchorage or in some remote cabin, someone was chopping women into pieces and throwing them into the sea. Cutter didn't blame Lola for wanting to find the guy. Given a choice, he wouldn't have been going to Juneau. He would have been on the ground, hunting.

CHAPTER 11

Lori Sovoroff Maycomb looked skyward, toward the wispy white waterfalls high on Mount Juneau, and banged the back of her head softly against a pillar outside the federal building. Midday sun, a welcome gift in Southeast Alaska, warmed her face. Shoulder-length black hair blended with the dark marble façade of the pillar. She was thirty-one, going on sixty. Some days she felt even older. Her husband had often told her she was pretty, but she knew her nose was a little too crooked and her cheeks a little too high for that to be so.

A gaunt twentysomething lady and an older blue-haired woman, both not smart enough to get out of jury duty, stood soaking up the sun by the bronze pelican sculpture. Another juror, this one with a pointy beard, tried to impress the women with the urban legend that there had been some mix-up with the artwork and a federal courthouse in Florida got the bald eagle sculpture meant for Alaska. Sounded cool, but Lori Maycomb knew the truth was much more mundane. The guy who ordered the art for Juneau just liked the pelican sculpture.

Maycomb thought of correcting him, but remembered the edict from Judge Forsberg barring anyone from speaking to a juror. The guy wouldn't believe her anyway. He'd read it on the Internet and he wanted to believe—so, done deal.

Sitting on truth made Maycomb jumpy. It always had.

She hoped the unlit cigarette hanging from the corner of her lips might calm her, trick her body into thinking she was getting a little nicotine. It did not. Waiting for a source to call was murder on her nerves. It made her itchy, like she wanted to crawl out of her own skin.

The Skeletor-looking creeper slouching in the pickup across Ninth Street didn't help either. He was gawking at her again, thinking the bill of his baseball cap hid his stares. He'd been there when she left for a sandwich, waiting for somebody, and had spent the last ten minutes since she returned stealing glances. She thought about flipping him off, but, judging from his stares, he'd probably like that.

She was surprised the downtown parking Nazis hadn't run him off already.

Her cigarette drew side-eyed glares from the yoga pants and Patagucci-wearing hipsters trotting up and down the steps on their lunchtime mail runs. None of them actually challenged her. If they had, she would have pointed out that the sign on the wall said NO SMOKING not NO HOLDING AN UNLIT MARLBORO IN YOUR MOUTH.

She checked her phone, cursed to herself at how undependable most people were, and did a mental count of how many cigarettes she had left in her self-imposed daily allowance. Not enough, not when she had to put up with this kind of tension. Sitting in court gave her too much time to think. And now it was almost time to go back upstairs for another unbearable half day of listening to lawyers tell the portions of truth that were convenient to their narrative.

She'd ducked out of the trial fifteen minutes before the

noon recess, expecting a call from her source. The call was supposed to blow things wide open. But it hadn't come. Maycomb had walked down Willoughby to beat the lunch rush and grab a venison burger at The Sandpiper, thinking the call might come while she ate.

Nope.

So back to court she'd come, stalling as long as she dared before heading back up where she'd have to turn off her phone. Maybe she'd chance an evil eye from one of the marshals and leave the phone on vibrate. It might piss off the judge, but at least a contempt charge would liven up her day.

This trial was a big deal for Juneau. Conspiracy to distribute heroin—black tar, which was still just heroin, but sounded far more evil in a news story than China White or Mexican Cinnamon. The trial should have been interesting, but legal rules and lawyer brinksmanship kept getting in the way of the narrative. Van Tyler, the hotshot assistant US attorney, was making his case with boat manifests and chains of evidence. He'd yet to produce anything close to a smoking gun. She hoped something would break soon, or she'd have a whole load of "This is Lori Maycomb reporting on absolutely nothing from the Juneau Federal Court. Back to you, Matt."

Oh, the Hernandez brothers were guilty as hell, but that didn't make them interesting people. Van Tyler would never have brought this case to trial if he didn't know he could win it. It wasn't a fluke that the federal government had something like a ninety-two percent conviction rate. But those pesky juries were always a wild card—and Tyler just wasn't winning their hearts. He wasn't from Juneau, or even Alaska. He came from somewhere back east and gave off the definite air that he thought himself just a tad smarter than everyone else in the courtroom. Even Judge Forsberg was obviously put off by his demeanor, which wasn't doing him any favors.

Maycomb checked her watch for the fifth time in as many minutes, then glanced at the guy in the pickup. Her auntie had taught her early on that an animal could tell if you were looking at it from far away, by the whites of your eyes. It worked with people too, and the bag of bones across Ninth Street was definitely locked in on her.

He pretended to look down at something in the seat. Tapped his hand on the steering wheel, trying to be non-chalant. He was too far away to hear, but she imagined him whistling what he thought would be an inconspicuous tune.

Her source had warned her that the Hernandez brothers were nowhere near the most dangerous people involved with this trial. There were elements that would do anything to keep information from seeing the light of day—people who would "grind your body into crab food and dump it into the Gastineau Channel."

Maycomb shuddered, then took a deep breath, getting control of herself. She'd been through far too much to be frightened by a scarecrow who wouldn't even get out of his truck.

Still no call from her source. Dammit. She'd have to go up soon, pass through the humiliating layers of security screening and all the guys with guns. She was a reporter, paid to be observant. Might as well have one more ciga-rette while she observed the guy in the pickup, see what he was up to.

She found a spot by the wall, out of the way, to minimize being hassled by any of the chai latte crowd, and pretended to look at her phone while she watched. The longer she looked at him, the more she realized this guy was more of a worm than a snake. She began to doubt herself. He probably had nothing to do with the Hernandez trial—if he was even watching her. Maybe he was just attracted to women with crooked noses and overly high cheekbones.

So far, her source was coming off as more than a little maudlin, promising a tale of danger and corruption.

Maycomb tried to ignore the creeper while she finished her Marlboro. She thought about the book she was writing, or to be more precise, the book she was going to start writing. Any day now. If it were true that every shitty thing that happened to a novelist could be chalked up to research, then Maycomb had enough material to win a Pulitzer. Some people whined that they didn't deserve all the shit they got in life. Lori Maycomb had earned every heartache and inflamed joint. All of it. The argument could have been made—and her sister-in-law made it all the time—that she had it far better than she deserved.

She pondered the taste of a whiskey, pushed the thought away, and savored the last of her cigarette. Her phone buzzed in her pocket, making her jump, but rescuing her from her pity party.

About damn time.

Instead of her source, it was her news director. He wanted an update.

"Nothing yet."

She studied the guy across the street. Maybe he did have a little bit of snake in him. She caught his eye this time and didn't look away, staring at him hard instead, letting him know she'd seen him. Knew his face.

He started the truck and drove away. His leaving should have made her feel better, but it didn't. She couldn't shake the feeling that he'd simply moved to stare at her from a different vantage point.

Shuddering again, she turned to hustle through the front doors, suddenly glad for the layers of security and all the guys with guns.

CHAPTER 12

Dallas Childers leaned into a gradual curve on the little Yamaha XT250 dual-sport, turning off Glacier Way onto Vanderbilt Hill Road, tracing the route from Lemon Creek Correctional to the federal courthouse. He'd watched the transport go by that morning from the parking lot of the Dragon Inn. They were making it easy—two prisoners, two marshals, one car. A dedicated kid with a cap gun could take them all out.

Childers had learned about choke points in the Marine Corps. This interchange in front of him now was perfect. A death funnel, perfect for what he had in mind. Egress might be tricky after he took the shots. Getting his ass outta there was nine-tenths of his strategic plan—but surprise was on his side. Shit like this just didn't go down in a sleepy little town like Juneau. The shock of shattered glass and quarts of blood would lock the attention of any passersby onto the marshals' sedan. Childers wouldn't need to look. His Nemesis Vanquish would be dead on target. And he knew from experience what a .308 round would do to a car window or a human brain pan.

He used his toe to downshift, smiling behind his helmet visor. They'd be talking about this ambush down at the

Viking Bar for years, and everywhere else too. No one would ever figure out who pulled it off, but they'd talk about it, and that was good enough for Dallas Childers. He was too slick to get caught, too careful. The Yamaha was stolen. He'd burn it after, just to be sure he hadn't left any DNA behind. It was crazy how often you got cut running through the brush and didn't realize it until later. He didn't want to get caught because some twig scratched his face and a drop of his blood or sweat got on the handlebars. Being a shooter was about paying attention to details—wind direction, humidity, angle of the sun. Now that he was no longer putting warheads on foreheads for Uncle Sam, he had to watch his own DNA as well. Hell, he'd heard the CSI suits could get markers from the condensation of your breath. He'd burn everything after the hit—bike, helmet, clothes, all of it. The beloved .308 Vanquish would go over the side too, deep into the water of Stephens Passage. The entire setup was a piece of expensive art—ten grand including the bolt action rifle, suppressor, and optic—but it was still just a machine. Dollarhyde had already bought him another one.

Childers rolled on the throttle, staying just under the speed limit as he passed the tidal flats of the Gastineau Channel and the crumbling concrete "stumps," bases of long-gone antennas for the FAA. A stiff wind shoved the bike right, thankfully pushing back the stench of the landfill. A copse of tangled willow and birch trees ran along the road on his left, just before the junction with Egan, the main thoroughfare between Mendenhall Valley and Juneau proper.

The little Yamaha was light, a street-legal dirt bike. He'd stash it in the willows and set up well before the marshals got there. This didn't require a ghillie—one of those shaggy suits worn by snipers to blend into their surroundings. The grass was thick, and the scrub willows exploded with spring foliage. The entire thicket off the side of the road was one big ghillie suit. He just needed to wear neutral colors—urban camouflage that wouldn't draw second looks while he was on the bike—and then disappear into the mottled shadows of the trees.

This morning would have been better, when the driver was nearest his side of the road, but these guys were US marshals. He wanted to get a look at how they did things first

He'd stayed in the Marine Corps long enough to deploy twice, the last as a scout sniper where he learned the value of surveillance. He was meant for that kind of life and would have still been in the thick of it too, but for that bitch in Okinawa. She completely lost her shit after she sent him the wrong signals and he tried to help himself to a little Japanese squeeze. Her brother had tried to defend her honor and got his ass beat for the trouble. The fight had not only been enjoyable, it had saved Childers from the brig. The brother turned out to be a low-level enforcer for the yakuza, so Childers was able to claim self-defense. It wasn't his fault he was a better fighter than the Japanese thug. In the end, the Marine Corps decided that they wouldn't send Childers to prison, but they didn't want him around either.

He'd returned home to northern Idaho and practiced his shooting, working the odd backhoe job until he got on full time at a silver mine in Wallace. The foreman identified him immediately as someone who could help "sort things out." Childers ended up bloodying his knuckles for management by the end of the first month. Higher-ups at the mine eventually learned that their new backhoe operator had skills far beyond the bucket. Soon, he was sorting out a few of their most sensitive issues. Most of the time he just tuned up troublemakers. Once in a while, though, some hardcase ended at the bottom of an abandoned shaft or flooded gravel pit deep in the Coeur d'Alene Mountains. Unfortunately, one of those hardcases Childers helped disappear turned out to be a shirttail relative of the Shoshone County Sheriff.

The boss started tying up loose ends, and Childers figured he might end up at the bottom of a mine shaft himself. He abandoned the stuff in his apartment and drove all night to Seattle, where he caught a boat to Alaska. People like Grimsson and Dollarhyde were magnets to bent men like Childers. It didn't take long for them to find one another. The job at the Valkyrie mine was a perfect fit. Equipment work was steady, and there was just enough sorting out to hold his interest. He'd never taken out a fed before—or any kind of cop—but they didn't have magical tactical powers. Hell, these marshals drove with their heads so far up their asses that he'd be able to pop everyone in the car and then ride away without breaking a sweat. Sure, he could get the needle in Terre Haute—if he got caught. Which he would not.

Their sedan looked like a rental or something. No armor, no cage, not even any tinting. If he'd known it was going to be that easy, he would have brought his .308 and popped the two gang bangers and both deputies that morning instead of wasting time on surveillance.

Still, prep was half the fun—wiping the fingerprints off his rifle and each twenty-round magazine, just in case one got left behind. He liked to prepare for the unexpected. He didn't plan to use more than six rounds—eight max, since he was shooting through glass. With any luck, he'd get the angle right and the first round would shatter the near passenger window, then continue on to splash the driver. He'd take an immediate follow-up shot in any case, just to nail down the marshal behind the wheel. He had to keep the car in place at all costs. The marshal in the passenger seat would go next—before he even figured out he should draw his gun. Childers anticipated getting at least one of the bangers in the back seat before the car crashed, depending on the angle. The last guy would be a sitting duck, chained up and seat-belted in the back. Childers could take him with ease even if he tried to hunker down.

His scope was set for match-grade copper jacketed rounds. No need for any fancy armor-piercing or hollow-point stuff. The shots wouldn't be from that far away—less than a hundred meters. At this range, .308 rounds would cut through the cheap steel like butter. Trijicon red-dot optic with 4× magnification would be plenty. Yep. Six to eight shots would do the trick—but he always brought more than he needed. Ammo didn't do any good if it was back in the truck. Besides, Childers knew firsthand, humans did bizarre shit when they got shot. Some dropped their guns if they only believed they'd been shot. A few fell over and died from a wound that by all rights should never have been fatal. Others soaked up massive amounts of lead and still shot back, just flat refusing to die. He'd watched more than one Marine with part of his face blown off continue to engage the enemy. *Oohrah.* But skinny Iraqi kids did the same thing sometimes, so you could never tell. Childers hoped for the best, but always planned for things to go sideways.

He did a slow three-sixty, checking his immediate and far surroundings before he settled in. It sucked to set up your hide under a hornets' nest—another thing he'd learned from experience.

Juneau PD was just a couple of blocks away, but the worker bees would be out on the street. The guys at the station were, well, the kind of guys to hang around at the station. He didn't worry too much about them. If things went too sideways, the Salmon Creek trailhead wasn't far. The nimble little Yamaha would do seventy in a heartbeat. He could get well into the mountains before anyone could stop him. Juneau was buzzing with helicopters, but it would take a while before they got organized enough to get up and look for him. Even then, the forests were just too thick.

It was just after lunch. He had time for the caffeine from his last cup of coffee to wear off before he took a leak and settled in behind the rifle. Schimmel was his ears at the courthouse. The goofy bastard didn't have to do much, just sing out when the marshals' sedan rolled out of the underground garage, and then follow behind at a distance.

It was a good plan. The way Childers figured it, everyone on the prisoner transport would be dead by nightfall.

CHAPTER 13

"Lola and I will take care of the jail run," Cutter said to Senior Inspector Scott Keen. Both men stood in the gallery at the back of the courtroom, out of earshot of the two prisoners.

Inspector Keen, tasked with security of both the judge and the court proceeding itself, swayed a little, stunned into slack-jawed amazement by Judge Shawna Forsberg's ruling shortly after they'd come back from the noon recess. He'd known it was coming. Everyone had. But hope sprang eternal that the judge would consider the logistical nightmare sequestering a jury would be for the Marshals Service and the individual jurors.

Cutter had seen it coming immediately after the judge took the bench, felt it in the mood of the court. Her demeanor had changed from earlier in the day. She'd obviously made her decision. Her high-back leather chair could have swallowed her up, and that morning, she'd let it. Now, she sat perched on the edge of her seat, obviously mulling heavily on the tens of thousands of dollars she was about to cost the American taxpayer in the name of justice.

She'd heard a couple of housekeeping arguments from both sets of counsel. Cutter hadn't paid much attention to the content of the motions. Instead, he sat and got a read on the mood of the court participants—observing body language and listening to the subtext of what was said. As a deputy marshal, Cutter's job was to make sure the prisoners showed up on time and behaved themselves during court. If they did not, he administered the necessary measures to make them. A judge might bang his or her gavel and demand order—but it was a deputy marshal who cajoled or muscled everyone into compliance. A judge wanted some guy to remove his ball cap in the courtroom—it was someone from the US Marshals Service who made him do it. If a juror didn't show up for court—the judge sent deputy marshals to knock on their door. As long as things ran smoothly, Cutter didn't worry about the guilt or innocence side of a court proceeding. Paraphrasing the immortal words of actor Tommy Lee Jones in the movie *The Fugitive*, he "didn't care."

The lead assistant US attorney—or AUSA—had stood at the lectern for fifteen minutes straight, apparently enjoying the sound of his own voice as he addressed the court about the medical problems of a witness who needed to be brought up from Seattle. Vital information for the wheels of justice, but one of the many boring bits of minutia that deputies had to take in every day when they pulled court duty.

The Hernandez brothers leaned on their elbows at the defense table, to the left of the lectern. Both of their attorneys were court appointed at taxpayer expense, despite the fact that the brothers surely had several cash stashes they'd conveniently left off of their financial disclosure forms at the time of their initial court appearances after arrest.

Half a dozen members of the audience were nodding off in boredom ten minutes after returning from lunch. Only a couple seemed truly interested in the proceedings. A young Native woman perched on the edge of her seat on the second row, the area reserved for journalists. She was dressed professionally—for Alaska—with well-worn KEEN hiking shoes, stylish polyester slacks, and a pullover fisherman's sweater of natural wool. She turned every two or three minutes to look over her shoulder at the double doors at the back of the courtroom, as if she were expecting someone to burst in with news that would exonerate or convict the defendants. Cutter couldn't tell from her expression which side she was on—if any. She appeared to be as interested in the show being put on by the lawyers as he was.

Lawyers were always filing motions to exclude evidence or for a summary judgment, extolling the virtues of their freshly scrubbed clients who looked nothing like they did at the time of their arrest. Cutter had thought it maddening when he was a young deputy, all their posturing for the judge and jury, even outright lying to make a client look less like his real self. Deputy marshals saw the defendants outside of the brightly lit, sanitized courtrooms. Deputies listened to them yammer as they shuffled in belly chains, handcuffs, and leg irons down narrow hallways back to the cellblock. Deputies brought them their lunch, handed them toilet paper, escorted them to rooms to see their attorneys. The judge might order a defendant's white supremacist tattoos covered for the jury. The family could bring a new suit of clothes. But deputies were everyday witnesses to the uncensored versions. They were privy to offensive ink, knife wounds, and colostomy bags that juries never saw. Deputies listened to prisoners curse their fate and watched them break down and cry. Deputies were cordial, friendly even, but never friends.

From what Cutter had seen, Judge Shawna Forsberg understood.

She'd come to the bench from fifteen years at the Federal Public Defender's Office after working five at the state level. Cutter had talked to a couple of the senior deputies in district who'd known Forsberg as a fierce advocate for her clients in court, no matter how heinous their crimes. When word came down of her nomination, everyone believed she'd be a pushover judge—but the opposite held true. Some of the defendants called her Frosty Forsberg, and not just because of her silver hair. She ruled her courtroom with an iron hand, maintaining cool detachment, absolutely unmoved by stories of rotten childhoods, poverty, attention deficit disorder, or any of the litany of excuses attorneys used to justify the criminal behavior of their client. She'd heard the stories before, used many of them herself, and wasn't buying any of it now that she was on the bench. It made perfect sense when Cutter thought it through. Some of the most lenient judges he'd ever seen were former prosecutors—likely wanting to balance the scales for all the people they'd sent to prison. The strictest were often former defense attorneys. Judge Forsberg was the closest thing to a hanging judge on the federal bench in Alaska. If he was forced to work court, Cutter preferred the decorum she expected in her trials. She thought out her rulings carefully, but once she made the decision remained unmovable to all further arguments.

When she decided to sequester the jury, no amount of fast talking from the defense or objection from the government was going to change her mind. Yes, she knew it would be expensive. She knew it would be difficult. But in her mind, it was the "rightest and safest" thing to do.

Five minutes later, the blue-blazered court security officer brought in the fifteen jurors—twelve primary and three alternates. They sat in stunned silence at the news.

Judge Forsberg explained the details of sequestration, reading word for word from her well-crafted order so there would be no question when the marshals enforced the rules she was imposing.

Each juror would hand over his or her cell phone to a representative of the US Marshals Service. They would be driven home to retrieve a week's worth of clothing and toiletries, medications, etc., after which they would be driven to a local hotel by a deputy marshal. There, they would each be assigned a private room. They were to have no contact with anyone outside of the court or jury room—including each other—unless supervised by a deputy marshal. Jurors would be permitted a phone call to their significant other each evening. This call would be via land line in a specially prepared room in the hotel and monitored by a deputy marshal. Jurors would be escorted to breakfast and supper by a deputy marshal. Novels, approved by the court on a case-by-case basis, were allowed, and movies—chosen by Inspector Scott Keen, the deputy marshal in charge—would be shown each evening in a common area of the hotel. Judge Forsberg thanked each juror by name for his or her sacrifice, noting that there was "no service save military service more vital to the nation than that of a juror."

The judge did not utter the exact words, but the content of her order made it clear. The jurors would be virtual prisoners of the US Marshals Service for the duration of the trial, which was expected to last two more weeks.

It was not yet 2:00 p.m., but Forsberg dismissed court for the day, directing the marshals to get the jury settled so they could all resume work bright and early the next morning.

She nodded at the court security officer, who said, "All rise for the jury!"

A man in a too-large polo shirt at the end of the jury box swayed on his feet as his plight sank in. The woman beside him dropped her notebook. Two more fell back in their seats. One juror, a swaggering guy the judge had already warned about wearing too much cologne, overtly eyed two middle-aged women in the row ahead of him. The look on his face said he was imagining possible conquests. Cutter resolved to have a little chat with the would-be Casanova. Juror love affairs happened all the time. The loneliness of being sequestered just helped speed up the process. Only the juror on the front row, nearest the bench, was smiling. She was a small thing, with mouse-brown hair and a startled look in her wide eyes as if someone had just set off a string of fireworks under her chair.

Cutter leaned over to Keen. "What's the deal with the one on the end?"

The inspector glanced up from his notebook. "Maddie Davis," he said. She's got three kids under five years old at home. If I had to guess, she's imagining a hot bath and two weeks of hotel-room solitude about now."

The jurors filed out and the judge adjourned court until 9:00 a.m., before leaving the bench, disappearing through the door to her chambers, contemplating, no doubt, the whirling shit storm she'd just put into motion.

"At least somebody wins," Lola said, walking up in time to get the gist of the conversation. "So, we're hookin' and hauling?"

Cutter gave her a nod, then looked at Keen. "Unless you want us somewhere else?"

"No, that's great. I've got a command post and rooms for all the jurors plus eight deputies at the Sheraton. With the two out-of-district deputies from Oregon plus the two each coming up tomorrow from western and eastern Washington, we should be good to go."

Marshals Service personnel customarily referred to the judicial district a deputy was from rather than the city, especially in states with larger populations that had more than one district. Western Washington meant Seattle. Eastern Washington was Spokane.

Keen peeled a credit card–size motel room key off a stack from the pocket of his suit jacket and handed it to Lola. "It's not far from the courthouse and they have a restaurant. I have two vans set up to take everyone home to grab their clothes. We'll eat dinner in the hotel and I have the command post covered tonight. Once you get the prisoners back you can get yourselves settled—so you guys can help me tomorrow with the day shift."

Prisoners were rarely restrained in front of the jury, so the two deputies and one contract guard from Juneau Police Department waited to hook up the Hernandez brothers until the door shut behind the last juror and the judge.

"We'll get them back to Lemon Creek," Lola said, taking a set of chains, cuffs, and leg irons from the JPD officer, a guy with a stark gray flattop that he'd probably had since the Marine Corps, judging from the Eagle, Globe, and Anchor tattooed on his forearm. One of the two deputies, a new guy named Lardon, up from the District of Oregon, held on to his chains. The outline of his issued ballistic vest was visible under his white cotton shirt and tie. Cutter figured it was the kid's first assignment after the Academy. Not that it wasn't smart to wear a vest; it just wasn't common for court duty. Lola held out her free hand, ready to take the chains, but the kid shook his head, clenching his teeth like a chargy horse, full of excitement and twitching nerves.

"I got him," he said. "I don't mind hookin' up these broke-dick assholes—"

Lola shot Cutter an amused side-eye. He raised a hand, motioning the kid to the end of the table.

"Sir?"

"Listen," Cutter said, keeping his voice low. "You're new. I get that. But we don't talk to prisoners that way here. It shows—"

"Disrespect." The kid cut him off and gave an emphatic nod. "I get it, sir."

"No," Cutter said. "Interrupting me shows disrespect. Talking to a prisoner like that shows weakness. These guys have been around the block many, many times. They respond to calm surety much better than strident bluster. The day will, no doubt, come when you need to kick somebody's ass. Let it be the prisoner's fault, not yours for spooling him up."

Deputy Lardon stood and blinked, clenching his teeth again. Instead of asking him if he understood, Cutter stood silently, letting him process the information.

"Copy that," the kid said at length.

"Outstanding," Cutter said. "Now, look at the door and pretend like I'm giving you instructions to take care of another matter so these assholes don't think I just chewed you out."

"I thought we weren't supposed to call them that."

Cutter shrugged. "We're not," he said. "But that doesn't make them any less so."

Lardon stood and listened for thirty seconds, then went to the back of the courtroom to check in with Inspector Keen for his next assignment.

"How come he gets a vest?" Raul, the eldest Hernandez brother, asked, pointing at the young deputy with his chin while Lola passed the belly chain around his waist.

She slipped the big link at the end of the chain through the smaller link, before inserting the jaws of the handcuffs through the same larger link and then around each wrist. This locked the chain in place and kept the prisoner's hands confined low at his belly. It was an operation she'd done so many times she could do it by feel, keeping an eye on the prisoner.

"What do you mean?"

"I mean that new kid gets a bulletproof vest," Raul said. "We're the ones in danger. We should be gettin' vested up too every day."

Cutter put the belly chain on Reggie, the younger brother, then had him turn and kick an ankle up so he could put on the leg irons.

Reggie gasped. "Damn, bro. That's some big-ass magnum cannon you got. You blow somebody's leg off if you shoot 'em with that thing."

"Not likely," Cutter said, tapping Reggie's ankle so he switched ankles. He knew the drill.

Reggie craned his neck around to look at Cutter over his shoulder. "You mean . . . you shoot to kill?"

"Let's just say, it's better you don't get shot."

Finished, Cutter had Reggie take a seat so he could talk to Raul. As in tracking—and most things in life—it was important to pay attention to the little nuances when dealing with prisoners.

"What's this about a vest?" Cutter asked. "Something happen that makes you believe you need protection like that?"

Raul shrugged. "We hear things. You know, through the

prison grapevines, threats, what do you call it . . . termination orders. That kind of shit."

"Be more specific," Lola said.

"Like it would be easier on a lot of people if we were out of the picture," Reggie said, backing his brother's play. The spider web tattoo covering his neck and lower jaw made it difficult to see him as a victim.

"You need to take that up with your attorneys," Lola said, giving the pat answer to ninety percent of any prisoner's questions.

"We already did that shit," Raul said. The brothers looked quickly at each other, drawing strength. So often, the toughest gang banger cried like a scared little kid after he got inside the joint. "They say we should talk to the prosecutor, turn snitch, tell him what we know."

"Sounds like a plan," Lola said.

"Sounds like you're trying to get us killed," Reggie said. "That's what it sounds like."

"Okay," Cutter said. "Humor me. Hypothetically, if you were going to hit a guy in your shoes, how would you do it?"

Reggie scrunched his nose, squinting like it hurt to think that hard. At length, he said, "I'd hire somebody to shiv me in prison. Some lifer who gots nothin' to lose since Alaska don't have the death penalty. Hypothetically, I could get somebody whacked for a couple cases of ramen noodles."

Cutter turned to Raul. "How about you? Let's have your plan."

"Easy," the elder Hernandez said. "I'd hit the prisoner transport as you come out of the federal garage. You guys are sittin' ducks out there."

The smug look on his face said he'd obviously thought about this very thing.

Scott Keen entered the well of the courtroom through

the waist-high swinging doors from the gallery, checking to see what the holdup was with transport.

"Let's get these guys some vests," Cutter said.

Keen's brow shot up. "Seriously? Since when do we let prisoners dictate the level of security on a jail run?"

"Come here a minute," Cutter said, motioning toward the end of the table again. "I want to run something by you—"

"Finally," Raul Hernandez muttered with a smirk. "A deputy with half a brain." He raised his voice a hair. "Tune that one up like you did the last one, boss—"

Cutter wheeled, nose to nose with the elder brother. The intensity of his whisper could have peeled paint. "Let me make sure you understand something. I don't like you. I don't hate you. Fact is, I don't give a pinch of shit about you one way or another." He waved an open hand around the courtroom, causing the outlaw to flinch. "My friends and I protect this institution, which means you enjoy the benefits of our protection along the way. Respect us, and we'll show you respect."

"Okay, okay—"

"But you piss me off and I give you my word that I will march back there to the judge's chambers and get an order to duct tape your mouth shut. Are we clear?"

"Honestly," Lola offered, giving the prisoners a sad shake of her head. "Duct taping your mouth shut would probably be safer for everyone. My partner doesn't take much in the way of guff before he completely loses it. You get murdered, he gets fired. We're all stuffed. No one wins. Well, society wins, I guess. . . ."

"That'll do, deputy," Cutter said. His prayer meeting finished, he went to the end of the table to join an astonished Scott Keen and lay out his plan.

CHAPTER 14

Across the courtroom, Van Tyler, the dark, pompadoured AUSA who looked like he could be on the cover of *GQ* magazine, chatted with the goateed case agent from the DEA as they stacked papers into a cardboard file box. His female assistant came in through a side door, walking quickly, head up, phone in hand, obviously bearing news. She had long legs and the propensity to wear form-fitting wool sweaters, which drew leering looks from both prisoners until Lola gave them a low growl. Out of breath, she leaned in and whispered something to Tyler, before handing him the phone. The attorney's face lit up as he read. He gave the DEA agent a quick fist bump and then rushed out the side door with his assistant, leaving the agent to take care of the file box.

Lori Maycomb had arrived in court a hair late from lunch. She didn't learn until she tried to get through the security checkpoint that the judge had suddenly banned all telephones, instead of just ordering them turned off, and didn't have time to run it out to her car. The court security officers working the front post were both retired JPD and knew her from the public radio station. They agreed to hold her phone in the Marshals' Office so long as she didn't tell anyone else they were being so accommodating.

Now, with court over, she couldn't get the phone back fast enough. A sequestered jury was big news and her bosses would want to know. Greta Nguyen from the *Juneau Empire* newspaper had been in the courtroom too. She was probably already down at her car phoning in a story so her editors could get something up on the online edition.

Maycomb took a right outside security and hustled down the hall. The marshals would bring prisoners out of the courtroom soon. They would lock down the hallway and their office until they got everyone ready for transport to the basement via freight elevator. Her phone would be trapped until they were done. She made a left past the elevators and found the Marshals' Office still open. A CSO named Dale Winslow was inside with his back to the door. His dark blue blazer hung over the back of a chair and he stood in white shirt and gray slacks, staring out the window through a pair of binoculars at the misty-green slopes of Mount Juneau, which loomed above the city. Five years ago, before he'd retired, he'd stopped Maycomb on suspicion of driving under the influence. He'd let her go with a warning since she was less than a block from home. He was white, but married to a Tlingit woman, and was known to be less of a hard ass than some.

The office was stuffy and dark, with industrial carpet that had probably been on the floor since shortly after statehood. The obligatory photo of the president and the attorney general hung inside the entry, though a little crooked since few bosses ever came here to check. Otherwise, the only decoration on the drab green walls was a large poster of the US Marshals Top Fifteen most wanted fugitives and an OSHA poster about blood-borne pathogens.

Lori cleared her throat. "Whatcha looking at up there, Dale?"

"Mountain goats," Winslow said, excited. He motioned her forward, like a grandpa wanting to show her something cool.

"Just here to pick up my phone," she said.

Winslow sighed. "Suit yourself. But they're pretty neat goats."

He opened the lap drawer of the desk in the cramped front office. He shuffled through a pile of rubber bands, boxes of staples, and a half-dozen staple pullers, until he found her iPhone, then slid it to her.

"Looks like you missed a call or two."

She gasped when she checked her call log, unable to contain her disappointment. "Nine. I missed nine—"

"Sorry, kiddo," Winslow said. "Maybe they left messages."

Lori was already on her way out the door, hitting redial. Her source wasn't the type to leave messages. Her heart sank when she got no answer. Any source sitting on a story with as much potential as this one wouldn't keep calling forever. At some point, they would go looking for someone else to talk to. Someone who was available. Someone who answered the phone. Maycomb sent a text via Signal, supposedly secure, but it was still crickets by the time she reached the street. She pulled up short when she saw the skinny guy in the pickup was back, watching. Half panicked, half pissed, she lit a cigarette and strode up the street toward her car.

* * *

"Hey!" Dean Schimmel's timid voice came across Dallas Childers's earpiece as soon as he answered.

"'Hey' doesn't tell me shit about what's going on, numb-nuts," Childers said. His hide in the willows gave him a perfect line of fire to the road, but he'd forgotten his mosquito dope and the toothy little bastards were eating him alive. "Give me details."

"O . . . okay," Schimmel stuttered. "You're not gonna like it, though."

Childers wanted to rip his head off. "I'm not gonna like what? Just tell me when they leave the building."

"They're leaving now," Schimmel said. "But it's not just them. There's a Juneau PD car in the lead. A big guy and a Polynesian lady in the prisoner car. Two more marshals in another sedan following."

"What?" Childers slapped a mosquito that was drilling straight into his forehead. "They're running a full-blown motorcade? Did you spook them?"

"I . . . no," Schimmel said. "Nobody's said a word to me. That reporter from the radio was here, but she left already."

"Okay," Childers said, wondering what Dollarhyde would say about this. The guy wasn't much on failure. "I'll call the boss. You stay with them."

The phone rang just once, as if Dollarhyde was waiting, ready to snatch it up, hungry for news. Childers gave him all he knew, which wasn't much.

"That's fine," Dollarhyde said, surprisingly chipper. "I was about to call you anyway. Another matter has come up that needs your attention. It's tricky, and last-minute, but I'm sure you're up to the task. You got a pen?"

Childers took a tattered notebook and pencil stub from his shirt pocket and lay it in the grass beside the stock of his Nemesis .308.

"Tell me what you need me to do."

Childers took in the instructions, made a few notes that no one but he would understand if the book fell into wrong hands, and then ended the call. He began to disassemble the rifle while he called Schimmel back. He slapped another mosquito on his face.

Schimmel picked up, still breathless with nerves. Childers cut him off before he could puke more nonsense into the phone.

"Shut up and listen to me," Childers snapped, unscrewing the Vanquish's removable barrel from the action and slipping both pieces into his backpack. "I'll explain the rest of it when we're not on the phone. First, I need you to get a boat—something fast—and meet me in Auke Bay."

"At the marina?"

"No, dumbass," Childers said. "The roundabout in the middle of town. It's a boat. Of course I want you to meet me at the marina."

"Got it," Schimmel said. "Auke Bay."

CHAPTER 15

Levi Fawsey sat at the desk in his father's study, staring down in disbelief. A tear plopped on the first page in the open folder.

His chest tightened, his throat convulsed, making it impossible to do anything but whisper. "*What have you done?*"

He'd sent Donita into the other room. Away from this, before his father came home.

Levi's dark looks and athletic prowess meant he never had to try very hard to be popular. It didn't hurt that his father was a state senator. Of course, that job paid shit wages in Alaska, but his dad also ran successful car dealerships in Juneau and Anchorage—and spent much of that money on bail and attorney fees for his only son.

Levi's superman curl had gotten him dates with every single cheerleader on the squad. He'd started for the varsity basketball team since he'd been a sophomore, driven a new Mustang from his dad's inventory every year, and never had to sling pizza dough or drop French fries like the other guys he knew. With good looks and a healthy allowance, he'd never really had to be particularly nice to anyone.

Oxycontin found him when he was nineteen after a knee injury heli-skiing with friends behind Mount Juneau. He'd met Donita when she was picking up her mom from rehab. She wasn't like the other girls. He actually had to put in effort with her. She didn't see his superman curl or his uncanny ability to shoot three-pointers all day long. Unlike everyone else, she saw him for the junkie he was. But she also saw promise.

He pushed away from the desk, trying to figure out what he had to do.

The folder had been open when he came in. He closed it and slid it back into the lap drawer, where he thought it belonged. It was going to be up to him to take care of this. His father wouldn't do it, but the men he worked with might. And they would be brutal. His stomach did flips. For the first time in months he craved a hit. Something to dull the fireworks flashing in his brain. Something to help him relax.

But Donita was on the other side of the door. No. She deserved better than that.

He leaned forward, rubbing his eyes with the heels of both hands.

"Oh, Dad," he whispered, lip quivering, wanting to spit. "What am I supposed to do now?"

CHAPTER 16

Van Tyler slipped on a pair of Maui Jim sunglasses to protect his baby blues against the glare coming off the Gastineau Channel. The tortoise-shell frames matched his dark hair, which was important, especially with Ensley in the car.

He turned right off Tenth Street onto Egan Drive, heading northwest toward the airport.

"We're supposed to meet in three hours," he said, loosening his tie, glancing sideways at his leggy assistant. He hoped he looked cool, nonchalant. He was a damned good lawyer, but not much of a playboy. In truth, long hours at the US Attorney's office kept him so underwater as far as a social life was concerned that he hadn't been on a date for over six months. He would never have dreamed Ensley Rogers would be interested in him at all. They were both single, so there was no problem there, but he was also her boss—and that was definitely a problem. Grant Henry, the US Attorney, took a dim view of workplace romance. He'd made it clear from the day he was appointed that any dalliance by one of his assistants with administrative staff would be viewed as sexual harassment. It made no difference to him if the staffer said he or she was a willing participant in the affair. They could get another job and date all the assistant US attorneys they wished, but so long as they were employed by the Department of Justice, subordinates could not give consent to their bosses. It was a smart rule, one that Tyler himself would likely have enacted had he gotten the nod for US Attorney—but those legs . . . those tight wool sweaters . . . Ensley Rogers didn't just say yes, she screamed it.

She'd been the one to bring up the fifty-mile rule. An FBI agent had once flirtingly told her that the normal rules did not apply when you were more than fifty miles away from your house. His ring, he said, could stay in the night-stand drawer until the end of the assignment. That agent had taken up cigars, which his wife hated, saying he would blame the odor on other agents when he returned home.

"You're not wearing a ring," said Ensley, who was eleven years Tyler's junior at somewhere around twenty-six. "And I'm not trying to get you to take up cigars. I'm just saying the US Attorney and his stupid rules are five hundred miles away. What we do on our own time is none of his business, and anyway, no one here cares if I sneak into your room at night."

She was a GS 7, knocking down somewhere around thirty-eight grand a year. Maybe she wanted to marry a lawyer. Or maybe she just liked him. Ensley was a solid nine on the Richter scale of smoking-hot women, but it's not like he was an ugly bastard. He was reasonably fit. Ambitious enough that he'd probably be criminal chief if he won this trial. So what if she just wanted to marry a lawyer—so long as *he* was that lawyer, it seemed like a pretty good deal for both of them.

Given such rock-solid reasoning, Van Tyler had crumbled like cheap concrete, throwing caution and his career to the winds. It was heady stuff hanging out with a younger woman. He liked it, and did everything in his power to keep it rolling, going so far as to confide far too much about things that should have remained confidential, and even bringing her along for a meeting with a confidential source. He should have brought Anthony Hale with him, the case agent from the DEA, but Ensley's legs won out. Tyler decided not to tell Hale about the meeting until it was about to go down.

Ensley checked her Fitbit. "Three hours, huh?"

"Yeah," Tyler replied, contemplating the bombshell this informant would throw into the trial—though he had another bombshell in his passenger seat. "I need to go back to the hotel and get out of this monkey suit."

"The hotel sounds like a good idea," Ensley said. She took his hand as he drove out onto Egan, guiding it to the hem of her dress, which was conveniently above her knee.

They were staying at the Super 8, way out by the airport. Her idea. It was quieter, with fewer scrutinizing eyes than the Sheraton or Baronof, more upscale hotels, but both downtown.

"I guess we have a minute," he said, his mouth going suddenly dry.

Ensley wasn't one to pout. She was too aggressive for that. Instead, she pushed his hand off her thigh and folded her arms as if it was all the same to her.

"It takes twenty minutes to get there," Tyler said, working through the timeline in his mind. "Even from the hotel. And we need to get there early."

Ensley brightened. "I get to come to the meeting?"

"Sure," Tyler said, regretting it as soon as he said the words. "But you have to stay in the car."

"Okay," Ensley said. "So where is it?"

"Some kind of remote chapel. The Shrine of St. Therese."

He took a chance and put his hand back on her thigh, letting his little finger sneak under the hem of her skirt. She didn't push it away. "I'd never heard of it."

Ensley shuddered. "I've been there," she said. "It's a little stone church surrounded by humongous trees. Out on this quaint little peninsula. Quiet. Kinda spooky, really."

She was so beautiful.

Tyler nodded to himself. "Good place to meet a secret informant then."

"I suppose," she said. "Only one way in and one way out, unless you have a boat. It's a ways out past Auke Bay."

CHAPTER 17

The guy at the corner market where Mim bought firewood suggested Auke Bay was a good place for a picnic.

The twins were going spastic with unbridled energy by the time Arliss picked them up. Lola came with him, which was great because she always played with the boys. Arliss wasn't one to download much after a day at work, but he told Mim enough she got the gist of what was going on. The sequestration sounded like it was going to be a hassle, but the judge had recessed court early, and Arliss didn't have to be back until the following morning.

It sounded like he'd not been happy with the level of security on the jail run and upped it, ruffling a few feathers of the inspector who'd planned everything. Mim was glad to hear he'd erred on the side of extra security. Frankly, the idea of driving around in a car with a couple of shackled drug dealers in the back seat terrified her. Arliss did that every day.

The fog and drizzle that had hung over Juneau when they arrived that morning turned into what Ethan used to call "severe clear." Rainbows graced every waterfall, and impossibly green mountains rose straight up from a sun-dazzled sea. Mim had heard all kinds of stories about Southeast Alaska's "liquid sunshine," the endless fog and rain—but today turned out to be the perfect afternoon for a picnic.

Lola was playing some word game in the back seat with the boys before they'd gone a mile. Mim felt sorry for her. Most of her large and boisterous family had moved back to the Cook Islands, and it was easy to see that she missed their noise. She had the twins call her Auntie Lola, which, Mim hoped, might make her feel more like part of the family.

Arliss had given each boy a knife to strap to his belt, making them promise to leave them sheathed until he got them set up with some sticks to carve. Fortunately, they made it to Auke Village picnic area before the boys forgot that rule and shredded the upholstery in the back seat of the rental.

As was his custom, Arliss took a moment to get a lay of the land as soon as they arrived. He made no secret of the fact that each of his four previous wives had chided him for the way he checked out everyone at a restaurant when he walked in the door. Mim had even joked when he'd gone to church with her that it looked like he was trying to find someone to fight before he sat down.

"Trying to see if there's anyone there who needs fighting," he'd said, only half joking.

Their rental car shared the small, roadside parking area with a lone Toyota. There was a rusted copper van parked a hundred yards away at another pull-off. A quick look through the huge evergreens over the railing showed there were at least two wood pavilions and several fire rings on the gravel beach fifty yards below. A tiny stream tumbled down the steep incline beside a set of expanded metal stairs. Mim's tolerance for other people was much greater than Arliss's, which seemed to hover somewhere around immediate family plus . . . well, just immediate family was best. There seemed to be enough room here for several groups to picnic without bumping into one another. The boys scrambled around the rental, throwing spruce cones at each other. Matthew slid to a sudden stop, trying to sound out the Tlingit name of picnic area number three, written on a sign above the railing.

"Ts'eegeeni," he said, surely butchering the pronunciation.

"Magpie," Michael read the word above in his usual of-course-it-is tone, as if he'd always known that *Ts'eegeeni* meant magpie.

The boys raced down the stairs, making it halfway to the ocean before Arliss whistled them back to help with the picnic stuff.

"What Grumpy Man-Rule am I thinking of?" he said when they came trudging up the metal steps.

Michael scratched his head.

Matthew groaned. "A man doesn't play until the chores are done. . . ."

Cutter had the boys' full attention when he let them build the fire—using a fire steel and a couple of cotton balls dipped in Vaseline he'd brought from home for that purpose. He told Mim he'd graduate them to natural tinder like birch bark scrapings, but for now, he wanted them to be successful.

They inhaled two hot dogs apiece, used their knives to whittle little spears out of some dry spruce sticks, and then went off to explore the beach with Lola, leaving Cutter and Mim sitting in canvas camp chairs by the fire.

Alone.

Arliss took out his pocketknife and began to carve on a piece of dry cedar he'd found beneath the trees. Mim leaned forward in her chair, warming open hands at the fire, and thought how much Arliss was like Ethan. Her late husband had doodled in a notebook with a pencil when he was deep in thought. Arliss carved. The little squint of their eyes, the raised brow, and frequent nodding of the head as they worked through some silent problem to their own satisfaction—it was similar enough to bring tears to Mim's eyes.

One of the chief reasons she'd gotten along so well with Ethan was his propensity to sit quietly in the same room, just being. Arliss had that quality in spades. They talked on the phone now all the time whenever he was away on assignment. She whined about her shift at the hospital. He'd ask about the kids, checked on the house when there were problems with the water heater or dishwasher. They were like a married couple. Sort of. But when they were together, in those quiet moments in the living room or at the kitchen table when the kids were asleep, they spent great swaths of time going about their own business, content to sit in the same room without a word. She loved that about him. That he gave her space—but still occupied that same space himself, quietly, without demands.

The resin in a spruce log popped like a firecracker, causing Arliss to look up from his carving and poke at the coals. He smiled, which often looked forced when he did it for other people, but appeared to come naturally with Mim. She started to ask him what he was thinking, but decided she didn't really want to know.

Pocketknife in one hand, hunk of wood in the other, Cutter rolled his shoulders—just like Ethan used to do. He looked around, checking out his surroundings as he did every few minutes.

A group of three women—all on the large side, though Mim was not one to judge—sat in folding chairs down the shore watching their small children splash in the chilly water. They were maybe fifty feet away, just within earshot when the breeze was right. The rough language they used made Mim happy Lola had taken the boys in the other direction. A couple of guys in leather vests sat at the picnic table above them, drinking beer. They laughed periodically—and loudly, in the way that drunk people laugh when they've washed away the inhibitions that help them get along with those around them.

Arliss didn't say anything, but Mim could tell he was keeping an eye on the men at the table.

Another woman, this one looked like she might be Native, with dark hair and bronze skin, walked toward them on the beach. A child of seven or eight meandered beside her. The child, Mim thought it was a boy, though he had incredibly long, curly hair that hung well past his shoulders—kicked a soccer ball as he slogged along in cheap black gumboots. Every so often, he'd get a burst of energy and dribble the ball forward, kicking it at a rock or piece of driftwood.

"I saw her in court today," Arliss observed, nodding toward the Native woman, his knife poised above the carved wood. "She's a reporter, I think—"

Just then, the boy kicked his soccer ball directly into the women. It bounced off a camp chair, went airborne, and then beaned one of the kids playing in the surf.

One of the seated women, who wore a sleeveless T-shirt and an extra-wide pair of Daisy Dukes, wallowed up and out of her chair to retrieve the ball. She threw it back to the little boy, frowning and shouting something Mim couldn't hear.

The boy took the ball and dropped it to the gravel.

The heavyset women turned back to whatever they were

doing. The men at the table picked up their beers and started laughing again.

Mim sighed. "What are we doing, Arliss?"

Cutter, already carving again, glanced up from the chunk of cedar. "We're . . . What do you mean?"

Mim leaned back in her chair, facing the sky, feeling the breeze and sun on her cheeks. "I don't know, I just think—"

A startled cry from the beach cut her off.

Apparently, the little boy with long hair had done something to anger the woman in Daisy Dukes again. She began to scream curses at the smaller woman, then grabbed the ball and threw it into the water. Hands on her hips, she watched the ball long enough to be satisfied it was going out with the waves, then wheeled and marched up the gravel beach so she was face to face with the Native woman. The men at the picnic table were up too, beer bottles in hand, making their way out to surround the cowering woman.

Mim's first instinct was to check on her boys, who thankfully were a couple hundred feet down the beach in the other direction, hunting for shells. By the time she turned back toward the brewing conflict, Arliss was sprinting that way.

Of course he would go. There was about to be violence. He wouldn't want to miss that.

CHAPTER 18

L ori Maycomb walked the gravel beach, deep in thought. She liked coming to the Auke Village picnic areas with her seven-year-old son and think. Locked in a semi-fugue state, she was only vaguely aware of the other woman, and paid just enough attention to Joseph to make sure he didn't get in trouble—almost. She was thinking about her novel, which was to say that she was thinking about her failures. It would be a compelling dumpster fire of a book to be sure. Every journalist she'd ever met wanted to write a book, but most seemed to struggle to find something to write about. Lori was sure the tragic soap opera that was her own miserable life would make for a *New York Times* bestseller. It was the nature of human beings to want to stand and watch other people's misery—and her sad sack of a life could certainly provide readers with plenty of that. The trouble was, other than her journal, she'd never written anything longer than the copy for a radio story. In the end, she thought she might be able to fictionalize the journal—not make it more sensational. Oh, hell no. She'd have to tone it down from reality. No one would believe that one life could be so raw.

Joseph dribbled his soccer ball a few yards ahead,

pitting himself against the periodic rock that stuck up from the gravel. Every now and then, he stooped to study some interesting tidbit on the beach, often popping them in his mouth. Like her, he was a person of the water. He'd been able to identify limpets, oyster grass, and the tiny holes in the sand from the digging foot of the razor clam by the time he was four. When the tide was out, the table was set, and despite her many shortcomings as a mother, Lori had worked very hard to pass on the knowledge of her ancestors. She'd fed Joseph from the water since he was old enough to chew. His father had been grossed out the first time Lori pried a little hat-shaped limpet shell off a rock, dug out the sweet flesh inside, and fed it to their son. But he'd come around—like he always did.

Joseph was remarkable at soccer, but his oversize gumboots wreaked havoc on his aim.

Lori apologized to a crazy-eyed lady when he sent the ball flying her way, and had just settled back into her novel-writing stupor when she heard Joseph yelp. Apparently, the woman decided she wasn't done with her screaming fit.

Lori shielded Joseph with her hip and stammered out another apology. It went against her nature to grovel, but there were three women, each easily half again her size, and she had her own child to think about. It was a soccer ball for crying out loud. People kicked them. But this woman had the scrunched-up face of a person who was looking for something to be pissed about. The two cows sitting beside her and the meth-head-looking dudes who'd come over from the picnic table all looked too twitchy for her to say what she was really thinking. Sometimes it was better to bite your tongue and offer the verbal equivalent of rolling over and showing your belly.

The crazy-eyed lady continued to curse over the top of

Lori's apology. She picked up the soccer ball with two beefy hands, grunting at the effort of bending at the waist, and then threw it as far as she could into the ocean. She didn't have much of an arm, but the water got deep enough fast.

The men from the table egged the big woman on, taunting Lori with jibes because she was Indian. It was bizarre behavior, out of place in Juneau even for a couple of meth-heads. The men edged closer, crowding within a few feet of Lori, goading the other woman not to "put up with her Native shit."

And then a very large blond man came running down the beach, directly toward them, growling like an enraged bear.

Startled by this stranger's sudden appearance, Lori assumed he would stop a dozen yards out. She recognized him from court, one of the deputy marshals. He was obviously the chivalrous sort, and having seen the others gang up on her, he would now try to deescalate.

But he kept coming, on a collision course with the two men.

The marshal appeared to home in on the largest of the men, who at six-two was about the same size. He slowed to a walk a dozen yards out but didn't stop advancing.

"Get behind me," he said. Not the least bit out of breath, his voice was as calm as if he'd just walked up to ask the time.

The larger of the two meth-heads took the man's slowing for a stutter in his resolve. "You're kinda outnumbered here. This bitch disrespected our friend and—"

"I saw what happened," the marshal said. "You all need to step back."

The big woman in short shorts scoffed. "Or what?"

The marshal motioned to Lori. "How about you go wait with my friend by the fire?"

The tall meth-head took a tentative step forward, looking like he might shove the marshal in the chest. He was sorely mistaken. He believed they were still in the dance-like, posturing stage of a conflict, but the marshal wasn't the sort to dance. The marshal established his dominance with a straight jab to the tip of the tall aggressor's nose, hitting the staggering man twice more in the face before he slumped to his knees.

Meth-head number two bowed his head and rushed forward, bellowing something nonsensical, and earned himself a knee to the face, which laid him out flat in the gravel.

One of the women had started to take a video with her phone.

The wide woman who'd started it all bent to help the taller meth-head to his feet. "Get up and kick his ass, Gino—"

A Polynesian woman with her T-shirt rolled above her muscular arms trotted up and stood beside the blond man.

"Police," the Polynesian woman said. "US Marshals. Recommend you stay down, Gino." She strode toward the gaggle of women who were crowding in around Lori again. Like her blond friend, this Polynesian marshal plowed ahead, flat handing two of the big women when they came at her. Her raw power at once cleared a path for Lori to move away and displayed her strength to the cursing women.

"Go!" the lady marshal snapped at Lori, shoving the woman shooting video in the chest, ordering her to move away. The phone flew out of her hand. For a second, Lori thought it was going in the water, but the Polynesian woman snatched it out of midair. "Don't want to lose the evidence of your asshole-ness," she said.

Two boys about Joseph's age ran up behind the lady marshal. One clenched his fist, the other, a little blond boy, held a big piece of driftwood like a sword and glared at the men on the ground like he wasn't beyond bashing them in the head. His frown looked remarkably like the marshal's. A woman in a ponytail rushed in a moment later. She grabbed both little boys and dragged them away by their shoulders. Lori took her own son's hand and followed her.

Of all the people gathered on the rocky beach, the woman in the ponytail looked the most ferocious—a mother bear protecting her cubs.

CHAPTER 19

Anchorage

Constance's eyes grew wide at the sound of all the chimes. Even the doorbell in the Liptons' house sounded rich. It was one of those long, drawn-out things like you'd hear at a church or from a fancy grandfather clock. The girls weren't supposed to have anyone else over. Three was the limit. Audrey's mom had said so before she went to catch her flight and left them to their own devices.

Audrey looked at her watch—an Omega, expensive for a high school girl, but not unheard of in south Anchorage. "Right on time," she said. She was sixteen and knew things.

Evelyn Brant moved her dark eyebrows up and down, then shivered in anticipation. "This is going to be so awesome."

Constance smiled and bounced a clenched fist on her knee, hoping she looked as excited to be there as the girls expected her to be.

The doorbell chimed again and Audrey got up from her spot on the floor, careful not to spill her glass of wine. Her pajama pants were pushed up above her calves—she was volleyball captain at South High, so she had great calves.

Cotton balls separated freshly painted toes, and she did an exaggerated heel walk, shaking her butt like there were boys in the room as she went to answer the door.

All three girls' parents knew where they were—but had no idea of their plans. What Constance's mom called getting into trouble and what Audrey Lipton's mom called getting into trouble were miles apart. Ms. Lipton didn't want her daughter to do anything that would get her arrested. Constance was sure her mom would think not going to jail was a pretty low bar.

Constance's mother often warned her to stay away from Mountain View or Spenard—parroting her Uncle Arliss with dire warnings of midnight murders, gang violence, and . . . insert ominously heavy music . . . drugs. What a joke. There were as many drugs to be had in the neighborhoods around Huffman and O'Malley as there were in Mountain View or midtown. Everything was just more expensive.

The midnight murder part—well, that was true about those parts of town, so Constance was happy to cool her heels at her new friend Audrey Lipton's bajillion-dollar house, surrounded by woods but still in south Anchorage. And anyway, for all Constance knew, her Uncle Arliss had installed some government tracking app on her cell phone. It was usually such a pain to have a law enforcement uncle, but Evelyn Brant had told her parents she was staying over with Audrey and Constance—playing the "her uncle is a US marshal" card to get them to sign off on the deal. She left out the part about Audrey's mom flying out of the country.

Audrey's mom was some kind of bigwig with an international shipping company. She was divorced and traveled a lot, mistakenly believing that because sixteen-year-old Audrey was an honor student at South High School, she could manage a couple of days at home alone without getting into trouble. No more than two friends over at once. That was the rule. It made Constance wonder if Audrey's mom had ever been a kid herself. Did she really believe that three teenage girls left to their own devices for two days and two nights over spring break could possibly keep from getting into trouble?

Audrey's mom smoked weed herself once in a while, to relax, so it wasn't like she was going to come home and smell anything that would make her freak out. She was more worried about her expensive booze and locked the cabinet with a combination that Audrey happened to know was her own birthday.

In truth, Constance didn't know what was supposed to happen that night, except that Audrey said they were going to "partay," which to Audrey usually meant smoking weed and snitching some of her mom's wine. At least, that's what Constance had heard. She'd never been invited to Audrey's house before and she didn't know Evelyn except from geometry class.

Audrey was gone long enough for Evelyn to tell an entire story about her mom's stepdad, who killed some guy who owed him money and now he was doing twenty years in Spring Creek down in Seward. "Hey, maybe your uncle knows him," she said, as if Arliss knew every murderer in the Alaska prison system.

"Maybe so," Constance said, hoping she sounded friendly instead of condescending.

Audrey came back with a small brown paper bag, rolled tight and wrapped with a rubber band. It was about the size of a fat cigar. She dropped it on the quilt next to her pizza plate and flopped down beside it, careful not to smudge her toes or jostle her wineglass.

"For laters," she said, pushing the paper bag aside.

"That was way easier than I thought it would be," Evelyn said, nodding at the paper bag.

Audrey took a bite of pizza. "Just like Uber Eats," she said. "But for the good stuff. You should have seen that girl's shoes." She nodded at Constance. "I mean, you *want* your shoes to look trashy for that whole goth, emo thing you have going on, but this poor girl didn't have a choice. I invited her in for some pizza, but she said she had somebody waiting for her in the car."

"That was nice of you," Constance said, feeling stupid as soon as she said it.

Audrey held up the bag and grinned. "Be nice to your dealer, they'll be nice to you."

Evelyn cocked her head, eyeing her friend with a sly smile. "Is that what I think it is?"

Audrey raised her wineglass and took a slug—like she was slamming down a Gatorade or something.

"Indeed it is," she said.

Evelyn's hand shot to her mouth. "You got tabs?"

Constance hoped the electric jolt she felt in her gut didn't twitch on her face. She'd been prepared to smoke a little weed, but tab acid—LSD—was . . . just . . . she did not want to think about what her mom would do.

Constance had seen tab acid at school, perforated paper with colored designs on each tiny square where there was presumably a drop of LSD that would be absorbed when you put the paper under your tongue.

"Have you done it before?" Constance heard herself say. There was a dumb question every other minute. At this rate, she'd never get invited back.

"It's all good," Audrey said, taking another bite of pizza.

"We'll do it one at a time, so two of us make sure the other one doesn't run into the street naked or something."

"This is totally sick," Evelyn said, stifling a giggle. "I can't believe you invited your dealer in for pizza like that."

"She's not my dealer," Audrey said. "She just works for my dealer."

"Did you give her money?" Evelyn said.

Audrey nodded.

"Did she give you drugs?"

She nodded again. "I guess she is my dealer. We could have painted her nails for her. I really do feel sorry for her." She leaned forward, as if confiding a secret. "I think they have her turning tricks on the side, poor kid. Anyway, I figure if we fed her and let her hang out a while, she'd bring us a little extra when she comes back tomorrow."

Constance bit her tongue.

Audrey and Evelyn had been friends since elementary, so they did most of the talking. Both of them acted sorry for the girl who'd come to the door, but they were happy to buy drugs from her. Evelyn was nervous because her dad had decided he was going to have her randomly drug tested after somebody's kid at their church had almost died of a heroin overdose. Constance ate pizza and listened, wondered if her mom might have her drug tested when she got back from Juneau. She'd never mentioned it before, but it sounded like something she might be paranoid enough to try. If her mom ever found out Constance was in the same house with LSD, she'd have her peeing in a cup daily.

Constance thought she heard something outside the front door but fought the urge to look that direction like a scared kid. Instead, she channeled her Uncle Arliss without thinking. "You're not scared of having that girl know where you live?"

"Lighten up, Lolita!" Audrey was always coming up with weird phrases like that. She patted Constance's arm like a wise old auntie. "It's the twenty-first century. Everybody knows where everybody lives. If you can't find out for free, you pay some website a couple of bucks. My mom met this guy online last year who screwed her over somehow, thinking she'd never be able to track him down. She flew to Chicago and put a dead salmon in his car. It will not do to piss off my mother. . . ."

Like having acid delivered to your home address, Constance thought, but didn't say it. She really needed to go to the bathroom. Evelyn interrupted her thoughts. "When are we going to try it?"

"Step back, Sriracha," Audrey said, scolding with another of her oddball phrases. "I said it's for laters. You gotta take it slow sist—"

The doorbell chimed again. There had been someone outside.

Evelyn's hand covered her mouth.

Audrey scowled, as if getting everyone murdered would prove her wrong.

"Maybe it's your parents," Constance said, looking at Evelyn.

Audrey, too brave or foolish for her own good, was already up. She slid the rolled bag of drugs under the couch. She spoke over her shoulder as she walked. "If you hear me talking to the cops, hide the wine."

Evelyn rocked in place, toying with the pacifier that hung from the ribbon around her neck. Constance sat frozen in place, straining to hear the conversation down the hall. She was so scared she forgot she needed to pee.

Then Audrey laughed out loud. Not a nervous chuckle,

but an honest belly laugh. "Ladies," she said as she came around the corner with a short, square-ish Hispanic girl. "I'd like you to meet our mule, Imelda." She grimaced. "Sorry, I shouldn't call you a mule, I just meant—"

Imelda smiled. "Is okay. I bring you your *chochos*, so I guess I am your mule " She paused and looked around the living room, obviously in awe. Her brown eyes sparkled in the dazzling white of the tile and walls.

"No men here?" she asked, running a hand along the back of the couch.

Constance thought it would have been better not to let a stranger know they were all alone, but Audrey shook her head.

"Nope."

"Good," Imelda said, still looking at the couch like it was some kind of museum piece.

She said she'd taken a cab, but the cab had left her. She was going to call her boyfriend but decided she could stay and eat some pizza like a normal girl. Likely story. She was probably inside casing the place for her friends to rob it. Constance had heard so many stories from her uncle that she couldn't help but brace herself and wait for Imelda's friends to bash in the door with guns—but no one did.

Imelda seemed like a regular kid once she settled in. And nicer, more genuine than Audrey and Evelyn.

Constance had never been one to paint her toenails, and if she had, it would have been black. Audrey had only bright colors—and pink, which Constance detested unless it was in the shape of a skull or something that looked rad instead of girly.

Imelda inhaled four pieces of pizza, laughing, trying to hide the fact that she was so ravenous. In the dim light of the porch she'd probably looked okay, but her frayed jeans and oversized T-shirt stood out starkly against the pristine furniture. Her hair was cut short, like a boy's almost, and needed a good wash. She wore no jewelry, not even a watch, but her cell phone case had a little string of fake pearls hanging from the lanyard hole in the corner. It was an older phone, at least four or five years, and the face was webbed with cracks.

Audrey offered to give her a pedicure—mainly as an excuse to get her to wash her feet. It wasn't quite as forward as saying, "Hey, girl, you could use a shower."

Imelda seemed overwhelmed at all the different bottles of polish. Audrey suggested they go with a different color on each toe.

"You are much too nice," Imelda said.

"No biggie," Audrey said, painting the nail of her drug dealer's little toe bright yellow. From her tone, Constance decided Audrey was nice too, just super messed up.

Constance worked on her own toes, but kept a wary eye on the door for the home invasion that she felt sure would go down any minute. She'd already decided to throw a chair through the back window and jump out the moment the front door opened.

Oblivious to danger—and just about everything else—Evelyn rested her chin on her hiked-up knees as she filed the nail of her own big toe. She asked, "Where are you from?"

"Guatemala," Imelda said. "My mother and sisters will come up too when I send them enough money. It is very dangerous where they live."

"You came to Alaska all by yourself?" Constance asked.

Imelda groaned and gave a sad shake of her head. "I paid

a man, or, I mean my mother, she paid him. He got me as far as San Diego . . ."

Constance felt like she might cry. Imelda was only a year older—sixteen—and all alone in Anchorage. She worked for some guy moving his drugs and doing God knew what else for him. She never called him her pimp, but the bruises on her arms and neck were clear enough. Constance began to suspect that Imelda accepted the invitation for pizza and a pedi because the alternative meant going back for some more rough stuff.

Imelda stretched out her legs in front of her when Audrey finished. She wiggled her toes, moving the cotton balls in between each one.

"I am so very grateful to you all," she said, sniffing back tears. "But you girls should be careful. I do not think you know the kind of man who sell you *chochos*. If he came here . . . and saw you are alone . . ."

Audrey fished the rolled paper sack out from under the couch. "Come on," she said. "I'm tired of being sad." She held the bag out to Imelda.

"Oh no, no," she said. "No for me, thank you. They will make me take pills with them when I go back. But that is all right. When I am with them, I do not mind being out of my head."

Constance wanted to scream. "Then don't go back. We can help you."

Imelda gave a soft laugh. "It is not so easy. He would hunt me down."

Constance started to mention her uncle Arliss, but Audrey saw it in her eyes and changed the subject.

"Brighten up, Betty! I said I'm tired of being sad. Let's play a game."

Evelyn bounced up and down. "Truth or dare! Let's play truth or dare."

Constance studied the bruises on Imelda's wrists, the worry lines in her pretty face. Yeah, a truth game with this poor girl was bound to cheer everybody up.

CHAPTER 20

"You wait here," Van Tyler said. The parking lot at the Shrine of St. Therese was a few hundred feet off the road, tucked into a dark forest of huge spruce and towering hemlock. He'd driven past the lot first, hoping to get all the way out to the shrine by car, but found the road to the caretaker's home and public restrooms blocked with a brightly painted little sign that directed him to go back the way he'd come.

Ensley put a hand on his forearm, cocking her head like she knew better. "You said you'd never been here before," she said. "I have, so I should show you where to go."

"Nice try," the attorney said. "You already told me there was only one way on and off. I'll be fine."

"We're the only car in the lot." She took out her phone and opened a game with colored bubbles. "Looks like we got here first. Your informant is probably going to park right here. Maybe I'll go ahead and get the information and cut you out of the deal."

"Just stay in the car," he said. "I'm serious."

She gave him the most noncommittal shrug he'd ever seen and went back to playing on her phone, popping bubbles with her thumbs.

Van Tyler knew he should pull rank, but he held his tongue. This girl was hot, but sometimes she made him want to punch a wall. She didn't have to do a damned thing he said. He'd given up all rights to be her boss as soon as her panties came off the first time. Before that, really. When they'd just flirted, talked about it in deliciously juicy double entendre. She had him over a barrel and she knew it—but oh, what a barrel that was. He shook his head, resigned to his whipped lot in life for as long as it lasted. He wasn't breaking any laws, or even any sacrosanct moral code, just office policy. It was only his career at stake. But if this informant came through with the promised information, his career would be able to weather a lot of storms.

He eased the door shut. The parking lot was all mossy stone and brown shadows beneath the enormous trees. It felt like a graveyard—not the kind of place you slammed a door. A gravel path followed the gentle slope down between the buildings, toward the sea. A small, tree-covered hummock rose out of the water at the end of a narrow spit, perhaps a hundred yards long. The stone chapel where he was supposed to meet the informant would be out there, completely hidden by the trees.

Basketball-size rocks landscaped with shrubs of ash and juniper lined the gravel path. This had been built by humans, but there had likely been a path to the island for millennia, exposed by falling tides and disappearing when they rose. It made for the perfect sacred island. There was a word for such an island mound connected to land by a spit . . . Tyler's vocabulary was far superior to the other AUSAs in the office. It was better than most people he knew except for his father, who had a true photographic memory. He was *eidetic* if a person wanted to use the precise word—which Van's father always did.

He continued out the spit toward the little bump of land. . . .

What was that word . . . ?

Tyler thought about looking it up on his phone but decided he'd let the back of his brain do the work while he focused on getting the Hernandez brothers convicted along with everyone else who had anything to do with smuggling a boatload of black tar heroin into Alaska.

He took a deep, cleansing breath of sea air to clear his head. There were no clouds, but it was getting late, and an evening haze hung over the distant snowcapped mountains across the Lynn Canal. The water was glass calm, undulating like quicksilver in the long light. A man in an aluminum skiff fished off the gravel bar north of the shrine. The path climbed gradually into the trees, and a humble gray chapel of gray melon-size river stone came into view. It resembled a small fort.

Still trying to think of the elusive word for this kind of island, Tyler walked the circumference of the grounds twice, stopping at each of several religious statues, halfheartedly reading their inscriptions, killing time. He expected someone would approach him in the shadows like a Cold War spy. No one did, so he pulled open the polished timber door and went inside the church.

Ensley Rogers stuffed her phone in the pocket of her jacket as soon as Van walked down the little hill between the buildings and out of sight. She'd suffered from FOMO before anyone gave it its own acronym. Fear of Missing Out. Never being the type to wait in the car—not for anybody—she wanted to see this informant for herself. Like that *Hamilton* song, she wanted to be in the "room where it happened"—in the thick of things. Most of all, she wanted to protect Van. He was a good guy, even if he was a little preoccupied with his cool hairdo.

Her leg began to bounce. Her fingers drummed the center armrest. After what seemed like hours, she pulled out her phone again to check the time.

Seven minutes.

Her leg bounced harder. The finger drumming became more intense. She'd planned to introduce herself when the informant arrived, like a good assistant, and then walk out to the shrine together. But no one showed, and she began to think the meeting was already going on. Without her.

Van would be mad if she followed him, but she'd make it up to him later.

She got out, easing the door shut so it didn't make a sound, and snugged her jacket up tight around her neck. She wasn't chilly. The dark shadows and towering trees just made this place spooky as hell. She checked her phone again.

Fifteen minutes. That was long enough to wait.

The tiny bud in Dallas Childers's left ear clicked with static a moment before Schimmel's discombobulated chatter came across the air. He was in the boat, fishing, watching, supposedly ready to give a heads-up when anyone approached the shrine. Childers had had the attorney in his sights for three full minutes before the idiot had said a word about it.

The voice-activated radios were encrypted, better than cell phones for this job. Childers did not want to leave his position on the gun to push or swipe any buttons needed to take a call. It was a good thing, too. The witless US attorney had walked within ten feet of his hide. This time, Childers wore a ghillie suit, uneven strips of multicolored burlap that matched the thick foliage of highbush cranberries and devil's club. He'd dug into the duff and decaying spruce trunk, covering himself with debris. A multicam sniper veil draped across the rifle's optic, breaking up the outline to any casual observer. But in the end, Childers stayed hidden because the lawyer, like most people, walked around with his head up his ass. Obviously nervous, the guy looked everywhere but saw little.

"I . . . I think . . . he's gone in the church," Schimmel stammered.

"I can see that," Childers whispered, hyperaware of his own breathing. The tiny mic was so close to the corner of his mouth that he was nearly eating it, so a whisper was plenty loud. The door was around the corner from his hide, out of his view, but he could see Tyler through the window now.

Schimmel started jabbering again. "Tall brunette just started your way from the parking lot."

"A female?" Childers confirmed. Surprised. "Alone?"

"Yes and yes," Schimmel said.

"Recognize her?"

"I don't know," Schimmel said. "Maybe. No. I mean, I never saw her at the mine offices or anything. She's pretty."

"I'm gonna need more than that."

"Tall, dark hair, long legs."

"Copy," Childers said, unwilling to waste anymore breath with a guy whose intel was useless. The description didn't sound familiar to him either.

A female informant. That was interesting. Maybe she worked for one of the senators. Maybe she was one of Grimsson's old whores. It didn't matter. Childers's job wasn't to figure out her motives, just to keep her from following through with them. She was meeting at a lonely church with a government attorney. That checked the only box he needed in order to move forward.

Eye on the scope, he watched the light change abruptly in the windows, flashing brighter, then getting dim again. She'd opened the front door and gone inside. The attorney stood in the middle of the chapel. He raised his arms, obviously animated about something—as if he were extremely surprised.

Taking both of them from this angle was problematic. Childers would have to wait for the woman to move into view, if she ever did. Following up would be messy—going inside to hunt down the survivor, risking someone else stumbling in on the action. Childers didn't mind messy, but he preferred something a little cleaner. Moving only his thumb, he pressed a small button on the transmitter he'd taped to the stock of his rifle. Childers still couldn't see the woman, but inside the building, the attorney's head snapped up and he began to move toward the stairs that led to a small loft at the back of the sanctuary, and directly into the field of fire. The informant was, no doubt, already spilling her guts, which made Childers's job clear.

Van Tyler and Ensley Rogers turned at the same time to look toward the loft. Tyler's momentary anger when she'd come through the door had quickly turned to relief that he was no longer alone. He'd read that at least one of the priests was buried in a crypt under the podium.

Ensley crouched like a startled bunny, her eyes fixed high on the back wall of the chapel. "What's that noise?" Clicking static came from somewhere behind the small balcony. Tyler could see the rounded tops of what looked like metal folding chairs over the railing.

"Sounds like a stereo speaker powering off and on," Tyler said. He cocked his head to one side, squinting to study the exposed beams in the shadows above, the corners of the tiny church—the logical places for a sound system. He half expected to see frowning gargoyles perched on their haunches. There were neither. The loft balcony ran the width of the chapel with a waist-high wall of painted concrete that would allow those seated above to hear the sermon or liturgy or mass or whatever happened to be going on in the front. The top half of a door to what looked like a tiny storage room was visible on the end opposite the stairs. The entry doors were beneath it, as was a table where people could leave donations for bottles of holy water or rosary beads. There was a stone fireplace in the corner, beside two modest-looking confessional cabinets of dark wood.

"You think your informant's already up there?" Ensley said. She crowded closer, nodding toward the door to the upstairs closet.

"Maybe," Tyler said, his mind in overdrive. Everything about this seemed wrong. "But the fireplace is directly below. It's got to be a mechanical room or something." The clicking grew louder. Less random. He took Ensley by the elbow and nudged her toward the exit doors. "We should go."

"What?" She gasped, slack-jawed, incredulous. "I can't even . . . You go back to the car if you want to. Maybe your informant left you a recording, or a burner phone. That would be cool, right? I'm gonna check it out."

Tyler's grip tightened on her elbow. "Listen to me. Raul and Reggie Hernandez are extremely dangerous people. The kind of guys who saw off heads on their home turf. Nothing's to say their people didn't bring their saws to Juneau." The words sounded pitifully maudlin when they left his mouth, but only that morning he'd reviewed a file about the brothers' cartel affiliations. Something about empty churches had always scared him, and standing in the chapel he couldn't get the bloody photographs out of his mind. He whispered, "They are bad. I mean, really bad."

"I know," Ensley said, her voice soothing. Certain. "That's why I'm so proud of you. Somebody has to fight them." Instead of yanking away, she reached across and took his hand, pulling him with her toward the steps.

"Okay, okay." He took a deep breath. "But I'll go first. You shouldn't even be here."

Childers had yet to get a clear shot of the woman until they started up the stairs. From that point, both she and Tyler were in view all the way to the top, so he decided to wait. The balcony offered the perfect sight picture, the perfect line of fire. Easy. The rifle's optic pulled them close enough that he could see the woman's chest tremble with each breath.

Working like a cricket, the tiny electronic noisemaker projected a maddening click that was almost impossible to locate. It gave the target something to focus on, while Childers lined up his shot—like whistling at a mule deer to get it to stop midflight.

Childers found himself wishing he'd planted a listening device. Dollarhyde and the old man would be highly interested in the conversation that was surely going on right now. The girl had probably spent the last five minutes venting her spleen to the Mr. *GQ* US Attorney. It would have been nice to know—but in the long run, it wouldn't matter, so long as

Childers did his job. The attorney surely knew too much by now. He couldn't be allowed to walk out of this church.

Childers held a small sand bag under the butt of the rifle with his left fist, tucked in next to the pocket of his shoulder. He squeezed it slightly, adjusting his point of aim so the scope's crosshairs rested at the base of the brunette's ear. He'd take her first, at once stunning the attorney with the sudden carnage and blocking his retreat down the stairs with her body.

Childers wondered idly if her diamond earrings were real as his finger tightened against the trigger.

Van Tyler coughed, spattering blood on the concrete wall. Behind him, Ensley's lifeless body pinned his legs to the floor. He'd tried to catch her, thought she'd tripped or something. But . . . he shuddered at the thought of her beautiful face. It was just . . . gone.

Had there been an explosion? No. Somebody had shot them. Breaking glass . . . Ensley's last word . . . He struggled to make sense of it all—needing air, losing blood. Her death had been mercifully quick. She'd teetered there, standing, one minute chattering about how scared she was—

Tyler felt a meteoric pain in his jaw, like he'd been struck with a hammer. Then, everything went quiet. He lost all sense of time.

They were on the floor now, behind the concrete balcony wall. He knew he was wounded, bad, but didn't want to touch his head for fear of what he'd find. His left ear was on fire. The light inside the quiet church, already dim, began to fade. He felt himself drifting above his own body. Nothing made sense. Why had they even come here? And why was his secretary with him? All that had been crucially important just seconds before was suddenly so meaningless.

His eyes drooped, his head too heavy for his neck to keep it upright.

The informant . . . That's right. An informant was going to meet him on this little mound of rock. . . . He chuckled softly, struck with a moment of sudden clarity as darkness enveloped him. A pained half smile crossed his lips and then fell away.

"Tombolo." That was the word he'd been trying to remember. . . .

CHAPTER 21

Cutter raised a wary brow as Lola's cell phone began to play "We Know the Way" from Disney's *Moana*. He didn't particularly care for ringtones that sounded like anything other than a normal phone, but this one suited Lola Tuakana Teariki. Mim had gathered up the twins and invited the Native woman and her son to the campfire so they didn't have to listen to the two sullen men and a very angry woman continue to curse. Cutter had them sitting cross-legged on the ground for now. The men's hands were secured behind their backs with cuffs, the woman's with a pair of disposable, shoelace-like restraints Cutter habitually carried in his pocket when he was armed—meaning almost always. The other two women slouched in their camp chairs, splitting their attention between the playing children and their friends. The Alaska State Troopers were on their way.

Lola answered the phone, keeping an eye on Cutter and the prisoners while she listened intently.

At length, she ended the call and stared at the screen. "Nobody's coming," she said.

The woman who took the video shot to her feet. "What do you mean nobody's coming. You people should be the ones in handcuffs. That Indian bitch is the one who started it."

Cutter ignored the woman, cocking his head, waiting for Lola to tell him as much as she could in front of the others.

"That was AST dispatch," Lola said. "They said we can either take them to jail ourselves, or get their names and fill out a report." She motioned Cutter a few steps away from the group and then leaned in close so she didn't have to whisper. "There's been an incident a couple of miles up the road. Troopers are asking for our help."

The whispered words "Van Tyler" and "murdered" were all the explanation Cutter needed for the moment. He took photos of the prisoners' IDs, gave them the main number to the Marshals' Office in Anchorage, and then kicked them loose. The tallest of the two men rubbed his wrists where the cuffs had been and glared, muttering something about the "equalizer" in his truck.

"You know," Cutter said, giving him a contemplative nod, "if I see you again today, I'd be afraid for my life—and I get twitchy when I'm afraid for my life."

The woman in short shorts may as well have grabbed the man by the ear the way she dragged him off the beach.

Lola called Inspector Scott Keen to make sure he was up to speed on the situation, and that he was setting up a protective detail on Judge Forsberg. Any murder was a big deal, especially during a trial, but the murder of a government attorney was a tripwire event that kicked a load of protective measures into motion. More than that, it was a megaphone for the killer—letting all those involved with the trial know that no one was safe.

The Native woman and her son were nowhere to be seen when Cutter and Lola made it back to the campfire.

"She leave already?" Cutter asked.

"She got a phone call that really spun her up," Mim said.

"Just said thank you and then rushed away." Mim nodded down the beach. "You let them go?"

Lola shrugged. "Guessing we got the same phone call she did."

Mim hardly said a word from the time Cutter told her about the murder to when she dropped him and Lola off in the wooded parking lot at the Shrine of St. Therese.

She sat in the parking lot with her window down, looking at him like she was just seeing him for the first time.

"You'll get a ride?"

He nodded. "Sorry about this."

She gazed through the trees, toward the direction of the church, keeping her voice low. "So they're asking you to hunt the killer."

"I don't know," Cutter said. "This is an FBI case, but both resident agents are out of town at the moment. I'm sure they're sending an army of them from Anchorage and Seattle."

He patted the van door to get Mim on her way. "I'll call you as soon as I know what's going on." He could tell from the look in her eye that she was already seeing Juneau as murder-town USA and didn't want her kids anywhere near it.

Apart from the political intrigue of a state capital or the hubbub of ten thousand tourists disgorged from the cruise ships each day during the summer, Juneau was a sleepy little town. Murders didn't happen every day, or even every year. Virtually every law enforcement officer in the area responded to see how they could assist.

Three Alaska State Trooper SUVs, two Juneau police cars, and a US Forest Service Suburban already occupied the parking lot.

Cutter unclipped the circle-star badge from his belt and fished out the metal chain hidden in the leather backing so he could hang it around his neck. Lola followed suit as they walked.

"You know," she observed, holding up the silver star at the end of her chain as they walked along the packed gravel path in the mottled shadows of towering trees, "I was so happy to get this after graduating the Academy that I used to prop it up on the steering wheel of my G-car so I could look at it on the way in to work."

Cutter chuckled, but didn't admit that he'd done the same thing.

A thirtysomething woman with frizzy red hair and a stern look met them at the base of the hill on the little island. She had the rushed look of someone on a serious mission. Her green rain jacket and brown Xtratuf rubber boots made Cutter think she might be Forest Service, but as she got closer, he saw the Juneau Police Department badge around her neck.

"You're the marshals," she said, extending her hand to Lola first. "Detective Rochelle Van Dyke, JPD. Everybody calls me Rockie."

"Detective," Cutter noted, introducing himself.

"I heard on the radio you had some issues with Lori Maycomb at the Auke Village picnic area. Hope she didn't give you too much trouble."

"No worries," Lola said. "Wasn't her fault she ran into those assholes."

Detective Van Dyke shrugged. "Yeah, well, you'd be surprised. The girl attracts trouble."

"You've dealt with her before?"

"Oh yeah," she said. The detective took a deep breath,

changing the subject. "Anyway, you got a lot of friends in the Anchorage FBI office?"

"We get along well enough," Cutter said.

"I guess," Lola said.

"They don't want us to touch anything," Van Dyke said. "Guess they're afraid we'll get local PD cooties on it or something. The agent on the phone seemed especially animated when the trooper told him we had marshals on the scene." She leaned in. "To be honest with you, I think he's afraid we might arrest the bad guy before they get here."

"We're here to help," Cutter said. "We can work perimeter if you need us out here."

"Oh, hell no," the detective said. "I guess the trooper major in Anchorage is buddy-buddy with your chief deputy. She tells him you're a hell of a tracker."

"I do some tracking," Cutter said.

"Interesting. I didn't know that was even a thing anymore, but the major wants you to take a look. This is a Trooper deal until the Feebs get here. JPD is just here to help as well."

An older man who looked like he was someone's favorite uncle met them at the door to the stone chapel. A silver comb-over matted to his pink scalp with stress sweat. Canvas suspenders bracketed the ponderous belly of a rumpled buffalo-plaid shirt.

The detective gave him a little nod like they knew each other well. "These are the marshals," she said. "And this is Roy. He's the caretaker here at the shrine. He found the bodies."

That explained the stress sweat.

Roy dabbed at the corners of his mouth with a wadded red bandana.

"I was taking care of the crocus beds up by the retreat

building," he said. "Heard some odd pops, so I came out here to check. Thought it might be the furnace, if you want to know the truth. Then there was all that blood on the wall as soon as I looked up at the loft. I didn't see any shell casings, so I figure the killer must have used a revolver. I mean, a semiauto would have left casings on the floor, right?" He shook his head, dabbing at his mouth with the bandana again. "I never saw anything like it. The poor girl . . . I . . . I figure they were shot at close range—"

"Thank you," Cutter said. "We're here in a supporting role. I'm sure the FBI will want to ask you some follow-up questions. Please excuse us while we check in with the troopers."

"Mind if I wait out here," Roy whispered. "I could use some fresh air."

"The FBI would likely prefer it," Lola said.

"He means well," Detective Van Dyke said as soon as they were inside and the heavy timber door shut behind them.

Cutter paused, turning a complete three-sixty in place.

Van Dyke pointed toward the raised dais at the far end of the sanctuary, beyond the two rows of simple wooden pews. A wooden crucifix hung in front of three tall windows.

"Fist-size hole in the glass on that window on the right," she said.

"So much for Roy's revolver-at-close-range theory," Lola said.

Van Dyke gave a tired sigh. "He watches a lot of *CSI.* Any tracks will be outside, but the major figured you'd want to see the victims first." She pointed to the stairs at the far back corner opposite the entry door. "They're up here."

Lola started that way, but Cutter tapped her elbow.

"I've seen plenty of dead bodies," he said. "No need to look at two more if it doesn't serve a purpose. I doubt we'd find much sign up there anyway except for possibly some of Roy's vomit."

"Someone knew what they were doing," Cutter said five minutes later, after they'd gone outside to look at the area beyond the window with the hole in it. He stood well back, unwilling to disturb any possible evidence FBI techs might be able to find in the forest duff. People almost always left something behind—a bit of thread, urine, even an eyelash could tell a story. Cutter had once spent two days sifting a gravel driveway for a piece of a broken tooth—and found it.

In any case, the scene told him plenty from a dozen feet away. As far as direction of travel, Cutter had little doubt that the shooter had been picked up by a boat.

He explained it as he went, mainly for Lola's benefit, but Detective Van Dyke listened with rapt interest.

"The flat of that old stump provides a good rest," he said.

"And a perfect line of sight to the window," Lola said.

"This guy knew his way around a sniper hide," Cutter said. "He trimmed the lower branches on this spruce and pruned back the foliage on the highbush cranberries to give him a clear line of fire but still give him a good place to hide. See how the twig ends are snipped off at right angles? They're not cut with a knife, but with small pruning shears— something a sniper would carry in his kit."

He nodded at the stone church, gritting his teeth, thinking through the ramifications of going inside. He wasn't squeamish, not by a long shot, but he wanted to take a look at the tracks before he risked clouding his judgment by seeing another person he knew with his brains blown out.

"I've changed my mind. I do need to check on a couple of things now that I've had a chance to look at the ground."

Detective Van Dyke provided paper shoe covers for both Cutter and Lola, allowing them to walk up the stairs without transferring in debris from the outside. Cutter didn't think he'd find actual tracks. This shooter was too much of a professional to risk coming inside to admire his handiwork. Still, there was more to the art and science of tracking than simply looking at footprints.

The upper end of the Alaska State Troopers chain of command was comprised of a colonel and two majors. Major Chris Terry, the less senior of the two, or "minor" major, had come to Juneau on the same flight as Cutter for meetings with the governor's protection detail. He'd assumed command of the scene until FBI brass arrived. Terry was an affable man with sandy hair and a pencil-thin mustache, trimmed to the regulation corners of his lip. Like a good boss, he talked little and listened a great deal while Cutter briefed him on what he'd seen outside.

As Cutter suspected, the scene added a layer of answers to what he'd seen outside, as well as new questions.

The young woman's torso draped across Van Tyler's legs, which at first glance would indicate she'd been shot second and then fallen across his body. But that didn't seem right. Tyler was in the lead, with Ensley behind him. The shot had killed her instantly—the explosive damage to her skull left zero doubt about that. Judging from the blood spatter, she'd been bunched up close to Tyler, crowded in, maybe even clutching the back of his jacket. His back was covered in her blood. He'd been facing away when she was shot. He'd turned then, catching one in the jaw. If Tyler was the target, then Cutter guessed the shooter had taken out the girl first, dropping her at the top of the narrow stairwell. It was something Cutter would have done—had done—if he wanted to block the escape of a group of bad guys at a choke point.

The real question was why Ensley Rogers was even there. She was a secretary, not an investigator or a paralegal. Van Tyler was a smart guy. He'd obviously come to meet someone in the middle of a high-threat trial with nexus to drug cartels.

Cutter had seen Ensley that morning, when she'd come into the courtroom to deliver a message to Tyler. As always, she'd been dressed to the nines. He'd noticed then how they seemed close, comfortable in each other's space, but hadn't read too much into it at the time. People could say the same about he and Lola Teariki. If you worked with a person long enough, you could become something like siblings. Under the circumstances though, Cutter wondered if this might be a little different. One thing was certain, this was not the kind of meeting where you brought your secretary.

He could smell Ensley's perfume, obscenely stark now amid the metallic scent of blood and gore. Both had taken the time to change clothes after court, though they'd seemed in a hurry when they left. Cutter had heard that Tyler had opted to stay at a hotel near the airport. Their personal relationship mattered little in the great scheme of things, but it did paint a picture.

The attorney had come to the shrine to meet someone— and she'd tagged along, likely to spend every off hour together that they could. It might mean nothing at all, but it would complicate the investigation, add to the conspiracy theories on the Internet.

Cutter stood at the balcony rail, looking across the small chapel. It was maybe seventy feet from where he stood to the broken windows. The shooter had been another hundred feet or so beyond that. An easy shot.

"Okay," Cutter said. "Your call, Major, but I'd suggest you pull back and secure the scene until the Bureau agents get here."

"That's it?" Major Terry asked, like he expected a little more out of Cutter.

"I'm supposed to look at the ground," Cutter said. "Tell you what I see."

"A couple of snipped bushes and the order of the shots," Van Dyke said. "I sure as hell hope we find a little more evidence than that."

"FBI techs might find something," Cutter said. "But this is a lot, really. The shooter knew Van Tyler was going to be here, in this spot, at this time—far enough in advance to set up a shooting position. That means there was a plan—either to lure him here, or to kill him and the person he was supposed to meet. It's highly likely that Tyler told someone who that person was."

"Maybe we'll find something on his cell phone," Lola offered.

"Maybe so," Cutter said. "In any case, this gives the Bureau something to work on."

A woman spoke from somewhere below, out of sight from the balcony. Detective Van Dyke's head snapped up as if she recognized it immediately and she leaned over the balcony. Major Terry saw who it was and shook his head, making his way down the stairs to call the AST colonel on his cell.

Van Dyke barked to the woman below. "You need to wait by the parking lot with the rest of the media."

Lori Maycomb, the Native woman from the beach, stepped into view, both hands open, palms out.

"Come on, Rockie," she said, just short of a plea—like she knew it was fruitless, but had to ask anyway. "Gimme something broad for the six o'clock news."

"JPD isn't in charge here, you know that," Van Dyke said. "Trooper public affairs office will put out a statement. Get your ass back to the parking lot before you get me in trouble."

Maycomb stuffed her tape recorder in the pocket of her jeans and ducked out the door.

"Aren't you afraid she'll stop and talk to Roy?" Lola asked.

Van Dyke shook her head in disgust. "Serve her right if she reported his theory."

"She seems harmless enough," Lola said.

"Don't let her little act fool you," Van Dyke said. "Oh, she's all goodness and virtue at first—but that little bitch is just one lie after another when you get to know her."

Lola shot Cutter a look, startled at the sudden vehemence in the detective's voice. "You've arrested her before?"

"Don't I wish," Van Dyke said. "No, my maiden name is Maycomb.

Lori was married to my brother. I'm pretty sure she killed him."

CHAPTER 22

"**Y**our guy had one job!" Harold Grimsson pounded his fist on the top of his desk. "One simple job."

Dollarhyde was accustomed to the shouting, especially when they were on the island, away from listening ears. Screaming was the way Grimsson conducted business. If he was happy with your performance, he slapped your back and yelled his praises. If he was upset, he pounded whatever he had at hand—and screamed his displeasure until spit dribbled down his skunky beard. He might even stab you with the end of his damned pipe.

"I want him to take care of the leaker," Grimsson went on. "Is that hard to comprehend? The informant. The person selling information. The one who can bring this whole operation down around my ass if they connect me with that heroin. But, oh no, your expert marksman and his magic rifle didn't shoot the one person I wanted shot. He had to murder the US attorney and, for God knows what reason, some secretary."

"In his defense," Dollarhyde said, "the secretary came up the road after the attorney. The spotter naturally assumed she was the informant. When Childers saw her talking with the attorney, he assumed she'd passed on sensitive infor-

mation and did what he believed was necessary to protect
you. It was an unfortunate, but understandable error."

"See!" Grimsson railed. "Right there. That's a shitload
of assuming going on. Your guy's error might have been
understandable if the leaker wasn't still in play, and as yet
still unidentified. Do I need to remind you that an avalanche
of federal agents is about to fall down on top of us—because
your man killed one of their own? That gives dozens more
ears for our unidentified leaker to whisper into. You understand me here?"

"I do, sir," Dollarhyde said.

Grimsson put his tirade on pause for a moment, heaving
to catch his breath, wiping froth from his beard. "Tell me
you have some idea who the leaker is? My money's on your
man, shizzle or schnitzel or whatever the hell his name is."

"Schimmel."

"Whatever," Grimsson said. "He was the one who identified the assistant as our leaker. That makes him likely."

"Kind of a reach," Dollarhyde said. "Don't you think,
sir?"

Grimsson's eyes narrowed, obviously working hard to
rationalize his conspiracy theory. "The man's awfully
jumpy. Seems like he's carrying around an ore car full of
guilt."

Dollarhyde grunted, nodding to show he was still personally engaged in his ass chewing, no matter how mis-
guided. Grimsson jumped through a lot of hoops to ensure
that the lion's share of his business was legal—hence all
the extra effort for the archeologist on the road project to
the new dig. The cadre of people who knew about the rest
of it was relatively small—maybe a dozen. All of those reported directly to Dollarhyde, and each of them knew too
well what would happen if they flipped.

The tone and pitch of Grimsson's voice changed, causing Dollarhyde to grunt out of habit, though he'd not been paying attention.

"Are you even listening to me?"

"I am," Dollarhyde said. "While at the same time trying to solve our problem."

"Tell me what you are going to do about Schnitzel."

"I don't think Schimmel is our rat."

"It's someone who works for me." Grimsson pounded the desk again, knocking a pencil to the floor. "I can feel it. Hell, for all I know, it could be you."

"Also doubtful," Dollarhyde said.

"Your swift denial inspires buckets of confidence."

"You can be sure I'm not the informant, sir," Dollarhyde said. "I've done too much of your . . . heavy lifting, shall we say. If your ship sinks, I go down as well."

"That may be true. But someone in my organization is making deals. I've gotta tell you, I don't like that Schnitzel kid very much. He smells . . . wrong to me."

Dollarhyde leaned back in his chair, steepling his fingers together, professor-like. "Childers is pissed, too, sir. He feels like Schimmel made him look bad, let him down."

Grimsson gave a nod of approval, jabbing at the desk with his index finger. "Now, I like that Childers kid. He doesn't mind getting his hands dirty."

"He'll take care of Schimmel."

"Take care of him?"

Dollarhyde held up an open palm and shook his head. "Not kill him," he said. "Just tune him up, tell him to pull his head out of his ass."

"A tune-up from Dallas Childers . . ." Grimsson chuckled softly, rubbing remnants of saliva off the desk with the cuff of his sleeve. He picked up his pipe, thinking this through. "Schnitzel's going to wish he was dead. . . ."

CHAPTER 23

It always amazed Cutter how quickly the FBI could drop into a scene with a dozen black Pelican cases and put down roots like an invasive species of khaki slacks and blue windbreakers. In this case, they were welcome, but they made no bones about the fact that they were the ones running the show. "Right-of-way by tonnage," Grumpy had always called it. The FBI was in charge because so many of them showed up. They ran all the databases, got the latest in crime-solving technology, and had the personnel to stand up an army. The agency was a byzantine labyrinth of culture and regulations, seemingly incapable of making the simplest decisions without checking in with some muckety up the chain of command at the Hoover Building. But if the need arose—like when someone murdered an assistant US attorney, decisions were made on the spot and agents appeared to materialize out of thin air.

Assistant US attorneys were not technically criminal investigators, but they were part of the executive branch—the top twigs of that branch, really. As such, they were considered part of the law enforcement family. Petty squabbles over jurisdiction would return, but for now, the death of one of their own pushed everyone together toward the same goal.

Mostly.

"They just had to bring Beason." Lola Teariki leaned forward in her seat so her elbows rested on her knees. "That guy—"

"I know," Cutter said. "Chief wants us to help out, so we'll help out."

Lola chewed on her bottom lip in thought. "His boss's boss is here, so maybe he'll play nice."

Cutter nodded. "Maybe," he said, but couldn't bring himself to believe it.

FBI Special Agent in Charge Skip Warneke had arrived in Juneau on the 9:51 p.m. flight with fourteen agents from the Anchorage field office. Warneke and six of his agents who specialized in crime scenes had gone straight to Shrine of St. Therese. For some reason known only to him, the SAIC had elected to bring Charles Beason, a supervisory special agent notorious for his apoplectic temper and utter contempt for anyone who was not part of the Bureau. Beason had come to the Juneau federal building to set up the command post with the remaining seven agents. A mix of special agents from the DEA, ATF, DHS, and four troopers from the Alaska Bureau of Investigation who'd been on the flight came with him. The National Marine Fisheries sent two criminal investigators, as did the Coast Guard. Both would liaise with other maritime assets in Southeast Alaska should they be needed. Eight more FBI agents were in the air, arriving on the 11:02 flight from Seattle.

Most of the men and women gathered in the courtroom command post had worked with Van Tyler—discussed cases, shared a beer. Many of them knew Ensley Rogers, at least by sight. This was not just a murder investigation or a manhunt for some random escapee. Members of their family had been murdered. This was personal, and the urgency in the room was palpable.

Judge Forsberg went on the record long enough to release the jury from her sequestration order and declare a mistrial on United States v. Hernandez without prejudice. Some of the jurors looked worried about threats, but she explained that since they would have nothing further to do with the case, there was no reason for anyone to harm them.

The jury gone, Forsberg approved the use of her courtroom as a command post for the ad hoc task force—and then got out of the way, remaining on hand and available to review any search warrants the FBI might require. Deputy marshals, formerly charged with the sequestered jury, now staffed protection details on both the judge and the remaining assistant US attorney who'd been working with Van Tyler. Both the Marshals Service and the FBI were in the middle of conducting threat assessments.

Scott Keen tried to fold Cutter and Teariki into his two protection details, but Chief Phillips ordered them to assist the Bureau task force since they'd already put eyes on the scene.

Mim and the kids had returned to Anchorage—away from the danger.

Whiteboards were rolled in from the clerk's office. Access to all but a few support staff was limited, especially from the US Attorney's office since they were possible witnesses to Van Tyler's plans before he was killed. FBI technicians wired secure Internet to the telephones and computers that appeared to sprout up from every table in the courtroom. Two junior FBI agents recently out of

Quantico came along as gophers. They set up urns of coffee on tables in the back with sandwiches from the grocery deli around the corner. Everyone knew they were in this for the long haul—until they ran down the person who pulled the trigger. One agent worked on getting Tyler's cell phone records, while others conducted interviews with anyone who'd had contact with Tyler or Rogers.

Charles Beason stood at the front of the courtroom with the Chief of Juneau Police Department and Major Terry from the Alaska State Troopers, hopefully making sure to de-conflict the agencies' various roles.

Cutter recognized a Forest Service uniformed law enforcement officer named Tarrant in the jury box. He started that way when his phone began to buzz in his pocket. The caller ID was blocked, which meant it could be a political pollster or a government number.

Cutter nodded toward Officer Tarrant, getting his attention, then turned to Lola before answering the call. "I need to take this. Would you mind asking Tarrant not to leave before I get a chance to talk to him?"

"No worries, boss," Lola said, happy to have a mission.

"Arliss Cutter?" the voice on the other end asked as soon as Cutter accepted the call.

"Speaking."

"This is Skip Warneke."

Cutter had met the Anchorage FBI boss a couple of times at leadership breakfasts he'd attended with the chief, but he doubted the guy would have been able to pick him out of a lineup. He sounded pleasant enough.

"What can I do for you, sir?"

"Jill Phillips said we're working together on this one?"

"Yes, sir," Cutter said. "Here to help."

"Yes, well, I'm out at the scene. Seems as though there

are no surveillance cameras here or on the highway leading this way. There was no one on the grounds but for a gardener named . . ."

"That would be Roy," Cutter said after waiting a beat so he didn't cut off the SAIC. He wanted to help, not interrupt.

"That's the guy," Warneke said. "He's got a bunch of theories that are less than helpful."

"I hear you," Cutter said, suddenly distracted when Charles Beason marched across the courtroom directly to the jury box, where Lola was delivering Cutter's message to the Forest Service LEO.

Warneke was still talking on the other end of the line. ". . . so I'd like the report of your observations of the scene ASAP."

"Of course." Cutter started toward the jury box as the FBI supervisor crowded into Lola's personal space. Had it been another person, she might have punched Beason in the beak to get him to step back, but the guy was a boss at another agency—and Lola Teariki had a natural propensity to obey authority.

"My report is finished," Cutter said to Warneke. "I'll email it and my sketches to— Excuse me just a moment, sir—"

Charles Beason had just committed a cardinal sin of management. He'd poked Lola in the shoulder with the tip of his finger to drive home some point. Cutter was close enough to hear the last bit of his side of the conversation. It dripped with condescension.

". . . already gave him an assignment. Now stop with your bullshitting and get out of his way so he can go do what I asked him to . . ."

Lola raised her hands, like she was either going to comply or slap Beason in both ears.

Cutter took the two steps to the jury box in one bound.

Lola saw him coming and shook her head. "No worries here, boss. I'm good."

Cutter ignored the wave-off and spoke directly to Beason. "I asked her to stop Officer Tarrant for me while I took a phone call."

Beason sneered. "Is that right? Well, you can—"

Cutter moved to within two feet from the FBI supervisor. Both were large men. If anything, Beason was a hair taller than Cutter's six-three.

Cutter kept his hands at his sides. His voice was direct, but measured, like a firehose on full blast but with a focused stream. "Let me be clear. Put that finger on one of my deputies again and you and I will have a serious problem. Is that understood?"

Beason was smart enough to see the don't-test-me look in Cutter's eyes. He took a half step back, raising his hands in retreat. "Look, it's been a long day and—" Beason paused, regaining his emotional footing after Cutter's sudden appearance. "You know what? I'm not going to stand around and get schooled by a couple of court monkeys. You are here in a supporting role. The old man wants your report on the crime scene, like yesterday."

"The old man?" Cutter asked, knowing full well who he was talking about.

"Warneke," Beason said. "The special agent in charge. Matter of fact, I should just call him right now and have him tell your boss you're impeding my investigation. They'll pull your ass out of here so fast it'll make your—"

Cutter pushed the cell phone out in front of him.

Beason flinched, apparently thinking Cutter was about

to hit him. His head cocked sideways when he realized it was a phone.

"What's this?"

"You want to talk to Warneke?" Cutter said. "Here he is."

The SAIC's voice spilled out of the speaker as Beason held the phone six inches away from his ear.

"Yes . . . I mean no . . . Yes, sir, I know it's *your* investigation, not mine . . . No, sir . . . I mean, I may have touched her on the arm with the tip of my finger . . . No, sir . . . I only . . . Yes, sir."

He passed the phone back to Cutter. Warneke gave him a curt apology and then ended the call.

Beason spoke through clenched teeth, seething. "You could have told me he was on the line."

"Honestly," Cutter said, "it's lucky for you he was. You know my reputation."

"For being a hothead?"

Cutter shook his head. "For not putting up with assholes."

"Listen," Beason said. "We're all under stress. I'm just trying to do the right thing."

"Bullshit," Cutter whispered. "Stress doesn't turn us into idiots, it lays bare the idiot we already are. I don't care if you're having the worst day of your life. Touch one of my deputies again and we'll both be out of work."

"What's that supposed to mean?"

"Figure it out," Lola said, following Cutter out of the jury box.

CHAPTER 24

Constance Cutter's secret would top anything Audrey or Evelyn could dream up—but telling it was a nuclear option. Imelda clutched her knees to her chest, jaw locked like she'd rather look at her new multicolored toes or do just about anything besides play confession. All the girls were smoking weed now, even Imelda. Their game of truth or dare had devolved into tell the shittiest little secret about your life that you can think of. Evelyn was finishing up with a story about some nasty thing her jailbird uncle had done to one of her cousins. Constance would have to go next—

Her cell phone buzzed on the floor. The weed made everything foggy, surreal. She sat and watched for a few seconds. Her mom . . . She coughed. It was her mom! She cursed under her breath, suddenly aware that she was holding a joint in one hand. Just one more fight for her brain to wrestle with.

Constance put a finger to her lips, shushing the giggling girls, and worked hard to calm her breathing. There was nothing to worry about. Her mother was hundreds of miles away. At least she hadn't tried to FaceTime.

"Hi, Mom."

"Are you all right?" her mom said. "You sound odd."

It was a test—and Constance wasn't falling for it.

"I'm fine," she said. She started to ask how things were going, but decided she shouldn't sound too interested. That would arouse her mother's suspicions for sure. "What's up?"

"Your Uncle Arliss has gotten busy with his work. I'm bringing the boys home."

"Tonight?" Constance said, wondering if she sounded like a terrified rabbit.

"We get in a little before midnight. You go ahead and spend the night with Audrey, but I'll pick you up in the morning."

"Mom—"

"Gotta go," her mother said, leaving no room for argument. "Be ready in the morning. I'll be there by nine o'clock."

Constance stuffed the phone in the pocket of her pajama pants, then fished it out again to make sure it was locked and not about to butt dial her mother back.

In some small way, she was glad her mom was coming home. It gave her a good excuse not to try the tab acid. Someday maybe, but not yet. She'd made plans for weed, though. Audrey had loaned her a pair of pajama pants and a T-shirt. Her own clothes were in a plastic garbage bag. She'd shower in the morning and then put on her fresh clothes right before she left.

Evelyn reached the end of the story about her uncle. Audrey curled her nose and called him a perv. Imelda nodded slowly, her face passive, as if such gross behavior was commonplace.

Sitting on the floor, Constance bounced the back of her head against the couch cushion, dizzy from the marijuana. Mulling over her secret.

Arliss had wasted no time in moving to Alaska after her dad died. Constance had seen the way he looked at her mother, knew the stories about when they were kids. The more she was around him, the more Constance saw certain resemblances, mannerisms—things she couldn't ignore.

The thought of it made her sick.

She desperately wanted to fit in with these girls, but this wasn't the kind of secret you just threw out there—or maybe you did and that's what made you cool.

She stared at the smoldering remnants of her joint on the saucer beside her and leaned back to stare at the ceiling, blocking out Audrey and Evelyn's goading.

She'd have to make something up. Up to now, it had only been a suspicion, but the weed made everything so much clearer. The evidence was all there in living color. Still, there was no way she was going to tell her new friends that her uncle Arliss was her real father.

CHAPTER 25

Skip Warneke divided the ad hoc task force into squads, all but one of them led by an FBI agent. Charles Beason was subdued if not contrite. Still acting as Warneke's field commander, he put Cutter in charge of a small team that included Lola, Detective Van Dyke from JPD, and Forest Service LEO Tarrant.

This investigation was likely to be a marathon, not a sprint. They would eventually work in shifts, but the first few hours were crucial, so everyone expected to pull an all-nighter. Most of them wouldn't have had it any other way. Warneke began to rotate squads out to grab a quick meal a little after ten p.m.

Cutter's squad was one of the first to go.

The Hangar restaurant was normally closed at that hour, but Rockie Van Dyke knew the manager. Under the circumstances, he'd agreed to stay open until midnight. Three squads would have time to walk over and eat in-house. He'd make to-go boxes for everyone else.

Cutter wasn't hungry, but he'd learned long ago that food, sleep, and bathroom breaks should be taken whenever and wherever they were offered.

A hostess with smudged mascara around drooping eyes

waved them in with a stack of menus. She stared at the floor as she moped her way to a corner table. The large influx of clients was a windfall to the restaurant, but the mostly to-go orders meant the staff would lose out on tips. Rockie reminded the hostess that most of the task force was from out of town, on government per diem, and she would personally ensure that they sent over a large tip envelope to thank the staff for their extra effort. The girl brightened, some, but still slogged back to her station.

A waiter came over next—long beard, man bun, skinny jeans, and checkered flannel shirt. To each his own, Cutter thought, but he'd work hard to make sure that if the twins decided to grow beards and wear flannel, they'd have calloused hands from an axe. Soft hands or not, Fake Lumberjack was much more chipper than the hostess.

Lola and Officer Tarrant went with Detective Van Dyke's recommendation and got halibut and chips. Cutter ordered a bowl of clam chowder and twice the normal amount of oyster crackers. Mixing crackers into his soup until it was more cracker than soup was his guilty pleasure. It had driven Grumpy crazy.

Van Dyke, Tarrant, and Lola chatted quietly, discussing investigative theories and performing the crucial initial steps of any ad hoc team by testing the water and getting to know one another's personalities. Cutter let Lola carry the water on the butt-sniffing stage and let his eyes drift around the restaurant. The two-story blue Wharf building that housed the Hangar restaurant and a few other shops was located directly on the water. Floor-to-ceiling windows along the seaward wall looked out over the Gastineau Channel and the twinkling lights of Douglas Island to the west. Cutter was sure there would have been a killer view of the water if it hadn't been dark outside. A few locals had wandered in as well, taking advantage of the later hours. Management didn't care. So long as they were paying their staff overtime, they might as well be making money.

The same sad-sack hostess who'd seated them now hovered over a man sitting in the corner booth, facing the wall. She spoke in hushed, but highly animated tones. Cutter could tell from the tension in the hostess's body language that they were having a disagreement. The man, obviously agitated by something she said to him, stood up quickly and tried to push his way past. The hostess hip-checked him, blocking his exit from the booth. She covered her face with both hands—and began to cry.

Cutter was on his feet in an instant, barking from across the restaurant.

"Hey! Everything okay?"

The hostess nodded. "I'm fine. He's a friend of mine. . . ."

The young man waved Cutter away. "We're good," he said, barely louder than a whisper. He rubbed his face and collapsed into the booth. The kid looked like a star football player who'd just lost the championship. His eyes were red from crying—and crying men were often the first to shove a pencil in your eye.

"I gotta be honest," Cutter said, watching the man's hands, his pockets, the area of the waistline that was visible. "You don't look fine."

Cutter heard footsteps padding up behind him. Before he could turn, Lola said, "Just us, boss."

Detective Van Dyke stepped beside him, tilting her head sideways to whisper, "That's Levi Fawsey. Senator Fawsey's son."

"Senator Fawsey?" Cutter said. He knew his federal reps but wasn't up to speed enough on Alaska politics to know more than a couple of state senators.

"He represents Juneau," Van Dyke said. "Bazillionaire owner of a couple of auto dealerships here and in Anchor-town."

"Ah," Cutter said. "That Fawsey—"

Senses heightened, Cutter caught a glimpse of movement at the entry with his peripheral vision. Lori Maycomb stood by the hostess podium, neck craned, scanning. She zeroed in on Levi Fawsey at once and marched across the restaurant, looming over the table. She ignored Cutter and her former sister-in-law as if they weren't even there.

Both hands on the table, she leaned in close, nose to nose with the cowering young man. "Where is she?"

"Leave me alone."

"Tell me what you've done with her!"

Rockie Van Dyke stepped forward and grabbed the reporter's elbow. "Hey, now. Come on."

Lori jerked away. "He's done something to her, Rockie. I have a witness who saw her leave with him in his boat earlier this evening." Her chest heaved as she fought back tears. "She's not picking up or answering texts. No one's seen her. . . ."

Van Dyke folded her arms across her chest. "Seen who?"

The hostess spoke next. "Donita Willets. That's who I just asked him about. Donita called me earlier. She was really upset about something. Now she won't answer my texts."

"Maybe she's out of range?" Lola offered.

"Donita loves her phone too much to go out of cell ser-vice," the hostess said. She turned to Fawsey again. "Please, Levi. Just tell us where she is. She's in trouble. I can feel it."

He leaned forward, banging his forehead on the table. "I . . . I'm sorry . . ." He began to weep in earnest now. His hands dropped to his lap.

"Levi," Van Dyke said. "You're making me really nervous. Keep your hands on the table where I can see them."

He complied, but kept crying, his face sideways on the table in a growing puddle of tears and snot.

Lori Maycomb moved closer again. "She called me too, Levi."

"Do you know where she is?" Cutter asked, bile rising in his throat.

Head still on the table, as if he was waiting for someone to cut it off, Levi blurted: "She fell, okay! We were out on the boat . . . and she just fell out."

The hostess gasped. Lola caught her as she sank to her knees.

"I tried to save her," Fawsey croaked. "But it was just . . . too cold. She went under . . ."

Detective Van Dyke held her radio to her lips, ready to get a rescue going that direction. "Where did she go over?" Van Dyke banged her free hand on the table. "How long ago?"

"North," he sobbed. "It's been too long. I'm telling you, she's gone. I tried to save her. Nobody can find her."

"Go ahead and stand up for me," Van Dyke said. She kept her voice low and steady, but Cutter could tell she was rattled. "You got any weapons on you?"

He shook his head, raising his hands to shoulder height, obviously having been through this before.

Van Dyke cuffed him behind his back.

"Anything in your pockets that'll hurt me? Needles? Fentanyl?"

"No," he said, sniffing, trying to rub his nose against his shoulder. "Will someone please call my dad."

"Sure," Van Dyke said. "You're not under arrest right now. But you were beating your head against the table so hard, I was afraid you were going to hurt yourself. I want you to listen to me, Levi. A girl's life is at stake. I need you to tell me exactly where she fell out of your boat."

"I'm sorry," he said. "I . . . I can't remember."

"Where were you going?" Van Dyke asked. "A particular bay, hangout spot? Anything?"

"She's just . . . gone."

"Okay," Detective Van Dyke said. "Now you're under arrest. Let's go."

Lola helped the teetering hostess to a seat in the nearby booth before she collapsed. She kept the one that was covered with Levi Fawsey's snot and tears secure for a possible sample of "free-flowing" DNA.

"I'm sure JPD will have a few questions for you," she said.

The young hostess gave a shuddering nod and buried her face in her hands.

Lola stepped back and whispered to Cutter, "What do you think, boss? Girl goes missing on the same day an AUSA is murdered. You always say you don't believe in coincidence."

"It's not a coincidence," Lori Maycomb said.

"And you know this how?" Cutter asked.

"Because Donita Willets called me this morning. She was paranoid about something. Would only talk in person. She was supposed to get in touch with me around lunchtime to schedule the specifics of a meet. Then the judge made us leave our phones outside the courtroom, so I missed her calls."

"Wait," Lola said. "This missing girl was a source?"

"She was," Lori said. "And I'm betting that when she

couldn't get hold of me, she set up a meeting at the shrine with Van Tyler."

Lola watched the door where Levi Fawsey had been led away. "Pretty damned convenient for her to jump in the ocean and drown."

CHAPTER 26

The throw rug in Dean Schimmel's filthy apartment was too dirty for him to notice the muddy boot print.

A near-constant adrenaline dump throughout the day left him too exhausted to be jittery.

He kicked the door shut behind him, slouching under the enormous burden of the bone rattle. It may as well have weighed a hundred pounds. At least a dozen times he'd considered throwing the damned thing into the sea, but the notion of a half million—or even half a thousand dollars— made him hang on to it a little longer. Things weren't going so well since he'd scooped up the rattle from the shaman's grave, but then, they hadn't been all that great beforehand either. Maybe it wasn't the bone rattle that was cursed, but Schimmel himself. If that were the case, then maybe the rattle was a good thing.

Maybe, just maybe, things would start looking up.

Schimmel had a bunk in one of the ATCO trailers out at the Valkyrie mine. It was dry and comfortable enough, but still smelled like other people's feet. On his off weeks, he lived in a miniscule efficiency apartment on Douglas Island, a couple of blocks from the Breeze Inn. He kept a spritz bottle of Febreze inside the front door, though there was no one here to blame for the stench but himself.

Childers was pissed at him. The guy had nothing against shooting a girl, but shooting the wrong girl meant they had probably scared his target away—and that made him mad. But what was Schimmel supposed to think? Some chick he'd never seen before came up the road fifteen minutes after the lawyer like they were going to meet. Dollarhyde and the others had the luxury of blaming him now, but every last one of them would have made the same call. They'd get over it.

Probably.

Schimmel gave the room a couple of squirts of Febreze and then headed for the bathroom. Experience told him to bring the bottle with him. For some reason, Schimmel's body was programed to need the toilet every time he got within a block of his house. He could go for a day or two at the mine, but at home, all he had to do was cross the bridge to Douglas Island and his guts started to gurgle. The two gas station corn dogs he'd wolfed down earlier probably hadn't helped.

He kicked off his pants, cracked open a Bud Light, and sat on the john, beer in one hand, air freshener in the other, staring at the peeling paint and thinking about the day.

It had taken Schimmel six hours to get home from the time they'd sped north away from the shrine. Childers got out at the Auke Bay Marina, where he picked up his motorcycle. It was there that Childers had gotten the call from Mr. Dollarhyde about the screwup. He'd told Schimmel to hide the skiff and they'd sort it all out in the morning, but it was obvious he was pissed.

Schimmel had slowed down near town, putzing past the abandoned tug boat that was anchored in the middle of the channel so as not to draw attention to himself. He'd loaded the skiff on a trailer at the marina north of the city, and then, covering it with a blue tarp, backed it in with a dozen other aluminum skiffs just like it.

He didn't like it when Childers talked about "sorting everything out," but he'd worry about tomorrow, tomorrow. For now, he had other things to worry about.

Anyone else would have taken one look at the grimy tub and run, or at the very least, run for some shower shoes. Schimmel knew it was dirty, but he reasoned that it was his dirt, so he'd be immune to whatever bugs it held. Naked and chilled, he reached behind the door and grabbed the towel hanging on the peg. It was stiff and slightly sour, but was cleaner than anything else he had. He dropped it on the magazine rack that still held a couple of water-crinkled *National Geographic* magazines from the previous renter. Schimmel had yet to crack one open, but it seemed cool to have reading material in the john.

The apartment was cramped and old, but the water heater worked very well. Steam rolled out from the shower curtain, fogging the mirror by the time Schimmel stepped into the grimy porcelain tub.

He bowed his head, feeling the super-heated water scald his scalp and neck, washing away three days of dirt and grit.

He caught a hint of the cheap coconut shampoo he preferred, the plain white store-brand bar soap in the caddy at eye level.

Feeling better, lighter, he grabbed the soap and began to hum.

Schimmel wasn't much of a reader, but he'd heard somewhere that most guys only washed their crotch and their armpits when they showered, letting the spray of water clean everything else—more or less.

Fortunately for Dean Schimmel, he always started with his pits.

The initial sensation was one more of uneasiness than pain. Something . . . not quite right. The sting of hot water against his skin made him think he'd imagined it.

Right-handed, he'd raised his left arm and rubbed the bar of soap liberally around his armpit, sliding it across his chest before transferring to his left hand to repeat the process. Another sting, this one sharp enough to snap his eyes closed. He winced, horrified when he glanced down to see streaks of meat oozing red lines across his chest. Blood poured down his sides, spilling from deep gashes under his arms. His left nipple was sliced completely in half, exposing yellow globules of fat. The water at his feet turned rusty red.

He grabbed the shower curtain with his free hand, pulling the flimsy rod down on top of him. Collapsing, he sat on the edge of the tub, blood pulsing from between the fingers of the fist that held the soap. He opened his hand tentatively, moving it under the stream of water to wash away the blood. A deep cut at the base of his thumb smiled back at him, pulsing geysers of blood. He gagged, not so much at the sight of his wounds, but from fear. Who would do this? If they were going to kill him, they should just kill him. It took a special kind of sadistic mind to put razor blades in a guy's soap. He could have cut his junk off. . . .

Dollarhyde. It had to be Dollarhyde. That guy was a psycho, always licking his lips, watching everyone else's pain. You could see it in his eyes.

Schimmel kept his arms down, his hands clenched into fists. This controlled the worst of the bleeding. Blood spurted from his thumb when he grabbed the crusty bath towel and held it against his chest.

He had to get out of here. But for that, he'd need money.

He knew a woman at a gallery downtown who would buy the bone rattle. She'd pay him shit, but at least she'd pay him. . . .

He lifted the towel away to examine the wounds. Thin, scalpellike lines crisscrossed his chest. He gagged again at the sight of it. Not life-threatening, but still bad. Whoever had sunk razor blades into his soap hadn't cared if he died or not. Curtains of blood cascaded down his chest and belly, dripping onto his naked thighs. He pressed the towel back to his flesh, wincing from the acid pain under each arm. He struggled to keep from hyperventilating.

Tape. He needed tape. Lots of tape. And gauze.

And he needed to get the hell out of Juneau.

CHAPTER 27

Ephraim Dollarhyde's desk at the main offices of Valkyrie Mine Holdings suited his personality. The rich mahogany was polished to a reflective sheen and smelled slightly of lemon and tung oil. Imported wood seemed sinful with all the beautiful cedar and spruce in the area.

Inside the desk, locked in a flat metal safe, were files that could burn down the company and put Grimsson in prison for a very long time. Using them would implicate Dollarhyde as well, of course, but he'd been to law school. He knew the first rat to the table got the best deal—and he had a lot to bring to the table. It was far too early for that—but it paid to have insurance. Especially with the informant still out there.

The irony of the situation was not lost on him—trying to ferret out this informant before he was forced to turn informant himself in order to save his own skin.

There were only a few people to choose from. His money had never been on Dean Schimmel. The buffoon was hardly smart enough to hide his intentions this long. No, Schimmel was a perpetual screwup, but he wasn't the type to be setting up secret meetings with the US Attorney's office. The timeline didn't work out for that anyway. The same went for

Dallas Childers, though he was mercenary enough. In some ways, Childers reminded Dollarhyde of a younger version of himself. More intense on the outside maybe, fortunate enough to have been able to exercise some of his baser passions in war. Dollarhyde had always had to operate in the shadows, convincing some employer that a heavy hand was necessary to keep order. Still, the timing was all wrong for Childers to be the snitch. He'd been waiting to take out the prisoner transport when the meeting with the AUSA was set up.

Dollarhyde tapped an unsharpened pencil on the desk, racking his brain.

One of the senators? Maybe. But they both had a hell of a lot to lose.

The phone rang. It was Fawsey, speaking ninety miles an hour.

"My son has been arrested," the senator said, breathless. "JPD has him now, but I'm told the Troopers are pursuing charges on suspicion that he murdered his girlfriend."

"Did he?" Dollarhyde said, processing, looking at this from all angles.

Fawsey gasped. "Of course not."

"I have to ask, sir," Dollarhyde said.

"Levi's not like that!"

"Ah," Dollarhyde said. "But how would you know?"

"I would," the senator said. "Believe me."

Fawsey ran down everything he did know, which wasn't much, then dropped the bombshell. "My contact with the Troopers office said the FBI is coming over to speak with him."

"The FBI?" Dollarhyde mused. "They have their hands full with this other murder. . . ."

"They want to hold him as a material witness," Fawsey said.

"To what?"

Dollarhyde's office door flew open and Harold Grimsson barged in, both hands planted on the desk, glowering. He obviously also had a source at the Troopers, or JPD, or somewhere.

"What in the—"

Dollarhyde cut him off. "I have Senator Fawsey on the line right now, sir."

"Put him on speaker!" Grimsson boomed.

"Harold," Fawsey said once Dollarhyde hit the button. "I will fix this. I only wanted to make sure we're all on the same sheet of music."

"Oh, we are," Grimsson said. "But what about Levi? What music is he singing from?"

"What do you mean?"

"If the FBI wants to talk to him, then they think he knows something about that AUSA's murder. Does he?"

"No . . ." Fawsey said, sounding hollow. "I mean, how could he? I don't know anything about it."

Dollarhyde went back to drumming the pencil. "He hasn't told them anything. Otherwise, it would be raining red lights and sirens. If they don't have a body, it'll take them a minute to make a murder charge stick. The feds may try to hold him, but a material witness has the same rights as anyone arrested for a crime. You have to see to it he makes bond."

"What about this dead girlfriend?" Grimsson asked. "Donita something."

"Willets," Dollarhyde said.

"They have her body?" Grimsson asked.

"No." Senator Fawsey's voice dropped to a hoarse whisper. "I can't imagine her knowing anything either."

"You and Levi get along well?" Dollarhyde said, trying to calm both Grimsson and Fawsey. Tempers and emotion would get them in real trouble.

"Yes," Fawsey said. "Normal father and son stuff, I suppose, but he's a good boy. We talk."

"Be honest," Dollarhyde said. "Is there a chance he got rid of the girl to protect you? Maybe she heard something she wasn't supposed to?"

Grimsson was having none of this. "You stupid bastard. What could your kid possibly know? Do you keep black and white glossies of our business meetings on your desk?"

"I think they were in my office a few days ago when I got home, using my sofa to . . . you know. I made a few phone calls that may have mentioned our relationship, some of the problems—all with my lawyer. Don't worry about him. It's covered by privilege. If they happened to overhear anything, it's not much. But I needed insurance."

"Insuring what?" Grimsson fumed. "That we all go to prison?"

"I didn't give any specifics."

Dollarhyde kept his voice even, though he found it next to impossible. "You gave them enough to rouse their curiosity so they could do a little digging."

"I'm not even sure they were there," Fawsey said. "I found the blanket later, after I'd left and come back."

"Okay," Dollarhyde said. "We'll send an attorney to see that the boy gets out of jail as soon as possible. Tell him to agree to cooperate for now. We'll get a bond set. File a writ. Whatever it takes."

Grimsson nodded.

"Do you understand me?" Dollarhyde prodded Fawsey to answer.

"Yes."

"Good." Dollarhyde ended the call. He dropped the pencil and leaned back in his chair, rubbing his eyes.

"We'll see what he does when he's free," Grimsson said. "If he goes into hiding, he's a rat. If he comes to us for help, I'll break out some of my best whiskey and we'll celebrate that he did what he needed to do and sunk the nosey bitch to keep his father out of jail."

CHAPTER 28

"Shoulda been us, Cutter," Lola Teariki said, exhausted, so her Kiwi accent made him *Cuttah* again. "We're the ones who arrested Levi Fawsey. We should be in on the interrogation."

Cutter stood at the reception desk of the Four Points Sheraton hotel downtown, eyes on his roller cases, waiting for the clerk to code his room key. He'd opted to move out of the lonely Vrbo and closer to town now that Mim and the kids had returned to Anchorage.

"Technically," Cutter said, "Rockie Van Dyke arrested him."

"She may have slapped the cuffs on him," Lola said, "but you made first contact."

"This is her city."

"It's our country," Lola said. "My badge says *United States* Marshal."

"Let me know how that attitude works for you," Cutter said. "Jurisdiction games are for . . . that other agency. It just pisses everybody off when we need their help—which, I might point out, is every time we go into the field."

Lola scuffed her boot on the lobby floor. "I guess so—"

Cutter's phone buzzed. The caller ID was blocked.

"Speaking of that other agency," he said before answering. "Cutter."

"Where are you?" It was Charles Beason. "Where do you need me?" Cutter said.

"Troopers are telling me the Fawsey kid is scared."

"Scared of who?"

"He's not giving that up yet," Beason said. "He says he'll cooperate so long as he has protection. I've already spoken to the judge. She's issuing an order for the USMS to babysit."

"Teariki and I will head to JPD right now," Cutter said. He kept his voice cheerful, unwilling to give Beason the satisfaction of a whine. Babysitting prisoners and witnesses was in fact the job of the Marshals Service. Cutter didn't mind. By and large, most protected witnesses were just outlaws who made it to the negotiating table before their coconspirators. Listening to them, observing their habits, helped Cutter learn what made them tick so he could catch them the next time. He dropped his gear in the hotel room, hung the DO NOT DISTURB sign on the door, and met Lola back in the lobby.

The clear day had given in to steady rain, turning the roads pitch-black, but most residents had gone to bed, making it a quick drive up Egan toward the airport.

Rockie Van Dyke met them at the employee entrance around back of the PD. Hair plastered to her face with rain, she was spitting mad.

Her mood was contagious. Cutter cocked his head, suddenly wary. "What's the matter?"

"He's gone," Van Dyke said. "I went to get something from my car and ended up taking a phone call from my husband while I was out there. Dipshit's attorney slithered in and produced a writ before I made it back in."

"A writ . . ." Cutter mused. It made sense. This kid was a senator's son, and the old saying was a judge was just a lawyer with a senator for a friend. State politicians didn't wield the terrible cosmic power of a US senator, but they surely knew a few judges willing to sign a writ to get someone out of jail. Levi Fawsey was not yet in federal custody, which made it a fairly simple process.

Lola shot an astounded look at Cutter. "They can't just snatch him away from us."

"I knew you guys were coming with federal paper," Van Dyke said. "I would have stalled if I'd been here, but my night lieutenant doesn't like to make waves."

Lola's eyes narrowed, and she cocked her head in thought, pooching her lips out slightly. "So, Daddy's closing ranks around his little murderer."

"I don't believe the girl's dead," Cutter said. "The way Levi talked about her in the present tense. He was a raw nerve of emotion when he came into the restaurant tonight, and not just because he got caught. Someone who's that upset because his girlfriend fell overboard would have sent out a Mayday to the Coast Guard, the Troopers—all ships at sea. I'm not so sure he wouldn't have jumped in after her. And he certainly would have dragged the first person he met back to the spot he last saw her."

Van Dyke's nose turned up in disbelief. She shook her head. "Why all the theatrics then?"

"Oh, he's definitely hiding something," Cutter said.

"Still," Van Dyke said. "If Donita Willets is still alive, then why didn't he just go home and keep his mouth shut?"

A wide smile spread over Lola's face as she caught up

with Cutter's line of thought. "Because he wants somebody to think she's dead."

Irate pounding came from the back door. It had to be Charles Beason. Only he would have the brass to demand entry to a police station where he didn't work. He blew in like the enemy side of a claymore mine as soon as Van Dyke opened the door.

He focused his anger on Cutter.

"I just heard." Beason's head was shaking like it might fall off the end of his neck. "You let him go!"

"His attorney got him out with a writ," Cutter said nose to nose with the FBI supervisor. This wasn't going to be the ass-chewing Beason thought. They were both supervisors, but Beason liked to slip in the fact that FBI supervisors were GS 14s while those of Cutter's ilk were lowly 13s— for now. "We weren't here yet," Cutter said. "But even if we had been, you didn't provide me with a warrant."

"So this is my fault?"

Cutter didn't move. "According to you, Fawsey was scared and wanted to cooperate on his own."

"If you worked for me—"

Now Cutter gave a slow shake of his head. "Charles," he said. "If I worked for you, I'd be in jail."

"Okay, boys," Van Dyke said. "If you two are done pissing on your territorial boundaries, how about we make a plan and decide what to do next?"

"All right," Beason said, still fuming. "What is it?" He was used to throwing his weight around without having anyone to throw it back.

Cutter gave him a quick rundown of his theory, relaxed again, like they were all part of the same team.

Van Dyke had come on board with the idea that the

Willits girl was alive. "Levi does seem to be more insistent that we'll never find her than any details of how she died."

"That's an odd thing to be so sure about," Lola mused, more to herself than Beason. He didn't listen to people of her lowly station anyway.

Beason rubbed a hand over the dark stubble on his face, exhausted, which explained but gave him no excuse for being even more of an asshole than usual. "So you think he's hiding the girl to protect her from someone?"

"I believe we need to look at that possibility," Cutter said.

"Why didn't he just bring her in?" Beason asked, still not buying in. "This town is crawling with FBI agents."

"There is that," Van Dyke said.

"Hang on a minute," Lola said. "This kid is a senator's son. Senators can run in some pretty shady circles to get themselves elected. Maybe it's one of his daddy's friends that he's scared of. Maybe he's so used to important people being dirty that he wasn't going to chance turning his girl-friend over to the authorities until he does his due diligence. I mean, Daddy did writ him out in the middle of the night right before he was going to cooperate. Maybe someone doesn't want him to talk because whatever the girl knew . . . or knows . . . he knows too."

"That's not good for him," Van Dyke said.

"I know, right?" Lola said. "There's no way Levi Fawsey is going to convince the people he's scared of that Donita Willets fell overboard. They're apt to be a little rougher in their interrogation methods than we would have been. And he flipped in about ten seconds for us. At the best they'll ship him off somewhere, out of our reach. Worst case, he tells them where she is and they kill him and Donita both."

Cutter and Van Dyke nodded at the logic. Lola's theory

made enough sense that even Beason listened to her—
for now.

Cutter checked his watch. It was almost three in the
morning. If Donita Willets was still alive, they had to get
to her first.

DAY THREE

CHAPTER 29

It was a quarter to four by the time Cutter got back to the Sheraton and his head hit the pillow. His alarm woke him at six fifteen. He'd learned in the army that if he couldn't get four hours, then he woke up more alert from a two-and-a-half-hour REM sleep cycle than trying to milk out another half hour.

He grabbed a quick shower, then dressed in water-resistant Fjällräven pants and a gray lightweight wool shirt. His meeting wasn't until seven, and it was in the restaurant downstairs. He didn't have to hurry, but he wanted to call Mim before she left for work.

Six thirty-five. He'd give her five more minutes. That gave him a chance to check his gear.

Among other things, his daypack held an extra set of black merino wool long johns, Ethan's mammoth ivory 3DK sheath knife, and an extra pair of wool socks. He didn't want to come back to the room no matter where the hunt for Levi Fawsey and Donita Willets led.

He pulled on his Xtratuf rubber boots, which felt more like slippers than the work boots he was accustomed to, and then peeked out the curtain to check the weather. Lights twinkled in the darkness behind the Hangar restaurant and the boats along the wharf. Rain zipped through the bright halo around each streetlight below. Fog and darkness completely obscured the Gastineau Channel and Douglas Island beyond.

Exactly the way he'd left it.

Earbud in his ear, he took out his pocketknife and the small chunk of wood he'd been working on, and then slid down to sit on the floor to carve with his back against the wall. It gave his hands something to do while he talked to Mim.

She'd sent him a text telling him she and the boys had made it home safely. Like they were a real family. They were. Just not the way he'd imagined it, thousands . . . no, tens of thousands of times since he'd met her at that bait shop on Manasota Key.

Ethan had been almost eighteen then, much more at ease with himself and the ladies. Mim had naturally ended up with him, even though Arliss had met her first. He'd been too taken with her to say a word. Too smitten with her peaches-and-cream skin to move. He'd just stood there, feet rooted in the peeling linoleum floor of that sweaty bait shop while Ethan talked and moved, and swept Mim off her feet right under Cutter's nose.

That's what Arliss got for having a cool older brother.

That single moment in that bait shop had torn the rudder right off his boat. Left him drifting until he'd found himself in the army—and all that other mess. That at least had given him direction, purpose, even if that direction kept him teetering on the edge of getting fired or put in prison.

Then Ethan had gotten killed, leaving Mim and her kids alone. And for some reason, Arliss found himself unable to move or speak again. In everything else he was a paragon of strength, but when his sister-in-law was involved—

Mim answered.

"You're up early," she said, sounding even more exhausted than Cutter felt. He could hear the thick, clickiness in her speech that told him she was just out of bed, hadn't had her coffee. Her text said she was going in to the hospital to cover another nurse's shift—since she was home anyway.

"Can't believe you're going in," Cutter said, turning his knife so it shaved off paper-thin slivers of wood, toward his thumb, exactly what he taught his nephews not to do.

"I owe her a shift," Mim said. "I wasn't asleep anyway."

"Constance okay?"

"She's got friends." Mim heaved a long sigh. It was content, and full of emotion, and such a perfect sound that Cutter nearly sliced his thumb.

"I told her I was picking her up at nine," Mim continued. "But now it'll be after work. She didn't sound disappointed. I'm just glad she's got girls her age to talk to. No sense in wrecking her evening just because you had to work."

"I am so sorry about that," Cutter said. He stopped carving and let his head fall backward against the wall so he faced the ceiling, eyes closed.

"That's okay," Mim said.

"Listen," Cutter said. "We didn't get a chance to talk after—"

"What happened on the beach?"

"Yeah—"

"That was . . . I don't know . . ." Mim paused, gathering her thoughts. "I thought I'd seen you lose your temper that time at the indoor track."

I didn't lose my temper, Cutter thought. That time or this one. *Losing my temper is ugly, something I never want you to see.*

He said, "Fights are nasty business. Better to end them as quickly as possible. I hate that you had to witness that. Sorry the boys had to see it."

"I get it," Mim said, her voice hushed. "Really, I do. It's just that it seemed so one-sided, like those guys never had a chance." She caught herself. "Don't get me wrong. I wanted you to win. It was just . . ."

Cutter waited for her to finish. When she didn't, he helped her out. "Violent?"

He could hear her nod over the phone. "Yes, and gruesome. That look in your eye. I have to admit it scared the crap out of me. For a minute I thought you might murder those guys."

Not even close, Cutter thought.

"It's just a lot to process," Mim said.

"Are the boys okay?"

"Are you kidding me?" Mim said. "They're fine. If I'd let them say ass they'd never talk about anything except how proud they are to have a badass uncle."

"I am sorry," Cutter said again.

"You're always teaching them Grumpy's Man-Rules. I guess I just thought they'd be a little older before they'd get the live demonstrations. Anyway, like I said. A lot to process."

They didn't speak for a time; Mim was making coffee from the sounds of it, while Cutter worked on his carving and tried to suss out any hidden meaning in the things she'd said—or hadn't said.

"There we go," Mim said at length. "I'll be human again in five minutes. Listen, I gotta get ready for work."

"Me too," Cutter said. He was already a minute late for his meeting downstairs.

"Call me later," Mim said—her way of saying she didn't think he was wrong for beating the crap out of someone in front of her boys—or, if she did, she forgave him for it.

CHAPTER 30

McGivney's sports bar was dead ahead as soon as Cutter got off the elevator in the Sheraton lobby, so he didn't have far to go. He was only two minutes late, which was twelve minutes later than he liked to be. Grumpy's rule: Ten minutes early was right on time.

Lola was still up in her room, on her way to the gym. That girl was always in the gym. She planned to spend the morning running down leads with Rockie Van Dyke, who wanted nothing to do with Cutter's breakfast appointment.

Lori Maycomb was waiting at the center booth along the wall, looking out the window at the rain. A soccer game was on the big screen behind her, above her head. Argentina vs. Brazil. Lionel Messi dribbled the ball down the field like it was tacked to the end of his shoes. Messi was the twins' favorite player. Arliss had bought them both number 10 jackets at a soccer store six months before, when he'd gone back to Miami Beach to testify in an old case, from before he'd gotten the supervisor's job in Alaska.

Maycomb turned when he approached the table, and stood up to shake his hand. She wore a synthetic hoodie with a Native design that Cutter took for a raven holding a circle in its open beak. Wool pants were tucked into her

Xtratufs. A waterproof daypack peeked from beneath a damp raincoat on the seat beside her. There was a wobbly, but fiercely determined look in her eyes. Cutter had seen it before—in the mirror. She was someone who'd hit bottom, hard. On the up-bounce, but not quite yet in control of her surroundings. She wore no makeup that Cutter could see. Her eyes were puffy, probably from lack of sleep. Cutter felt her pain there. Her fingernails were chewed to the quick, black hair pulled back over her ears with a pink, no-fuss elastic hair band, like she was going out to play tennis instead of helping Cutter find a missing girl. There was a notebook on the table and a cheap blue Paper Mate pen that looked like a dog had gotten hold of the cap. Judging from her fingernails, Cutter suspected the damage had been done by Maycomb. The notebook was closed and the chewed cap was still on the pen—good signs in Cutter's book. If anyone took notes, he wanted it to be him.

She tilted her head toward the bar. "He's bringing coffee in a second." Her voice was soft, direct, and she looked him in the eye.

"So," he said, hoping to break the ice with a little small talk. He was far too tired to force anything close to a smile. "Maycomb—like the county in *To Kill a Mockingbird*."

"Culture points to you," she said. "Arliss Cutter, like Little Arliss in *Old Yeller*."

"Touché," he said.

"Thanks for meeting me," Maycomb said. "I'm sure Rockie has filled you in with all sorts of horror stories. Sad to say it, but most of them are probably true."

Cutter waved away the thought—for now.

"We needed to talk," he said. "You may be the only person we have as far as a lead to Donita Willets."

"I told the FBI everything I knew yesterday," she said.

"Which wasn't much of anything, I'm afraid. Whatever got the poor thing killed, she hadn't had time to tell me about it."

Cutter let the waiter pour their coffee and take their order. Scrambled eggs and toast for her, eggs over medium, bacon, and pancakes for him. He hoped to get so busy tracking down Donita Willets that he wouldn't have time for lunch. He stirred a couple of spoonfuls of half-and-half into his coffee to soothe his gut, and then let the waiter go back to the kitchen before he pitched the new theory—off the record, which meant Maycomb couldn't use it in a story.

"So she isn't dead?" Maycomb said after he'd given her the bones of it.

Cutter eyed her over the top of his raised coffee, deciding how much to tell her. Some, or she'd clam up. He took a sip and set the cup on the table. "We're thinking not. But we need to find Fawsey in order to find her."

"Before whoever did the Tyler-Rogers shooting out at the shrine kills her too."

"Yep," Cutter said.

The waiter came back with their order. Maycomb nudged the syrup toward him.

"No thanks," he said, lifting his eggs on top of the pancakes with his fork before breaking the yolks. "I'm not in a very sweet mood."

Maycomb put both hands flat on the table. "I promise, if I had any relevant information, I'd share it with you."

"*Any* information," Cutter said. "Even irrelevant."

"I don't have that either."

Cutter cut a bite of pancake, sodden with egg yolk. "You may have it but not know it."

"My friend in Anchorage said I should be careful of you," she said.

Cutter ate another bite. "Good advice."

"Don't you want to know what my friend told me?"

"Nope," Cutter said. "I stopped caring what people think about me a long time ago. I know who I am and what I know. I want to know what you know."

"Well," Lori Maycomb said. "I know that you probably saved me from a beating yesterday. That woman on the beach would have pulled my hair out by the roots if you hadn't shown up. Who knows what the guys would have done to me."

"Stood and laughed," Cutter said, serious.

"Maybe," Maycomb said. "Anyway, I owe you. Most people wouldn't have stepped in like you did."

"Don't know about that," Cutter said.

Maycomb heaved a heavy sigh, looking around the restaurant. "I'm just saying, not everyone could have handled those people the way you did."

Cutter kept eating his pancakes.

She prodded. "Are you from Alaska?"

"Florida." He took a sip of coffee.

"Aren't you the king of pithy answers."

Cutter shrugged, fork and knife in hand. "Harder to misquote."

"I'm not the enemy, you know."

"That's the thing," Cutter said. "You kind of are. Journalists and cops are at cross-purposes ninety-nine percent of the time. I cannot count the number of occasions where ten seconds got taken from some interview with me and put on an endless out-of-context loop that distorted the truth into something ugly and interesting, just so it would get ratings—or clicks or whatever."

Maycomb gave a slow nod, staring down at her index finger as she drew tiny circles on the table. "I get it, you'd just as soon your work stayed in the shadows, hunting the swamps and dark holes of the world."

Cutter shrugged. "That's where the rats and roaches like to hide."

"Is that what you think they are? The people you hunt? Rats and roaches?"

"Hey, it's your metaphor," Cutter said. "But I guess I do. Human rats and roaches, worthy of human rights, but sometimes not so much human kindness."

"I guess that's the difference," she said. "You'd prefer to work in the dark. Journalists want to shine the light on things."

"And there you go," Cutter said. "That is exactly what I mean. In my experience, it's the angle of that light you're shining that's the problem. Straight down, hold-nothing-back lighting is just fine, but tilt that light a little up, down, or sideways and the shadows on one side get longer or shorter. The truth is distorted."

"A philosophical marshal," Maycomb said, looking at him, but still doodling on the table with her finger.

"*Deputy* marshal," he corrected. "And don't get me wrong. This isn't an indictment of every reporter out there. I'm all about a free press. It keeps everybody honest. I just prefer not to be the one to talk to them."

"How about we be the one percent," Maycomb said. The circles with her finger turning into jabs against the table as she came to some conclusion. "How about you and I work together."

Cutter gave her an it's-not-so-easy grimace. "To get your story or get to the truth and find Donita Willets?"

"Both," she said. "But Donita Willets first, definitely."

She piled a mound of scrambled eggs on her toast and took a bite. "Listen," she said. "My sister-in-law hates my guts. She's made it clear to my news director that the station will get nothing if he assigns me any story regarding the police or public safety. I cover Native issues for public radio. Harmless."

"Native issues?" Cutter said.

"Yep," she said. "I'm Tlingit and Unangan."

"Unangan?" Cutter said, interested. Culture had a great deal to do with behavior.

"Our word for Aleut," she said. "My mother's family was from here, Tlingit. My father's father was Tlingit as well. But my father's mother was from the Pribilofs. She was brought here during World War II. The United States government, in its infinite wisdom, decided to rescue the people from St. Paul and other islands in the Aleutians from advancing Imperial Japanese troops. Sounds like a deal, right? But they dumped them in internment camps here in Southeast. My grandmother ended up in Funter Bay."

"I read about that on the plane ride down. Tragic," Cutter said. "An old salmon cannery."

"In the *Anchorage Daily News*?"

"Yep."

Maycomb beamed. "That was my piece."

"Good writing," Cutter said. "Bad times. I guess German prisoners of war were held here in Southeast as well."

Maycomb nodded, apparently pleased he'd actually read the whole article. "The German prisoners got dry barracks, decent food—and heat. My grandmother was with the group that got plunked in the rain and mud at that broken-down salmon cannery at Funter Bay. Not fit for a goat, let alone American citizens . . ."

"Sounds like it," Cutter said.

"The war ended and the government shipped the ones who hadn't died of flu or dysentery back to the Aleutians to work the seal harvest—except my grandmother. She'd fallen in love with a Tlingit boy who used to help deliver their meager supplies. I'm thinking of writing a book about her."

"I'd read a book like that," Cutter said.

Maycomb ate a bite of toast, settling herself again after getting so personal. "The point is, there are a lot of Native issues for me to write about. Those guys who came after me on the beach called me an Indian bitch. Not just bitch, but *Indian bitch*, as if that made it worse somehow."

"There was a lot about them that wasn't right," Cutter said.

"Anyway, thank you."

"What's the deal with your sister?" Cutter asked, changing the subject.

"Sister-*in-law*." Maycomb put both hands on the table again to steady herself. "Well . . . for starters, she wants to take my son. She thinks I'm a shitty mother and wholeheartedly believes she could do better."

Cutter let out a deep breath. "Because you're Native?"

"No," Maycomb said. "Because I'm a drunk. I could deal with it if she were just another Indian-hater. That would put her a hundred percent in the wrong. Trouble is, part of what she thinks is absolutely true. I am . . . or at least I was a shitty mother and an even worse wife."

"You appear to be doing well now," Cutter said.

"Looks can be deceiving," she said. "I mean, I am sober. My birthday was yesterday if you can believe it."

Cutter knew enough alcoholics to understand she meant her sobriety birthday. People who attended AA called the anniversary of when they were born their "belly-button birthday." Their "birthday" celebrated the first day they had remained sober—and that was far and away more momentous than the belly-button kind.

"I'm a recovering drunk, but I'm still a drunk," Maycomb continued. "Leave me alone with a six-pack—and at some point, there's a good chance I'll have to do my research and drink it all, just to see if I'm still an alcoholic. And when I say drink, I mean drink." She faced the window as she spoke, staring into the fog. "My husband—Rockie's brother— he was such a decent soul. Poor guy watched me go back to the bottle again and again—and never once said anything about kicking me to the curb. I mean, I was already there on my own, but he never mentioned divorce or taking our son from me."

Head still bowed, she glanced up at him, embarrassed. "Sorry to vomit the sordid details of my life up on the table."

"Hey," Cutter said. "I asked."

She gave a soft chuckle. "You know how to pick a recovering alcoholic out in a crowd?"

Cutter remained stone-faced.

"Don't worry," Maycomb said. "She'll tell you. I guess we get so used to making amends and admitting we have a problem that we start to believe everyone wants to hear about it."

"Like I said, I asked."

"Yeah, well, you didn't ask for all . . . this . . ." Her voice trailed into a whisper as she locked on to something on the street outside.

Cutter turned, leaning forward to get a look at Maycomb's sight line.

Juneau was waking up. People were just beginning to emerge from warm houses onto chilly streets black with rain. A man in orange Grundéns overalls and floppy black rubber boots pushed a wheelbarrow toward a waiting boat, illuminated by a string of work lights. A couple of young women walked side by side toward some early-morning job downtown, dressed Juneau-sheik with tasseled Nepalese wool beanies, name-brand rain jackets, and skinny jeans tucked into their Xtratufs. Another woman, a mom or nannie, pushed a tandem jogging stroller with a clear plastic rain hood across the heavy timbers of the wharf toward a line of parked cars. She balanced a flat of coffee cups on top of the extra-wide stroller.

The skinny guy looked out of place, uncomfortable, like he'd been dropped off at the wrong address or escaped from solitary confinement.

"See that guy with the scruff and the red bandanas tied around his hands?"

"Yep," Cutter said.

Cutter estimated the man was about six feet tall. Thin, but not the healthy kind. All bone and skin, like an addict—the kind of person Lola would have said survived on the "smell of an oily rag." He had a bouncing stride that looked as if he was loping when he walked. One arm stayed close to his chest, the other hovered over his belly, elbows tight, like he had a broken rib or some other injury that hurt him when he moved. He was probably thirty, but carried himself like a very old man.

Cutter shot the reporter a quick glance, then returned to Bandana Hands.

"What about him?"

"I saw him sitting in a truck in front of the federal building yesterday."

"Post office, maybe?" Cutter said.

"Maybe. But he was there when I left for lunch and there when I got back. I was waiting for a call from Donita. Maybe I'm just being paranoid, but I can tell when someone's watching me, and he definitely was."

"You know him?"

"Never saw him before yesterday."

Cutter was already on his feet. He peeled two twenties off the roll in his pocket and left them on the table.

The double doors in the lobby slid open automatically when Cutter approached, letting the cool air from outside hit him in the face like a damp washcloth. Bandana Hands crossed under the glow of a streetlight, shooting a nervous glance over his shoulder as he walked north from the Wharf building. His collar was turned up against a steady drizzle, but he'd left the hood of his raincoat down, presumably so he could keep his head on a swivel. He was hinky about being followed, which made Cutter want to follow him all the more.

Lori Maycomb stood inside, well away from the entrance.

"Wait here," Cutter said, and stepped out the door at a trot. He moved obliquely, like he was going straight to the restaurant. Bandana Hands flicked another look over his shoulder, saw Cutter, sized him up like a grazing gazelle deciding if it was time to run. He looked at the hotel entrance—then froze, mid-bounce. His face fell, not really a frown, more like he was melting in the rain. Cutter followed his gaze to find Lori Maycomb standing at the hotel doors.

"Fantastic," Cutter muttered to himself. Bandana Hands tucked his head—and bolted.

CHAPTER 31

Cutter knew a thing or two about chasing people. The smart ones—and there were very few of those—just took off, trying to make the most of any head start. Experienced crooks did the same, even if they weren't smart. Bandana Hands was neither.

Animals—humans included—tended to follow the path of least resistance when they moved. Some trackers called this the "natural line of drift." Grumpy called it "funneling."

"Ten guys walk out of hunting camp to take a dump at different times of the day, nine of them get funneled to the same spot and end up planting a boot in somebody else's crap."

It was human nature to take the easier way, to let the terrain dictate direction of travel.

Bandana Hands followed that logic—at first.

The Gastineau Channel lay to his left, a twenty-foot drop from the wharf. The streets and alleys of downtown were to his right, but that was all uphill. Bandana Hands's legs told him it was better to run parallel to the street instead of crossing it and having to work to gain elevation.

Cutter was fast and this guy was injured. It wasn't anything close to a fair footrace. Cutter gained ground with every stride. Pumping his arms. Feeling the familiar bump when his elbow touched the Colt Python on his hip. It was good to open up, to run all out after someone who needed to be caught. He'd already zeroed in on the spot between Bandana Hands's shoulder blades where he'd give a little shove. Tackling was for rookies who'd never broken a rib on some felon's boot heel. Another ten steps and it would all be over but the paperwork.

Then Bandana Hands saw the lady with the jogging stroller. Maybe that had been his goal all along. He juked between two pickup trucks, rounding up so he was face-to-face with the startled lady. The back door of her Subaru was open, where she'd been bent over fastening one of her kids into a car seat. The other, a child of two or three, stood at her mother's thigh, all but eclipsed by an oversize yellow rain coat.

Bandana Hands scooped up the child as he ran by, wincing with pain, but digging into a sprint.

Directly toward the water.

Cutter was right behind him, ten steps away, maybe less, but it didn't matter.

Bandana Hands ran along the edge of the boardwalk until he cleared a waiting tug boat that was moored stern to the wharf, and then tossed the screaming toddler over the side like a piece of garbage.

Five more steps and Cutter would have had the son of a bitch. No little shove now. A human sled ride to the ground, face-first. But the kid was in the water. New terrain that dictated Cutter's direction of travel.

He took a scant second at the edge to locate the yellow raincoat sinking beneath the surface. The water was black as stone. For all he knew, there *were* stones down there, big ones, just deep enough they didn't scrape the bottom of a boat, but plenty shallow to break your neck if you dove from the wharf.

The glint of yellow raincoat faded from sight, so he jumped anyway, feetfirst.

Cutter braced himself, waiting for impact, but felt only cold water. He bobbed up quickly, forcing himself not to draw in a gasping lungful of the frigid water. The guy with the wheelbarrow had made it to his boat. Spotlight in hand, he was shouting, pointing over the side. Cutter caught a glimpse of yellow again. He took a breath, kicked his feet above his head, and piked into a dive, pulling himself deeper into the darkness with powerful strokes.

Cold blackness closed in around him. A life-long scuba diver, he was as at home in the water as he was on land, but he'd not taken time to clear his ears. Ten, fifteen feet down, he heard the familiar squeal as his Eustachian tubes tried to equalize the pressure against his eardrums. He wiggled his jaw back and forth, tasting salty water.

His lungs tightened. His hand brushed something in the darkness. Lost it. He drove himself forward, kicking as hard and fast as he could while still wearing the rubber boots. He found it again. Smooth. Slick.

His fist closed around the edge of the raincoat, then a fragile little hand. Pulling the tiny child to his chest with both arms, he looked skyward, kicking even harder now, willing himself upward.

He surfaced a dozen yards from the boat and the man with the spotlight. Seconds counted, so he flipped the little girl on her back, resting her on his forearm. His body blocked the spotlight, leaving her small face looking fragile and chalky pale in his shadow. He checked for breathing. Nothing.

Lifting the child to him as he swam, he gave her two rescue breaths before he made it to the boat.

The man in orange Grundéns reached down and took her, pulling her on board.

"She's still not breathing!" he yelled, alternately talking to Cutter and the child. "Come on, baby girl. I already called nine-one-one! Come on, wake up, kiddo." Cutter pressed himself up onto the stern platform and then scrambled over the side in time to find the man patting the little girl on the cheeks. Her mother, who had another baby to worry about, was just working her way down the ramp from the wharf. She called out her daughter's name.

"Brie! Brie!"

Brie lay on the deck of the fishing boat, the hood of her raincoat pulled back to reveal a tangle of dark hair across a pale forehead. Her eyes were closed.

"I'll do CPR," Cutter said to the man, dropping to his knees. Seawater spilled from his boots as he knelt, ran from his sodden clothing, puddling the deck and dripping on the little girl. He tilted her head gently, opening her airway. "Get back with nine-one-one and stay on the line. Tell them no breathing. No pulse." He wanted the man to have a job. Something to do so he didn't get in the way.

She'd been in the water less than a minute. That wasn't enough time to cause brain damage, but the shock of hitting the cold water had caused her to take a reflexive breath. Cutter had brought her up from the bottom, but her lungs were full of water.

She was on dry ground, but still drowning.

She was so small that Cutter gave rescue puffs of air, held back with his chest compressions to make sure he didn't break a rib.

Two breaths, thirty compressions.

"Come on, Brie!" Cutter said. "Come on, kiddo."

Two more breaths—

She gagged. Then spewed a geyser of water, coughing and spitting and crying. Her mother crowded in to take her, handing off her smaller baby to a soaking wet Cutter.

An ambulance arrived four minutes later, put little Brie on oxygen, and then sped away to the hospital with her mother and sibling.

A second ambulance arrived shortly after. Cutter refused care but did accept a wool blanket that he wrapped around his shoulders. He was fine. Cold, wet, and supremely pissed. But fine.

Lori Maycomb recounted how she saw Bandana Hands get in a skiff, probably stolen, and disappear into the fog toward Douglas Island. She stood in the rain with Cutter now, staring across the channel at nothing but cold gray darkness.

"No idea what his name was?" Cutter asked for the third time.

"Sorry, no," she said. "I've never seen him before yesterday." Cutter pushed his chin toward Gastineau Channel. He was shivering now and needed both hands to hold the blanket tight around his neck. "What's directly across from us?"

"Forest, mostly," Maycomb said. "Neighborhoods, schools, a few restaurants and stores. But mostly forest. The Treadwell Mine is there. It's abandoned. Caved in about a hundred years ago. Huge place. There are lots of old buildings, moss-covered ruins, really, like something you'd see in an Indiana Jones movie."

"Takes a special kind of bastard," Cutter said, his teeth chattering.

"To toss a kid in the water like that?" Maycomb said.

"No." Cutter looked up at her. "To hunt a guy like that down."

CHAPTER 32

Special Agent Beason, who must have been sleeping at the courthouse, screeched down Willoughby and across Egan in his rented Tahoe. He jerked to a stop on the wooden wharf directly behind Cutter and Maycomb. He left the engine on, the headlights glaring, which only served to piss Cutter off more than he already was. Cutter continued to look the other way, even when Beason addressed him, forcing the FBI agent to come around and face his own blinding headlights if he wanted to talk.

"You let another one get away," Beason said, turning to follow Cutter's gaze into the fog. For once, he didn't rant. His idiocy was ingrained, but he was too exhausted to rail.

"Yep."

Cutter had worked for and with people like Charles Beason before. The FBI didn't have a corner on the asshole market. The Marshals Service had their fair share, as did the army, even the pizza joint where he'd worked in Port Charlotte when he was seventeen. It was best to ignore them. Let them derail their own careers—or, in some cases, inexplicably promote. Those people were uncanny at their ability to discern which asses needed to be kissed and which ones they could kick with impunity.

"You're not being fair." Maycomb hooked a thumb over her shoulder, up Egan toward the hospital. "Cutter had to choose between saving a drowning child and catching the guy."

Beason glared at her, acting like he'd just realized she was there. "And who are you again?"

She extended her hand. "Lori Maycomb. KTOO. Assuming you're with the FBI, I talked to a couple of your agents yesterday."

"Maycomb?" Beason recoiled as if he'd been smacked in the face. "You need to beat it." He turned to Cutter. "Donita Willets was this woman's informant. She's a person of interest herself, in case that little investigative tidbit slipped by you. I don't know what you'd call that in the Marshals Service, but we—"

"We call it not being a dick while we're interviewing a witness," Teariki said. "You should try it sometime."

Cutter snugged the blanket a little tighter, past caring. Beason's grumbling was directed at him, so he shrugged it off.

Lola had trotted across the street, crowding into the group, thinking she needed to be there to keep Cutter from pulling Beason's head off. She'd heard the last. She handed Cutter a dry shirt she'd grabbed from his room after he'd called her.

"That's enough, Lola," Cutter said. She held the blanket while he stripped out of his wet shirt and slipped on the new one, feeling better instantly. The Fjällräven pants were clammy but relatively dry already.

Lola wedged herself farther between Cutter and Beason, holding up the blanket with both hands, like a matador. She spoke over her shoulder to Cutter. "What? You know you wanted to say it yourself."

"I'm good," Cutter said, buttoning up the shirt. "He can be a dick to me. Just not my people."

"Well," Lola said. "You're *my* people. . . ."

Fortunately for Beason, Rockie Van Dyke pulled up in her SUV, interrupting his response. The detective ignored Maycomb altogether when she approached the group. "Hey. Dispatch got a call from Mary Dutchik two minutes ago. She's a scanner fan, monitors JPD radio more than a rookie patrol officer on his days off. She heard the call go out about the pursuit and the little kid in the water. Sounds like she had an appointment with a man this morning who wanted to sell her a Tlingit shaman's rattle. According to her, this guy had bandages on his hands."

"Where is she now?" Lola asked.

"Her shop's right around the corner. We can walk there."

"Can I come?" Maycomb asked.

Beason started to protest, but Lola cut him off, looking at Van Dyke.

"Your caller said this guy was trying to sell her a shaman's rattle. Native culture is probably going to be germane to the investigation."

Cutter looked at Maycomb with a wary eye. He hated to agree with Beason, but he wasn't completely convinced either. "You familiar with shaman's rattles, things like that?"

"Of course," Maycomb said. "I'm happy to help however I can."

"Settled," Lola said. "It might be good to have someone along who has more than a cursory knowledge of artifacts."

Rockie Van Dyke closed her eyes, the muscles in her jaw tensing. "You say so. But she'll let us down. I guarantee it."

* * *

"Odd deal all around," Mary Dutchik said. "Strange men aren't exactly at a premium around here, but this one is especially weird." Dressed in a fashionable wool cardigan and matching gray gabardine slacks, she reminded Cutter of one of his high school English teachers. Short silver hair was still wet from a walk in the early-morning rain. She looked tired, as if she'd come in earlier than usual. It made sense. Cutter couldn't imagine the foot traffic at an art gallery would be very heavy at seven in the morning when there were no cruise ships in town.

The waist-high display cases contained an assortment of engraved silver and gold bracelets and other Native carvings of spruce and cedar. Each item was set against black velvet to make it pop from its surroundings and neatly spaced so it stood out from everything else. The cases formed a U on the three sides of the showroom—all but for the storefront itself, and a small gap that led to what Cutter assumed was an office or storage area.

Bright lighting gave the gallery a sparkling feel, like a high-end jewelry store. Wooden masks of Raven, Bear, and men with twisted faces hung on the wall above the cases between similarly painted canoe paddles and other art. Like the totem poles Cutter had seen around Southeast Alaska, the predominate colors were red and black. Everything was beautiful, bright, and expensive. No made-in-China tchotchkes here.

"And the artifact," Mary Dutchik continued. "That was very unusual as well. As far as I know, most Tlingit rattles were carved of wood. Raven steals the moon, Frog, man, that's the general motif. I've seen some with small deer dewclaws tethered to the outside that sound when the rattle is shaken. Others have stones inside a carved, gourd-like hollow. The thing is, wood rots, so only a very few authentic artifacts have survived that are older than the late nineteenth or early twentieth century. Those were discovered on expeditions in the early 1920s—"

"Robbed from graves," Lori Maycomb whispered.

Dutchik shrugged. "That's sad, but it is the truth. In any case these would have rotted as well but for the fact that they were found and put in museum collections."

"The one from this morning," Cutter asked. "Do you think it was authentic?"

"I believe so," Dutchik said. "But it was different. The body of this rattle looks like it was made of animal horn, likely Dall sheep, boiled so it could be shaped. A length of long bone—probably from the same sheep that provided the horn—made the handle."

Cutter looked directly at Maycomb. "And that's unusual?" he asked. "A . . . bone rattle?"

She gave a noncommittal shrug. "But it makes sense. Some Tlingit traditions say the first animal hunted after the great flood was a bighorn sheep. Many taboos are associated with the animal. Hunters going after sheep could not have sex for a day before a hunt. Their wives refrained from heating water and did not comb their hair during the duration of the hunt, for fear of combing their husband off the high cliffs where he was hunting. Bones would have been important to a Tlingit shaman, part of a hard versus soft duality of nature. Shaman often wore ceremonial aprons with bits of bone and hoof dangling from the front. A rattle made of sheep horn and bone might have held some serious power. Any carvings on it?"

"Raven," Dutchik said. "Frog, maybe."

"Yehk," Maycomb said. "Shaman had spirit helpers who often took the form of animals. Yehk."

"Look at you," Van Dyke sneered. "Guess you did prove useful after all."

"Did he tell you where he got this rattle?" Beason asked.

"I asked him," Dutchik said. "But he refused."

She pursed her lips and shook her head, looking even more like Cutter's high school teacher. "I told him the artifact's provenance was vital in order to be certain it's from a private collection and not robbed from some grave."

Maycomb scoffed. "Which still translates as robbed from a grave, just not recently."

"True again," Dutchik said. "Modern collectors want to share the blame with somebody who went on an expedition a hundred years ago. It makes them feel less dirty." The gallery owner had obviously covered this ground before, probably with the people who'd provided all the contemporary Native art for her to sell.

"How much would something like this be worth?" Cutter asked. "If it's authentic."

"Two or three hundred," Dutchik said.

Lola gasped. "Two hundred bucks seems like chump change for a one-of-a-kind bone rattle."

Dutchik laughed out loud. "Oh no. I meant two or three hundred *thousand*. The man who brought this one in had done his research. He knew of a Raven rattle that recently sold for over half a million dollars."

"Five hundred thousand reasons to commit murder," Beason said.

Cutter nodded, eyes half closed, the kind of nod that said he didn't agree at all but was in the process of thinking things through.

"Doesn't make sense," he said at length. "How much would you have given him?"

"Nothing remotely close to that," Dutchik said. "I have

a small fund I use when I want to buy things and get them back in Tlingit hands. He knew I wouldn't give him much when he came through the door."

"How's that?" Beason asked.

"Well," Dutchik said. "He told me about the half-million-dollar sale, then said he was willing to take 'pennies on the dollar.' I said I could give him a few thousand."

"So," Beason said, accusingly. "Did you?"

"I did not," Dutchik said. "I told him I needed to examine the artifact in person, have it appraised. He had several photos of it on his phone, from all angles, but he refused to show me the actual rattle."

Beason brightened. "Does he plan to bring it back, do you think?"

"I believe he had it in his pocket the entire time."

Cutter tapped the top of a glass display case, still thinking. "I want to go back to something you mentioned a minute ago. You said, 'the man himself *is* especially weird.' It sounds like you've met him before. Is that how he knew you might be the person who would buy something like this bone rattle?"

"Oh, sorry," Dutchik said. "I didn't make that clear, did I? He came into the gallery once before, about three months ago, and sold me a large formation of crystals. I paid him in cash. He didn't give me his name then either."

"Crystals?" Cutter mused.

"Quartz," Dutchik said. "Big ones, like something you'd see in Superman's lair or something. This formation was about the size of a soccer ball. He said he'd found them in a mine."

"Do you know which mine?" Detective Van Dyke asked.

"I'm not certain," Dutchik said. "But I've only seen crystals like that come from a mine near Port Snettisham, to the south. Not surprisingly, it's called the 'Crystal Mine.'"

Cutter shot a glance at Beason to see if he had any further questions. The FBI agent shook his head. Grudge match or not, both were professional enough not to let it bleed into their interviews.

"Okay then," Beason said. "Thank you for your time, Ms. Dutchik. Do you think you'd be able to help a sketch artist put together a drawing of this man?"

"I'll do better than that," Dutchik said. She removed one of the wooden masks from the wall. Cutter guessed this one was a bear from the rounded ears and big teeth.

Dutchik removed a small camera from the mouth of the mask. "Bear is always watching. Most of the art I have in here is one of a kind, quite valuable."

Beason put on his all-knowing FBI hat. "Studies show that it does more to deter theft if people can see the cameras."

Dutchik smiled sweetly. "I don't want to deter them," she said. "I want to catch them in the act and send their thieving butts to jail."

Lola patted Dutchik on the shoulder and gave her a wink. "If you were twenty years younger, I'd give you an application."

CHAPTER 33

"The Valkyrie is also out near Port Snettisham," Lori Maycomb said, as soon as they were all out of the gallery and walking up Franklin Street. "I did a report about the mine owner a couple of months ago. Harold Grimsson. Fancies himself a modern-day Viking." She sneered. "My piece was a feel-good story about all the philanthropic work his mine does for the community."

Van Dyke bristled. "You have a problem with the industry that built this area, put us on the map?"

Maycomb, arguing from the high ground, was having none of it. "Technically, my people built this place, and we were 'on the map' eons before your people got here. But to your question, I love iPhones, computers, electron microscopes, and all the other things built with metals we dig out of the ground. I've done stories on both of the bigger mines in this area. They're great. No problems at all there. This Harold Grimsson character just rubs me the wrong way. You know, the kind of handsy, condescending jerk who calls you 'sweetie' and 'hon' and looks at you with X-ray vision."

"She's not wrong about that," Van Dyke said. "Grimsson is a weasel. A big weasel with a beard that looks like a skunk."

"His wife supposedly drowned in the bathtub," Maycomb

said. "Way out on his little private island. No witnesses. Odd circumstances if you ask me."

Van Dyke scoffed, climbing back on her hating-horse. "So now you're a homicide detective? Give me a break, Lori, and let us do our jobs."

Maycomb shrugged it off. "Anyway, Grimsson donates money to the library, supports Juneau Douglas High School sports, provides a lot of jobs—so he buys himself the title of hero. But he's been cited something like twenty-seven times for safety and land-use violations. Indigenous groups have sued Valkyrie Mine Holdings because the mine is lo-cated right on top of our ancestral lands. A couple of months ago, Grimsson was trying to get an old right-of-way approved as an existing road so he could dig another hole . . . or at least, dig deeper in an old one. Apparently, there's still a lot of gold in them thar hills. Most everyone was surprised when he got approval so quickly, but there were rumors he had a couple of politicians in his pocket."

"Senator Fawsey?" Lola mused.

"That was the whisper," Maycomb said. "But nothing was ever substantiated."

"Maybe that's what Donita Willets was going to substan-tiate," Lola said.

"Grimsson had to get approval for a road on his own claim?" Cutter asked.

Van Dyke nodded. "The Tongass is one hundred percent roadless. If there was no old road there already, there can't be any new road now. . . ."

Beason rubbed his face again, squinting hard as his thoughts cut through the exhaustion. Cutter didn't blame him there. Few things were less exciting than land claim disputes—but it was often the boring particulars that pro-vided motive for murder.

The agent blew out a forceful breath, trying to wake up.

"Okay," he said. "Check and see if JPD or the Troopers have had any calls for service out at the Valkyrie or dealt with any Valkyrie employees recently."

The man was a level 10 jerk, but he was also a decent investigator.

Van Dyke gave him a thumbs-up, stepping to the back of the group, bringing up the rear while she called her office.

"How far away is this Port Snettisham?" Lola asked.

"About thirty miles south of here," Maycomb said. "On the north side of Stephens Passage."

"And the Crystal Mine?" Cutter asked. "Who operates that?"

"No one," Maycomb said. "It's been closed for decades."

Beason's phone rang at the same moment Van Dyke trotted forward, catching up with Cutter.

"Turns out we did get a call for service," she said. Beason put his cell phone to his ear and, for a time, tried to listen to two conversations at once. In the end, he brightened, said, "Is that right?" and then fell to the back of the group to concentrate on his own call.

"Go ahead," Cutter said to Van Dyke.

"JPD got a welfare check request yesterday from a Mrs. Merculief in Anchorage. She said her son, Isaac, is an archeologist working on contract at Valkyrie mine. She hasn't heard from him in two days."

"Why would the mine need an archeologist?" Lola asked.

"Some contracts require it," Maycomb said. "I imagine that was one way Grimsson got his go-ahead to push through construction on the old corduroy road easement, even though it's been proven to be on our ancestral grounds.

An archeologist on-site would make sure nothing was damaged or disturbed."

Cutter's eyes widened. "Like a bone rattle."

"Exactly like a bone rattle," Maycomb said.

"Anyway," Van Dyke said, looking miffed that Maycomb was still playing explainer when she had more to say. "Initial calls to Valkyrie Human Resources say Isaac Merculief hasn't shown up for work for two days."

Maycomb's phone rang next. She checked the caller ID, then said, "Sorry, have to take this."

"What do you think, boss?" Lola asked, looking at Cutter. "Go show a screen shot of our runner to the people at Valkyrie Mine Holdings, see if they know him?"

They'd made it back to the hotel lobby.

"And dig a little deeper into this archeologist," Cutter said. "Beason may want to ask Judge Forsberg for a warrant so we can take a look at any reports Isaac Merculief may have on file." A hard shiver racked his entire body. Standing in the warm hotel made him realize how chilled he'd actually become. "First, I'm going to put on dry pants."

Lola and Van Dyke went to the lobby couches to wait, while Beason with his phone call was near the front door, out of earshot. Still shivering, Cutter pressed the button to summon the elevator, but Maycomb walked up and put a hand on his arm, stopping him.

"That call was from my radio station," she said. "I asked a friend to do a little research. He found video on YouTube from when Levi Fawsey's father was running for senator. I just watched a couple of minutes of it. I think it's going to give us a direction to look for Donita."

"Outstanding," Cutter said. "I'll change and we'll watch it on the way to Valkyrie's main offices."

Lori Maycomb fiddled with an unlit cigarette and chewed on her bottom lip.

"I'm banned from Valkyrie mining offices because of some of the questions I asked when I was doing my story. Rockie would love nothing more than to arrest me for criminal trespass if I go back."

Cutter chuckled, his teeth chattering badly now.

The elevator doors opened, offering an escape to a hot shower.

"You go do whatever it is you're going to do with that cigarette," Cutter said. "I'm going to put on some dry clothes."

Beason finished his phone call and yelled out for Cutter to wait.

He let the elevator shut without him in it. Released a tremulous breath. Wouldn't that be something? Dying of hypothermia in the hotel lobby.

"What's up?"

Beason grinned. "Looks like all of this is going to be moot."

"How's that?"

Beason winked, like they were suddenly old buds. "The Hernandez brothers have agreed to cooperate in exchange for a plea deal. They'll provide us with the answers we need."

"What about Donita Willets," Cutter asked. "It's not suddenly moot to her."

"I'm not saying that," Beason growled. "But I can only do one thing at a time."

Cutter gave him a half grin. "That's what you have us for. You're going to keep a lid on this? Right? It leaks that the Hernandez brothers are talking, that just turns up the heat on Donita Willets."

"Don't tell me how to do my job," Beason growled. "Of

course we're keeping a lid on it. I wouldn't even have told you if Warneke hadn't ordered me to. It's bottled up tight. No one outside FBI leadership and the US Attorney's office."

Only fifteen or twenty people then, Cutter thought. Buttoned up all right. Like the Hell's Angels' famous credo: "Three could keep a secret—if two of them were dead."

CHAPTER 34

It was relatively easy for Schimmel to steal a skiff after he'd tossed the kid. Everyone had been focused on the rescue, allowing him time to give the fuel priming bulb a couple of squeezes and set the choke on the outboard. It was a thirty horse, not a great deal of compression, but yanking on the starter rope was excruciating and sent arcs of pain across his chest and under both arms. The motor coughed and sputtered, but started after the third try.

Schimmel sat on an overturned paint bucket at the tiller, throttle cranked wide open, running blind across Gastineau Channel through chowder-thick fog. Fortunately, it was the wrong time of the year for cruise ships, or he would have risked being crushed and chopped to chowder himself. The cops would be after him as soon as they pulled the kid out of the water. They'd probably shoot him if the kid drowned, or beat the shit out of him at the very least. What was he supposed to do? Let that big guy catch him? He didn't know what that guy was selling, but he didn't want any part of it.

Halfway across it dawned on him that the cops had radios. The channel was barely a mile wide, less in most places, but they didn't even need to drive across the bridge to catch him, or wait to fish the kid's body out. They'd just call across and whatever troopers or JPD cops who happened to already be there would be waiting for him on the other side, probably all lined up at the harbor ready to blow his head off as soon as he rounded the breakwater.

He turned south, down the channel, past the tank farm and the sewage treatment plant to his left. He thought of running all the way to Stephens Passage. Auclair would hide him if he could get to the Valkyrie, but that was a no go. The wimpy fuel can in the skiff was only about half full, not nearly enough juice to get him thirty miles, especially not at this speed.

He turned to look behind him, winced at the pulse of pain it shot through his razor wounds, then slowed a hair, straining his ears, listening for pursuing boats in the fog.

Feeble lights told him he was abeam Douglas Harbor to his right. He slowed even more, cheating more to the middle of the narrow channel, hoping he could sneak past any waiting cops.

Schimmel had to get out of town—not so easy when the only way in and out was by boat or plane. Childers would know. Yeah. That was it. He'd give Dallas Childers a call. Childers would come meet him, tell him what he should do.

Tears welled in Schimmel's eyes when Childers picked up on the second ring. He was gruff, dismissive when he answered, but he was always that way. It didn't mean anything.

Schimmel gave a quick rundown of what had happened, trying not to cry, leaving out the part about taking the shaman's rattle from the dig.

"So what do you think I should do?"

Silence.

Schimmel didn't worry. Childers was probably trying to figure out the best way to get him out of here.

"I know a place," Childers finally said. "It's kind of a climb, but it'll get you away from the cops."

Schimmel listened to the directions and then turned the boat farther south toward the old Treadwell Mine. He felt better knowing that Childers was on his way. Yeah, he was gruff, unpolished, but he was the closest thing Dean Schimmel had to a friend.

CHAPTER 35

Harold Grimsson pounded the arm of his leather chair with the flat of his calloused hand. Dollarhyde's voice poured from the speaker of the cell phone on the table beside him. The condescending bastard was telling him there was absolutely no way to kill the Hernandez brothers.

"Oh," Grimsson said, sloshing the whiskey in his other hand as he smacked the chair again. "There's always a way."

"True enough," Dollarhyde conceded. "If you accept the risks that go along with it."

"What do I pay you for?" Grimsson's voice rose nearly an octave. "Let me ask you that. I told you I wanted those little pendejo rats dead, what? Two weeks ago? You assure me that you'll take care of it and then come back with nothing but excuses. My ancestors would have cut your head off with an axe!"

"Mr. Grim—"

"Don't you Mr. Grimsson me! You gave me certain expectations when I hired you. Was it all a bag of shit?"

"No," Dollarhyde said. "It was not all a bag of shit." His voice was even, unflappable, as it always was, the mocking, ginger-ale-sipping, self-righteous son of a bitch. "I suppose

I could get myself arrested and then shank both brothers myself during chow . . ."

Grimsson found himself nodding in agreement. He scooted forward in his chair and took a bracing slug of whiskey. Finally. A good idea. "Now you're thinking like the guy I pay you to be. I know you don't have the balls to do it yourself, but you could get your boy Schnitzel to do it."

"Schimmel."

"Shitzle, Shamwow. Makes no difference to me what his name is. I mean the weird bag of bones. Have him go break a bottle over some JPD cop's skull. That takes at least one badge out of the equation, and he can do the Hernandez brothers when they toss his ass in Lemon Creek."

"He's connected with Valkyrie," Dollarhyde said.

"Always with the why-nots," Grimsson said. "So what if he's connected with Valkyrie? Half the people in jail have probably dug ditches or broken rock for me at one point or another in their miserable lives. I want you to make this happen."

"Yes, sir," Dollarhyde said. He sounded unconvinced, but Grimsson didn't doubt he would do as he was told.

"Now," Grimsson said. "That other thing . . ."

Ephraim Dollarhyde ended the call and pitched the cell onto the blotter at the center of his desk. If it had been possible, he would have shot Grimsson through the phone lines. The arrogant fool thought he was oh-so-much smarter than everyone around him. Normally, that's what Dollarhyde wanted him to think. The inertia of such monumental hubris made him easier to steer in the right direction. Dollarhyde had been the brains behind every important decision since he'd come aboard. Oh, Grimsson believed he was running things, but the idiot was too caught up in his whiskey-addled bravado. *Kill him. Dump that. My grandfather would have cut your head off with an axe.* In truth, Grimsson's forefathers were cod fishermen for as far back as Dollarhyde could see. Still a rough lot, to be sure, but not the horn-helmeted, axe-wielding Vikings of legend Harold Grimsson liked to trot out there with every threat he made. And he made a lot.

Dollarhyde was the man behind the power. The chamberlain to the shogun. The special adviser with the king's ear. But all too often kings and shoguns started to believe their own bullshit and forgot who propped them up. They began to think they were invincible, above the laws of probability and physics. Bulletproof.

Dollarhyde's phone pinged, showing he'd missed a call. It was from Senator Fawsey. The brainless idiot had left a voice mail. An actual voice mail . . . Dollarhyde buried his face in both hands. These people were so incredibly exhausting. It wasn't as if voice mails could be discovered by the FBI or anything . . . Groaning, Dollarhyde listened to the message.

As stupid as it was to leave the information, it was promising to hear.

According to the lawyer who'd bailed him out, Levi Fawsey had taken off at a dead run as soon as he hit the JPD parking lot. Childers and two other trusted men had rushed in to scour the area, checking the boy's apartment and all his old haunts. He'd gone to ground. Disappeared. Senator Fawsey's message said he had a couple of leads where his son might be staying. Thankfully, he didn't leave the locations on the voice mail. He'd call when he knew more.

Dollarhyde deleted the voice mail, opening the app that was supposed to overwrite everything on his phone seven times. NSA-level protection, the app claimed. In reality, Dollarhyde knew the voice mail was still out there, on Fawsey's phone, or just floating around in the phone company cloud, waiting for the FBI to grab and use it to bury everyone.

Done is done, he said to himself, and punched in the number for Dallas Childers.

The former Marine answered on the first ring

"Yeah."

"It's me," Dollarhyde said. "How's Schimmel?"

"I just hung up from him."

"So he's alive . . . ?"

"For now," Childers gave a soft chuckle. "He's hurting, though. You're not going to like what he told me. Apparently, he was downtown and some cop took out after him. He said he had no choice but to run. It's all over the news."

Childers filled him in about the kid in the water.

Smart, Dollarhyde thought. Smarter than he gave Schimmel credit for.

"Did he say why he was downtown? Why the cops were after him?"

"Nope," Childers said. "We're supposed to meet in half an hour. You still think he might be the rat? That could be why he was running. If some deal went south or something."

"Not likely," Dollarhyde said. "Find out what you can when you meet."

"You want him alive after the meeting?"

Dollarhyde thought about that. "Grimsson has a job for him, so, yes, keep him alive."

"Unless he's the rat."

"Yeah," Dollarhyde said, knowing there wasn't much of a chance of that. "Unless he's the rat."

CHAPTER 36

Changing into dry clothes after being soaked to the skin for two hours was nearly as good as a nap. Though, Cutter had to admit, the cold water had drained him. A nap would have been welcome, if he'd had the time.

Bobby Tarrant arrived as Cutter stepped off the elevator into the lobby. Everyone, including the Forest Service LEO, stepped into the parking lot and crowded around Maycomb's iPhone.

The YouTube video her friend at the radio station had found turned out to be a campaign commercial, produced during Fawsey's first run for a seat on the state senate a decade before. His car dealerships had already made him wealthy, a man separate from the masses. It helped to be an everyman in Alaska politics—someone whom the people identified with, someone they could trust. It was hard to trust someone with money.

Cutter had spent a good portion of his career helping State Diplomatic Security with dignitary protection, dropping him into the grease of politics and politicians. Standing by the wall, radio pigtail trailing from his ear, pistol hidden under the tail of his jacket, while they talked their schemes and dreams and situational ethics right in front of him, as if he were nothing more than a potted fern. Sure, there were a handful of rich and honest people in politics. But then, in Cutter's experience, there were only a handful of rich and honest people period.

Fawsey was a millionaire, not a billionaire. He could lose his fortune with a couple of bad business deals, but was still rich enough that he risked seeming snobbish and out of touch with everyday folk. He wasn't nearly rich enough to be worshiped, so he had to establish himself as a man of the people—a bona fide Alaskan.

That's what the commercial was for.

Set against the incredibly beautiful backdrop of the Tongass National Forest, Fawsey stood with his pretty wife and handsome son in front of a tall yellow cedar. He recounted his years as a young father, working his way through school at the University of Alaska Southeast campus. How he and his wife worked at a fish hatchery south of Juneau, turning their son, Levi, loose every summer from the time he was ten years old to explore the mountains behind the hatchery. The forests, Fawsey said, were his son's home for five years, and remained so to this very day. He extolled his virtues as a free-range parent, letting the wilderness help raise his child. He compared it to the kind of governance he represented—the kind of government Alaskans liked.

The kind of government that stayed out of your way.

Maycomb pocketed her phone when the video ended.

"It's a long shot, she said. "But if Donita Willets is still alive, I'd bet Levi Fawsey stashed her somewhere out there. Behind the hatchery where he used to explore as a boy."

Van Dyke sneered. "That narrows it down to . . . Oh, I don't know. How far can an energetic kid hike in the five years between the time he's ten and fifteen?"

"Still," Cutter said, refusing to acknowledge their feud.

"It gives us a place to start." He thought for a moment, then turned to Tarrant. "Bobby, is there a chance Forest Service has maps of any cabins in that area around the fish hatchery? If Fawsey was going to hide her anywhere, it's likely to be in some kind of dwelling."

"There are a couple of obvious ones," Tarrant said. "But I'm guessing he'd want something more off the beaten path than a recreational use cabin. We have a burn list that we've determined need to be destroyed. Rangers stumble on them usually while they're in the backcountry—illegal structures put up by squatters, hunters, and such. Takes a while to get around to torching them though, so there are a few out there. The weather has to be right."

Lola smiled. "Don't want Smokey the Bear starting the fires."

"No kidding," Bobby Tarrant said. He turned toward his green Tahoe, but spun immediately, seized by an idea. "I'll round up some air assets and find out which officers are familiar with that area around the hatchery. I'm sure we'll have plenty of topo maps, but I may have something better. I know a guy."

CHAPTER 37

Lola went with Detective Van Dyke to the Valkyrie Mine Holdings main offices in the Mendenhall Valley, leaving the hatchery lead and Bobby Tarrant's "guy" to Cutter. The offices were not much to speak of. A bored receptionist sat behind the counter playing games on her phone. The lobby was small, with two ratty avocado-colored chairs that looked like they'd been manufactured sometime around statehood and a low coffee table with a few dusty mining magazines. It reminded Lola of some of the shabby clinics she'd visited in the emerging nations of the South Pacific. She half expected to see a line of tiny black ants climbing the wall.

The receptionist looked up from her game of Candy Crush long enough to glance at Rockie Van Dyke's badge.

"We need to check on someone who may have worked here," Van Dyke said.

"You'll want to talk to Elaine in HR." The girl went back to her game without picking up the desk phone, pushing an intercom, or even yelling over her shoulder.

"Is Elaine here?" the detective said at length.

The girl heaved a dramatic sigh, rolling her eyes like a

teenager. Lola thought she must have been the boss's daughter or something—maybe his mistress.

She picked up her phone, searched for the right button to press, and then paged Elaine from HR to come to the lobby.

Lola opened a folder containing a couple of screen shots from the surveillance video of Mary Dutchik's gallery camera and spread them out on the desk. In one, Bandana Hands's gaunt face peered almost directly at the camera. He was bent and crooked, his expression twisted with pain. "Wonder if you've seen this foldy-uppy guy before."

"That's Dean Schimmel," the girl said. "He's a—"

A heavy-set woman in a blue sweatshirt and tight jeans poked her head around the corner from the hallway behind the reception desk. It was almost a tactical quick peek, like Lola would have done were she searching a house for an armed fugitive.

"These detectives are asking about Schimmel," the receptionist said.

The woman introduced herself as Elaine, the Human Resources manager. She looked at the photo.

"Yeah," she said. "That's Dean Schimmel all right. I'd recognize his skinny ass anywhere. What'd he do now?"

Van Dyke raised an eyebrow. "Now? What's he done before?"

"Nothing, really," Elaine from HR said. "Drunk driving, maybe some weed. Stuff like that."

"He threw a baby girl in the ocean," Lola said, her words coming out like they tasted bitter.

The receptionist looked up from her game. "No shit?"

"No shit," Lola said. "He didn't want to talk to us, so he just snatched the kid away from her mother and pitched her in the drink like a piece of garbage. All so he could get away."

"So," Van Dyke said. "Dean Schimmel still works here, then?"

Elaine nodded. "A general laborer out at the mine." She pulled up a roster on her iPad. "He's supposed to be out there now, but it looks like he banged in sick for the last two days. They sent him back to town to see a doc."

A tall man with slick black hair came around the corner of the hallway. He carried a stack of files in one hand and a leather lawyer's briefcase in the other. Ready to walk out the door, he wore a raincoat and rubber boots over jeans and a powder-blue button-down.

"Shred these," he said, handing off the files to Elaine, before peering up at the two women standing in his lobby. He gave Lola the once-over, as men often did, and then glanced back at Elaine, obviously feeling like he'd walked into something that was beneath his interest.

"These are detectives," Elaine said, as if warning him not to say anything that would get them all in trouble. "Asking about Dean Schimmel."

Lola caught a flash of something in the man's eyes. She was relatively new compared to everyone else on the task force, with just over three years on the Marshals Service, but she had an instinct for creeps—and this guy was one. He set off all manner of I-got-somebody-chained-up-in-my-trunk alarms as soon as he came around the corner. She'd misjudged bad people before, by hoping they were decent, but she'd yet to be wrong when she thought there was something "off" about someone.

Lola fished her credentials out of her rain jacket. "She's a detective. I'm with the US Marshals."

"Ah," the creepy dude said. "The Marshals . . . I suppose they're calling in the big dogs for the murder."

"We were already here," Lola said. "Sorry. I didn't catch your name."

"Ephraim Dollarhyde," the man said.

"And what's your position here, Mr. Dollarhyde?"

"Lobbyist, adviser, that sort of thing."

Van Dyke showed him the screen shot.

"That does look like Schimmel." He looked genuinely surprised. "What happened to his hands?"

"We were hoping you could tell us," Van Dyke said. "So you know everyone who works at the mine by name? Even the laborers?"

"I should," Dollarhyde said. "I oversee the background checks when they're hired, but I confess that I don't know that many. I only know that's Schimmel because we were just talking about firing him."

Elaine turned and looked at him, eyes blank.

"And why is it that you were talking about that?" Lola asked. "I'm afraid I'd have to talk that over with our lawyers before I went into any details about an HR matter. Can I ask why you're interested in him?"

The receptionist spoke up now. "He killed a little kid."

Dollarhyde recoiled as if he'd been slapped—a little heavy on the dramatics, like he wanted them to think he was just hearing the news.

"The kid didn't die," Lola said, locking eyes with Dollarhyde. "But she could have. If he calls in, tell him the police and the US Marshals are looking for him. Tell him this place is far too small for anybody to hide very long."

Dollarhyde excused himself and disappeared out the front

door. He walked briskly to the parking lot, where he got into a white pickup and drove away.

Lola and Van Dyke thanked Elaine and tried to look nonchalant as they hustled out to their vehicle.

"He turned left," Lola said, buckling her seatbelt. "Hope he's not going to the airport."

Van Dyke stayed well back, taking an outside lane when the white pickup made a U-turn to head south.

Lola slid down in her seat as he passed, going the opposite direction. "You think he saw us?"

"Probably," Van Dyke said. "I mean, those girls would have called and told him we bolted out the door as soon as he left."

"I wonder," Lola said. "That one chick was too busy with her game to be bothered, and I get the sense that Elaine isn't a big Dollarhyde fan."

"Hope you're right," Van Dyke said as she made a U-turn of her own and then punched it to bring the white pickup back into view. It was still going south, past the turn off to Mendenhall Glacier.

"Not for nothing," Lola said. "But your sister-in-law seems like she's trying awfully hard. I have a couple of alcoholics in my family. Staying sober for a year is . . . well, that ain't no small deal."

Van Dyke clutched the steering wheel until her knuckles turned white.

"What do you want me to say? That she's not a piece of trash? I can't do that. Because she is. She was in Anchorage for over two weeks last year doing God knows what all, while my brother stayed at home with the kid sick with worry because he didn't know where she was." Van Dyke turned to look Lola full in the face. "That kind of worry can kill you. Did you know that? It killed my brother. The artery in the side of his head just delaminated. Cut off the blood flow to his brain. He was probably dead before he hit the ground."

"And Lori was still in Anchorage?"

Van Dyke shook her head. "No, she was home. My stupid brother took her back. She boohooed and told him she was getting sober. But the damage was done. Just because you 'make amends' with someone after you cut their throat doesn't make everything all hunky-dory."

Lola stared out the window at the dense evergreen forests that lined the road. The white pickup was the only vehicle that she could see, ahead or behind.

"Shit!" Van Dyke pounded on the wheel. "I should have thought of that."

The pickup made a left into Auke Bay.

Lola craned her head, looking for some hint as to where he was going. "What?"

"That's the way to the marina," Van Dyke said. "He's going to get on a boat."

CHAPTER 38

Dallas Childers was a strong man, but he hadn't focused much on cardio since he'd separated from the Marine Corps. It took him a while to make the hike up to the agreed-upon section of the old Treadwell Ditch, not far off the Mount Jumbo trail and the Treadwell Glory Hole pit, long since flooded when the mine collapsed on itself in the early nineteen hundreds.

The eighteen-mile ditch was an engineering feat in and of itself, especially when you considered that it was built in the late nineteenth century. Cut horizontally along the side of the mountain, it collected runoff through dams of timber and rock and a series of steel pipes and chutes blasted into the rock. Streams large and small, fed by Juneau's frequent rain and melting snow, tumbled down from the icefields in the high country above to fill the ditch. This massive amount of hydropower was channeled down the mountain to the Treadwell, Mexican, 700 Foot, and Ready Bullion mines that made up the Treadwell enterprise. There it was harnessed to run the stamp mills used to crush the gold-bearing ore when it came out of the mountain. Treadwell ran over nine hundred such mills, with hammers that looked like organ pipes. The moving water turned a flywheel that turned an offset camshaft, lifting the hammers the size of small telephone poles and letting them fall in turn, smashing the rock to get at the gold, day after day, night after night. Childers was half deaf from the roar of his backhoe, but miners back in those glory days must have gone a little crazy with steel pounding away at tons of rock all day and all night but for Christmas and the Fourth of July. Those two days must have been hell on the miners. The silence after all that constant racket . . . That would be off-putting as hell.

Childers's boot slipped on a piece of rotting wood as he turned off the main trail to cut directly across the mountain. The forest was littered with fallen trees, snot-slick with moss and rain. Broken branches stuck up here and there like mossy punji sticks. Even side-hilling required a lot of up and down. It was a good place to break a leg.

He grabbed the nearest branch to keep from falling. It happened to be devil's club. He let a muffled curse through clenched teeth, brushing the stickered leaves and stalk out of the way with the forearm of his raingear. The thorns were small, hairlike, just enough to piss him off. He hiked on, keeping his body upright on the angle so his feet didn't squirt out from under him. He wanted to get well off the established trail. Too many people down there for what he had in mind.

Hikers were like rain in Juneau. They didn't come along every day, but they could show up anytime. You had to figure them into every plan when you went into the backcountry. The Treadwell Ditch Trail was nearby, as were the Mount Jumbo and some smaller trails near Paris Creek, the stream that fell over the rocky cliffs and into the flooded Treadwell Glory Hole, hundreds of feet below. The trails were well groomed, far too apt to draw a crowd for any kind of clandestine meeting, even early in the morning. Hell, especially early in the morning. That's when all the algae-juice-swilling health nuts got a few miles in before plopping down in front of their computers. A random encounter wouldn't pose much of a problem. Most of them looked to be clueless when they ran, buds jammed into their ears, staring at their feet. Childers would be able to walk up and clobber most runners with a rock before they ever knew he was there. Still, he might as well avoid it if he could. That way, he could focus his efforts on Schimmel. He stopped picking his way over the mossy deadfall long enough to laugh at that thought. What a joke. Like Dean Schimmel would take any effort.

The moist earth and lush vegetation of an old growth forest had a way of eating sounds. It was even worse in the fog. Ravens croaked here and there in the treetops, a porcupine snuffled by. And water. There was always water trickling or dripping somewhere. If you didn't stop to listen, you might think the mountain was as quiet as a tomb.

Schimmel sat on the edge of an old timber dam, head down, swinging his legs like a bored schoolkid. Childers was tempted to sneak up just to scare the shit out of him and see if he keeled over like a fainting goat. Childers made it to within ten feet before he even looked up.

Schimmel brightened and slid off the old logs to land on his feet.

"Thanks for coming, man," Schimmel gushed, looking like he might cry with joy. Clueless little prick.

"Yeah," Childers said. "What the hell happened to you in town?

That thing with the kid . . ."

"I know, right?" Schimmel said. "I had to do something." He lifted his shirt. "Look what that sadistic bastard Dollarhyde did to me."

Childers gave a low whistle, admiring the outcome of his work. The flaky little puke looked like a redneck Frankenstein. Childers counted three long slashes and two shorter ones crisscrossing his chest from armpit to armpit. Blood oozed from under each arm, coating the otherwise ghostly pale skin of his ribs. His left side was worse than his right, which made sense, Childers thought. Short pieces of duct tape ran the length of each wound like oversized butterfly bandages. The tape did a decent job of keeping the deep gashes closed, not necessarily a good thing since it trapped the infection that already turned Schimmel's chest into a swollen mass of pink tissue.

"Damn," Childers whispered, sounding sympathetic despite how humorous this was. "You need help. Can you walk?"

Schimmel nodded. He dropped the tail of his shirt, wincing like a baby again. "Hurts like hell, but I made it all the way up here."

"Follow me," Childers said. "I know a quicker way down. You can tell me what happened on the way."

"I can't figure it out," Schimmel said, staying close as the two men picked their way over, under, and around deadfall and devil's club. They weren't going far, but Childers took the hardest route, just for the fun of it. Schimmel followed like a dutiful puppy.

"Why would Dollarhyde cut you up?"

"No idea," Schimmel said. "He'd kill me if he wanted me dead, but this is just sick, man. Razor blades in somebody's soap, I mean, that takes somebody twisted beyond belief to do that. I coulda sliced my nuts off."

"You didn't?" Childers asked, hiding his disappointment.

"No!" Schimmel's face pulled back into a grimace as the thought settled in on him again. "Something is seriously wrong with that dude."

Says the guy who tossed a baby into the drink to save his own ass, Childers thought.

They reached a relatively flat spot on the mountainside. The undergrowth had thinned. A misty breeze was blowing away the fog, and Gastineau Channel was visible through a gap in the trees. Paris Creek waterfall chattered and hissed as it fell over the sheer drop just a few feet away.

Childers raised his open hand. "Hold up a minute. Catch your breath. You sure it was Dollarhyde?"

"Who else?" Schimmel said. "I mean, an old girlfriend maybe, but I haven't had a girlfriend in over a year." He gulped, started to breathe harder, even though they'd stopped. "Listen . . . I gotta tell you something." His lips pursed like he was about to pop with important news.

Childers's mood darkened. He didn't like surprises, and this sounded like a big one. "What is it?"

"You remember when we hit that Indian grave?"

Childers groaned. This was so painful.

"I remember it like it was two days ago." He snapped his fingers. "Spit it out. Just say what you're trying to say."

"Well . . . you didn't see it, but there was a rattle down there in the rocks."

"A what?"

"Like an Indian witch doctor's rattle. Spooky as hell. A raven or something carved on it." Schimmel sniffed, his chest heaving like he was on the verge of breaking into tears. "You were busy talking to Dollarhyde. I woulda tossed it back, but that kid, Merculief, said rattles like this one could go for half a million bucks."

Half a million. So, that's why he'd gone into town.

"How much did you get for it?"

"I'm sure this one is cursed," Schimmel said. "Everything in my life just turned to shit as soon as I picked it up."

That didn't start with some Indian rattle, Childers thought. He resisted the urge to throat-punch the pathetic turd. "How much?"

"I didn't sell it yet."

Schimmel reached under his rain jacket and pulled out a bundle wrapped in a flimsy plastic grocery store bag. He pushed it to Childers like it was on fire.

The rattle did look old. The bent horn body was chipped and still flecked with bits of dried mud from the dig. A long, white bone was fixed to the horn to form a handle. Something was carved on the horn, a face maybe, or a bird, but Childers didn't care. He didn't know a damned thing about archeology or Indian treasures, but he knew that this bone rattle would be worth some serious coin.

Schimmel winced, dabbing at one of the wounds on his chest where blood seeped through his shirt.

Childers stifled a grin. *Got him good there.*

Schimmel gulped back another sob. His rheumy eyes flicked from tree to tree in the shadows above, the clearing below. He stopped his whimpering long enough to orient himself. "Hey, are . . . are we above the Glory Hole?"

Childers looked toward the sea, as if that location hadn't occurred to him. "It's down there somewhere."

In truth, the mountain fell away over a near-vertical rock wall—just a few yards through the trees. The open pit entry into the Treadwell Mine—flooded to form an eerie, crystalline lake when the mine collapsed in 1917, lay some two hundred feet below.

"Thought that's where we were." Schimmel licked cracked

lips, consoling himself. His eyes continued to flit herky-jerky through the trees. "I mean, I just want to get rid of the thing. I guess I don't know for sure if it's cursed, but I don't want to take any chances either. Half a million is way too much to expect. I know that. But that bitch at the gallery would only do a couple of thousand . . ." He brightened. "Hey, maybe you know somebody. We'll split the money. Hell, I only want a cut. Sixty-forty's fine by me."

"Sixty-forty?" Childers shook the rattle as if he was testing it. It seemed awfully sturdy for something that had been in the ground for a couple hundred years. The dirt or seeds or whatever it was inside made an earie whooshing sound.

"Sixty-forty," Schimmel said again. Hugging himself, he leaned against a rotting log, rocking back and forth like a junkie who needed a fix. "I mean, seventy-thirty is good too, if you know a place to sell it. I just don't want to be the one to hold on to it anymore. I mean, I think it might be why Dollarhyde put razor blades in my soap."

"I'll hold on to it." Childers gave the rattle another shake, if only to watch the shudder run up Schimmel's broken body each time he did it. The chilly mist was making him hungry. Time to speed things along. "Wanna know a little secret?"

Schimmel leaned closer, ready to hear it. "Dollarhyde didn't put the blades in your soap."

Schimmel blinked and gave a nervous laugh. "What do you mean? Then who?"

Childers took a threatening step toward him, crowding his wounds, forcing him to backpedal or be run over. Schimmel fell, scrambled to his feet. Tears of betrayal and pain ran down his face.

"But . . . why?"

Everyone Childers had ever killed up close asked something like that. *Why?* He continued to advance, chasing Schimmel around a tree. Arching his neck, he loomed above the terrified man, making sure to put Schimmel's back to the drop. Childers shook the rattle again, terrorizing the sobbing little pussy. Forcing him backward without ever laying a hand on him.

"Why?" Schimmel begged again, falling over his own feet as much as the deadfall. Fresh blood soaked the front of his shirt.

"I mean, I thought . . . I thought we were friends."

"Not even close," Childers said, swooshing the rattle.

Schimmel began to hyperventilate, mewling like a baby. He stopped when his heels reached the lip of the cliff, teetering there. Jagged rocks and the flooded pit waited below. His head fell sideways, bewildered, like a puppy after you kicked it. "I mean, I never did shit to you."

"You pissed me off," Childers said, smug. "And you made me look bad by marking the wrong girl when we were set up at the shrine."

"What?" His voice a stunned whisper. "I . . . I made you *look* bad? You hid razors in my soap because I made the same call anyone would have made?"

"About the size of it," Childers said. He moved forward, lifting the bone rattle like a club—careful of his own footing.

Schimmel stepped back a hair, somehow catching himself, swimming in the air with his hands.

Childers gave a tired sigh. He was getting bored.

He took another step forward, holding the bone rattle out in front of him.

"Kill me if you're pissed." Schimmel stared at him, mouth open, eyes like dinner plates. "But razors?"

"I always wanted to see what would happen." He shook the rattle again.

"But—"

"Ssshhhh," Childers said, mimicking the whooshing sound, and gave Schimmel a little push.

CHAPTER 39

Levi Fawsey woke to the smell of frying bacon. His eyes felt as if they might pop out of his head from the hard-cry hangover. The bedroom was unfamiliar, with Hopi Indian dolls on the dresser and paintings of cactus on the walls. It took a minute for the haze in his brain to clear enough that he remembered where he was.

It came back to him in a rush. He'd gotten away.

He looked at the clock. He couldn't believe he'd slept so late. Fear and the long run to the Jepsons' house had used up his last ounce of energy. Still—he was here, safe and warm—and Donita was not.

He was lucky to be alive.

Levi had never met a mob lawyer until the chunky guy with the bald head and a fancy suit got him out of JPD custody. Well, maybe he wasn't a mob lawyer, but a cartel lawyer. And wasn't that the same thing? Levi knew this attorney sure wasn't there to represent him. His father's man—or more likely Harold Grimsson's. Levi had seen more than his fair share of lawyers, DUIs, a couple of drug busts, but nothing since he'd gotten serious with Donita. He knew most of them in Juneau: the law-and-order ones who chided you for misbehaving; the flakes who came to court

rumpled and unprepared like they'd been the ones who
spent the night in the drunk tank. They always told you
everything was going to be okay, though they seemed not
to believe it themselves. And then there were the slick,
cufflink-wearing big-money guys in silk suits and thousand-
dollar shoes who would sell you to the wolves for a pay-
check.

The guy who got him out of JPD's mitts was one of
those wolf-feeders. "There are things we need to discuss,
Mr. Fawsey," he'd said as they walked out the back door of
the PD.

Levi was sure this was mob-lawyer talk for "somebody
will be along in a minute to yank out your fingernails while
they ask you some questions."

Levi ran the other way before the door shut behind them,
leaving Fancy Suit with an agitated frown on his fat face
and a cell phone glued to his ear. He was calling out the
cavalry.

Levi made it over six miles, spurred on by worry and
guilt over Donita. His dad's friends, the Jepsons, kept a
summer house off Mendenhall Road. They spent every
winter in Scottsdale and usually didn't come back until
April. Levi knew where the key was. His dad would eventually look for him here, but it would take time, hopefully
long enough that Levi could come up with a plan. Donita
had wanted to go to the police, but Levi had talked her out
of it. If his dad was dirty—and he was dirty as hell—then
there was no way to know who else was in on it—the cops,
judges, prosecutors.

As it turned out, his dad was waiting for him in the
Jepsons' living room when he got there, glasses down on
the tip of his nose, looking sad and angry and scared all at
the same time. They didn't talk right away. He told Levi to

sleep. He'd keep watch and they would "straighten everything out" when Levi woke up.

And now his dad was downstairs in the kitchen, frying bacon like the old days when he worked at the fish hatchery—before Levi's mom died and before his dad had become a senator and lost his soul. Maybe his dad's soul had always been lost, but Levi had just been too young to notice. It didn't matter. His dad was here now, cooking bacon—ready to straighten everything out.

Levi dressed quickly, putting on the same clothes he'd worn the day before since that's all he had, and made his way into the kitchen.

His dad stood over a cast-iron skillet, white shirt untucked, sleeves rolled up. He still wore his reading glasses. A large mug of coffee sat beside a stack of folders that spread across the kitchen table where he'd been working, probably all night.

"What are we going to do, son?" he asked without looking up from the bacon.

"What do you mean?"

Now he glanced up, peering over the top of his readers. "I mean, what are we going to do about the girl?"

Levi didn't plan to tell him where Donita was, or even let him know she was alive. His dad was up to his neck with Harold Grimsson. Donita knew it. Now he knew it too.

"Was she trying to go to the police?" his dad asked. "You should have called me. Trying to handle things yourself just digs a deeper hole for both of us."

His dad was questioning him without asking questions that might implicate him. So far, he didn't seem sure if Levi had killed the girl in order to protect him or hidden her out somewhere. And Levi couldn't tell which option he preferred.

The senator moved the pan to a cold burner but didn't bother to take out the bacon. He wiped his hands on a rag and tossed it on the counter. "I don't mind telling you, son, I'm more frightened than I've ever been in my life. The people I'm . . . The people we're dealing with are not nice people."

"I know that, Dad," Levi said. "Don't you think I do? I mean, that US attorney and his assistant were murdered. That could have been me and Donita. Have you thought about that?"

"Son . . ." The senator closed his eyes. "You have got to tell me where she is."

"Why, so they can shoot her in the head? And then murder me too? Is that part of the plan?"

"No!" Senator Fawsey said, incredulous. "It's better you came here instead of staying with that lawyer. Everything is coming to light now anyway. Juneau is crawling with FBI agents. They should be able to keep us safe."

Levi rubbed his eyes with the heels of his hands. "What are you saying? That you'll turn yourself in too? Because from what I saw you're in this shit—"

The senator gave a solemn nod. "I've done a lot of things since your mother died. Things I'm not proud of. Things that disgust me even as I stand back and watch myself doing them. Murdering that US attorney crossed a line. I'm not going to be a part of that."

"Where does that leave us?"

"Let's you and I go get your friend, and then we'll all talk to the FBI together."

"You're sure?" Levi studied his father's face. He looked sincere—but he was a politician. Faking sincerity was a vital skill. Still, Levi knew his dad. This seemed genuine.

It was a weird feeling being proud of your dad because he was admitting to being mixed up with a bunch of killers.

"Remember the big mine we hiked to a couple of times behind the hatchery?"

The elder Fawsey chuckled, his gaze soft, nostalgic. "You used to call it the Lumberjack when you were younger."

"Right," Levi smiled. "I knew it was logging related. THE CROSS CUT. Donita's in the big stope we rappelled into that time from the top."

"You called it the Great Hall."

Levi nodded. "She's got water and food. But I'm sure she's going bat-shit crazy without her phone."

"Thank you for telling me, son—"

Ephraim Dollarhyde stepped into the kitchen from the hallway at the rear of the house. His goon, Dallas Childers, came in on his heels, but cut around to run interference as soon as he had enough room to maneuver. Both of them wore latex gloves.

"Yes," Dollarhyde said, brimming with contempt. "Thank you very much . . . *son.*" His gaze narrowed. "Do you realize how much work you've caused me, you sneaky little prick?"

Levi eyed the pan of hot bacon grease, but Childers leveled a Glock at his chest and shook his head.

"Are you kidding me, Dad?" Levi said, heartbroken. "How could you be a part of this?"

"I only wanted—"

"You stood there and lied right to my face. . . ."

"Relax," Dollarhyde said. "Daddy didn't call us, if that's what's got your panties all askew. We were looking for you as hard as he was. His phone pinged off a tower a quarter mile away. A quick search showed he'd called this landline a few months ago. He didn't rat you out on purpose. He's just not a very smart daddy. Sorry."

Dollarhyde reached in his pocket and pulled out a blue-steel Taurus revolver. "There was a break-in at your house last night. I think our young Levi snuck in and took your gun after he fled the jail."

"I don't understand," the senator said. "I don't have any handguns. And even if that were mine, Levi's been here all night."

"Maybe so," Dollarhyde said. "But the police don't know that. Everyone in Juneau is looking for you, Levi. They know you're distraught. Mr. Kostis, the attorney whom you treated rudely when he got you out of jail, will testify that you were so up in arms about the crimes your father was involved with that you saw no other way out but to kill him."

Dollarhyde shot the elder Fawsey twice in the chest with the revolver. The senator stood there, blinking sadly. He looked at Levi and opened his mouth to speak.

Dollarhyde shot him again.

"Enough of the sentiment."

He sighed, turning to a terrified Levi. "And then you turned the gun on yourself."

Dallas Childers had holstered his Glock during the senator's murder. He grabbed Levi and spun him into a full nelson.

"I have to apologize," Dollarhyde whispered. "But this is only a five-shot revolver." He was close enough Levi could smell the sickeningly sweet odor of peppermint on his breath. He pressed the gun to Levi's temple. "I hate head shots, I really do, but I can't risk anything else with the only two rounds I have left."

A single round was plenty.

Childers didn't turn away. He grinned, letting the kid's body fall naturally to the floor.

Dollarhyde dabbed a piece of gore out of his eye—backsplash was inevitable—and stooped beside the body. He put the revolver in Levi's limp hand, lifted his arm so the trajectory wouldn't look like he'd shot from the floor and then fired at an interior wall. Crime scene techs would surely swab the boy's hands. The final shot ensured gunpowder residue was where it should be.

"You think they'll buy it?" Childers asked as they left out the back, avoiding the prying eyes of any neighbors. "Fawsey said he didn't have any guns."

"Please," Dollarhyde said. "This is Alaska. Everybody has guns. Even Democrat senators." He took out his phone and thumb-dialed Grimsson's number.

"Yes, sir," he said after listening to the obligatory rant. "You're going to love this. The little bitch is hiding in a mine." He gave Grimsson the rundown on the location. "I need to grab some supplies. We'll meet you at the marina in an hour."

CHAPTER 40

Cutter parked the SUV in front of a narrow two-story blue house off Mendenhall Loop. It was tucked back among tall spruce trees as big around as his tires. An aluminum skiff and a Honda SUV took up most of the gravel driveway. Bobby Tarrant's friend, Tom Horning, was supposed to be a good guy, but Cutter parked at an angle anyway out of habit, giving both he and Maycomb door posts for concealment and minimal cover as they exited the vehicle. Rhythmic, metallic pinging came from behind the house, wafting through the trees. A small wire-haired dog, the color of toasted toffee and just as sweet, bounded out from around the porch. She sniffed Cutter's and then Maycomb's hands in turn, then decided she liked Maycomb better and stayed glued to her heels.

Cutter followed the pinging sound around the corner of the house, to find a red-bearded bear of a man under the roof of a detached shed hammering away at an anvil. He looked to be in his early thirties, hiking-fit, accustomed to carrying a pack—a physique that came from work, not a couple of hours a day at the gym. He wore a long-sleeve shirt and a thick leather apron that was scarred and burned as if he'd been working hot iron for most of his life. A propane forge hissed in the corner of a heavy-duty work table to the man's right, the horizontal opening that ran along the front forming a molten orange mouth. Hammer in one hand, blacksmith tongs in the other, the man was in the process of transforming a red-hot railroad spike into a knife blade. Two more spikes in varying flattening and twisting stages of becoming knives lay on the metal workbench alongside the anvil.

"Thomas Horning?" Cutter asked.

The man plunged the tongs into a bucket of water, sending up a hiss of steam, and then turned off the forge.

He shook Cutter's hand with the calloused grip of a man who was accustomed to swinging a three-pound hammer.

"Call me Tom."

Cutter displayed his credentials, to ease any concerns, but Horning waved it away. If he was worried about Lori Maycomb being a journalist, he didn't show it.

"Bobby told me you guys would be coming by. I love talking about the wild places around Juneau."

"This is beautiful work," Maycomb said. She reached to touch one of the unfinished knives on the table, grabbing it before Horning could warn her. She let go immediately, recoiling to put her index finger in her mouth.

"A little hot for you?" Horning said.

"Nope." Maycomb grinned, still sucking on the finger. "Just doesn't take me long to look at a railroad spike."

Horning chuckled. "Should have a sign, I guess. Metal glows cherry red around fifteen hundred degrees—but a three-hundred-degree spike looks pretty much the same as it does at ambient. I can get you some salve. I make my own from balsam poplar."

"I'm okay," Maycomb said. "Really."

"Let me know if you change your mind," Horning said,

hobbling around the anvil. Cutter noticed for the first time that the man's left leg was in a plaster cast to the knee.

"You're probably thinking, why didn't Bobby mention the guy had a broken leg."

"Crossed my mind," Cutter said.

"He didn't know," Horning said. "I haven't seen him for a couple of weeks."

"Misstep hiking?" Maycomb asked.

"Fell out of a helicopter," Horning said, as if that sort of thing happened to him every day. "I found an old ninety-pound anvil up behind Mount Juneau. Chopper cost me eight hundred bucks for the eleven-minute round-trip flight to go get it. I was so worried about bashing a hole in the helicopter's floor that I fell out the door when I was strapping the damned thing in. Only about fifteen feet, but it was enough to fracture my fibula. Otherwise, I'd be guiding you guys instead of drawing you maps." Horning opened his back door and waved them inside.

"We appreciate any help you can give us," Cutter said.

Typical of Alaska homes, including Mim's, there was a dead-air space called an arctic entry inside with a second door, trapping warm air inside during the winter. Cutter and Lori kicked off their Xtratufs.

Cutter had been in hundreds of houses over the course of his career. Potential witnesses, fugitives, and sources came from every culture and socioeconomic strata. It was more common for deputies to be disgusted than impressed—but Tom Horning's house was like some sort of intrepid adventurer's museum.

A Marlin .45-70 Guide Gun hung on wooden pegs inside the door on the stairwell leading to the second story. Stainless steel to withstand the weather, big-loop lever to fit a gloved hand. Perfect, Cutter thought. Floor-to-ceiling shelves held tents, backpacks, and sleeping bags of assorted size and temperature rating. Cross-country skis stood against the far wall of a small living room. It was cluttered but clean, and looked as if it was rarely used. Two shelves to Cutter's right were devoted entirely to mountaineering boots, crampons, ice axes, and coils of climbing rope.

Horning made a little smooching sound. "Come on, Kat."

The dog scampered up the stairs ahead of him.

"Your dog's named Kat?" Maycomb said, smiling.

"Yeah," Horning said. "My wife said she'd never get another dog after our last one died. So, she brought home little Kat." He showed them upstairs. "Sorry about the mess," Horning said, swinging his broken leg up to thump against each step as he followed the dog. "My maps and computer are up here. Keeps me in shape."

Large photographic prints of Horning's expeditions covered the walls of the stairway. Pack-rafting under cobalt-blue glaciers, his beard covered with frost while climbing frozen waterfalls, wearing a hard hat while rappelling into hopelessly black mineshafts. The prints catalogued virtually every kind of Alaska adventure, but by a count of three to one, the photos showed Horning and his friends deep underground. It was clear by the time Cutter reached the top of the stairs that hiking, climbing, and rope work were a means to an end.

Tom Horning's passion was exploring mines.

Cutter counted at least five rock-climbing helmets of assorted brands and colors when they reached the single large room on the second floor. Each helmet had a headlamp strapped to it. Three more lamps, a little larger, and likely more powerful, rested in chargers on the desk next to a twenty-inch computer monitor. An orange helmet, probably Horning's favorite, sat on top of a Panasonic Toughbook on the other side of the desk. Climbing rope, ascenders, rappelling brakes, and harnesses from a recent adventure— before the helicopter fall—were spread out on a tattered love seat. Dozens of poster-size charts and maps, rolled into tubes with rubber bands, leaned against the corner opposite the computer desk. Bright yellow weatherproof Pelican cases were propped open to reveal thousands of dollars in cameras and lighting equipment.

Lori Maycomb gave a low whistle. "I think we've come to the right place. Your wife do all this with you?"

"Most of it," Horning smiled. "She's a badass. A quiet badass, but still a badass. Works at the library. Her superpower is putting up with this mountain of gear." He shoved the ropes on the love seat aside. "Take a load off."

"I feel like we've stumbled into Indiana Jones's house," Maycomb said.

Horning smiled. "Not hardly," he said. "But I did just order a bullwhip from Australia. Always wanted one." He sat in the swivel chair at the computer desk, propping his leg on a hard plastic camera case. The dog jumped in his lap and curled up, one eye on their new guests. "Bobby said you're interested in the area around the old hatchery. Hoping to save some young woman who's hiding there or something."

"That's right," Cutter said. "He said you might have run across some old off-the-grid cabins."

"I know of a couple cabins," Horning said. "But I'd lay odds that if she's hiding, she'll be in a mine. Bobby mentioned Levi is involved. He's come on quite a few group hikes I've led, back before the oxy got ahold of him. Decent kid, really. Anyway, he seemed like he was familiar with several of the adits up there behind the hatchery. I have maps of that area if you'd like."

"That would be helpful," Cutter said.

"When you say mines," Maycomb asked, "are you talking like caves? I know Juneau was built on mining, but I've never been in one."

Horning gave his dog a scratch behind the ears. "Caves, pits, shafts, rooms big enough to hide a cruise ship, you name it. The city as we know it sits on tailings, basically the insides of Mount Roberts and Mount Juneau. The AJ mine runs for miles through the mountain, the entire length of town with multiple levels connected by drifts, raises, and winzes—basically chutes and ladders. The area you're talking about by the hatchery wasn't worked as extensively as some, but there are a couple of good mines up there—and a lot of places to hide. I guarantee you, you could walk within twenty feet of some of the mine openings and you wouldn't realize you were there if you didn't know what to look for."

"What *do* you look for?" Cutter asked.

"Tailing piles, mostly," Horning said. "They'll be grown over with moss and plants now. All the rock has to go somewhere, so it ends up piled outside the opening. You look for shapes that don't belong, something manmade. I've found hidden mine entrances by following the river of cool air flowing down the hillside. Ambient temp in the mines stays in the mid to high forties once you get away from the entrance, a little warmer when you go deeper underground. If there's airflow, it's easy to feel the breeze pouring out in the summer."

Cutter made a mental note, as he always did when he learned some new bit of information that would help with tracking. "I'm trying to imagine someone hiding inside a mine. Wouldn't methane be a danger?"

"Oh," Horning said. "There's all kinds of stuff in a mine

that could kill you. Rotting wood gives off CO_2, displacing oxygen. Methane, as you mentioned, is a problem. Rotten ladders, old planks set over hundred-foot drops—covered with a thin layer of sediment so you don't see them with even the brightest light, giant icicle-mites near some openings, cave-ins, and just plain old bumping the shit out of your head. And all that's not counting the Tommy knockers." He pronounced it *knacker*.

Maycomb frowned. "What's that?"

"Welsh miners believed in little leprechaun dudes who knock on mine walls," Horning said. "Some say they're malevolent, but most believe they're the ghosts of dead miners who knock to warn you of an impending cave-in. Just settling rock and timber supports, but it's awfully easy to grow a vivid imagination when you're four hundred feet from daylight." He chuckled. "And then there are the spiders. Some walls are covered with thousands of harvestmen—daddy longlegs. Though I guess they're not technically spiders."

"I'm okay with spiders," Maycomb said. "It's crawling around in tight spaces that creeps me out."

"Sorry," Horning said. "There can be more than a little of that."

Horning steadied Kat, the toffee-colored dog, in his lap as he spun the chair to access his computer. A couple of clicks of the mouse brought up a sectional map of a large mine. Viewed from the sides, the multiple layers, connected by up-and-down shafts, resembled a maze.

"By far, most places are big enough to stand up and walk in," he said. "But some, especially if you want to hide, might mean getting down on your hands and knees." He clicked through a couple of photos, stopping on one that showed a rock face at the end of a tunnel. A closer look revealed a two-foot gap at the bottom of the wall. "This used to be open to shoulder height," he said. "But there was some shifting over the last couple of years and now it's all but blocked. There's a big stope on the other side, but you have to belly crawl to get there."

Maycomb squinted, scrunching up her face, looking like she might be sick to her stomach. "That's . . . groovy . . ."

Cutter leaned forward to get a better look at the screen. "A stope?"

"Open room where the ore body widened out," Horning said. "There's a big one on the mountain above the old hatchery you're talking about. You have to rappel over a hundred feet to get into it. You could easily fit four or five of these houses inside that one."

"Those tailings should be fairly easy to locate," Cutter said.

"I've got maps," Horning said, tapping the side of his head. "Up here, but also on my iPad. I'll drop them to your phone if you want."

"Thanks," Cutter said. "That will give us a start anyway."

Horning rubbed his pup behind the ears and gave the computer mouse a click, bringing up a video. "Here's what you can expect."

Both Cutter and Maycomb crowded closer to the monitor. Cutter took more mental notes of the slide-prone earth around the entry, the old timbers, low-hanging rock, the dripping water, and the complete darkness at the edges of the headlamp's beam. This particular mine—Horning called it an adit—was a simple tunnel, head high in most places, that ran straight into the mountain. "What are these pockets in the wall?" Cutter asked.

"Looking for other veins of gold?" Maycomb said.

"Good guess," Horning said. "But those are where miners

would stand to get out of the way of the blast when they were blowing more rock."

"Are you kidding?" Maycomb gasped. "They're what? Three or four feet deep?"

"Not kidding," Horning said. "Remember, we're talking the turn of the last century, the nineteen hundreds. Guess they weren't too savvy about overpressure dangers to your innards. They just wanted out of the way of flying rock."

"Is this one behind the hatchery?" Cutter asked.

"No," Horning said. "This is up Perseverance Creek. I'll drop you the maps of the ones behind the hatchery too."

"Thank you," Cutter said. "If you have a paper map as well, I'd pay you for it. Sort of a sailing thing. I navigate with GPS, but like to have paper charts."

"Smart," Horning said, startling the dog as he gave the side of his plaster cast an impatient smack. "I wish to hell I was going with you. I know every inch of those mines. There are two or three there that would make for good hide-outs, I think." He looked up, seized with a sudden thought. "You'll need gear. I'm happy to loan you some if you want. From the sound of it, you're a two- or three-light guy."

"Or more," Maycomb said.

Horning shooed the dog out of his lap and got up to putter around the room. "I like to carry at least two head-lamps and a handheld flashlight." He began to gather helmets, lamps, and climbing rope. "You ever rappel?" he asked Cutter.

Cutter gave him a thumbs-up. "Army Ranger. I taught high-angle tactics for a bit."

"Good enough for me," Horning said. He handed them each a climbing harness to try on and then looked through a box on his desk until he came up with a carbon monoxide detector and an O_2 meter.

"You have to remember," Horning continued, "it's a kinetic environment down below. You'd think solid as rock—but things are always moving. ASAR—Alaska Search and Rescue—will come and get you off a mountain, but they don't do mines. PD, fire department, the Troopers, Forest Service—none of them train to do mines rescue."

"So," Maycomb said. "Who do people call when they get in trouble—say, if someone is overdue from going into a mine?"

Thomas Horning rubbed a hand through his beard and then gave his dog another scratch behind the ears.

"Me."

CHAPTER 41

Donita Willets played the beam of her headlamp across empty tin cans, half-melted candles, and rotting dynamite crates—all of it over a century old. She couldn't help wondering if her bones might stay in this same dark hole until they, too, would be considered antique.

Levi had taken her to explore a couple of the other old mines above the hatchery, but never this place. He called it the Great Hall, and even he rarely came here. He'd always said he wanted to keep it secret, between himself and the few others who already knew about it. Too many trips to the opening would beat a trail into the fragile vegetation, and then everyone would be able to locate the otherwise unremarkable hole behind the unremarkable rock on the side of the mountain.

She'd thought him a little paranoid. This was too tough a hike for most vandals or the sort of people who dropped McDonald's cups and beer cans on the ground. But now she was glad he'd left the place hidden.

Levi had tearfully gotten her settled before shimmying back up the rope, alternately sliding each ascender, and using the attached loops to slide step by step. He seemed to dangle there forever, but each foot upward left her feeling more and more alone, a tiny and insignificant dot at the bottom of this enormous space. He'd lowered another case of water down—she'd need that—and left the rope and ascenders hanging in place, in case she needed to get out.

Being stuck here terrified her, but it was better than the alternative.

Donita Willets wasn't a large person to begin with, barely five feet tall. A hundred five pounds after a big breakfast. But the cavernous rock stope made her feel miniscule. As a child, she'd imagined mines would be quiet, tomb-like. In reality, they were a riot of noise—if you took the time to be still. Rocks fell from the ceilings and skittered down ledges at a near-constant pace, clattering to the piles of other rocks that had fallen before them. Water oozed from cracks and pores in the ceiling, tapping against wet stone or dripping into black pools. Once in a while, the mountain itself groaned, quietly, like it didn't really want to bother her, but needed to crack its back or move a leg or something.

Donita wore her raingear, slept with the rock helmet on her head, and hummed songs her grandmother had taught her in order to stay relatively sane. Water dropping into puddles sounded like Raven's call. Donita's mother had been Raven moiety, so Donita was Raven, and she found the sound comforting.

The beam of her headlamp was powerful enough to cast shadows over the bumpy stone walls, but the black around the edges swallowed the light. She'd walked the entire cavern as soon as Levi yelled goodbye, noting the old shovels, ladders, buckets, and other equipment the miners had simply abandoned in the hole when they quit digging.

It was incredibly interesting, an underground museum from 1908, but mainly, she wanted to make certain she was the only one down there.

In the dark.

It was easy to see why Levi called it the Great Hall. All the mines he'd taken her to before had been relatively straight tunnels in the rock. What people thought of when they pictured a mine, something out of a movie with timber supports on the low-hanging ceilings and a stope that was maybe the size of a large bedroom. The Great Hall looked bigger than all those other mines put together. It had taken over half of their 150-foot rope to rappel in. There was a small ledge about fifteen feet below the entrance, and then an undercut that left them dangling on a free rappel with no place to put their feet for the last fifty until they reached a pile of clattering shale that gradually sloped another twenty feet to the relatively flat floor. Levi described the shape of the Great Hall as looking like a semitruck and trailer. Donita thought of it more as a gigantic dung beetle, like she'd seen in *National Geographic*, with the arched ceilings and sloping walls of the ovular Great Hall forming the largest part of its body. A relatively smaller bubble comprising the beetle's head was opposite the end from where they'd rappelled down. The larger space was an open cavern over a hundred feet at its tallest point, half again as long, and ninety feet wide. A rough, oblong dome, it relied on its shape for support. The twenty-foot ceilings of the beetle's head had four support stone columns evenly spaced in the forty-by-forty-foot room. These columns had once been more robust, thicker, but greedy miners had chipped away at the goldbearing diorite, "robbing" the very rock that kept the roof from caving down on their heads, leaving the remaining columns small enough now that Donita could almost get her arms around them.

There was a crystalline-blue pond at the far end of the beetle's head. Roughly twenty feet in diameter, a narrow ledge ran around the far end, where the beetle's mouth would be. Even with her powerful headlamp Donita couldn't see the bottom of the pool. She could tell it was a flooded tunnel, leading to God knew what labyrinth of other shafts and stopes. The water looked pure enough to drink, but she didn't dare risk the cyanide, arsenic, and other toxic minerals.

She'd brought plenty of batteries, a small gas stove, toilet paper, a lightweight cot to keep her off the rocks, a sleeping bag, some books, drawing materials—she loved to draw—and enough water for two weeks if she was careful. Her food would last twice that with her present appetite, which was basically nonexistent.

It was hard to think about eating with men like Ephraim Dollarhyde and his musclebound stooge, Childers, hunting you. She'd seen them around Levi's dad before, along with Harold Grimsson. That guy was evil, but he was money evil. Linking up with drug cartels evil. Pushing heroin on the streets of Juneau evil. He hurt people who got in his way, or who could rat on him—but it was always a business deal. Dollarhyde and Childers had that look in their eye like they would hurt you for the fun of it, just to listen to you squeal.

Levi didn't admit it, but his dad had been strung out on pills most of the time since Levi's mom died—stressed from politics and the secrets that went with it. The senator hardly ever noticed when Donita hung out up in Levi's room, waiting for him to come home from work or run to the store. Their house was nice, more comfortable than her little apartment, and Levi's dad was rarely ever there. But then she'd overheard him talking to Dollarhyde and his creepy pal Childers. The conversation had been about heroin and the drug trial that was all over the news. That had roused her curiosity enough that she did some snooping in the senator's office after he left the house. She'd listened in on a couple of calls between him and Grimsson, all about some road project he'd pushed through the process, and that Grimsson was the money behind the heroin in the Hernandez brothers' boat. Levi's dad must have wanted leverage, because she caught him spouting stuff on his voice recorder after the call with Grimsson that no self-respecting politician would ever want put on any kind of record.

Donita thought of going to the police, but with Senator Fawsey dirty up to his eyeballs, corrupt cops weren't exactly out of the realm of possibility. That's why she tried to talk to Lori Maycomb, that reporter she'd met at a couple of AA meetings with her mother. Maycomb had a pleasant radio-voice. Trustworthy.

Then Donita had heard Levi's dad talking to Dollarhyde about a murdered archeologist out at the Valkyrie mine. She'd known from the start it was dangerous, but she didn't think anyone would get killed. That kind of stuff only happened in the movies, not in sleepy little Juneau. She'd panicked when she couldn't get through to Maycomb and decided to go straight to the US attorney. He'd be interested in Grimsson's connection to the guys on trial.

But someone, probably Childers, had blown the attorney away right before she was supposed to meet him. Donita and Levi had driven up just as the brunette woman had walked out toward the shrine. They'd waited, heard the faint pops of suppressed rifle fire. The cops had kept all the details to themselves, but Donita knew the US attorney and a woman were dead, murdered by shots that had been meant for her.

She'd wanted to run, to go as far and as fast as they could, but Levi said it was too risky. They'd just come after her. He was a good man, but a horrible liar. She doubted he could pull off the story about her accidental drowning. Best case scenario, the cops would think he murdered her.

In the end, it seemed better to hide than to run. So she trusted Levi to become a better liar overnight.

And here she was.

She'd looked behind every support pillar twice, checked the clear water to make sure there wasn't something lurking there. Found the small alcove that the miners had used for a privy a hundred years ago. Then, she'd set up her cot in the back of the Great Hall, near where it necked down to the beetle head, on a spot with the fewest chunks of fallen rock.

She tried to read, lit a candle for emotional comfort—and to make sure she still had plenty of oxygen—but her mind began to play tricks on her. Her grandmother had told her too many stories of demons and witches and wily shapeshifting land otters and frogs who kidnapped young girls and took them to their underwater homes. The first time Levi had taken her to a mine he'd told her about Tommy knockers, little green goblins who lived deep in recesses of the mountain, sometimes evil, sometimes nice. Sitting there on her cot, a tiny dot in a massive man-made cave, it was hard to believe anyone who lived in this oppressive darkness could be anything but evil.

She sat on the edge of her cot, clutching her knees to her chest, sobbing, quietly, because she didn't want to disturb the mountain any more than it wanted to disturb her.

She might eventually lose her mind in this self-imposed

solitary confinement, but consoled herself that her cell was big and not some cramped hole where she had to crawl around on her hands and knees. The entrance was well hidden. As long as they didn't know she was down here, she was safe.

If Ephraim Dollarhyde ever figured out where she was hiding, he wouldn't have to waste time and energy rappelling down to look for her. All he had to do was drop the rope and leave her stranded until she starved to death—or blow the entrance and shut her up for good.

CHAPTER 42

Cutter called USFS LEO Bobby Tarrant as soon as he left Tom Horning's driveway. The hatchery where Fawsey had worked was in Berners Bay. Almost forty miles north by boat from Auke Bay Marina, it was only seven miles from the northern end of the Glacier Highway, the road that led out of Juneau. Cutter hoped to have someone with a Forest Service boat meet him with a skiff at the terminus instead of wasting the time to drive all the way into Juneau.

Rather than call and argue with Special Agent Beason while he waited for Tarrant to work out the logistics, Cutter contacted Lola and asked her to pass along what he planned to do. UNODIR—Unless Otherwise Directed—he planned to go straight to the abandoned hatchery and see if he could pick up Levi Fawsey's tracks. UNODIR meant he was informing FBI task force command, but due to exigency, moving forward without permission. There was no time to sit around and debate this. Much better to err on the side of doing something.

Tarrant came through. A white pickup pulling an aluminum skiff rattled through the trees at the Echo Cove boat launch twenty minutes after Cutter and Maycomb got there.

USFS Ranger Karen Sakamoto didn't park, but made a wide U-turn and expertly backed the fifteen-foot Smoker Craft down the ramp in one shot, stopping just short of the water.

"Sorry I couldn't get you anything larger," Sakamoto said, a hint of an East Coast accent in her voice. She went around to the back of the skiff, inserted the drain plug in the transom, and detached the metal motor brace that kept the 30-horse outboard from bouncing on the trailer. "This one's hell-for-stout though, and the little Honda should do well over twenty knots with both of you. You know how to drive a boat?"

"I do." Cutter threw his gear over the side. "I appreciate you getting here so fast. Do I need to sign a Forest Service receipt or anything?"

"Nope," the ranger said. "This is my personal Smoker Craft. Bobby said you were in a hurry. I already had her hooked up to go fishing later." She jumped back in her pickup and put the boat in the water. Maycomb held the bowline from the side of the ramp while the boat floated off the trailer.

Cutter thanked Sakamoto and left immediately, taking the little skiff north along the low, tree-covered hills of Echo Bay. He lost cell service five minutes later, making any further orders from Charles Beason moot. The satellite phone would allow Cutter to communicate, but he'd keep that turned off until he needed it.

Lola was likely already at Tom Horning's with Van Dyke, picking up more lights, helmets, and rope. Not the sort of partner to let Cutter twist in the wind, she would follow, whether Beason approved it or not. And anyway, the chief would back whatever they did when she knew there was a life in danger.

A brisk sea breeze held the rain at bay for the time being, but low clouds still boiled over the mountains. Cutter sat at the back of the skiff, hand on the tiller of the little thirty-horse outboard. The GPS said they were making a solid twenty-one knots with the two of them and minimal gear, which felt even faster in the chop. Enough spray flew over the bow as they raced across the waves that it might as well have been raining. Cutter didn't care. They were moving forward. That's what mattered.

Lori Maycomb sat midships, facing him. She'd pulled her hair back with a couple of elastic bands. A chilly wind pinked her oval face, slightly bewildered that he'd allowed her to come along. She nodded at his belt, eyeing the worn leather pouch that was half hidden by the rain jacket, opposite the Colt Python.

Leaning toward him, she raised her voice over the roaring engine and the chatter of the boat against the waves. "What's with the medicine bag?"

"It was my grandfather's," Cutter said, offering no more information.

She sat back, looking at him for a time, then said, "You're thinking that you'll be able to track them?"

"I plan to try," Cutter yelled. "Levi and Donita would have had to take a boat out there. If they came this way, we'll find where they docked. There'll be some sign."

Maycomb chewed on that idea. "Might be all we find is bear sign."

"Maybe," Cutter said. "We'll poke around. Two people can leave a very distinct trail if you know what to look for."

She leaned in, wanting to hear everything. "And you know what to look for?" She sounded more impressed than skeptical.

"This terrain is different from where I grew up," he said,

able to speak at a little more normal volume now that she'd moved closer. "I've done some tracking in similar forests on Prince of Wales Island."

"Yeah," Maycomb said. "But was it chasing murderers?"

Cutter chuckled. "As a matter of fact, it was. . . ."

She grimaced at the thought.

"That *has* to be different from Florida."

"Different and the same," he said. "People move across the ground, they leave sign. Grass, downed trees, dirt. It might be slow going, but I can follow a trail if we can pick it up."

"Thanks for letting me come with you."

Cutter gave her a nod.

"Why did you anyway—let me come with you, I mean?"

"Two reasons," Cutter said. "Donita Willets is your informant. That means she trusts you. I imagine she thinks everyone is trying to kill her right now. She might not come out of hiding if some ugly-looking guy like me starts poking around. She could be armed. I could get hurt."

"She does trust me," Maycomb said. "What's the other reason?"

"The main reason," Cutter said. "I don't like the way your sister-in-law treats you."

"Let me get this straight," Maycomb said. She'd missed a lock of hair with her elastic bands and a gust of wind blew it across her face, wet with spray. "You let me come because Rockie Van Dyke didn't want me to?"

"About the size of it," Cutter said.

"That's about the coolest thing anybody's ever done for me," Maycomb said, more to herself than Cutter.

* * *

Heavy chop at the entrance to Berners Bay forced Cutter to tack into the waves to keep from swamping the little skiff, curtailing their conversation for the time being.

Lori Maycomb had seen plenty of men who knew their way around a boat, but the ones Cutter's age usually made a little show of it. They wanted you to know that they knew what they were doing. The behavior was evolutionary, she supposed. *Look at me. I can make fire. I can catch you fish. I will keep you safe on the open sea. I would be a good mate.*

Lots of people said they didn't care what others thought. Apparently, Arliss Cutter was one of the few who actually meant it. He did what needed to be done and then moved on to the next thing. Oddly, his behavior only made her want to watch him more closely.

Thomas Horning had loaned them a nautical chart for the area. Cutter folded it so he could look at the relevant section through a gallon-size ziplock bag he kept on his knee. The chart allowed him not only to orient himself with landmarks and terrain as they headed south, but to tuck in relatively close to shore while avoiding boat-eating rocks that lurked under the surface.

The concrete tanks and dark brown wood of the abandoned hatchery appeared through the mist less than half an hour after they left the Echo Cove boat launch. Below the hatchery, a smooth gravel beach dropped quickly to a newish wooden dock. A painted US Forest Service sign marked the trailhead that disappeared uphill into a heavy thatch of devil's club, cow parsnip, and sky-touching spruce. Behind the dock, a treeless point of black rock jutted sixty or seventy feet from the shore, forming a natural jetty.

Cutter eased off the throttle, but instead of motoring to the dock, he swung out, arcing well away from the point. Lines of rock like that rarely ended abruptly, instead trailing into the sea just under the surface, like hidden teeth, waiting to rip the bottom off a boat.

"We're not tying up at the dock?"

Cutter nodded at the point. "Levi's still missing, so we have to assume others are actively hunting for Donita. That kid doesn't strike me as a very convincing liar, so whatever he knows, the bad guys will know soon enough."

"Still," Maycomb said. "I thought we were going to track them."

"We are," Cutter said, looking down at the chart before bringing the skiff abeam the rocky point. "I'm hoping to hide the skiff. Hopefully it'll give us a slight advantage if—" He stopped, cursing under his breath. "Looks like they beat us here."

Another aluminum boat bobbed nearshore on the far side of the natural jetty. Slightly larger than the Smoker Craft, this skiff was much older, dented and scraped. A fifty-horse Suzuki hung off the transom, kicked up to keep from damaging the prop in shallow water.

His left hand on the tiller, Cutter's right dropped to the gun on his belt.

Cutter scanned the shoreline—shape, color, movement—anything out of place among the thicket of devil's club and forest. They were less than fifty yards from the shore now, easy pickings if someone was hiding with a rifle—certainly closer than the killing shots at the shrine. Consoling himself with the flimsy knowledge that no one had shot them yet, Cutter pulled the tiller toward him and turned the Smoker Craft in a smooth arc toward the other skiff.

A bright yellow rope ran from the bow to a scrubby

clump of willows, far above the line of driftwood and other flotsam that signified the high-tide line. They were at low tide now. White shells, likely the leftovers from a sea otter's dinner, littered the gravel bottom. Cutter guessed it to be around three feet, deep enough to keep the boats from going dry. The natural jetty offered protection from ocean swells. An anchor, also off the bow, allowed the boat to swing while keeping her from drifting onto the rocks.

"Valkyrie boat?" Lori mused as they came alongside.

"Good guess," Cutter said. "But only a guess. There's nothing to identify it one way or another. It's hidden off the main dock, but that could just be someone who doesn't want to get their boat stolen." Pulling the other skiff closer, he leaned across to feel the motor with the back of his hand.

Some residual warmth still lingered on the block, but it had been here long enough to cool substantially.

Cutter scanned the shore again and located the likely trail. The foliage on the dense scrub was slightly blanched where the lighter underside of several leaves had been turn upward, almost woven together when someone had pushed through. He reached over the side and unhooked the rubber hose that ran between the outboard motor and the fuel jug, taking it with him.

The boats gave a hollow clunk as they bumped together. He pushed away and then flipped the Honda's transmission into giving himself enough room to turn around in the deep water before heading around the point to the dock. He held up the black fuel hose.

"I've chased more than my share of fleeing boats in my day," he explained. "Worst case, that skiff has nothing to do with us and they have to wait a little to get their line back."

"Not sure that's the worst case," Maycomb said. She pulled her jacket tighter around her neck, chilled by the breeze—and the situation. "I get that this is faster than rigging a shore line and anchor, but aren't you worried about tying us up in the open?"

"I'm not tying up for long," Cutter said, hopping out and wrapping the bow line quickly around a rusted cleat. He lifted his pack onto the dock beside him. The rock helmet, rope, and other gear had wreaked havoc on his system and he had to dig through his pack to find the satellite phone. "You take the skiff and get out of here. I'll catch a ride back with—"

Maycomb frowned. "What about letting me come along because Donita trusts me?"

"It was stupid of me to put you in this kind of danger," Cutter said. "I'd hoped we'd get her to safety before anyone was the wiser, but that is obviously not the case."

Maycomb grabbed her pack and stood. "You didn't *put* me in danger."

"Look," Cutter said. "These people have already committed at least two murders. If you'd seen the bodies in that chapel, you might be a little less inclined to come along and risk getting your skull blown open."

"I don't scare," she said.

"And I don't have time to argue."

Maycomb stepped out of the skiff, defiant.

"Then you don't have time to arrest me. Don't fret. I'm not after a story. But I am worried about Donita. Let me help. You know good and well you need another set of eyes."

Cutter grit his teeth.

"There won't be time for you to smoke."

"Okay." She wagged her head. "I just quit."

Cutter punched Lola's number into the sat phone.

"What's your ETA?" he asked as soon as she picked up.

"We have the gear," she said. "The Hernandez brothers are spilling their guts, naming their cartel jefes and just about everyone they can think of."

"Anyone local?" Cutter asked, eyes on the tree line.

"No," Lola said. "But they're giving damning information on enough kingpins that the DEA and FBI have climbed into bed with the little bastards. I'm thinking they'll be in WITSEC with new names and respectable jobs before you know it." The disdain was clear in her voice.

"Okay." Cutter asked again. "Your ETA?"

"That's the thing, boss. Beason has everybody and their dog running down the heaps of leads the Hernandez brothers are puking up. He thinks that's the best way to find Donita Willets."

"He could be right," Cutter said.

"No," Lola said. "I'm going with your gut. It's just taken us a bit to get a boat. Everything's organized now and we're driving out to Echo Cove to launch."

"So how long?"

Silence while she conferred with Van Dyke.

"We'll hurry," Lola said when she came back on the line. "Forty minutes, tops."

Cutter briefed her on the second skiff.

"Now I'm really going with your gut," Lola said.

"We can't be sure it belongs to our shooters," Cutter said. "Beason will argue that it's hikers or something, but see if you can get a couple of the other teams heading this way. It wouldn't hurt my feelings if you could get a Coastie Jay-hawk to fly over the mountain."

"Copy that," Lola said. "Sit tight and we'll be right there."

"I'm not waiting," Cutter said. "You just follow my tracks."

"Hang on a sec," Lola said. "What if I get lost?"

"You'll do fine," Cutter said. He shouldered his pack and started toward the dark patch in the foliage. "You've been tracking for over a year now."

"Always with you!" Lola said. "Boss, don't do this. Wait for me to get there."

"Did Tom Horning give you a topo map with the mines located on it?"

She was breathing heavier now. "Yes." The Kiwi crept back in, turning it into a tentative *yis*.

"Then you know where we're likely to be going. Seriously, you'll do fine, Lola. Step by step."

"Okay," she said, still unconvinced. "Step by step."

"As fast as you can."

"Boss!"

Cutter kept his voice low, steady. "Not faster than you can. Like I said, you'll do great. Just use what you've learned. Gotta go so I can concentrate."

He started to end the call, but Lola stopped him. "Hang on, what about Lori Maycomb?"

"Still working that out," he said.

CHAPTER 43

Cutter found a patchwork of tracks in the mud right away. It was not uncommon for a moat of murky water to mark the transition zone between the gravel beach and the tree line. Left behind from high tides or storm surges, the water was usually stagnant and brown. Silty mud above and below the water made the perfect track trap.

Maycomb followed, but stayed ten feet behind, out of the way. To her credit, she kept her eyes up on the trees more than down.

"You're not going to try to talk me out of coming with you?"

"I told you I don't have time to argue," he said. "I meant it."

"Well, okay then," Maycomb said. "You won't regret it."

Cutter stooped to study the tracks. "I already regret it."

There were at least four, maybe five sets of footprints. One of them was considerably smaller, probably a woman. The edges of this one made him think it was a little older, but the recent rains made it difficult to tell. He made a quick sketch of the particulars—heel wear, length of stride, straddle—the width between tracks, and a couple of sole blemishes that might help him tell two of the larger sets apart—if he was fortunate enough to get clear prints, which was unlikely in forest duff. The most he could hope for were partial prints, but he was more likely to get scuffed moss, broken branches, and occasional heel digs. Stride and size of each track would be key. The smaller track had the corrugated ridgelines of an Xtratuf boot.

"It's like they issue these things," he muttered.

Willow was almost as abundant as devil's club, and it didn't take him long to cut a relatively straight shoot, about the diameter of an arrow and half again as long, and then glance at Maycomb. "Can I borrow those elastic hair ties?"

She rolled them off her ponytail at once. "See," she said. "Useful already."

"I'd have gotten by," Cutter said. "But thank you."

He doubled the bands so they fit tight around the willow shaft, and then rolled them over the end, one at a time. Next, he stooped over the mud where the clearest set of the two smallest tracks first appeared. Holding his stick in his fist, he put the tip at the heel of the forward track. The heel of the rear track was even with the leading edge of his fist. That gave him stride. He marked it by rolling the first elastic band to his hand. The second band went just forward of the first, indicating the length of the smallest track.

"Make sure you sing out if you see or hear anything," he said without looking up. If Maycomb was going to hang around, he might as well give her a job.

Finding tracks was straightforward through the mud, but there was far more to tracking than seeing footprints. Cutter took the time to scribble a few more sketches and then stepped to the edge of the mud. Sign in the way of heel digs, scuffs, and transferred mud was abundant in the duff, but it was impossible to tell whose track was whose.

Almost.

He crouched over the last track he could positively identify as belonging to the smallest set of Xtratufs. Keeping the rearmost elastic band so it lined up with the back of the heel, he played the point of the stick back and forth in a slow arc.

"I get it," Maycomb said. "You measured Donita's step so now the tip points you to the next track."

"I measured somebody's step," Cutter said. "The length of their stride. Not sure if it's Donita's yet. That's my best guess, though, so I'm going to follow it. But you are correct on how the tracking stick works."

He moved quickly now, following divots of leaf-littered duff and scrapes over mossy deadfall. The trees provided a thick canopy overhead, giving the forest a sense of perpetual twilight. It was so dense in some places as to block the rain, leaving the trail relatively dry but for seepage and runoff. The sign bushwhacked upward at first, skirting heavy thickets of devil's club and large outcroppings of rock, but generally heading due east. After a quarter of a mile, it turned south, side-hilling over the deadfall and basketball-size hummocks.

"Tailings?" Maycomb offered, panting from the endless up, over, and around they had to do to negotiate the mountain.

"I'm thinking tailings would have been crushed to get at the gold," Cutter said. "This could be an old rockslide."

"Got it," Maycomb said, saving her breath.

Cutter made exaggerated digs with his own heels every few feet, marking the trail for Lola. She was good, but still learning, and this wasn't the time for a test.

The wind shifted just a hair, but enough that he could hear the hiss of a waterfall.

Tom Horning's maps indicated two mines ahead, so it was impossible to tell which one they were going toward—if any. Oddly, the elevation lines on the topo showed a deep gorge a few hundred yards ahead through the trees, running straight down the mountain, blocking their path. He checked the map against the GPS.

"Must be a bridge up ahead," he said. "Or they turn—"

Eyes on the trail, he heard Lori Maycomb's plaintive sigh as the sound of the waterfall grew louder.

His hand dropped to the Colt instinctively.

"What is it?"

"A hand tram," she said, pointing through the trees at a set of cables.

Another few steps brought three cables into view, strung like powerlines across a deep ravine. A series of waterfalls boiled just uphill, throwing a cloud of misty spray. Across the gorge was a simple basket of bent steel and wooden benches hung from the cable on two pulleys. Cutter estimated it was seventy or eighty feet away. Someone had used it to cross and then left it on the other side.

Maycomb stopped at the trees, well away from the rocky edge. "How deep is it, do you think?"

Cutter moved to the square platform. Grabbing one of the steel posts where the cable attached on his side, he peered over.

"A hundred, maybe a hundred fifty," he said.

"Okay," she said, moving to join him. "As long as it's deep enough to kill me outright. I don't want to lay down there in agony for hours until someone can come down and get me."

"Guess that's one way of looking at it."

A nylon rope ran in a continuous loop through a series of metal guides the length of the cable, then through pulleys on both sides of the ravine. The metal car or hand trolley was attached to this rope.

Cutter had no idea when the hand trolley had been built. The steel piping was screwed instead of welded. Two small wooden benches were bolted to the floor on either side of the open frame, facing each other. There were no seat belts, and the frame itself provided the only handholds beyond the rope used to pull yourself back and forth. The pulleys and cables were rusted, but appeared to be in good condition—at least good enough to carry the previous load across that day. The newest piece of the setup was the rope, a spliced length of twisted mountaineering rope called Goldline. It was frayed, but serviceable, probably attached by Tom Horning or one of his group of adventurers sometime in the past year or so.

Cutter believed they might have pegged the trolley, making it impossible to bring over, but he gave it a stout tug and it began to move toward him.

"You can still wait—"

A loud pop came from the far side of the ravine. Cutter initially thought it was a gunshot, or some kind of sabotage to the line, but the hand trolley continued to squeak and wobble toward them. It took just under a minute to bring it all the way across.

"Get in!" he said.

To her credit, Maycomb complied without question.

Cutter stood on the opposite side of the trolley cage, balancing the swing as best he could. Both hands on the rope, he began to pull hand over hand. He needed to get them across as quickly as possible.

"Want to tell me what that was?" Maycomb asked, staring

straight across the gorge, as they swung, and inched, and swung some more. She and Cutter both avoided looking down at the silver line of churning water in the rocks beneath their flimsy basket.

Cutter kept pulling, but nodded to a silver canister tied to the pulley arm on which the trolley rode the cable.

"A flashbang," he said. "They set it and left it."

Maycomb closed her eyes and groaned. "So now they know we're behind them."

"They know somebody is," Cutter said. "If they're close, they could send someone back to check—and we're sitting ducks out here."

Maycomb reached up to grab the rope. Timing her efforts to match his, she began to help him pull. "Yeah, and you look like a cop from a hundred yards away."

Cutter stepped off the trolley as soon as they reached the other side, holding it steady for Maycomb.

"This way," he whispered, stepping toward a line of devil's club, fiddlehead fern, and alder on the uphill side of what looked to be Donita's direction of travel. "Try your best not to touch any of the vegetation."

"Yep," Maycomb said, breathless with tension. She mimicked Cutter's twisting dance to avoid disturbing the alder and berry leaves.

They needed to get off the trail as quickly as possible, but Cutter wanted to gain the high ground before he took a minute to see if someone returned to check their back trail.

He didn't have long to wait.

CHAPTER 44

The first shot snapped through the branches to their right, skittering leaves and narrowly missing Maycomb. Cutter spun at the staccato crack, pulling her down behind a thick-hipped hemlock that was wide enough to cover them both as long as their aggressors attacked head on. If there were three of them, as Cutter suspected, there was a slim chance of that. They'd simply fan out, using their own trees for cover while they flanked the couple and picked them off.

Whatever he was going to do, he needed to do it fast, before the others got organized. To do that, he needed intel. Rather than removing his pack, Cutter asked Maycomb to get the compact Leupold binoculars from the outside pocket. He rolled to the side, staying low to come up behind a neighboring stump of old growth, peeking out a good ten feet away from where he'd last been seen.

There were three all right. An older man with a huge black and silver beard and a man with slick black hair, each carrying a pistol. Slick carried a pack with a coil of climbing rope. The third man was younger, more muscular, with a killer look in his eyes that distance couldn't hide. A tough guy, and he knew it. He also carried a pack, out of which he took the components of a scoped precision rifle.

Cutter didn't take the time to get any more information. He had all that he needed to make a decision.

He belly-crawled back to Maycomb behind the hemlock tree.

Two more pistol shots skittered through the foliage. WAG shots—wild-ass guesses for now, but they'd settle down and zero in soon enough.

"We have to move," Cutter said. "Three bad guys. One of them is putting together a rifle—and he moves like he knows how to use it. Good chance he's the shooter from the shrine."

"We're here, right?" Maycomb whispered, pointing to a spot on the map just east of the ravine.

"Yep."

She traced a line on the paper with the tip of her finger, directly uphill. "That's a mine, isn't it?"

Horning marked his mines with triangles—deltas. This one was blue, underscored by three blue lines and the notation: *CC#2.* Cutter guessed this one to be no more than a couple hundred yards away. But every yard of it was uphill, with people shooting at them while they tried to find a hole in the mountain that Horning had warned them could be almost impossible to find.

Cutter tapped Maycomb on the arm so she'd look at him. He already had the Colt in hand. He passed her the Glock. "Know how to use this?"

She nodded. "My husband had one."

"Good," Cutter said. "When I say, give a slow five-count, and then shoot a couple of times in their general direction.

Don't stick your head around. Don't try to aim. Just make them shoot back at you."

"You want them to shoot at me?"

"Stay behind the tree and you'll be fine," Cutter said. "As soon as you hear my first shot, run as fast as you can for the mine, finger off the trigger. Hopefully, I'll be able to get them to put their heads down for a second or two so you can get a head start."

"What if they don't? Put their heads down, I mean."

"Then we'll have one less guy chasing us," he whispered. "Now, go on my first shot. And remember, finger off the trigger when you move. Ready?"

Maycomb gathered herself up to run and gave a snappy nod.

She had to be terrified, but she only looked determined.

"Start counting now!" Cutter rolled to his right, coming up behind the stump. He'd just come to a stop when Maycomb took her first shot.

Black Beard returned fire first. Slick waited a beat for Maycomb to shoot again. He was more deliberate, strategic, where Black Beard appeared to act on emotion. Good to know. Tough Guy had his rifle assembled now and lay on his belly behind the scope. Maycomb's shot had done the trick, and he was zeroed in on the hemlock, ready to pick her off as soon as she exposed herself to shoot again.

Tough Guy had found himself a trough in the forest duff, a small hillock that concealed most of his body. Only his boots and the front half of his rifle were exposed. Prone and steady, Cutter maneuvered the Colt so the front sight covered the rifle's action. He'd thought momentarily about shooting that Tough Guy in the foot, but decided he'd rather take the rifle out of the equation and deal with three guys with handguns.

He guessed the range to be less around forty yards. A reach for the pistol as far as pinpoint accuracy was concerned, but doable.

Maycomb's shots were already going stale, and the three men's eyes were starting to wander, looking for targets.

Cutter took a settling breath and, holding a hair high, pressed the trigger, sending a .357 round slamming through the magazine well of the rifle.

Tough Guy cursed, crawfishing into his makeshift foxhole away from the shot. Cutter fired toward his feet, but it was a snap shot and went low, kicking up dirt and moss. He wasn't a fan of spray and pray tactics, but sent another round into the brush where he'd last seen Slick keeping them down. Cutter dumped his three empty shells, the topped off quickly before scrambling after Maycomb.

Sprinting uphill felt interminably slow, but Cutter consoled himself that the men pursuing them were running up the same hill. He swung around a boulder the size of a car, caught sight of Maycomb through the trees, and adjusted his course toward her. She ran with purpose, and hopefully had the mine entrance in sight. If they could duck inside before the men got there, they might have a chance.

Cutter vaguely registered another shot as wood shards flew off a knee-high deadfall the same moment he hurdled over it. He cut right, keeping Maycomb in sight, no more than twenty yards ahead through the trees. She had to be getting close.

Hiding in a hole was far from optimum. Cutter could think of a dozen ways he'd assault an enemy in a tunnel, but he needed time to formulate some semblance of a plan— and outgunned and in the open, time was fast running out.

Cutter ducked right again, skirting a line of spruce trees he hoped might offer some cover, and nearly stepped into an oncoming bullet in the process. The shot sent dirt spraying at his feet. He sprang left as another round thwacked the bark next to his head. He was already running as fast as he could, but rounds snapping in from downrange had a way of adding a little adrenaline kick to his step. Digging in again, he scanned for Maycomb, who'd suddenly dropped out of sight.

More shots peppered the trees around him, forcing him to sidehill, away from where he wanted to go. A bullet slapped the ground to his left, sending him back the other direction. They were lobbing them in now, but with three people shooting, it was only a matter of time.

Two more shots popped in quick succession—from uphill.

Way to go, Lori Maycomb, Cutter thought.

Another two steps brought her into view. She'd jumped into the mine entrance and was now laying down cover fire to slow the assault on Cutter as he ran.

The Glock held only eleven rounds, and she'd already used two at the tree.

The shots behind Cutter kept coming, but they were wide and sporadic.

Maycomb rolled onto her side when Cutter approached, giving him room to slide into the narrow opening. A flat rock the size of a dinner table and covered with dirt hung over the mine's entrance, reducing it to a black gash in the mountain less than three feet tall and half again as wide. Cutter slid on his belly through a slurry of mud and rock, headfirst into the darkness. He came to a stop next to Maycomb's feet and scrambled back up the scree to assist her.

He reached into his pocket for an extra magazine for the Glock. "You okay?" he asked.

Maycomb nodded. Firing her last two rounds when she saw the fresh mag. Meant for a larger model, this one carried fifteen rounds hanging out the bottom of the magazine well.

"They're still coming," she said. "What now?"

"I have one more magazine of fifteen after that," he said. "So keep shooting, but be judicious. I'll try and make a call on the sat phone to get the cavalry here."

Maycomb answered, chambering a round and sending it downrange immediately.

Cutter extended the satellite phone's antenna and held it as far out as he dared to try to get a clear view of the sky. A flurry of bullets slapped the ground around his hand.

"Shit!" he said, jerking the phone inside and trading it for the Colt Python.

Another bullet smacked the overhang, sending shards of rock into the tunnel. Whoever was on that gun was a better-than-average shot. Probably Tough Guy, Cutter thought, chiding himself for not taking off the rifleman's foot when he had the chance.

Maycomb had the only semblance of cover in the form of a basketball-size lump of rock. Cutter rolled sideways, trying to find an angle or something to hide behind so he could look downhill long enough to take a productive shot.

"Let's have you move back behind me," he said. "Better that I do the shooting."

She gave him an emphatic nod and then fired three quick shots. "Cutter!" she yelled. "They're moving!"

"Moving?"

He and Maycomb were both half deaf from all the gunfire in the enclosed space.

"Two of them," she said. "One right, one left." She shimmied backward away from her rock, yielding the space to him.

He crawled into position in time to catch a glimpse of Slick and Black Beard working their way uphill on either side of the mine. He fired toward Slick, but it was wasted ammunition. He didn't have the angle.

Cutter pushed away from the entrance a couple feet and took one of the Streamlights from his pocket. A rock fell from the jagged roof, making him wish for the helmet, but there was no time for that. He rolled onto his back, surveying the area around the entrance, then playing the beam past Maycomb into the blackness. The tunnel would have been head high for the miners when they'd built it—a little shy of six feet. Cutter would need to remember to stoop. His light bounced off a narrow stream that ran down the center of the tunnel. Old boards and rusted tools lay here and there along the arched gray walls. Water dripped steadily from the uneven rock ceiling, plopping into the trickle. The sweet odor of decaying wood came from the rough-cut timber frame just inside the opening forming a shallow puddle in the mud and shale. Sodden and sagging, the wood looked more like the trigger to spring a trap than any kind of architectural support. The upright timber beside Cutter's leg was badly splintered, listing heavily as if it were carrying the weight of the entire mountain.

Gruff voices drifted down from outside. It was impossible to tell from where exactly, but a skitter of dirt and gravel falling from above the entrance told Cutter all he needed to know.

Cutter pointed the beam of his Streamlight down the tunnel again, found what he wanted, and then tapped Maycomb on the thigh.

"We need to move!"

Fist-size stones bounced inside the entrance, clattering against the rock and splashing into the puddle and punctuating Cutter's urgency.

Scrambling to his feet, he grabbed Maycomb by the hand and ran, splashing and sliding through the ankle-deep water and silt to put as much distance between them and the tunnel entrance as he could. Fifteen steps in he reached what he was looking for, a shallow depression cut a scant three feet into the rock. He pulled Maycomb tight against him so they both faced the wall.

"Cover your head," he managed to say, before a sullen *woomf* shook the mountain. A black wall of dust and stone blew into the tunnel on a gale-force wind, the pressure wave slamming against Cutter's lungs. Jagged chunks of rock rained from the ceiling. One of them slammed against Cutter's forearm, raised to protect his head. The sudden shock of the blow caused him to drop his flashlight into the muck at his feet, throwing the tunnel into complete darkness.

CHAPTER 45

"You hear that?" Lola Teariki said, standing at the tide-line of sun-bleached driftwood and rotting kelp above the old dock.

Rockie Van Dyke's hand dropped to her Glock.

"Gunfire?"

Both women had thought they may have heard a rifle shot on the way in, but the roar of the outboard motor covered everything quieter than a howitzer.

"Could be," Lola said. "Sounded deeper, though. A rumble."

"Probably my idiot sister-in-law starting a rockslide," Van Dyke scoffed.

"Due respect, Detective," Lola said, casting around the ground for tracks. "But you should give your damned blood feud a rest for a quick minute. I'm trying to concentrate here."

"Okay," Van Dyke nodded at the mud, not quite sorry, but professional enough to get back on task. "So what do you see?"

"Not a damned thing," Lola admitted. "And that's the problem. Cutter always says that everything that moves across the ground leaves some kind of sign."

She and Van Dyke had tied off next to the Smoker Craft and then walked directly toward the tree line in hopes of finding a trail—cutting sign, Cutter called it. Surprisingly, she'd found no fresh tracks at all, even in the willow-choked line of mud that ran parallel to the forest. They had to have crossed somewhere, so she walked north, scanning the beach.

"Cutter," she mumbled into the wind. "What have you—"

She stopped when she looked back toward the water and saw a skiff bobbing beyond a line of rocks that jutted into the cove. The sight of the new boat focused both women immediately.

"He said someone is already here," Van Dyke said under her breath.

"Keep an eye uphill," Lola said. She started for the trees above the skiff, getting a better picture now of what Cutter had meant on the phone.

You didn't need to be a trained tracker to locate a bunch of footprints in mud, but Lola had a moment of pride when she was able to suss out where Cutter had squatted to take measurements and make sketches. She'd seen him do exactly the same thing dozens of times. Another set of impressions stood well behind Cutter's. Those would be Maycomb's, observing Cutter work, just as Rockie Van Dyke was observing Lola now.

Lola looked up the mountain, trying to peer through the dense shadows of moss and brush and fallen trees.

Now came the hard part.

Behind her, Van Dyke held up the sat phone and shook her head. "I'm getting no answer from Cutter."

"Understandable," Lola said. "He'd have to be holding the antenna just right to get a signal in these trees."

She searched the willows until she found a straight branch and then bent it so it was taut at the base. Her pocket-knife cut through it like butter. She trimmed the leafy twigs along the length of her tracking stick and measured the stride between two tracks she believed to be Cutter's. He would try and leave her a trail, so in theory, his tracks would be easier to follow. In truth, it didn't matter. Lola wanted to save Donita Willets and arrest the bad guys, but it was Cutter she'd follow, wherever his tracks led. He was her partner. He needed her.

Urgency drew Teariki and Van Dyke up the mountain. The tracks became more difficult to find as soon as they passed into the woods. Lola slowed, doubting herself, using the willow stick the way Cutter had taught her, willing the tip to point to a track. Her eyes settled on something she thought might be the print of an Xtratuf in the dirt. Crouching, she took a shuffling half step and then held the stick over that spot, twisting her wrist so the point of the stick arced back and forth.

She gave an audible gasp when it crossed a divot she absolutely knew belonged to Cutter's heel.

She reached in her pocket and took out a roll of bright orange flagging tape, ripping off a foot of it and dropping it on the ground beside the good track.

"This is going to take all day," Van Dyke said. "Going from track to track."

"Agreed," Lola said. "That's why we're not going to do that."

"What then?" Van Dyke asked, brow raised.

"We're going to bound," Lola said.

"Okay . . ." Van Dyke said.

Lola moved forward as she explained. "Cutter knows heaps about tracking," she said. "And he's a terrific teacher.

I'm learning, but it helps if I hang what I learn on things I'm already familiar with." She studied the hillside ahead, looked down at her feet, then the area ahead again. "My dad's a sailor, a voyager. Loves the ancient ways of navigation our forefathers used to cross the Pacific in double-hull canoes."

She stopped to study a devil's club leaf that had been torn off the plant and now lay on the ground, bruised and darker green from being crushed under a boot. She marked it with tape as well and moved on.

"Anyway," she continued. "When I was a little girl, my dad used to sail with this friend from the island of Mongaia who taught him something called *Kaveinga* . . . and he taught it to me. In a nutshell, it's the same sort of thing I'm learning from Cutter."

Ten yards up Lola spotted a divot where someone, likely Cutter, had dug a heel into the mossy ground. She marked it with another piece of flagging tape and stood.

"Where was I?"

"Your dad and his friend from Mongaia."

"Right," Lola said. "*Kaveinga*. You locate a star on the horizon in the direction you want to sail, then steer toward that star. When it rises too high and out of line, you pick the next star that comes over the horizon at that same spot and steer to that one, until it's too high and out of line . . . and so on and so on. A path of stars. We're just following the azimuth between two known tracks as fast as possible until the next one presents itself, then adjusting course as needed. *Kaveinga,* but with tracks instead of stars."

"Sounds cool enough," Van Dyke said. "But you have to know which stars to look for. And what if there are clouds and you don't even have stars?"

"Yeah," Lola said. "Those would be problems. But I

prefer to focus on what we do have, and right now, we have stars—tracks."

Lola moved as quickly as she dared, going from heel divot in the soft loam here, a toe scuff in the moss there. She paused to study a stalk of cow parsnip. Waist high, it was the diameter of a large piece of celery. The leaves were green and healthy, not yet beginning to wilt. Fresh sap pooled around the broken stem. She'd learned the hard way that she was allergic to the stuff, using the stalks to sword-fight with another deputy at a party. Her skin had become hypersensitive to the sun wherever the sap had touched her, causing her to burn and scar.

Less than an hour into Lola's gut-wrenching first solo tracking effort, the woods began to clear. Dirt gave way to bedrock, making it difficult to find any clear sign at all. Lola kept moving in the general direction of what she'd already found, losing faith in her own abilities with each passing step. She brightened when the roar of a waterfall carried through on the wind. A crossing would give her a funnel, a track trap where she was sure to find some sign of Cutter. She broke out of the trees with Van Dyke in tow and realized immediately that she had something even better. The hand trolley waited on the far side of the ravine, meaning someone had used it to get across.

She was on the right track.

CHAPTER 46

Rock and gravel slid off Arliss Cutter's back as he pushed himself up on all fours. A high-pitched squeal assaulted his ears. His head felt as though he'd been hit between the eyes with a sledgehammer. The darkness was thick enough to cut.

Stunned, he coughed, trying to catch a breath that wasn't full of grit. He felt movement beneath him in the darkness, heard a muffled cry.

"Lori?"

She flailed blindly in the blackness, brushing his face with her outstretched fingers. "Cutter? Are you all right?" His ears rang so badly that her words sounded like they were coming from the bottom of a well.

He took her hand, held it tight to his chest. She'd admitted to being scared of tight spaces and this had to be terrifying for her. Cutter, who'd never been claustrophobic, found himself suddenly reeling and disoriented. He tried to speak, but coughed again, sputtering this time. "Light," he finally managed to say. The Streamlight he'd been holding was hopelessly gone, buried after it had been knocked or blown out of his hand.

Maycomb found her light first and flicked it on, pointing

toward the ground. Cutter squinted anyway, blinded by the relative brightness until his eyes adjusted. The timber supports were gone, buried under a mound of rocks that completely blocked the exit and sloped into the tunnel. Gauging from the location of their safety cutout, the first ten feet of the mine had collapsed from the explosion.

A rock the size of an axe head and just as sharp fell from the ceiling and clattered at Cutter's feet, narrowly missing Maycomb's head.

Cutter snatched up his pack. "Let's put our helmets on before we both get brained."

"They buried us alive," Maycomb said, breathing heavily. She pressed tightly against Cutter as she fastened her helmet under her chin and switched on the headlamp.

"Do you bend anywhere you shouldn't?" Cutter asked.

"I . . . No," Maycomb said. "Can . . . we dig our way out?"

"Eventually," Cutter said. "I need to know if you're hurt."

"I'm fine," Maycomb snapped. "We should start digging now so we—"

"We could," Cutter said. "You've been in tougher jams than this. Don't you think it's better if we take a breath, look at the situation from all sides."

Maycomb looked up at him, her chin quivering under the helmet strap. "O . . . okay . . ." she stammered.

"Good deal," Cutter said, trying to convince himself there was a way to get out of this and still reach Donita Willets in time. "You've got the CO and O_2 meters in your pack. Go ahead and check our levels while I take stock of ammo and other gear."

Cutter knew exactly what they had, but he wanted Maycomb to know, to understand that they were fine for the near term. That there was no need to panic.

They knelt facing each other, their packs between them, and he ticked through the gear—ropes, ascenders, foil blankets, candles, water bottles, thin gloves, jackets, extra headlamps and batteries, along with his regular everyday carry of a small knife, a small flashlight, and Zippo lighter. He had another six rounds for the Python. The Glock magazine had six rounds left, plus the one in the pipe.

Maycomb followed each item he pulled from the pack, but none of it seemed to register with her.

He reached inside like a magician pulling a rabbit out of a hat. "And toilet paper. My buds always bring a bunch of weapons and then forget to bring TP."

"I need a cigarette."

Cutter ignored her, pulling a gallon-size ziplock bag from the main portion of his pack. "And I saved the best for last. My nephews stashed some biscuits in here."

Maycomb looked up, blinking, a defeated look on her face. "That's the best thing in your pack? Biscuits?"

"I don't know," Cutter chuckled. "They're good biscuits."

"I'm going to start digging," Maycomb said.

"Okay," Cutter said. "Mind if I borrow your phone?"

She was on the verge of hyperventilating. "There's no way we get a signal in here."

Cutter kept his voice low and even. Calling her Captain Obvious wouldn't help matters at all. "I want to look at the maps you got from Horning."

"Whatever." She dug in her pocket. "It probably doesn't even work." She passed it to Cutter, who gave it back.

"I'm going to smoke."

"Nope," Cutter said. "Not in here, you're not. Password?"

She used her thumbprint and passed it back, then began to cast around the tunnel floor, presumably looking for something to dig with.

Cutter scrolled through several pages of map thumbnails until he found one that read *CC#2*. "Here's something."

"What?" Maycomb asked, her back to him. She'd found a rusted shovel, but it looked about to crumble in her hands. "Photos of biscuits?"

"That's cute," Cutter said. "No, come look at this." He lowered the phone so Maycomb could see. "CC#2 means it's the second entry Horning discovered into a mine named the Cross Cut." He used his thumb to swipe to the next page. This one displayed a sectional map of a large bubble-like stope complete with support columns. The entry was located at the top and necessitated a rappel to get inside. It was labeled CC#1. Opposite this areal entry was a shaft—a winze in mining terminology—dropping down to a secondary tunnel with the notation "to CC#2."

Maycomb read it three times, swiping back and forth between the two maps. "So," she said, still unconvinced. "We just go to the end of this tunnel, rappel down, and then end up in this big room with another way out?"

"According to Horning's map," Cutter said, tapping the screen.

"What about these marks?" she asked, pointing to a series of blue hash marks beside the down shaft.

"No idea," Cutter said. "But we need to go look."

A single tear rolled down Maycomb's cheek, creasing a line in the thin layer of dirt there. "Remember when I told you I don't scare?"

"Matter of fact, I do remember that," Cutter said.

Maycomb's jaw clenched, moving her helmet straps. "Well, this scares the shit out of me and I don't mind telling you. It makes my groin ache and my head spin and I feel like I'm going to keel over dead."

"Hey," Cutter said, completely serious. "I'm no paragon

of bravery. I want out of here as badly as you do. The map says it's about three hundred yards to the down shaft. We'll be able to decipher Horning's code when we get there." A sudden thought hit him. "Everything happened so fast, I never got to ask you. Did you recognize any of the men who were shooting at us?"

"The one with the black beard is Harold Grimsson," Maycomb said, as if it meant the end of the world. "He's the owner of the Valkyrie Mine Holdings."

"The other two?"

"I didn't get a good look."

"Grimsson," Cutter said. The name tasted bitter. "We need to get to Donita Willets before he does."

Thinking about the missing woman seemed to take Maycomb's mind off her own troubles and she followed dutifully, head down, behind Cutter.

Deeper in, the tunnel looked much the same as it had near the entrance. Here and there, a half-burned candle slumped in small alcoves along the wall, drips of snow-white paraffin running down the rock, frozen in time. Miners had written their names in soot from carbide lamps with dates going back as far as 1908. The remnants of an old dynamite crate made Cutter want to stop and look, but he kept going, methodically, checking every step for rotting boards and hidden down shafts—and all the other dangers Horning had warned them about.

Two hundred feet in, Maycomb's steps grew heavier, trudging along, kicking the water as she walked. The beam of her lamp pointed straight down.

"We're going to die in here," she said, blurting it out like she was trying to rid herself of a heavy load. "These walls . . . They don't seem to be getting closer to you?"

"The walls are fine," Cutter said. "Let's just keep moving forward. We're not going to die."

"You can't know that." Maycomb grabbed his sleeve, sloshing to a stop in her tracks. He turned and faced her. Logical arguments made little difference when someone was panicked. If anything worked, it was a calm, understanding voice.

"Let's keep going," he said. "Tom Horning's map says this is a way out."

She stomped her feet, splashing the ankle-deep water.

"Look," she said. "I'm not a stupid person. I'm not trying to be dramatic, but let's be honest. We could die right here in this mountain."

"We certainly will if we give up," Cutter said. "But it's much more likely that my partner will check in with Horning when they can't find us. They'll see that one of the mines on his maps has caved in, and somebody will come dig us out."

"You're forgetting the guys with guns up there," Maycomb said.

"That's true," Cutter said. He thought of Lola, coming to help him, and prayed she wasn't walking into an ambush. "So let's get moving and be our own rescue. We'll find a way out of the tunnels ahead. We have food and water to last a couple of days if we had to."

Maycomb sniffed, rubbed her nose with the back of her sleeve. "I'm just so scared."

"Me too," Cutter said. "But moving helps me keep that fear in check."

She sniffed again. "As long as you have biscuits . . ."

"There you go," Cutter said.

They began to walk again, side by side instead of single file.

Maycomb's chest shuddered with a single sob, but she shook it off. She glanced up at him, facing slightly away to keep from blinding him with her headlamp. "If there's a chance I'm going to die, there are some things I need to get off my chest."

Cutter gave a somber chuckle. "As sin eaters go, I'm not much—"

"I can never make amends," she said. "Not really. Not after all the things I've done to the people I love. But I've got to tell somebody, just in case . . . you know . . ."

"All right," Cutter said, steeling himself. If there was one thing he understood, it was trying to make amends.

CHAPTER 47

Lola Teariki wasn't exactly scared of heights, but she wasn't keen on smashing into the toothy rocks below either. She gave the rope attached to the hand trolley a series of sharp hand-over-hand yanks, pulling it toward her.

The open cage—what there was of it—swung violently back and forth, but stayed on the cable as it rattled and squeaked across the ravine.

"Careful!" Rockie Van Dyke said.

"This is what careful looks like, sister," Lola said. "If it's going to fall, I want it to fall before I get on it."

Other than the white marking on the pipe frame from an expended flashbang, the car looked in decent enough shape considering its age.

In the end, it held, and Teariki and Van Dyke pulled themselves across without incident.

Marks in the rocky ground that looked like several sets of tracks moved across the clearing and into the mossy undergrowth and chaotic deadfall. Scuffed moss and freshly broken ferns said at least one set of tracks, and probably two, headed straight up the mountain.

"High ground," Lola said, half to herself.

Van Dyke was focused on the shadows ahead on the sidehill as she took a drink from a water bottle in her pack.

"What?"

Lola pointed uphill with an open hand. "I'm thinking Dollarhyde, or whoever it is in that other skiff, set off the flashbang to let them know if they're being followed. Cutter would have expected them to come back, so he'd have looked for a high vantage point."

"Did they?" Van Dyke asked. "Come back?"

"I can't tell," Lola said. "But I'm staying on what I think is Cutter's track."

"You seem to know what he's thinking," Van Dyke said, following, pushing aside brush. She kept her eyes up and scanning while Lola tracked.

"Cutter's not particularly mysterious when it comes to tactics," Lola said.

"I don't know," Van Dyke said. "The big guy seems like a mystery to me. I mean, have you ever even seen him smile?"

"Not often," she said. "But when he does, you know you've earned it."

"He married?"

Lola gave a soft belly laugh. "When it comes to his personal life, that dude is Fort Knox and the NSA all rolled into an enigmatic ball. But tactically, you can always count on him to do the right thing, right now. He does have kind of a resting-killer face, but you have to work pretty hard to offend him personally. I'll tell you what, though, he will flat pull the head right off of anybody who mistreats someone he thinks is the underdog." Lola glanced up to make sure she had Van Dyke's attention. "An underdog like, say, your sister-in-law."

"That again?" Van Dyke waved her away. "I'm gonna

have to call bullshit. In this scenario, my brother was the underdog. His son is the underdog. If anybody needs their head pulled off, it's little Lori Lush."

"You say so." Lola shrugged. "But it seems to me she's trying. How many people do you know who don't even do—"

Lola held up a fist, signaling Van Dyke to freeze. A glint of metal caught her eye—and it could only be one thing.

Scuffs in the duff and moss had led her through the twilight forest to a large hemlock. The space on the uphill side of the tree looked different. Needles, twigs, and other debris had been moved around a great deal, piled up here and there to reveal fresh dirt underneath.

"Someone knelt here," Lola said.

But it was the glint of metal that had caught her eye. Something shiny pressed into the dirt, almost hidden.

Fired brass.

Lola used her pen to pick it up and passed it back to Van Dyke when she found another.

"Rectangular primer strike," the detective observed. "Glock." She dumped the spent casing in her vest pocket and continued to watch the surrounding woods for threats.

"Cutter's," Lola said, searching the undergrowth, trying to suss out what had gone on here from the signs on the ground.

"I thought he carried that big revolver."

"His grandpa's," Lola said, still searching the ground. "Technically, that's his backup. Per policy he has to carry a Glock, but if he resorted to . . ." She dropped to her knees next to a wide stump a dozen feet to the right of the hemlock, seeing something out of place, wanting a closer look.

"So," Van Dyke said. "They had a firefight here, but

there are no bodies, so something happened to break off the fight."

"Here we go," Lola said, pushing aside some rotten wood at the base of the stump to reveal two spent .357 cases.

"*This* is what I was looking for."

Cutter had reloaded here—maybe just topped off after a couple of shots, Lola couldn't tell. She decided not to take the time to search for more brass.

The spent ammo lit a fire in Lola's belly. Arliss Cutter was the most capable guy she'd ever worked for or with, but he was in trouble now. She could feel it in her gut. And if there's one thing Cutter had instilled in her, it was to trust that niggling gut when it spoke to her.

The terrain steepened considerably. Rotten logs bigger around than her waist crisscrossed the forest floor. Blacks and greens and browns ruled the day, smudging back other colors. The skids and scuffs in the ground grew deeper, more widely spaced. Lola imagined Cutter and Lori running. But were they running from someone or after them? Cutter would have done some of his tracking voodoo and figured it out. The bastard. He made it look so easy.

The tracks suddenly cut left into a depression that Lola guessed was an old trail. The ground leveled some, running along an exposed granite face just taller than her head. It was easier going here and she had to remind herself not to run faster than she could read the ground.

Then the tracks stopped.

A slab of moss-covered earth had sluffed down the mountain on a slurry of mud and gravel fifteen feet across.

"What do you think?" Van Dyke asked, breathing heavily from the fast climb. "Landslide?"

"Yep," Lola said.

But what had caused it? She skirted the loose gravel and rock, and found tracks on the other side, leading along the same overgrown trail.

"Let's hurry," Lola said, pointing up the mountain, urgency welling in her belly. "This slide looks fresh. Cutter's close. I can feel it."

CHAPTER 48

Under normal circumstances—above ground where people were meant to live—the tiny candle flame beside Donita Willets's cot would have hardly been noticed. Down here, in the darkness of her underground prison, it was bright enough she could turn off her headlamp unless she was reading. The little flame served three purposes. It told her there was oxygen, chased the darkness away from her little nest, and kept her from sliding any further into insanity.

Pacing beside her cot, she checked her phone. The intense glow from the screen reflected off her face, which she knew was slightly scrunched from the helmet straps. She'd thought of taking it off, but the frequent clatter of rocks falling from the high ceiling made her decide to sleep in it.

She kept the phone on airplane mode to save battery, but switched that off for a few seconds. Maybe a miracle signal would somehow beam down through the portal at the far end of the huge man-made cavern and bounce around on the rocks until it found her.

There was nothing, of course, but living in a pit could make you think crazy stuff.

She switched back to airplane mode and consoled herself

by swiping through some pics—Levi in his boat on a sunny day, looking happy; some old ones of her mom during the all-too-infrequent healthy times between rehab and falling off the wagon.

Sighing, she switched off the phone and set it gently under the rolled jacket she used as a pillow at the head of her cot.

Near the opening, a rock fell from the ceiling, bounced off the ledge, and then smacked the ground.

"That was a big one." She whispered to herself a lot now. Anything louder seemed freaky, out of place.

A second rock hit the ledge below the opening, then stopped. A shower of smaller stones followed, some piling on the ledge, others clattering to the floor.

"Levi?" she said, breathless, barely audible, even to herself. Finally, he'd come back and she could leave this horrible tomb. She snuffed out the candle, and all but ran to meet him, keeping to the edges to keep from getting brained by falling rocks. The angle of the portal let in very little light except for up on the ceiling.

Donita stood against the wall beneath the ledge next to the dangling ropes. She kept her headlamp on its dimmest setting so as not to blind Levi when he started down. Frantic to see his face again, she cupped a hand to her mouth to call up.

More rocks fell, which was weird. Levi was more careful than that. He had to know that she'd be down here, going stir-crazy waiting for him to come back. He was supposed to whistle before he came down, signal it was him and that she was safe.

She pressed her back against the rock face. Gravel continued to pour over the lip of the ledge—but no whistle.

The climbing rope to her right swayed, and then the

carabiner attached near the ground began to rise as someone started to haul it up. Levi had used this one to get out and then lower the water down to her. Someone gave the rope to her left a tug. Her ascenders still hung on the dangling line, one above the other. Anyone who pulled up the rope and saw them attached would know she was still down here.

She thought of trying to take them off, but the rope was already rising. She'd need slack to release the cam that held them in place. Instead, she drew the folding knife Levi had given her. Holding slack above the cut so anyone at the top wouldn't feel the sudden increase in tension, she managed to saw through the line moments before it rose out of her reach. The cut would look suspicious, but not as much as the ascenders at the end of a rope.

The ropes disappeared over the ledge. She clicked off her light and trotted as quietly as she could back around the wall to her cot. She switched the headlamp to a dim red glow, hoping it couldn't be seen from above, and then scooped up her bedroll and cot and shuffled behind the largest of the stone support pillars in the small beetle-head room. She chanced one more quick trip to get her pack and then ducked behind a second pillar with her back to the underground pool. She switched her headlamp off and waited. In the darkness behind her, droplets of water plopped into the underground pool. Rocks continued to chatter against the floor, echoing through the Great Hall.

Donita thought she heard voices, held her breath, still hoping it might be Levi. A whirring buzz suddenly pierced the darkness, whining loud enough to cover the noise of persistent rock fall. Bats? No. She'd been here long enough she would have seen bats. The whir grew louder, filling the cavern, bouncing off the rock. It seemed to be coming from everywhere at once.

The buzz of ten thousand bees.

It was almost on top of her now, waiting on the other side of the column, daring her to show herself.

Donita covered her ears and clenched her eyes tight, pressing tears of fear through her lashes.

Darkness was absolute—but it didn't matter. She didn't have to see to know exactly what it was.

CHAPTER 49

Lori Maycomb sloshed through ankle-deep water, shoulder to shoulder with Cutter. Every breath filled her lungs with more of the dark that never came back out, making her heavier and heavier until she felt sure she would collapse. The tiny pools of light from their headlamps were far too feeble to help her steady herself in the unbearable closeness of the mine. Cutter walked in silence, waiting for her to unburden herself, surely unable to imagine the things she'd done.

She jumped when he spoke, gasping in more darkness.

"You can change your mind," he said.

"No . . . I . . ." She looked sideways, aware of her lamp and not wanting to blind him. "What would you do if your wife got so drunk she woke up next to some guy in a homeless camp?"

Cutter walked in silence for a time. "I have no idea."

"Right answer," Lori said. "I'll spare you the lead-up, but my drunk brain told me booze was far more important than my husband and our little boy. I remember going to Anchorage to work on a story, and telling myself I'd just have a couple of beers at a little sports bar in midtown. A couple of beers turned into seven, and all the little bottles of liquor from my hotel minibar—even the baby Patróns, and I hate tequila. Every day for a week, I tried to outdo my previous record. The lady at the Brown Jug even started to cajole me when I went in. I stopped calling home the third day. By the fourth, I stopped answering my phone. The next day, I lost the phone in a bar somewhere. Six days in, I was trying to stumble back to my hotel room when I saw a drug store off Northern Lights that was having a sale on box wine. . . ."

Lori shuddered as the memories came rushing back.

"The next thing I know, I'm waking up in a tent under the trees in some greenbelt in midtown. I had no idea how I got there, or how I met the lump asleep beside me. I mean, I love my husband. I drink, at least I did, but I don't pick up men. Ever. And still, there I was, next to a toothless guy who somehow convinced my drunk brain that I should party with him in his tent."

She checked Cutter's face. Still impassive. He was a better sin eater than he let on.

"Anyway, he smelled like old socks and stale urine, but then, so did I by this point. My wallet was on the ground beside him, the money gone. He must have passed out before he . . . you know. I just . . . I puked right there on the tent floor, then again outside. I think I left a trail all the way to the road.

"Anyway, I ran until my feet bled, wanting to put as much distance between myself and the situation. Then I caught a glimpse of a reflection in the window of a Subway sandwich shop, a barefoot Native woman with a snotty nose and matted hair. It hit me like a train. *I* was the situation. It didn't matter how far I ran, I'd still be there. I tried to wash up in a coffee shop restroom, but the hipster barista ran me off in the middle of my spit bath."

Maycomb sighed, giving Cutter a pitiful look, not because she wanted sympathy. She just couldn't manage anything else. "So there I was, barefoot on the streets of Anchorage, with sopping wet hair and cry-swollen face. I fell down on my knees on the corner of Northern Lights and . . . I don't know where . . ." She began to cry but kept talking. "My heart was not strong enough to tell my drunk brain to quit drinking. People talk all the time in AA about rock bottom. Well, that day was my rock bottom—not that I'd nearly let some drunk guy go to town on me in his tent, but that I'd totally forgotten about my husband and son, the most precious people in my life.

"I flagged down the first Anchorage cop that I saw and told him I was a drunk and wanted to get sober. He believed the first part, but was not so sure about the last. Six days in detox, another month of in-patient, and they gave me my old job back at the radio station in Juneau. You know, the worst part? The worst part is that my husband took care of our little boy the entire time without a word of argument or threat. He never filed any papers, no protective orders, nothing to tell the courts what a shitty mother I was. I have no idea why, but he took me back—and then he died. Suddenly. A headache. Dead."

Maycomb slogged along in silence for several steps, then gave a halfhearted shrug. "It's pretty easy to see why Rockie hates me."

"You told your husband everything?" Cutter said at length.

"All of it. More than I told you."

"And he took you back," Cutter said. It wasn't a question, but she answered it anyway.

"Yes."

"Seems to me, that's all that matters. Detective Van Dyke

is going to think what she's going to think. My granddad used to say that we can't change someone else's mind, we can only change ourselves and let things shake out like they shake out."

"Sounds too simple."

"The principle is simple," Cutter said. "Following through with it's hard as hell. I'm not big on pop psychology, but I will tell you this—everybody on earth's got a secret sin. Something they know without a doubt is so much worse than everybody else's sins. Most of the time, they're not worse, they're just different."

"Have you got one?"

"Indeed I do," Cutter said. "And I will spend the rest of my life making amends for it."

"Will you—"

"Not a chance."

Cutter played his headlamp across the gray rock face at the end of the tunnel. Maycomb had given up a lot, but he wasn't the sort of guy to ask questions. If she wanted to say more, she was welcome to. Until then, he needed to reach Donita Willets.

Two rough-cut pieces of timber stuck a few inches above a dark void at the base of the wall. Cutter stood at the edge, toes against the ladder, looking down. The ladder was probably as old as the mine, well over a hundred years. Hand-hewn timbers formed the uprights, as well as the crosspieces. Water from the tunnel floor cascaded in a small but steady fall over the rungs, keeping them wet and, Cutter hoped, from wasting away to dry rot. In its day, the ladder had been hell for stout, capable of holding the weight of miners and heavy gear. But now . . .

Cutter put a boot to the top rung, pressed, but didn't commit.

"It's more hope and rust than it is wood," he said. "But it seems to be holding."

"For now," Maycomb said, unconvinced, Eeyore-like.

Cutter peeked over the edge, exploring the bottom to see what sort of jagged rocks and mining tools he would impale himself on if the ladder disintegrated. The shaft appeared to widen into a larger room below. The water pouring over the edge turned the bottom ground to a muddy slurry. For all Cutter knew, it was a bottomless pit of gunk, but a splintered dynamite crate and a rusted coffee can beneath the hole made him believe it was no more than a few inches deep. He dropped a rock the size of his fist, watched it splat and then sink halfway into the ooze. The water had to be going somewhere.

Bracing himself on the uneven rock wall, he leaned forward to point his light farther back in the open room. He slipped on the slick floor, caught himself, and then began to turn his helmet back and forth, scanning the muddy cavern below.

Maycomb's hand shot to her mouth when the beam illuminated something pale at the edge of the shadows. The shapes were too regular for rocks.

She gasped. "Are those bones?"

"Too big to be human," Cutter said.

"Aliens then," Maycomb groused.

"More likely a horse or a mule. Probably spent a good deal of its life underground, maybe even born down here without ever seeing the light of day. Odd that the miners would just leave the dead carcass to rot in this spot. It would have been a straight shot to cut it up like a moose and haul the pieces out. Something must have happened . . ."

"Like what?" Maycomb asked, eyes locked on the bones. Absent any sunlight to bleach them, the bones had absorbed the minerals in the mud that surrounded them, turning the color of a terracotta pot.

Cutter shrugged off his pack and set it on the ground.

"You're going to use the rope?" Maycomb asked.

"Nope." Cutter slipped on his thin Mechanix gloves to give him some level of protection from hundred-year-old slivers of wood. "But that pack is thirty pounds the rungs don't have to hold if it's not on my back. Drop it down to me when I get to the bottom."

Maycomb began to chew on a hangnail. She looked up at Cutter, then said, "I know, I know. No smoking."

Cutter used the lip of the shaft to lower himself into the hole, descending slowly. He added pressure gradually to each successive rung, one foot at a time, probing, testing, before committing both feet to repeat the process. He had a vague idea that he'd grip the uprights if one of the rungs gave way, letting his feet crash through while the shattering wood acted as a brake. But they held. The idea sounded insane anyway by the time he reached the bottom, like something from a superhero movie.

"Toss it down," he yelled when his feet hit firm ground.

Water gurgled somewhere in the shadows, like the last few inches of dishwater in a sink. He put his light on the bones first. A heavy-duty leather harness lay half embedded in the mud with the skeleton. Some of it had decayed along with the flesh that it rested against, other bits looked almost serviceable. A pear-shaped loop of rolled leather and several smaller straps lay in the mud beside the pelvis. Cutter recognized it as a crupper, the strap that went under the tail of a mule or horse with low withers to keep the saddle or harness in place. He was right. Likely a mule.

The fact that the animal had just been abandoned there at a well-traveled junction to rot began to eat at his curiosity. He scanned the room, trying to make sense of it.

Maycomb's voice tumbled over with the trickle of water from above. "I'm coming down," she said.

"Nice and slow." Mud sucked at his boots as he stepped to the base of the ladder to steady it. He sniffed the air, suddenly wondering if it had been gas that had killed the mule. If that were the case, he'd already be dead.

Maycomb made it down the ladder quickly, unwilling to spend any more time than necessary in a pitch-black tunnel by herself.

She brushed remnants of the wet timbers off her hands when she reached the bottom, and immediately began to chew on her fingernail again.

"It seems a little cooler down here to me," she said.

Cutter didn't say it out loud, but by his calculations, they were three hundred meters inside the mountain and six hundred meters deep from the peak. It didn't seem like a factoid a person with claustrophobia would want to know.

"Must have been a large pocket of ore here," he said, scanning the chamber.

The oblong room was roughly twenty by thirty feet, with an arched ceiling just higher than Cutter could jump. It was empty but for the dynamite box, the coffee can, and the old bones.

Closer inspection revealed that the gurgling sound came from the center of the room where water seeped into a down shaft, or winze, that had been backfilled with tailings.

"Must be another tunnel running beneath us," Cutter said. "Otherwise, this place would have . . ." His voice trailed off as he studied water marks, high on the walls. "That's what killed the mule," he said. "At some point, this entire chamber flooded."

Maycomb stared at the gravel sump in the center of the floor. "So somebody filled in our escape tunnel. Now we're basically screwed."

"No," Cutter said. The beam of his headlight bounced off the rock as he sloshed toward the far end of the room, away from the ladder. "The shaft we want should be back here."

He stopped cold when he reached it.

Maycomb came up beside him. "And . . . we're still screwed."

Like the one they'd come down on, a heavy timber ladder descended into the shaft—only this one was filled to the brim with crystalline water.

"Let's see your phone again," Cutter said, holding out his hand like a surgeon waiting for a scalpel. He'd never been one to panic, but this had him worried.

Maycomb dug the phone out of her jacket and passed it to him. "According to Horning's map," Cutter said, "in order to reach the larger stope—and the way out of this mountain—we have to drop down this winze about thirty feet, travel laterally through another tunnel for a hundred and change, and then climb thirty feet up another shaft." He ran a hand over the rock face at the back of the chamber. "The place we need to be is on the other side of this wall."

"Over a hundred feet," Maycomb said, chewing on her hangnail again. "Every inch of it under water. Might as well be on the moon."

Cutter stooped and pointed his spare headlamp into the flooded pit. The light faded to an eerie green shadow toward the bottom. The base of the wooden ladder was just visible in the deep. He dipped his fingers below the surface.

"Fifty degrees or so," he said. "About the same as the air. Chilly, but doable."

Maycomb looked up at him in horror. Her hair, absent the elastic ties since he'd borrowed them for the tracking stick, stuck out in all directions from under the helmet.

"Doable? Are you shitting me? Even if you could dive down twenty feet, then swim through what is basically a rock pipe full of cold water for a hundred-plus feet, what's to say the shaft out of the big room isn't backfilled like this one? The way you want to go might not exist." She spun away from him and began to pace, alternately folding her arms and then dropping them so she could chew on her nails. "That does it. Even the condemned get a last cigarette—"

Cutter put a hand on her arm.

"Let's have a biscuit," he said.

"You're out of your mind!" Maycomb snapped, eyes wide. She stepped backward, putting distance between them. "I don't want one of your biscuits."

"Suit yourself," Cutter said, willing himself to stay calm. "That water's awfully cold. Easy to get hypothermia if we're not careful."

"I'm not going in that."

Cutter took a bite of biscuit, washing it down with a slug from his waterbottle. "Completely understand," he said. "I'll go get help. We'll dig you out from the other direction."

"I'm not staying here by myself!"

"Lori," Cutter said. He was trying hard not to sound condescending. "We have only two choices here. It is safer for you to stay here, but I'm not making you do anything."

He took a biscuit out of the ziplock bag. "In any case, I need to use the baggie as a waterproof housing for my light." He put that biscuit in a second ziplock with two more and handed them to Maycomb. "Not sure how long it'll be before we get you out, so you hang on to these."

"Seriously, Cutter," Maycomb said. "We're talking about you going into a water slide that might be plugged on the other end. There won't be any place to come up for air. If the way out is blocked, then you have to make the same trip again—without a breath."

He peeled off his jacket. It would only slow him down.

"I happen to be a pretty good swimmer."

"Well." Lori wagged her head. "I'm a pretty good drowner."

"I thought you were waiting here."

"Alone?" Lori hugged herself. "Not a chance."

"I'll come back and get you," Cutter said.

She sniffed. "And what if you die?"

"Then you would have died too," Cutter said. "Make your way back to the entrance and start digging. Someone will likely get you out."

Maycomb looked stricken, like she might throw up.

"Likely? What does that even mean? Likely . . ."

"Better to be honest, don't you think?"

"No!" Maycomb snapped. "Not at all. I'd like you to paint the rosiest picture possible if you please."

"Good to know . . ."

Cutter winced, lowering himself into the crystalline water. Fifty-degree air was not bad. Fifty-degree water was bone-numbing. He'd considered taking off his boots but decided against it. He'd need them on the other side—if he got there.

"Cold?" Maycomb asked.

"Not at all," Cutter lied. Already exhausted and chilled to the core from his earlier swim from the wharf, his teeth began to chatter immediately. "Warm and toasty, like the water off Manasota Key, if I'm painting rosy pictures."

He flicked on the headlamp inside the sealed ziplock bag. All the air had been pressed out, leaving the baggie flat but for the small light. Submerged up to his neck now, he lowered the light into the water, illuminating the eerie scene below. The underwater housing appeared to be working, for now. Pressure and time and good old Mr. Murphy tended to break things during the most crucial moments.

One hand on the ladder, his chin quivering an inch above the chilly water, he gave her a rare smile.

"Seriously," he said, "everything is going to be just fine. I do this kind of thing every day."

CHAPTER 50

All the guys at the mine called Harold Grimsson the Wannabe Viking. Any real Viking would have been drinking from the old man's skull by lunchtime on the day they met him. The shootout had knocked him off his game—and his game was mostly a bunch of yelling and screaming to begin with, when Childers drilled right down on it.

Now Grimsson had them standing around the portal to the Cross Cut mine, while he tried to pull his head out of his ass and decide what to do. Dollarhyde was working the drone, looking for the girl. So far he hadn't seen shit, which was making Grimsson apoplectic.

"We should blow it!" Grimsson said. "Tell me you see her down there. Rig a charge, Childers."

Childers looked to Dollarhyde, who gave an almost-imperceptible shake of his head. *Belay that order.*

That's how it went, every time things went even a little sideways. The old man's booming voice and huge black beard gave him the appearance of a berserker. He often appeared to go crazy, but always within unspoken boundaries, which wasn't berserk at all when Childers thought about it. It was more like one of those sideeyed tantrums bratty kids throw where they constantly look at their mommy to make sure they don't go too far.

Most of his edicts came on the back of tyrannical rages riding a torrent of slobber and threats. But everyone who worked for him knew him for the kind of guy who bellowed until his eyes bugged, but then looked hard at the reactions of those around him before moving forward with any plan. He liked to stand around instead, hoping someone with a better idea would argue with him. That way, if their plan worked, he could take the credit because he was in charge. If it failed, he could rub their face in the fact that he should never have followed their advice to begin with.

It would have been funny if it weren't so tragic.

With nothing else to pound on during his rant, Grimsson slapped his own thigh, peered at the drone display in Dollarhyde's hands. "We'll blow it to hell and her with it . . ."

Dollarhyde did as he was expected and countered with a plan of his own.

"We *could* blow it, sir," Dollarhyde said. "But this is a large stope and we don't have a line of sight. That means the drone will only go back so far."

Grimsson wiped his mouth with the back of his sleeve. "But she was down there?"

Dollarhyde kept his eyes on the display. "Little doubt about that. Bottled water, a stove. Someone's set up a home."

"So we blow it!"

"We have two fixed ropes," Dollarhyde said. "One with the ascenders topside, the other with no ascenders at all. That could suggest she's down there, or that she came up on her own. For all we know, she's out there now, behind some tree, just waiting to slip back to town and spill her guts to the FBI."

"Send the drone in deeper!"

"That's a no go, sir," Dollarhyde said. "It just returns to where it last had line of sight. I'd guess there's twenty to thirty percent of the stope that's beyond our reach."

"I never expected *you* to go squeamish on me," Grimsson said.

Dollarhyde looked up slowly from the drone controller, staring daggers at the boss. "Mr. Grimsson, I will happily drop a rock on that child, or shoot her, or gut her, or, as you are so fond of saying, cut off her head with an axe. But to do that, we need to find her."

Childers took his eyes off their back trail long enough to watch Grimsson and see how he'd handle this. As suspected, the old man waved it off. Dollarhyde always seemed to know just how far he could push. That dude was about as wily as—

"Childers!" Grimsson snapped. "Get on one of those ropes and see if she's down there."

Childers looked at Dollarhyde for approval.

Grimsson gave him a little nudge on the shoulder. "Don't look at him! Get your ass down there and kill her."

Childers considered tossing the old man over the edge, and would have if he'd nudged him again. Some shit you didn't put up with, even from your boss.

Grimsson handed him the rope with the ascenders attached.

"I've got a rappelling brake in my pack," Dollarhyde said, apparently on board with the plan.

"There's a chance she has a gun." Childers's eyes narrowed, daring the other men to press him. "I'm not scared, but I'm not about to get my ass shot off."

Dollarhyde handed Grimsson the drone controller and then stooped to dig through his pack. "I wouldn't worry about that. Even if she does have a gun, I doubt she can shoot it."

Childers took the rappelling brake without speaking.

Grimsson hunched over the controller now, convinced he could make the drone perform better than Dollarhyde. "Find me something that says she's still down there. Then we'll bury her."

And me too, Childers thought. He ignored Grimsson altogether and said, "Mr. Dollarhyde, I'd suggest you come down with me on the second rope. Two sets of eyes will be better than one."

"You'll be fine," Dollarhyde said.

Grimsson flicked a hand toward the ledge, his eyes glued to the controller screen. "One of you get your ass on that rope."

Childers leaned in close to Dollarhyde, taking advantage of the moment the old man's attention was on the drone.

"I'm not going down there by myself."

Before Dollarhyde could counter, Childers pulled the bone rattle half out of his jacket pocket, enough to reveal the carvings and bent sheep horn. "I got this from Schimmel," he whispered. "According to that archeologist you dumped, this is worth at least a half million."

Dollarhyde's face lit up at that. "I'll hold on to it for you."

"Not a chance," Childers said. "You come down there with me. That way I know I have an insurance policy. A way out. We'll get rid of the girl and Grimsson and then sell this."

Dollarhyde gave a contemplative nod. Which was lucky for him, since Childers had already decided to shoot him in the face if he balked at the plan.

"What are you two women nervous about?" the old man snapped.

"Childers is right, sir," Dollarhyde said. "Two set of eyes will be better." He gave a wry smile. "But I'll take the explosives with me, just to keep everyone honest."

Dollarhyde didn't mind the dark or the height, but it made him feel weak that Childers had the advantage of experience when it came to rappelling. Still, he was a fast learner and he zipped down the rope. The headlights made them sitting ducks, which was more than enough incentive. His feet crunched against the gravel floor seconds behind the former Marine.

Dollarhyde drew his pistol the moment he unlatched his carabiner. He glanced sideways, drawing a withering squint from Childers.

"Get that outta my eyes!" the younger man hissed. "You're killing my vision."

Not one to apologize, Dollarhyde turned his head in a slow arc, playing the powerful light around the cathedral-like stope. He was smart enough to know that there was a hierarchy in situations like this, where title meant little to nothing. The one with the experience called the shots. Still, he pretended he was in charge of Childers—just like Grimsson did to him.

Childers aimed his headlamp at a small mountain of supplies—canned tuna salad, crackers, potato chips, and a couple of jugs of water. A couple of Pop-Tart wrappers littered the ground beside a half-burned candle on a flat stone.

"I think she's back there," Childers whispered. He motioned with his pistol toward a dark spot where the cavern narrowed and the ceiling dropped.

"Take a look behind those pillars," Dollarhyde said.

Childers put a finger to his lips and then stepped to

where he was cheek to cheek with Dollarhyde. "Switch off your light."

"Off?"

Childers's voice was menacing, viper-like. "You want to find her or not?"

Dollarhyde groaned, playing along.

There were few places darker than a mine. Certainly not caves.

Caves formed over time, a partnership with the earth. They were growing, living rock. Dollarhyde had always thought of mines as dead, the husk left over after a mountain was gutted of everything important, full of a darkness far beyond the mere absence of light. Childers's shoulder brushed his as soon as their lights went off.

Gravel rustled as he crouched to the ground. A faint clatter said Childers had picked up a rock. Dollarhyde could see absolutely nothing, but the sounds and movements beside him made him picture Childers drawing back like a baseball pitcher and then hurling the rock toward the stone pillars at the back of the stope. The crack of rock against rock was extra loud in the blackness. Childers repeated the process, two more times, each time turning slightly to throw toward a different pillar. Dollarhyde took a half step back to be certain he didn't catch one in the head from close range.

The third rock hit one of the pillars on the right, cracking like a gunshot. Between the clatter of stones and the splash as it hit the wet floor, Dollarhyde heard a sound that brought a smile to his lips.

A sudden rush of breath. Donita Willets, choking back a scream.

CHAPTER 51

Lori Maycomb stood over the flooded tunnel, gripping the sealed plastic bag tightly in a trembling hand. Cold, crystalline water swirled at her feet. Gray walls closed in around her. Her breath came in ragged gasps.

He'd abandoned her. Or, had she abandoned him? As terrified as she was to be left in the dark mine shaft, it had to be worse for Cutter. The pit in her gut told her to dive in and help him—but that was just crazy. She just couldn't do it. It was too deep, too cold, too dark. She'd surely die if she stayed put, but there were few things worse than drowning alone, deep in the bowels of a mountain—except for letting yet another person down at the end of her short and miserable life . . .

Darkness followed Cutter. In front, behind, above, and below, everywhere outside the blue-green bubble formed by his headlamp and makeshift ziplock housing, was a blurry wall of impenetrable black.

Legs above his head, he flutter-kicked downward, working to stay in the center of the shaft to avoid clouding the water with silt.

His arm movements made the light move wildly at first, throwing shadows against the jagged rock, disorienting and causing him to lose time zigzagging down the shaft to keep from bashing his head. He'd run into the pool wall once at speed, racing with Ethan when they were teenagers. The impact had nearly knocked him out. Pain used up precious oxygen. Here, with no place to surface, such a mishap would prove deadly.

Cutter saw the portal for the drift seconds after he started his dive. It was arched, about six feet high, like the other tunnels and shafts in the mine. He pulled himself down and around with his free hand, fighting the natural buoyancy that kept pressing him into the ceiling of the tunnel. His foot grazed the rocks. He turned to plane downward, bashed a shoulder into a jagged edge. The impact traveled up his arm as an electric shock, causing him to drop the baggie with the headlamp. He flailed for it, missed, and watched it sink behind him while momentum carried him forward. He extended both arms, putting on the brakes, which caused him to rise immediately. Rolling sideways, ensuring that his shoulder struck the ceiling before his head, he pushed off with one hand while swimming toward the light with the other.

He scooped up the light with one hand, careening upward like a submarine on emergency blow.

Cutter had calculated he'd need about forty-five seconds to traverse the 100 plus feet once he reached the tunnel, but that hadn't taken into account having to spend so much energy keeping himself off the top. His stupidity with the light had just added another eight seconds—an eternity when you're running out of air.

Buoyancy semi-controlled, he fell into a kick-kick-adjust-plane-downward-repeat rhythm.

His heartbeat throbbed in his ears. *Still less than eighty beats per minute*. Slow, he thought, considering the effort he had to make to keep from shredding himself on the rough ceiling—not to mention the relatively high probability of dying alone.

Had he been in a pool or a lake, Cutter could have traveled half again as fast for the first dozen yards, maybe even the entire hundred feet, but he had no way of knowing if he would hit a wall at the other end—and be forced to turn around and swim all the way back on the same breath. If Horning's map was right, a round-trip would be a little over two hundred feet—a little less than half the world record for underwater swimming. But records were set under ideal conditions.

Cutter pushed the possibility of a lonely death out of his mind and concentrated on his rhythm.

Seconds ticked by. His heart raced faster now, drumming in his ears until he could hardly hear himself think. His lungs screamed for fresh air. His throat tightened, begging to expel the carbon dioxide in his lungs, and the remainder of his oxygen along with it. To breathe was suicide, but his body was sending signals that it no longer cared about such logic.

He blew out a tiny cloud of bubbles, hearing them burble past his ears, a compromise with his lungs. Exhaling helped some with his buoyancy control, but cold and fatigue had cost him more than he'd thought.

There was no way he could make it back if he had to turn around.

Panic fell away at the realization. He sped up, eager to get to the end, one way or another. But the tunnel went on and on and on. The impulse to breathe was overwhelming, disrupting his kick cycle, impairing his ability to swim in a straight line, overriding all other thought.

The light flickered in his hand, went dark, then flicked back on again. Cutter kept kicking, but brought the baggie close to his face. As he suspected, the plastic bag had torn, probably when he'd dropped it or tried to grab it. Maybe it hadn't been watertight from the beginning. It didn't matter now. The headlamp was flooding.

Two more kicks and the light stopped working completely; the blackness closed in around him.

Swimming blind now, Cutter struggled to stay oriented. The whooshing squeal of his pulse echoed in his head. His shoulder struck the wall hard, jolting him with bone-numbing pain. There was surely a cloud of blood there, but he couldn't see it. He pushed away, as if fending off an attack. The movement pushed him upward, slamming him into the arched roof. Tooth-like outcroppings ripped at his shirt, gouged his flesh. Bubbles from his own escaping breath burbled past his ears as he careened upward again, a torpedo stuck in a closed tube.

CHAPTER 52

Donita Willets had recognized Childers and Dollarhyde while they were still sliding down their ropes. Light from the headlamps created long shadows, but there was no mistaking the cruelty on their faces. It was not enough for men like this to kill her by sealing off the mine.

They wanted to watch her die.

She cowered behind the support pillar farthest from the mouth of the Great Hall. Her back to the black pool, she'd run as far as she could. Levi hadn't left her with a gun, but she had the knife on her belt. She would not make it easy for them.

The men turned off their lights. Maybe they had night vision. Or one of those devices that looked for heat. She pulled her arms tight against her body. It was over if that was the case. She choked back a sob. It was over anyway, no matter what they had.

Something cracked against the wall behind her, splashing into the pool. Instinctively, she inched around the stone pillar, away from the sound. Another snap echoed in the darkness, then another, this one clacking off the rock inches from her head. She drew a quick breath, caught herself in mid-yelp, but it was too late. They'd heard her.

Now it was over.

Mumbled voices buzzed by the far pillar like angry wasps. They were close now, where the Great Hall narrowed to become the smaller beetle's head. Scornful laughter cut the darkness—and then quiet. Nothing but dripping water, the periodic clatter of rocks—and her own terrified breathing.

Then a strange hissing sound filled the cavern. It stopped, letting the dripping water and falling rocks take over for a time, before starting up again. At first she thought it was closer, behind her maybe—or to her right, or her left. The hissing sound grew louder, coming from everywhere at once. She'd been to Arizona, Texas, the places with snakes. If this was that, then there were hundreds of them, filling the Great Hall.

Sssssshhhhhhhh. Like a sinister rain.

It stopped.

"Donita!" a voice said, sneering. Childers. "You and me, we have some things to talk about."

The *ssshhhhh* started again.

"Levi sends his regards, by the way . . . at least I think that's what he was boohooing about right before I blew his brains all over the wall."

Donita's knees buckled at the revelation.

"Anyway," Childers sneered. "Your dude's not coming to rescue you, so you can put that shit out of your pretty little mind."

A sob caught hard in Donita's throat. Hopelessness washed over her.

Sssshhhhhhhh.

"You're Indian," Childers said. "Ever seen one of these before at your powwows or whatever you guys do up here? I guess it's some kind of witch doctor bone rattle. We got it from one of your buddies, next to a rotten skeleton." He chuckled. "The guy who had it before me thought it was cursed."

A voice yelled down from the portal above, echoing around the Great Hall. She recognized it as Harold Grimsson. "She down there? Somebody tell me what's going on! Kill the little bitch and get out!"

If Childers heard the orders, he ignored them—for the time being.

Donita couldn't see from her vantage point behind the stone column, but she imagined him shaking a Raven rattle.

Sssshhhhhh.

The horrible hiss threatened to swallow her whole. Tears ran down her cheeks. She wanted to plug her ears but was afraid to move.

"I don't know," Childers went on. "Maybe this thing is cursed. Hey, maybe the old bones we found it with belong to one of your Indian relatives. Maybe I should bury it down here with you. Put it under the earth again where it belongs."

Sssshhhhhh.

"You know what, though? This ugly old bone rattle is worth a buttload of cash. I think I'll just hang on to it for now. I don't believe in curses anyhow. Do you, Donita?"

Ssssshhhhh.

"What do you say? Ready to get this over with? If I remember right, you're not too hard to look at. It could be me on top of you instead of a ton of rock. At least one of us would enjoy—"

A voice pierced the darkness to Donita's left, somewhere near one of the other pillars.

"Now!"

It was Dollarhyde. He'd worked his way around while Childers talked.

"Took you long enough," Childers said.

Both men flicked on their headlamps, flooding the room with light but momentarily blinding them in the process.

"Come on, Donita," Childers said, menacingly, darker than the mine had ever been. "This is getting boring. Let's spice things up!"

"I see her," Dollarhyde said. "She's—"

An ungodly croaking sound filled the Great Hall, bouncing off the roof and walls. Water erupted from the black pool, like the tail of a great fish breaching the surface. Another deep croak rose from the blackness, followed by more splashing.

Adrenaline spent, Donita slumped behind her rock, numb. One way or another, she was about to die, either at the hands of these two men or this creature from beneath the mountain rising from the inky water.

She mustered the energy for a blood-curdling scream. Dollarhyde's scream put hers to shame.

Headlamp beams went crazy, bouncing this way and that as the men scrambled away from the dark form that emerged from the black pool. Dollarhyde screamed again— backpedaling into one of the stone columns, bouncing off to stagger toward Childers and firing wildly into the water.

CHAPTER 53

Thirty seconds earlier

Cutter dropped the useless headlamp and rolled onto his back. Facing a ceiling of stone fangs that he could not see, he hauled himself along, hand over hand, rock to rock. The thin Mechanix gloves protected his hands at first, but he bashed his forehead twice, nearly knocking himself out, before he learned to keep his arms relatively straight and his hips arched. In effect, he crawled across the top of the tunnel, creating the necessary distance to avoid ripping off his nose on a hanging crag.

Not quite two minutes into the dive now, the edges of his mind began to fray.

He could see perfectly now in the crystalline-green water. Grumpy swam beside him, younger, like when Arliss was a boy. Ethan was there too. No longer alone, Cutter decided to give in, to breathe. He wanted to talk to his grandfather again. To let go and stop the crushing pain in his chest. The cold water could have him.

Grumpy pointed a finger, silently chiding him. He'd have no talk of quitting. Ethan dolphin-kicked alongside, challenged him to a race—like the old days. And then Barb, his last wife, was there, her shoulder brushing his. She was always an excellent swimmer. Flowing hair enveloped her face in the water, long, like before the chemo. And her smile . . . she looked so much like Mim . . .

Mim.

Cutter pulled harder. The gloves were in tatters now, and he shredded his knuckles on the knife edges of rock, grabbing, hauling . . .

And then there was no more rock above him, only a column of water. He felt his lungs expanding, and the sensation of floating upward. He kicked, feebly at first, then harder as he realized he'd made it.

Light shimmered above him. People. Danger. The closer he got to the surface, the more his lungs expanded and the faster he rose. He knew he should slow, for safety's sake, but he had to have air. Caution was worthless if he drowned. He broke the surface like a missile, shooting out of the water almost to his waist. A long, croaking breath filled his lungs with sweet, wonderful air.

More light. Screams. Echoes.

Cutter inhaled deeply, feeling his vision clear with each lungful of air. He blinked, trying to get his bearings amid the chaos. Pistol shots boomed off the rock walls, slapped the water around him, forcing him to dive again, back into his airless tomb. Oblivious to the cold now, all he could think about was air. He needed to breathe.

Underwater, he kicked his way to the far edge of the pool, fifteen or twenty feet away from where he'd first surfaced. A stone outcrop no larger than his head offered momentary cover from the searching lights. He allowed himself two quick, shivering breaths, before reverting to slower combat breathing, abbreviating the cycles because of his hypoxia. In for a three-count, out for a three-count. Water drained from his ears. His pulse began to slow enough that he could discern voices.

"Holy shit!" It was Slick's voice—from the gunfight on the mountain. "What was that? A falling rock?"

"That wasn't no rock!" another voice said.

Tough Guy, the rifleman. Cutter had robbed him of the long gun, but he'd proven himself plenty handy with the pistol.

Cutter blinked, moved slowly to wipe the excess water out of his eyes. Both men wore climbing harnesses. Headlamps illuminated their faces, the beams playing this way and that, crossing each other, then stopping to study some spot before moving to another. So far, Cutter remained in the shadows.

The girl he assumed to be Donita Willets wasn't so lucky. Cutter could see her clearly from his vantage point. Tough Guy sent a round slamming into the stone column where she was hiding, sending her scurrying around it for cover. If she went too far, she'd expose herself on the other side.

She screamed again.

"Would you just shut up!" Tough Guy barked. He held something in his hand. The bone rattle. "Who else is down here?"

Something boiled in the black water to Cutter's right. He heard a noise he couldn't place. Tough Guy jumped at the sound. He dropped the rattle and spun toward it, using two hands to fire a couple of snap shots from his Glock into the middle of the pool.

Behind Tough Guy, Slick stooped to grab something from the ground. He spun on his heels, the light from his headlamp bouncing and bobbing on the far wall as he hauled ass back to his rope—bone rattle in hand.

Pressing against the rock deck, Cutter used the diversion to push himself up and out of the water. He'd intended to draw his Colt as soon as he was up, but cold and fatigue cramped his muscles. He stumbled forward on numb feet for the cover of a stone column—and almost made it.

"Hey there," Tough Guy said, his light settling on Cutter, still three feet from the rock support. "Got some friends in the water, do you?" The Glock was aimed directly at Cutter's chest. He had the advantage and he knew it.

Water drained from Cutter's clothes. His Xtratufs were full. Running would be a joke. He raised his hands to shoulder level, opening and closing his fists to get the blood flowing. He kept his voice low, soothing, trying not to look like too much of a threat, which wasn't hard considering he looked more like a drowned rat than a deputy US marshal.

"Only me."

"Bullshit!" Tough Guy snapped. The pistol remained rock steady. "Dollarhyde, cover the pond," he said, so focused on Cutter he wasn't aware that Dollarhyde was halfway up the rope. Cutter spoke again, drawing Tough Guy's attention back to him. If he felt suddenly isolated, he might go ahead and shoot. And Cutter needed a second or two longer to get the circulation back in his hands.

"I . . . s-swear." He didn't have to affect the chatter. "It's only me."

Tough Guy's headlamp bobbed slightly as he nodded to the Colt Python. "Mighty big *pistola* you got on your belt there, sport."

"For bears," Cutter said. He made a fist, held it, then opened his hand slowly.

"Bears?" Tough Guy tilted his head to the side, studying Cutter's face. "I know you," he said, anger welling up with each word. "You're the son of a bitch that shot my rifle."

Grumpy had taught both his grandsons the art and science of gun fighting, long before Cutter had joined the Army or come aboard with the Marshals Service. Speed and accuracy both counted, Grumpy always said, but neither were worth a damn by themselves. *"You might have the skill to shoot the nuts off a fruit fly at a hundred paces while sighting over your shoulder with a dental mirror,"* Grumpy would say, *"but if you can't do it fast, that kind of pinpoint accuracy is worthless."* It might not win many trophies, but exceptional speed with decent accuracy was far superior to decent speed with exceptional accuracy.

Tough Guy's face darkened. The Glock rose a hair.

Action was faster than reaction, but Cutter would have to draw, acquire his target, and fire. Tough Guy simply had to squeeze the trigger. Cutter relaxed his hands, letting them sag a couple of inches. He took a fluttering breath, which Tough Guy took for fear.

They stood a dozen yards apart. An easy shot if Cutter hadn't just been submerged for two minutes in muscle-cramping water.

Cutter picked a spot on the man's chest. Took another breath.

Settling himself. Hearing Grumpy's no-bullshit voice in his ear.

Demonstrating with his shot timer, Grumpy started every range day the same. *"A BEEP will be your signal to fire. When you hear the B, I want your gun hand dropping to that holster—the gun should be out and shooting your target by the EEP."*

Water splashed again to Cutter's right—

"B . . ."

Cutter's hand dropped to the Colt. Muscle memory acquiring the same grip his fingers had formed thousands of times. The pistol cleared his holster at the same moment Tough Guy's eyes flicked toward the splash—

". . . EEP."

Cutter shot him twice. The first round went low as the Colt was still coming up, slamming into his pelvis. The second punched a neat hole just left of center mass.

Cutter felt like his shots were on target, but he didn't stand and wait for a postmortem. He sprang for the cover of the support column as soon as he'd fired his second round.

Tough Guy cried out, the kind of bellowing roar a man made when mortally wounded. He was dead on his feet, but not yet out of the fight. Firing twice as he fell, he put two rounds into the rock directly beside Cutter's face, spraying his eyes with razor-like fragments of granite.

Cutter ducked behind the column, touched his cheek, felt blood. He couldn't open his left eye at all. The vision in his right was dim, blurry.

He heard Tough Guy fall, his pistol clattering to the rock with its distinctive polymer Glock rattle.

"Cutter!" It was Lori Maycomb's voice. Through the haze, he could see she was leading Donita Willets.

"Dollarhyde made it up to that ledge," Willets said.

"Tough Guy?" Cutter said, more than half blind now.

"You mean Dallas Childers?" Lori said. "You got him. He's down. Seriously, we have got to go now! When Dollarhyde makes it out, they'll blow the ledge. The whole place is coming down on top of us."

CHAPTER 54

Lola Teariki stooped to study a boot print that had crushed a mushroom underfoot. Streaks of bright red oozed from the flattened remnants of the bone-white fungus.

"This looks like blood," she said.

Detective Van Dyke worked a flank position, slightly ahead of Teariki a few yards to the side of the presumed trail. Her sidearm was out, where Lola's remained in its holster. Van Dyke took her eyes off the shadows ahead long enough to glance at the track.

"It's called bleeding tooth," she said. "Tooth?"

"A kind of fungus that grows around here," Van Dyke said. "Bleeding tooth. Devil's Tooth. Looks like drops of blood oozing out of that gnarly white flesh. Pretty gross if you ask me."

"Something new every day," Lola said. She was already moving, looking for the next discernable track.

The trees were smaller here, more widely spaced. Mottled shadows from the thinning canopy shifted with the breeze over a carpet of mossy ferns and stones. A few more steps revealed the entire side of the mountain, hundreds of feet across, was an old tailing pile. The guts of the mountain, now long grown over.

A raven *ker-lucked* in the treetops.

Van Dyke stopped in her tracks, raising her open hand.

Lola froze, listening. Wind rustled the spruce bows. A halfhearted rain pattered here and there on alder and ferns. Then she heard it too. Voices.

Now she drew her pistol, carrying it muzzle down, away from Van Dyke.

The women sidehilled slowly, stepping over and around fallen trees and mounds of rock. Springy moss and a recent rain masked their approach, but they needn't have bothered. Less than a half minute later they stood at the black mouth of a mine tunnel cut into the mountain. Two men, just inside from the sounds of it, were engaged in a fierce conversation, oblivious to the rest of the world.

"Throw me the damned thing," a deep voice growled.

"You put a knot in the rope!" This one was strained, higher. Angry-scared.

"Insurance," the gruff one said. *"Didn't want Childers sneaking up and cutting my throat. I hear pretty good, you know. Now pitch the rattle up to me."*

"You'll leave me," the scared man said, panting. *"Pull me up."*

"I will," the growler said. *"But you'll need both hands. Throw. Me. The. Rattle."*

Her Glock hovering just below her sight line at low-ready, Lola began to cut the pie, sidestepping slowly around the outer edge of the mine portal, bringing the dim interior into view inch by inch. Van Dyke did the same from the other side.

"Grimsson!" the tight voice said, frantic now, hollow

inside the mine tunnel. *"Wait! You're throwing away a fortune. Half a million according to the archeologist."*

Lola recognized the terrified voice as Mr. Dollarhyde, from the Valkyrie Mine Holdings offices.

"Hand it to me, Ephraim," Grimsson said. *"Then I'll pull you up."*

"Okay, Okay . . . Take it. Wait! What are you doing? Wait! I took all the explosives with me. . . ."

Grimsson's voice dripped with contempt. *"Turns out you didn't,"* he said. *"Like I said, I hear pretty well, you traitorous son of a bitch!"*

Lola button-hooked into the mine entrance, her back pressed tight against the wall.

Beyond the wooden frame supporting the arched alcove, the floor fell away into a huge cavern. Less than a dozen feet inside the portal, Harold Grimsson was on his knees, leaning over the edge, bone rattle in one hand, a black plastic box in the other.

"US Marshals!" Lola barked. "Do not move."

Grimsson remained on his knees, but half turned. His thick beard pushed to one side as he peered over his shoulder. Eyes ablaze, surrounded by dark rock and black pit, he looked like the Devil himself peeking down on Hell. Lola could not remember ever seeing anyone looking quite so much like the embodiment of evil.

"Marshals?" Grimsson said.

"Police, asshole!" Van Dyke said. "Stand up slowly."

Grimsson gave a slow nod, eyes closed. Groaning, he got to his feet.

Dollarhyde's whimpering voice came from the darkness. "Police? I'm down here. He was going to kill me. I'll tell you everything. The US attorney, the Fawsey kid, all of it. Just get me off this rope."

Grimsson turned to stare over the edge again, focusing the intensity of his wrath on the man dangling a few feet below.

"You worthless—"

Dollarhyde gasped. "You're going to kill me!"

"You and Childers had the same in mind for me!"

"That's enough!" Lola said. She nodded at Van Dyke, who gave the orders.

"Walk backward toward my voice, hands above your head."

"Shoot him!" Dollarhyde screamed. "He's got explosives!" Grimsson peered over the edge again and began to rail on Dollarhyde, ambivalent about the two guns pointed at him.

He shook the rattle at Dollarhyde, working himself into a frothy rage.

"You were never loyal to me! Always in it for yourself." Rattle in one hand, Grimsson pounded his fist on rock wall as he screamed. "I oughta cut your traitorous head off!"

"SHOOOOOT HIM!" Dollarhyde yelled. "Shoot him or we're all dead!"

Lola recognized the electronic controller, like a television remote, in Grimsson's fist—the same fist that he was now bashing into the rock wall in a screaming fit, oblivious to the fact that his thumb hovered a hair away from the button.

Grimsson's rage had reached a full lather. He drew back to pound the wall again.

Lola yelled for Van Dyke to move at the same instant she hooked around the rock the way they'd come in. Both women dove downward, away from the concussive rumble. Rock and fire shot from the portal like a cannon blast directly over their heads. A second blast followed on the heels of the first, knocked Lola off her feet, and sent her tumbling down the mountain.

CHAPTER 55

"Hurry," Maycomb said, "before I lose my nerve!"

Cutter turned his head, struggling to bring her into focus with his semi-good eye. "I'm going to need some help," he said.

She answered by grabbing the front of his pants, above his belt buckle, and pulling him closer.

The action was jarring in its intimacy. He pulled away instinctively, but she held fast.

"Trust me," she said. And tucked a flat stone under his belt. "Easier this way."

Above them, Ephraim Dollarhyde begged for his life.

Maycomb led Cutter to the edge of the pool.

Dollarhyde let loose a tattered scream.

"Time to go!" Maycomb flicked on the headlamp in her baggie and dove headfirst into the water. A bewildered Donita followed. Cutter took a deep breath and dove in behind them.

They swam hard, pulling downward, reaching the turn into the drift thirty feet down just ahead of the shockwave that propelled them forward like an unseen hand. Cutter rolled off the rocks, tumbling, trying to keep Maycomb's light in view through the blur. She bounced off the bottom, stunned by the force. He grabbed her hand, pulling her up. She in turn grabbed Donita, guiding her. With no need to conserve energy for a possible return trip, they swam quickly, breaking the surface together, back in the mine tunnel, a minute and seventeen seconds from the time they started.

The force of the shockwave had sent a geyser of water out of the shaft and knocked the wooden ladder sideways. Cutter straightened it and then stayed in the water, pushing Donita Willets while Maycomb helped her out of the flooded shaft. Spent, oxygen starved, and chilled to the bone, his teeth were chattering badly. He wondered if he'd have enough energy to haul himself up the wooden rungs.

He remembered the rock behind his belt buckle.

"Nice touch," he said, letting it fall before starting his climb.

Maycomb got another light from her pack, illuminating the tunnel, turning the water a cool aquamarine. She held her hand toward Cutter. "I was right behind you, watched you struggle with floating to the top. I didn't want to waste time looking for rocks while I held my breath, so I came back up and grabbed one here to help me be less . . . floaty."

The water had washed some of the debris from Cutter's eyes, but his vision was still clouded.

"Thank you," he said. "Guess you overcame your fear."

Maycomb scoffed. "The hell I did," she said, hollow, like she might cry. The aftereffects of stress caved in around her as surely as the mine. "I'm still scared shitless of tight places. I'm just more scared of staying in them all by myself."

Soaking wet, she folded her arms tight across her chest. "We made it out of there before Grimsson blew it, but we're right back where we started. Nothing's changed."

Donita spoke next, softly, still getting her bearings.

"You saved my life," she said. "That's changed. *Gunalchéesh*."

"Don't thank me yet," Maycomb said. "We're still stuck."

"But the explosions," Donita said. "Surely someone heard them."

"Maybe," Maycomb said. "As far as we know, everybody will think we all died in that cave-in."

"You're probably right," Cutter said.

"I am?" Maycomb said, crestfallen. "I thought we talked about this telling the hard truth thing."

"I'm not saying we're all doomed," Cutter said. "I'm saying we need to be our own rescue."

Donita began to sob, in shock. "Did Childers . . . ? Is Levi really dead?"

"I don't know." Cutter peeled off his sodden shirt and put on the merino wool top from his pack.

Maycomb changed into a dry thermal top as well, offering a crushable down jacket to Donita in place of her wet shirt.

"Do you think someone will look for us?" Donita asked.

"I think so," Cutter said. "But what I know is that we need to start digging from this side."

"And what if they don't?" Maycomb asked.

"Same thing." Cutter shouldered his pack. "We dig."

CHAPTER 56

An orange US Coast Guard Jayhawk overflew the mountain twenty minutes after the explosion. Five minutes after that, a Trooper helicopter touched down in the clearing above the cave-in. USFS LEO Bobby Tarrant, two troopers, and three FBI agents, including Supervisory Special Agent Beason, got out to find Deputy Lola Teariki and Detective Rockie Van Dyke, bruised and bleeding but alive.

Tom Horning was the last to exit the helicopter. Absent the plaster cast, he wore a dark-blue walking boot and fairly skipped down the mountain with the aid of two trekking poles.

He caught Van Dyke looking at the boot and gave a tense shrug. "I cut the damned thing off. Had an itch—to be up here helping."

"Thanks," Van Dyke groaned. Her hearing was shot from the blast and she spoke much louder than she needed to. "But it's kind of over now."

One of the troopers checked Lola and Van Dyke for trauma, while Beason stood and looked at the large depression in the mountain.

"Are we sure they were in there?"

"Grimsson, Dollarhyde, yes," Van Dyke said. "They were the ones behind the AUSA's murder."

Beason shook his head. "I don't care about that right now. Cutter and the reporter. Were they down there?"

Lola bowed her head, tears welling in her eyes. "They must have been." She sniffed. "We were behind him the whole way, all the way here."

"Did you see him go in?" Beason asked.

"No," Lola said. "I never did see him. He was always a mile or two ahead." She buried her face in her hands, muffling an angry sob. "But I was on his tracks."

Beason prodded. "Are you sure they were his?"

Lola nodded, her face still covered, her voice taut. "We found some of the spent cartridges for his Colt, then followed the tracks past the first cave-in, to where we came across Grimsson."

"What do you mean, first cave-in?" Tom Horning asked.

Lola stared up at the sky in despair as she explained the rock slide over the trail.

"Sounds like the second entrance to the Cross Cut." Horning gave the area where the blast had occured a tip of his head. "This is . . . was also an entrance to the Cross Cut mine."

Lola's jaw fell open. "You mean they could have gotten out at the other end?"

Horning grimaced. "The passages in between are flooded. But we should probably take a look at that other rock slide. That tunnel is open for a couple hundred yards before it reaches the water."

Lola lead the way, up and moving before the rest of them could make a plan.

* * *

Special Agent Beason found blast marks on the rocks above the first slide while Lola studied the tracks.

"You said you found Cutter's spent brass?" the FBI supervisor asked. He sat on a flat rock, on the slope of the hillside.

"Down there," Lola said. She pointed down the mountain into the forest.

"Let's think about this," Beason said. "Cutter and that reporter get in a firefight with Grimsson and then they run up here."

Lola and Van Dyke nodded in unison.

Van Dyke patted the flat rock. "So Cutter and Lori make a stand here. But the bad guys blow the tunnel shut, sealing them in."

Lola dropped to her knees and began turning over rocks, gently at first, until she found what she was looking for two feet in from the outer edge of the rockslide. She pointed to the Xtratuf track, faint but visible in the dirt. "I've been following the particular crease in that heel ever since the shoreline. That's Cutter's boot—and it's pointed toward the mouth of this tunnel, not away from it. He went inside, not past it like I originally thought."

Not daring to hope, she picked up a rock and sent it tumbling down the slope. Frantic with worry, she picked up another, and then another, clawing at the dirt and rock until her fingers bled.

Horning, seeing she was going to dig harder than anyone else, with or without tools, gave her the gloves from his back pocket.

Van Dyke, Tarrant, the troopers, and the FBI agents, including Charles Beason, joined in. An hour in, a team of deputy marshals showed up in a chartered helicopter jumping out with picks, pry bars, and looks of grim determination.

Most of them still wore business suits, straight from their protection details over Judge Forsberg and the surviving assistant US attorney. They'd heard what was going on and hauled in diesel-powered construction lights from the clearing a half mile away.

By sunset, the area around the mountain looked like a small city, with a first-aid station, rain shelter—thankfully it hadn't been needed—and Porta Johns. A trooper wife had sent up a plastic tote full of sandwiches, but so far, they'd remained untouched. Everyone focused on excavation.

Tom Horning ran the operation. He'd dug out enough old mines to know what made them tick—and how to open a mountain without having the rain-soaked earth crash down around his ears. His wirehaired dog, Kat, scampered around the dig, sniffing, helping.

An hour after dark, the little dog homed in on a particular spot. She whined, then stuck her toffee-colored snout in a narrow crevice, and began to dig. One of the FBI agents got down on all fours to listen, shouting that he thought he could hear tapping from under the rocks. Like ants, the group focused their efforts in that spot, careful not to cause another slide as they cleared away debris.

Kat barked.

"I see a hand!" one of the deputies yelled.

Lola redoubled her efforts. Tears streamed down her face.

"Fingers are moving," someone else said.

"That's Donita Willets's ring!" Van Dyke said. "Her aunt gave us a photo." She took the hand in hers.

Rocks began to fly off the mountain, exposing a forearm, and then an elbow.

Lola stepped back, allowing the others to work. She looked up at Tom Horning.

"The route in from here to that big room where Donita was supposed to be was flooded?"

"The stope," Horning said. "Yes."

"Could a person swim it?"

"Theoretically, yes, but they'd have to be a hell of a swimmer—"

Lola threw herself flat against the rubble, pressing her face to the rocks. "Hold on, boss, we're coming for you!"

Beason shot her a quizzical look.

"You hear him?"

"No, sir," Lola said, digging again, "but if Donita Willets was on the other end, and now she's here, then Cutter went and got her."

"And you know this how?"

Van Dyke gave Donita's little hand a squeeze where it stuck out of the crevice. She smiled at Lola. "Because he does the right thing, right now."

"Damn straight," Lola said.

Fifteen agonizing minutes later, they pulled the girl free of the slide. Lori Maycomb followed, coughing and sputtering. Van Dyke wrapped her wet sister-in-law in a wool blanket and led her to the first-aid tent, not quite forgiving her, but not ready to throw her back in the mine either.

Cutter crawled out next, soaked to the skin and covered in a layer of mud and shards of rock.

He swayed uneasily on his feet as he pushed himself out of the mountain. Lola caught him by the arm. Amazingly, he let her hang on and envelope him in a frantic hug. She would have kissed him if she thought he would have stood for it. He was alive. That was all that mattered. Unwilling to let him out of her grasp, she held him at arms' length, to check his injuries. His left eye was swollen completely shut. His right squinted at all the lights.

Lola held him up while the other deputies crowded in around him.

When he spoke, his words came slurred, drunk from shock and exhaustion, and to her delight, he leaned on her for support.

"What's going on? Y'all having a party?"

CHAPTER 57

The ophthalmologist in the Juneau emergency room dug six pieces of stone out of Cutter's eyes. Three of them bore flecks of gold. The doc put those in a tiny glass vial and sent Cutter on his way with a bandage over his left eye, an order for a good night's sleep, and a promise to go in for a follow-up when he got home. The flight back to Anchorage wasn't until after noon. He went to the hotel for his second hot shower of the day; then Lori Maycomb joined him and Lola for a burger at McGivney's.

"Rockie couldn't make it?" Lola said, when Maycomb showed up alone.

"Turns out it takes more than a near-death experience to unhate somebody," Maycomb said. "But she's trying."

"She'd better," Lola said, sipping her lemon water. Her hair was up, and sweat beaded across her forehead from her intense workout in the hotel gym. "Did Rockie tell you we arrested two of the women and one of the guys who threatened you on the beach?"

"She did not," Maycomb said.

Lola gave a satisfied nod. "Looks like they were all three former employees of Valkyrie Mines. Dollarhyde apparently brought them back on for some contract work. The lady from HR admitted to hearing him talk to them about convincing a Native reporter she needed to leave Juneau for a while."

Maycomb closed her eyes and sighed. "Thank you."

"How you feeling?" Cutter asked.

"Honestly," she said, "I feel like I need a cigarette."

Lola looked up from her water. "But not a drink?"

"So far, so good," Maycomb said.

"I'd think recent events proved you're tough enough to handle anything," Lola offered.

"Wish it worked like that," Maycomb said. "Gotta take it one day at a time, every time. As soon as I start thinking I'm tough enough to go this on my own—that's the day I'll screw it all up."

Cutter gave her an understanding nod.

"I'm fine, though," she said. "Really. For now, anyway. And I got some cool material for my novel."

Cutter passed her the little glass vial the doctor had given him. "This is all the gold I'll ever get out of a mine. I want you to have it. You saved my life. *Gunalchéesh.*"

Maycomb's jaw dropped. "You heard Donita say thank you in Tlingit one time and you remembered it?"

Cutter shrugged.

"I know, right." Lola spoke around the straw clenched in her teeth. "Welcome to my world."

Cutter's phone buzzed in his shirt pocket. It was Mim.

"Excuse me a minute," he said. "I need to take this."

"You're writing a book?" he heard Lola ask as he scooted out of the booth and walked toward the door, his phone still buzzing.

"Yeah," Maycomb said. "Your boss gave me the theme without knowing he was even doing it."

"How's that?"

Lori Maycomb sat transfixed on the door where Cutter had disappeared. "You'll have to read the book."

Cutter answered the call and found a bench outside under the hotel portico, where he could whittle while he talked. His hands were bloodied and sore from frequent collisions with rough rock, but he couldn't stand to have them idle.

"What did the doctor say about your eyes?" Mim asked first thing.

"I'll be fine."

"Fine you won't die?" she asked. "Or fine you'll have a cool eye patch?"

"Fine, I'll be fine," Cutter said, chuckling. "No cool eye patch, unless you think a white piece of gauze is cool."

"Seriously, Arliss," Mim said. "Your eyes . . . ?"

"He said I'll be good as new in a couple of weeks. The chief ordered me to take at least a week off."

"Good for her," Mim said.

Cutter paused with his knife, looking at the wood, seeing nothing. Later maybe. He folded the blade and put it away. Just as well, his depth perception was shot for the time being and he was likely to cut his thumb off.

"I'm really sorry about the way this wrecked your vacation."

"The kids are out of school for the rest of the week," Mim said. "I was thinking, we could start smaller, maybe drive down to Whittier, go through the tunnel, eat at the Swiftwater if it's open."

"The Swiftwater?" Cutter said, not caring where they ate. He was just happy Mim was going to let her boys hang out with him again after everything that had happened.

"Yeah," Mim said. "If that's okay. I really like their rockfish and chips. And we could walk the docks and look at boats. The boys would love that."

Looking at boats was Cutter's weakness, and she knew it.

"Well," Cutter said, testing the water. "My depth perception is going to be a little off for a few weeks with this eye thing. I just might walk off the pier into the water."

Mim laughed, the way she'd laughed when they were sixteen. "I think I can help you out with that."

EPILOGUE

Anchorage PD patrol officers worked four ten-hour shifts per week. It was great if you had family, or hobbies, or wanted time off, but all Joe Bill Brackett could think about during those three days off was getting back to work. He'd only had two days on his own before his first weekend. There was overtime duty, but the senior guys scooped that up—and Officer Brackett was about as junior as you could get in the APD pecking order.

His first night back he got punched in the ear, talked a young woman out of jumping off the A-C Couplet onto the tracks, and Tased a guy on meth who wanted to fight—he didn't intend on getting punched in the ear again.

All of that was exactly what he'd signed up for, but what he wanted to do was hunt down whoever was hacking up girls and dumping them into the ocean. He'd phoned the detectives three times over his weekend to check on status, until Sergeant Hopper called and told him to cool it in his no-nonsense Texas drawl.

It was raining now, but Brackett didn't care. He was back at work, and life was good—but for one tiny detail.

Officer Fluke's weekend usually only overlapped with his by one day, which was a blessing. Two shifts of that guy was a gut full. Unfortunately, Fluke had done a tour trade with another officer so he happened to be working.

And that worthless son of a bitch got the call.

A body off the Tony Knowles coastal trail near Bootlegger's Cove.

The call was North, Brackett was assigned to South, but he didn't care. He attached himself anyway.

Fluke waved him off over the air, but good old Sergeant Hopper countermanded him and told Brackett to "come ahead on."

All the way down by O'Malley when the call came in, it took Brackett a few minutes to get there, windshield wipers thumping, water spraying around his tires. He prayed that he wouldn't come across an accident on the way. He'd have to stop if that happened, giving Fluke far too much time to screw everything up. Brackett consoled himself when he realized Fluke wouldn't likely want to be out of his car for very long in this downpour.

Nearly there, Brackett slowed to work his way through the neighborhoods below downtown Anchorage. He drove down O Street until he got to Nulbay Park, where he saw other patrol cars.

Sandra Jackson, the uniformed investigator, was already there, sitting behind the wheel of her white APD Impala. The light of her phone lit up her face.

Brackett killed his headlights and parked behind her, grabbing his raincoat.

She rolled down her window when he approached.

"Hey, Joe," she said. Her expression was tight, grim.

"What do we have?" he asked.

She scrunched her nose, squinting, like her face hurt, then rubbed her eyes.

"Another girl," she said at length. "Or a piece of one, anyway."

"Shit," Brackett whispered.

"I was on the phone with Homicide just now," Jackson said. "We're supposed to hold the scene until they get here. In other words, don't go poking around and screw everything up."

"Is Fluke down there?"

She shook her head. "Fortunately, he's taken up a post under that awning, out of my way."

"Same MO?" Brackett asked, not knowing what else to say. He wanted to go down there but didn't want to piss off the homicide guys. They barely talked to him now.

She nodded. "Killer's getting sloppy, though. I took a couple of photos before Homicide told me to back off, if you want to see."

Brackett tried to sound nonchalant. "Sure."

She motioned him around to the passenger side. "You'll have to squish in by my MDT, but this way I can roll up my window."

The inside of Officer Jackson's car smelled so much better than his—like coffee and shampoo, where his smelled like . . . not that.

She passed him the phone as soon as he shut the door.

Brackett zoomed in to reveal a female foot, cut off just above the ankle. It was hard to tell from the photo, but the foot looked relatively fresh, like it hadn't been in the water more than a day.

Jackson pointed at the phone. "Like I said. He's getting sloppy."

The rain picked up, battering the windshield.

Brackett enlarged the photo all the way to reveal a tiny gold ring around the index toe.

"And look at her nails," Jackson said. "Each one is a different color. I guarantee you, somebody is gonna recognize this girl."

ACKNOWLEDGMENTS

The image of a lone deputy US marshal saving the day plays well in Hollywood or on the printed page, but I learned early in my law enforcement career it was better—and much safer—to ask for help.

And so it is with writing a novel.

As with every book, I spent hours talking, and in this case, walking, through the various man-tracking and fight scenes contained in *Bone Rattle* with my longtime friend and former partner in the US Marshals Service, Jujitsu Master Ty Cunningham. We sat around a campfire near his home in Southeast Alaska discussing human conflict, wilderness tracking, and long-range shooting.

A significant portion of the story takes place underground. Through a stroke of luck, a coincidental introduction from Ty's sister-in-law on an early research trip to Juneau put me in contact with Peter Nestler—jump rope master, multiple Guinness Record holder, and world class fine-art photographer. Visit his website. You won't regret it. Peter also happens to be a genuinely nice human being. He and his wife guided me on my first trip into an abandoned gold mine and then introduced me to a friend of theirs named Brian Weed.

As it turns out, Brian is a real-life incarnation of Indiana Jones when it comes to adventuring. He spearheads a group called Juneau's Hidden History (check out the amazing photos on their Facebook posts) and is surely one of the most knowledgeable people in the area when it comes to historic mining sites. Brian; his wife, Mareta; and their super cool dog, named Kat, opened their home to me during subsequent research trips and guided me on some incredible excursions underground. Many of the locations described in *Bone Rattle* are taken directly from these adventures.

The whole gang from Juneau's Hidden History invited me on several hikes and even hosted a dinner during my last research trip to Juneau. During the course of my visit, I wished many times that I didn't have a deadline so I could throw my hat in and join one of their adventures—over mountains, down rivers, or deep into some mine; it didn't matter to me.

Someday.

My dear friend Brian Krosschell answers countless questions about life in rural Alaska and provides a sounding board (and source) for many of my ideas.

Though this story is set in Alaska, much of it was written on the island of Rarotonga, ancestral home of Lola Tuakana Teariki. My wife and I have made many wonderful friends in the Cook Islands over the years—Bill Rennie, Peter Heays, Jolene Bosanquet, Carey Winterflood, George and Karleen, Amber and Jaret, Jean and Brian, Rod and Lily, Paul and Gabrielle, Mike and Pauline, Vikki, Naomi—all of whom contribute continually to Lola's character, culture, and my writing life in general during our stays in the South Pacific.

I have one of the best literary agents in the business in Robin Rue of Writers House. Gary Goldstein, my editor at Kensington, is a gem of a guy. More than just colleagues, both have become my good friends over the course of many years and a few million words. In fact, the entire gang at both Writers House and Kensington Publishing are nothing short of stellar.

My friends with the Anchorage Police Department and the United States Marshals Service continue to be a constant source of inspiration and guidance.

It's a fortunate writer indeed who has a partner who listens, plots, critiques, applauds, cajoles, and edits like my wife, Victoria, does for me. I was thinking the other day how patient she's been over the past three (almost four) decades, allowing me to disappear into my mind as I wrote several hours each day—half of that time getting nothing from publishers for my efforts but rejection letters.

In one way or another, all the best characters in my books are inspired by her.

RECIPES

Grumpy Cutter's Venison Stew

Note: Grumpy's version calls for venison and a Dutch oven. Arliss uses caribou and cooks it in an Instant Pot. Moose, bison, Dall sheep, musk ox . . . or even beef may be substituted.

3 tablespoons olive oil
1½ pounds caribou cut into cubes
1–2 teaspoons salt
1–2 teaspoons pepper
1 tablespoon Montreal Steak Seasoning (or similar)
½ cup red wine
1 large onion, chopped
2–3 cloves garlic, minced
3 cups beef broth
2–3 tablespoons Worcestershire sauce
3–4 Yukon gold potatoes, cut into big chunks
4–5 carrots, cut in big chunks
2 tablespoons cornstarch
1–2 tablespoons water

Add 2 tablespoons olive oil to the Instant Pot and turn on the SAUTE function. When the oil starts to sizzle add the meat and season with the salt, pepper, and Montreal

Steak Seasoning. Stir the meat until it has browned on all sides.

Scrape the bottom of the pot for brown bits as you deglaze with the red wine. Add the last 1 tablespoon of oil, onions and garlic and cook on the saute setting for two minutes, stirring with the meat.

Turn the Instant Pot off.

Add the beef broth, Worcestershire sauce, potatoes, and carrots. Lock the lid and check that the valve is set to seal. Set to cook for 35 minutes on HIGH pressure. It will take 7–10 minutes to come up to pressure. Cook on HIGH pressure for 35 minutes.

Allow for a natural release of pressure for 10 minutes when the cooking time is up, then move the valve for a final quick release of pressure. Meanwhile, whisk the corn starch and water together to make a slurry.

Add the corn starch slurry to the steaming hot stew, stirring continuously as it thickens. Stew is done and ready to serve.

Grumpy Cutter's Flaky Square Buttermilk Biscuits

3 cups all-purpose flour
2 tablespoons sugar
1 teaspoon salt
4 teaspoons baking powder
½ teaspoon baking soda
2 sticks butter, frozen (16 tablespoons)
1½ cups buttermilk
Melted butter

Preheat oven to 400°F. Prepare a baking sheet with a light spray of oil or cover with parchment.

In a bowl, stir together all the dry ingredients: flour, sugar, salt, baking powder, baking soda.

Grate the two sticks of butter and add to the dry ingredient mixture.

Gently combine until the butter particles are coated.

Next add the buttermilk and briefly fold it in. Transfer this dough to a floured spot for rolling and folding.

Shape the dough into a square; then roll it out into a larger rectangle. Fold by hand into thirds using a bench scraper. Press the dough to seal it. Use the bench scraper to help shape the dough into flat edges. Turn it 90 degrees and repeat the process of rolling it out to a bigger rectangle and folding and shaping it again. Repeat this process a total of five times. The dough will become smoother as you go.

After the last fold, and if time allows, wrap the dough in plastic wrap and let it rest in the fridge for 30 minutes. Otherwise, cut the remaining dough into 3-inch squares and place 1 inch apart on the baking sheet. Brush the tops with melted butter.

Bake at 400°F for 20 to 25 minutes. Let cool on a rack before serving—if you can wait that long.

Tips to remember:

- A buttermilk substitute can be made by adding one teaspoon vinegar to one and a half cups regular milk and letting it stand for a few minutes.
- Handle the dough lightly—don't overwork it.
- Freeze the butter. It makes it easier to grate and distribute it throughout the dough.
- For the very best results, your bowl and other utensils should be cold.

- Rolling and folding the dough 5 times produces the flaky layers—again, don't get too heavy handed.
- Shaping the dough into a square and cutting it into squares avoids waste and rerolling (and overworking) the scraps.
- If time allows, let the dough rest for 30 minutes, wrapped in plastic wrap in the fridge, before you cut into squares. This helps them rise tall in the oven without slumping or sliding.

Makes about a dozen biscuits.

**BONUS—turn the page for MARC CAMERON's
acclaimed Jericho Quinn novella,
Triple Frontier—available in print here for the first time!**

VENGEANCE HAS NO BORDERS

It's called the Triple Frontier—the volatile border zone
between Paraguay, Brazil, and Argentina, one of the most
lawless and deadly regions in the world. Where drug
lords, Middle Eastern terrorists, slave traders,
and dozens of other violent gangs operate with little
or no interference from the law. It's a corrupt sanctuary.
For special agent Jericho Quinn, it's the crossroads of
hell. Especially when his younger brother Bo gets caught
in the fire. Enlisted to protect the son of an
IT mogul on a South American trip, Bo and his crew
disappear after being kidnapped by a ruthless cartel.
Jericho amasses a cartel of his own to take on the most
vicious criminals on earth—far from home, without
U. S. government sanction, and without mercy.

Mess with the bull, you get the horns. Jericho Quinn style.

TRIPLE FRONTIER
A JERICHO QUINN THRILLER

by MARC CAMERON
National Bestselling Author

Read it now!

"Right knows no boundaries, and justice no frontiers . . ."
—Learned Hand

Nothing says "your prompt payment is appreciated" like the sight of another man's severed toe.

Justino Medina stared down at the open ring box on his coffee table, teetered for a moment on unsteady feet, and then collapsed into the cool white leather of his expensive couch. Fernando Richter did not offer a grace period. Delinquent accounts served two very important purposes: they demonstrated Richter's resolve to the other cartel bosses in *La Triple Frontera*, and they provided body parts to use as a billing notice for the next name in Richter's ledger.

Smaller sums might cost the debtor a finger or, as in this case, a big toe. If more was owed, more digits would be taken. From there, Richter moved to the teeth. Justino thought he would rather lose a few teeth than his fingers and toes, but Fernando Richter did not let his victims have a say in these matters. And in any case, Justino and his wife owed such a large sum of money, they simply did not have enough parts to cut off.

Angelica Medina came out of the kitchen carrying a

terracotta platter of baked cheese and *sándwiches de miga*—the trimmed whitebread finger sandwiches ubiquitous to Argentina. Two inches taller than her husband, she had high cheeks and the most exquisite of collarbones. She was absolutely breathtaking, well above Justino's station, and he knew it. Justino was bald, with an odd little ring of fuzzy hair like some kind of botched monastic tonsure. Angelica refused to let him shave his head or cover with a toupee. She, on the other hand, had thick black hair that she wore around her splendid face like the helmet of a beautiful Amazon princess. He could not understand why such an attractive woman had married a toad like him, unless it was because he could never bring himself to tell her no—as he should have done when she'd suggested they go into business with Fernando Richter, the Paraguayan boss most people referred to simply as "The German."

Angelica was a judge in the Misiones district court. As such, she was accustomed to order in her courtroom and the day to day activities of her life. Even a bloody toe on her coffee table could not dissuade her from afternoon tea and a subsequent two-hour siesta. She would certainly not be difficult to find if the time came for The German to start cutting.

Angelica gave her husband a peck on top of his bald head and then set the tray of food on the table, nodding at the bloody toe. "Cover that awful thing with a paper towel and have something to eat, my love."

She folded long legs under her bottom and sat down cat-like on the couch, leaning forward to spear a piece of baked white cheese with a wooden skewer the size of a large flat toothpick. A copy of *La Nación* lay on the couch beside her and she picked it up, flipping through it while she ate.

Justino sat with his mouth hanging open. "How can you be so calm?"

Angelica looked up from the newspaper and gestured with the wooden skewer as she chewed a bite of cheese. "What do you wish me to do? Weep? Chew my nails? I am a judge and you are a well-respected lawyer. We are intelligent people." She pursed her lips, the way she did when she was annoyed. "In any case, we have six days remaining."

"Six days with no prospects," Justino groaned. "My love, if we do not find the money to pay this monster . . ." He felt the overwhelming urge to chew his nails, but couldn't now that his wife had made it sound so cowardly.

This plan was completely insane, but for some reason, Angelica, one of the smartest women he knew, could not see it.

Going into business with Fernando Richter was dealing with a viper. He could be trusted to lie about everything but the time he would come to kill you. Not even an Argentine, he lived instead across the river, two rivers actually—the Iguazú that separated Argentina and Brazil, and the Paraná that flowed between Brazil and Paraguay—in Ciudad del Este, thief among many other thieves.

The Medinas knew of Richter. Everyone in the Tri-Border region did. One of Justino's clients had once said that The German had cut off his hand for nothing. Another man in the jail had overheard the conversation. "Liar!" the second man had said. "For nothing, The German only cuts off a few fingers."

Until now, Justino had been able to steer clear of any entanglements with the cartel boss and his violent associates. Then Angelica had gotten it into her beautiful head that they simply had to build an addition to their home. Like the devil who came when one uttered his name, Fernando

Richter had appeared from the other side of the river and offered to front them 1000 kilos of marijuana. The Medinas could, he said, take the drugs with a load of their soybeans bound for São Paulo, sell it there, and pay him after the fact. With Richter charging two hundred dollars per kilo they could double their money with buyers in São Paulo, easily paying him back his $200,000. It had seemed like easy money. The bulk of all the marijuana grown in Paraguay ended up in Brazil—and little of it was ever interdicted by authorities. Risks were minimal and the rewards were high.

Usually.

For the first time since they'd started shipping soy, their barge had been stopped by bandits on the Iguazú River. The marijuana had been stolen, leaving the Medinas no drugs to sell in São Paulo and therefore no profit to pay Richter back for his advance. He'd graciously given them one month to recoup his investment. In hindsight, The German had most certainly stolen the drugs himself. Justino had no doubt that his men had merely continued down the river to sell the marijuana in Brazil. Any money he got from the Medinas would be a windfall. If they did not pay him, he would simply kill them to keep up appearances. It cost him nothing, and from all accounts, he would probably enjoy it.

Justino leaned back and stared at the ceiling. They'd been happy before all this, padding their regular salaries and shipping income as *buscas panzas*. Literally *belly hunters,* they looked for pregnant women among the local population. Blue-eyed blondes of European heritage were preferable, but Guarani Indians were acceptable if that was all they could find. These indigenous women were so desperately poor that they could barely feed the children they had. It was usually a simple matter to convince them to sell one to a family who wanted to give it a better life. If the woman did not see the value of the transaction, Jelly or one of the other men who worked for Angelica would help them reach the right decision.

They had two such women now in the pipeline that were ready to pop, with couples from Buenos Aires prepared to pay ten thousand dollars for each baby. Any other time that would have been a great deal of money—but it was so far from what they needed that it might as well have been nothing at all.

"We could sell the house," Justino offered, still unable to eat. "Perhaps we—"

"This is our home," his wife scoffed. "And besides, no one would buy it in such a short time."

Justino groaned. "Then what do you suggest, my love? I happened to be quite attached to my toes and my teeth."

"Oh, Justo, you stupid, stupid man," Angelica said, without looking up from her newspaper. "We owe The German a great deal of money. He will surely cut off something much more important than a few toes and teeth."

"That does not help me feel better—"

Angelica held up her hand, judge-like, focusing now on something in the newspaper. "My love," she said, her leg suddenly bouncing with energy. "I believe I have found the answer to our prayers. Do you have your mobile?"

Justino fished into his pocket, holding up the phone when he found it, and trying desperately to control his breathing.

"Good," Angelica said. "Call Jelly and tell him to get the others together. We have a job for them among the *porteños*."

"Buenos Aires?"

"Yes, Buenos Aires." Angelica turned her copy of *La Nación*. At the top of the page was a photograph of what looked to be five handsome college students. Angelica tapped the face of the young man standing at the far left of the group. "I do not know about the others, but this one is worth a great deal of money."

Justino smiled at his wife and gave a long sigh. She was either crazy or brilliant. These young people looked to be riding their motorbikes on some long journey, an adventure Justino himself had dreamed of before he'd met Angelica. They had done nothing to deserve what she had planned. Still, something had to be done about the issue of The German. If these poor youths could provide the money to pay him back, well, then that was just the way it had to be. Justino took the paper, bringing it closer for a better look at the people who were about to pay for his mistake.

Four of them—two men and two women—were smiling. The fifth man, perhaps ten years older than the others, with shaggy blonde hair and piercing eyes, did not look happy at all.

Buenos Aires
Tuesday, 7:35 a.m.

Bo Quinn finished a breakfast of ham and cheese empanada and strong coffee and stepped out the side door of the Urbanica Hotel in the upscale Belgrano neighborhood to give the bikes one final check before the morning got underway. He was charged with the safety of the riders—and that started with their motorcycles. The morning was cool, a welcome respite from the weeks of riding in the heat. It was March—autumn in Argentina—and the seedpods were falling like miniature helicopters from the tall rosewood trees outside the hotel.

Mussed straw-colored hair brushed the tab collar of Quinn's Vanson jacket. His leather boots, once shiny black but now scuffed and a more respectable weather-worn brown, said he'd been at this riding business for some time. He bent at the waist and touched his palms to the gray paving stone, stretching his back and knees. Joints popped. Scar tissue complained. Old injuries—and there were many—ground bone on bone.

Bo looked after people. Some, he looked after by seeing that they got what they deserved. Others, that they did not.

Three of the riders under his stewardship who stumbled out of the hotel at that moment in varying stages of bleary-eyed stupor deserved to be protected. The fourth, a smarmy business school dropout with a perpetual case of bed-head, was another matter. The first three abided by Quinn's mandate of anonymity, but Matt King never met a photo of himself he did not love—and he posted all of them on his various social media accounts.

South America was no place to advertise the fact that you were a rich North American. Matt King either didn't understand, or he just plain didn't care.

Yesterday, Bo's fears had been born out when someone tipped off a reporter from La Nación to a photograph of the entire tour group on Matt King's Instagram account. They were all standing beside their bikes in front of the Urbanica Hotel like a bunch of carefree college students—as if one of their fathers didn't own a company worth upwards of five hundred million American dollars. It was just the sort of information you didn't want broadcast anywhere, let alone a country where quickly planned "express" kidnappings weren't exactly unheard of.

There was little Bo could do but cajole. He couldn't very well slap one of the kids he was supposed to be protecting. He did mention the incident in the nightly email to his employer the evening before, but so far, he'd received no reply.

Bo looked up and down the street at the morning traffic. It was normal, so far as he could tell. They'd make a run south to their next stop in Tandil to look at a few knife shops, and then end up in Bahia Blanca before dark. Hopefully, no one would be ballsy enough to try anything stupid against five American bikers in broad daylight. At least, the plan was to leave early and arrive before dark. Trying to get these guys going in the morning was trying to push a piece of wet spaghetti.

He checked each bike's tires while the group stowed their gear and checked emails for the tenth time that morning. Rich people didn't have to worry about pesky things like roaming charges and out-of-country cell data fees.

Two of the motorcycles were Harley Davidson Road Kings like Bo's. One was one a Ducati and the other, a Honda Africa Twin. All were loaded like pack mules with luggage and camping gear—though they hardly ever camped—leaning on side stands along the uneven walk in the chilly shadows of the hotel.

A tall woman sidled up next to the Africa Twin, eyeing Bo with a beautifully arched dark brow as she secured her tank bag. She wore armored riding pants similar to Bo's. Hers were black leather; his faded denim Tobacco jeans. A wide yellow headband swept back thick auburn hair, revealing a prominent widow's peak. Somewhere in her early twenties, Alma Cortez had impeccable taste about virtually everything but men. Bo would have loved to show her the error of her thinking, but sleeping with the girlfriend of a client seemed like a bad idea.

Alma's boyfriend moved in behind her to check the Ducati, textile riding pants drooping like he was carrying a load in the seat of his drawers. Matt King was the son of a real estate tycoon from Houston. The sultry Chilean girl had met him at a club in Dallas. His dark superman curl and quick wit had somehow concealed the more vaporous aspects of his nature, and for reasons Quinn could not fathom, she'd agreed to accompany King and his friends on this two-month motorcycle journey to the tip of South America. The young man seemed to realize the relationship was doomed and held on to it just a little too tight, never letting Alma get too far away for more than a few moments—especially around Bo.

"Alka-Seltzer," King demanded, rubbing his eyes with one hand while holding out an open palm.

Bo eyed the outstretched hand, weighing his options. In the end, he chose the one that wouldn't get him fired. "You borrowed the last from my kit yesterday."

King groaned. "Somebody's gonna have to go get me some more before we ride. My gut's on fire."

"I'll go," Alma said. "It won't take long."

Bo shook his head. "Nope," he said. "We're not going anywhere except as a group. Not after that photo stunt."

King rolled his eyes. "It's the twenty-first century, genius. People post stuff. Get over it."

"He's trying to help us, Matt," Alma said. "Cut him some slack."

Bo shrugged it off. It was something like this every day. Privately, he vowed never again to allow the offer of a large chunk of money to lure him into such a thankless job.

"There's a store a couple of miles away," he said. "We'll stop there on our way out of town so you can do the plop-plop fizz-fizz thing."

The other two riders, an attractive blond woman who was on the smallish side and an athletic young man with a shaggy beard attended to their own bikes. Eva Turcott and Steven Grey weren't quite engaged, but Bo was pretty sure it was going to happen any day now. The fact that Grey carried a diamond ring easily worth twenty grand in the pocket of his riding pants did nothing to help Quinn's fears.

The two lovebirds chatted quietly, oblivious to everyone else on the trip, and frankly, most of the world around them. Steven's father knew his son was in no mental state to ride to the tip of South America without a sheepdog to watch over him. Riley Grey was a biker himself, and had been friends with Bo Quinn since his dotcom company was barely a blip on the Internet. Few people even knew who Steven was, but he'd made the tabloids more than once and the elder Grey had decided it was a good idea to hire Bo to look after his heir. The state of the world made it an absolute necessity.

Bo threw a leg over his Road King and hit the ignition, letting the engine warm up while he slipped on his helmet and fastened the chin strap. For some reason, the others never seemed to realize it was time to get on their bikes until he started his.

When everyone was mounted and ready, Bo turned to look at the others before calling out over the Cardo Bluetooth on his helmet. Straddling their bikes, they looked like they did on most every other day of their journey—with Alma eyeing Bo in a flirtatious pout, Steven and Eva lost in a lovers' fog, and Matt's head up his ass.

Bo felt the first flutter of uneasiness ten blocks from the hotel when the truck in front of him slowed for a man with a hardhat and road construction flag past the Libertador tunnel. His brother, Jericho often said that the air smelled different just before a bad event. You just had to learn to recognize it. He took a deep breath through his nose, getting nothing but the sweaty odor of five thousand miles in the same helmet. "That's no help at all, brother," he whispered. Jericho would have called the nagging feeling in his gut by its Japanese name, *haragei*—"art of the belly." Bo tapped the rear brake with the toe of his boot and hoped he just needed to take one of Matt King's Alka-Seltzers.

The flagger directed the truck ahead to turn right, down a tree-lined residential street. Bo considered making a U-turn, but Matt hadn't quite mastered that basic maneuver and would have to duckwalk his motorcycle in the busy thoroughfare to go the opposite direction, slowing everyone down. The presence of a second flagger at the next intersection, assisting with the construction detour, brought Bo's nerves down a notch. The truck ahead made a left, paralleling the main street.

"Heads up," Bo said, mouth to the Cardo Bluetooth mic inside his helmet.

The truck in front of them slowed again, as if to make another left, forcing the riders to roll to a stop behind it. Quinn gritted his teeth as a dark blue van made the turn behind the group, looming larger in his side mirror. The van accelerated quickly, roaring up behind Eva Turcott and bumped her motorcycle hard. The bike went down, engine roaring, rear wheel spinning. Eva had to crawl to drag herself out from under it. Steven jumped to check on her. Sputtering with fury and adrenaline, he forgot his side stand and let his big bike fall on its side in the middle of the street.

Three men wearing black balaclavas poured out of the van while two more bailed out of the pickup. All five of them were armed with wooden clubs. Bo saw at least one pistol, stuffed down the waistband of the stockiest of the lot.

Bo and his brother had spent many hours talking tactics—with each other, and with their old man around campfires in Alaska. Admittedly, Jericho had had more opportunity to bring those tactics to play—and he agreed with their father that it was better to attack back through any assault. You didn't try to negotiate with five guys with clubs.

Assessing the situation in an instant, Bo used his right thumb to flick the small button on an orange device the size of a cellphone that was mounted on his handlebars. Alma's husky voice was the only one that came across his headset.

"Bo," she all but growled. "What do you want me to do?"

Quinn gave a tight smile at her ballsy attitude, but looked up in time to see a big guy with a pistol stuffed down his pants heading straight for her. Instead of answering, Bo gunned the throttle and plowed the front wheel of his bike directly into the one with the pistol.

The big guy's right leg bent unnaturally as eight hundred pounds of Harley Davidson motorcycle slammed into his thigh. Bo watched him fall, and gunned the throttle again, spinning the rear tire in an attempt to turn and face one of the other threats without dismounting the bike. The full-face helmet made it impossible to see everything that was going on around him. He heard the engine on Alma's Honda rev to his right, but before he could turn, something heavy slammed into the back of his head. He slumped forward, immediately losing control of the bike so the handlebars came around and slapped the tank. Stunned and seeing stars, he gave a valiant attempt to hop off, but something hit again, rattling his teeth and driving him to the pavement.

A third blow caught him across the shoulders, keeping him there.

Alma's scream buzzed in his earpiece as he sank into unconsciousness.

On the handlebars of Bo Quinn's downed bike, the satellite communications device flashed a message that his SOS and GPS location had gone out to the numbers he'd preprogrammed. The little man with the baseball bat who stood over him was panting too hard to notice.

CHAPTER 1

Heads down, shoulders heaving, Jericho Quinn and Jacques Thibodaux faced each other, circling for the fifth time in as many minutes. Quinn's dark eyes narrowed above a week's growth of dark beard. Thibodaux's high and tight haircut glistened with perspiration in the orange light that filtered through the spring foliage on the sycamore and oaks. Gravel crunched under their boots on the concrete driveway in front of Emiko Miyagi's colonial brick, a short jog from George Washington's Mount Vernon estate.

Copper skin and a dark beard left him with what his ex-wife called an ambiguous ethnicity. At an extremely fit thirty-seven, he could, and often did, pass for someone of Middle Eastern descent, a Native American like his maternal grandmother, or the deeply tanned son of an Irish fisherman that he was. His shaggy hair was just long enough to curl over the top of his ears.

At five feet-ten, Jericho had held the Alaska state Golden Gloves title in his weight classes through five of the eight years from sixth grade until he graduated high school, and had gone on to box for the United States Air Force Academy, winning the Wing Open his junior year. He'd trained in several martial arts, but leaned toward an ancient form of Japanese jujitsu—with plenty of striking mixed in with joint manipulation and throws. More than a series of techniques, it was a way of strategy. Beyond his years of training, he was an instinctive fighter, born with not only the physique and intelligence for close quarters battle, but the willingness to inflict maximum sudden violence on his fellow man when the need arose.

Officially a special agent with Air Force Office of Special Investigations, he'd been seconded, along with his partner, Marine Gunnery Sergeant Jacques Thibodaux, to the office of the national security advisor to the president. When they weren't working, they were training—and according to their instructor, Emiko Miyagi, there was always something to learn.

Thibodaux had Quinn by six inches and sixty pounds. The man was massive—but his were no mere mirror muscles. He had plenty of experience in the octagon, where he fought amateur MMA bouts under the name Dauxboy. The Marine's black eyepatch and an impossibly square jaw added a severity to his already imposing look. Still, his broad face generally held a smile, even in the middle of a fight.

Both men were strategic thinkers, and both knew there were rarely any winners in an actual fight—only those who lived, and those who lost. Real fights were car-wreck quick, emergency-room gory, and brick-to-the-head final.

The problem with fighting someone who sparred with you weekly lay in the fact that you started to learn each other's rhythms, discovering each other's tricks. The benefit, as Miyagi explained, came from the need to constantly adapt in order to conceal one's strategy. If an opponent knew you favored a series of exploratory left jabs prior to bridging the gap of distance, he or she would be ready for the attack long before it came. As such, both Jericho and Jacques varied their movements in an attempt to throw the other off his game.

Neither man was a tentative fighter, though Quinn was a skosh more thoughtful. Thibodaux tended to use his tremendous size to crash in and overwhelm, but when sparring with Quinn the big Cajun often switched things up—as he was doing now—circling, waiting for just the right moment to make his move.

Jacques stutter-stepped, almost tripping on a patch of gravel and glancing for an instant down at his feet. Quinn seized the opportunity and moved in, catching a strike to the nose for his trouble, feeling the cartilage grind under Jacques Thibodaux's forearm.

Neither man was the sort to take it easy in a sparring match; training had to reflect life in order to be beneficial. So, the two men battled like bulls at eighty percent, taking care not to cause serious incapacitating injury. Unfortunately, reality came with a good deal of pain. Each man knew his abilities—and his limits. If a blow would have defined the fight at a hundred percent—the receiver would have no problem conceding that fact. Eighty percent from the mountainous Cajun would be enough to flatten anyone, but Quinn knew how to move, and a broken nose was nothing new to him.

Quinn let his head flow with the Cajun's forearm, following up with machine-gun strikes to Thibodaux's liver and neck as he turned sideways from the momentum of his arm-strike. The big Marine's neck was protected by thick muscles, but Quinn knew it was folly to hit the man in his iron jaw. The liver strikes were sickening, even at eighty percent.

The six-foot-four Cajun winced, both hands raised in surrender. "Fairly certain that one chopped me down to your size, Chair Force." Even in defeat, the Marine couldn't help the little jab at the Air Force. Blood trickled from a small cut Quinn had given him under his left eye.

"Sorry about that," Quinn said, dabbing at his bloody nose while he nodded to the gunny's swelling wound.

Thibodaux waved him off, chuckling. "I ain't no Cinderella, *mi ami*. Lucky enough I had a pretty face when I needed it to catch Camille."

A compact Asian woman with her hair pulled back in a ponytail stepped onto the concrete driveway from the lawn. Emiko Miyagi wore a white t-shirt and khaki 5.11 cargo pants. The scooping neckline and thin material of the shirt did little to hide the intricate and colorful Japanese tattoos that covered her torso. As the men's instructor, she insisted much of their training occur in street clothes—and most often on an actual street rather than the padded floor of a dojo. In this case, the concrete driveway in front of her brick home provided for the realistic backdrop—as well as plenty of bruises and raspberries for all three of the combatants.

Miyagi was forty-seven years old—but could have easily passed for a woman in her mid-thirties. Where the two men under her tutelage had years of experience in fighting, Miyagi had trained as a killer from her early teens. There was something other-worldly about the way she fought, as if she could anticipate her opponent's moves even before they knew they were about to make them.

Her training sessions always ended with a short bout between the instructor and each man. The fights were not short because she planned them that way, but because it did not take her long to win them. Jacques was good, and Jericho was very good, but Emiko Miyagi was better—a lot better.

"I truly hate this fighting friends shit," the monstrous Cajun said, four minutes later as he limped across the circular driveway toward a stainless steel water bottle in the shade of Miyagi's porch. He kept his arm tucked in tight against his side, wincing from Quinn's liver strike and the machine gun beating Miyagi had given him to his floating ribs.

Quinn stood at the edge of the driveway beside his gunmetal gray BMW GS Adventure motorcycle and pressed a wad of tissue to his bloody nose. "I'm with you there," he said, sounding like he had a bad cold. Jacques Thibodaux knew how to throw a forearm. That was an undeniable fact.

Miyagi took a long drink from her own water bottle, then shook her head. "Are you such an excellent judge of character, Jacqueskun?" she asked, using the more familiar form of the Japanese honorific *san*. "Sometimes, those we believe to be our friends turn out to be something else entirely."

"Yeah." Thibodaux rubbed his ribs again and nodded. "I'm gettin' that."

Miyagi canted her head to one side and shrugged at her disbelieving student. "On more than one occasion I have found myself engaged in battle with those who should have cared for me. Each year we read of men and women who believe themselves happily married—until their spouse tries to murder them." She gave a little nod to drive home the seriousness of her point. "Just last week an Alexandria police officer's wife was arrested for attempting to poison him by putting rat poison in his spaghetti."

Quinn sighed, but kept his thoughts to himself. He was sure there were times his ex-wife had been mad enough to feed him d-Con.

The big Cajun gave an adamant shake of his head.

"I trust my Camille completely."

"I'm sure many of those involved believed that same thing about their own companion," Miyagi said.

Thibodaux set his jaw, glaring with his good eye. "I'm tellin' you, Camille wouldn't do such a thing."

"But suppose she did," Miyagi said. "What would you do then?"

"She wouldn't."

"But if she did?"

Thibodaux shrugged, as if it were all so clear.

"Then I'd eat the spaghetti. No point in goin' on if the last fourteen years have been a sham."

Miyagi smiled softly, displaying uncharacteristic emotion. "We should all be so fortunate to have—"

The chime of a cellphone cut her off, and caused all three to look at the black leather jacket lying across Quinn's BMW.

Thibodaux shot his friend a quizzical look. "What the hell, Chair Force? Since when did you start using a ringtone?"

A chill ran up Quinn's back. He kept his phone set to vibrate at incoming calls from everyone but the company dispatching his brother's emergency locator beacon.

He dug the cellphone out of his jacket pocket and answered it by the second ring. A male voice that sounded like a college student advised him that an SOS signal had been triggered at 7:46 a.m. local time on a device registered to Boaz Quinn. So far, the company had been unable to make contact with the registered number. Authorities in Buenos Aires had been notified but were not yet on scene.

Quinn looked at the TAG Heuer Aquaracer on his wrist and noted the time. It was 6:54 a.m. Eastern, an hour earlier than Argentina, eight minutes gone from the time of Bo's SOS. He asked the dispatcher to call him back as soon as he had more information, then hung up and started the protocol he and his brother had already worked out. When an SOS went up, it was too late to start planning.

First, he called Bo's cell, getting nothing but voice mail.

He scrolled through the list of contacts Bo had given him while he explained the situation to Jacques and Emiko. Both knew Quinn's brother was on a protection job in South America and they listened intently, stone faced. Neither had to say anything for Quinn to know he had their complete support. At length, Quinn found the number he was looking for and called the personal cell number for the man who had employed Bo's services.

"Riley Grey," the voice said.

"My name is Jericho Quinn. I just received an SOS message from my brother. Has anyone been in contact with you?"

The line was silent for a long moment. Quinn could imagine the stricken look on the face of the father at the other end. He'd been there himself.

"Steven?" Riley Grey whispered. "What about my son?"

"I don't have any more information yet," Quinn said. "I'd hoped you might have heard something."

"I . . . I haven't."

"Very well," Quinn said. "Bo's GPS puts them in Buenos Aires. Local authorities are en route to the coordinates where the SOS went up. I'll let you know when I get anything else."

"Any chance that this is a false alarm?"

Quinn took a deep breath. "It's possible," he said. "But unlikely. It takes two distinct movements to activate the SOS on his device—sliding a button sideways and then depressing it. Considering their location and your net worth, I'm afraid your son is a possible target . . ."

"I appreciate your honesty," Grey said.

Quinn looked at his watch again, though only seconds had passed since he'd done it last. "I'll call you back."

"Ten minutes," Grey said. "Even if you don't hear anything."

"I'll try," Quinn said. "Until then, I need to get started on some things. It's best to move quickly in this kind of event."

"You have experience with kidnappings?"

"I have experience with bad men," Quinn said. "Now if you'll excuse me, I need to make some calls."

"Wait!" Grey said, clinging to the call like a lifeline. "What are you going to do?"

Quinn groaned. He couldn't help but feel for the father's helplessness, but every moment he spent on the phone was time he could be moving toward Bo.

"I'm going to get a ticket on the next available flight to Buenos Aires out of Dulles. If this turns out to be a false alarm, I'll cancel. In the meantime, I need to be moving forward."

"I can help with that," Grey said, giving an audible sigh at being able to do something tangible. "I'm in Baltimore for meetings. My Citation is sitting at BWI airport right now. Are you closer to Dulles or Reagan?"

"I'm ten minutes from Reagan," Quinn said.

"Good," Grey said. "My plane will be waiting for you when you get there."

"And you?" Quinn asked, fearing the strings that always seemed to be attached to the goodwill of the rich and powerful.

"I broke my leg waterskiing in Tahoe three weeks ago," Grey said. "It kills me not to go down there myself, but I'll be more use to you working from here, providing resources."

"Okay then," Quinn said, relieved but anxious to end the call.

"Bo and I have been friends for a long time," Grey offered. "I don't know much about you, but I trust him completely, and I know he trusts you. He told me that you'd pulled his fat out of the fire on more than one occasion."

"And vice versa."

A tense chuckle came across the line. "Bo told me you'd say that."

CHAPTER 2

Anchorage, Alaska
1998

Fourteen-year-old Boaz Quinn drifted the back tire of his streetlegal Honda dirt bike, throwing up a rooster tail of gravel before coming to a stop in the alley behind the Lucky Wishbone restaurant. Four other motorcycles rolled in behind him. The other riders were all in high school, or at least they should have been.

Jace, a short kid with a wild look in his eye, slid to a stop on the cracked pavement and held up his hand in the dusky light.

"Kill it," Jace said, turning off his own bike. At eighteen, he was the oldest, and the mastermind of the would-be gang. Beef, a big Samoan who was about the same age, provided the smaller Jace with the muscle it took to be the leader. He looked ridiculous on his small dirt bike, but no one said anything about it. Chris was sixteen and already had a full beard. His mom also let him get a tattoo of a dagger on his arm, which Bo thought was pretty cool of her. Austin was a wiry kid with a long history of run-ins with the police. He'd been in and out of McLaughlin Youth Center dozens of times, which only added to his mystique among the gang. Bo was the youngest and the best rider of the group by far. He was maturing early, and looked older than he was. He could probably have given Chris a run for his money on a beard, but Bo's old man was having none of that.

Pete Quinn often said that if either of his sons didn't keep a decent haircut he'd take them out in the fishing boat and only he and the boat would be coming back. As big and tough as the elder Quinn was, it was an empty threat. He would, however, cut that shaggy hair himself, and the only thing he knew how to do was shear it down to the scalp. Bo wasn't about to let that happen. He was only fourteen, but old enough to taste the legal freedom of his new motorcycle license, and had recently discovered how much the girls in eighth grade loved his curly blond locks.

Fortunately for Bo, the Coho salmon fishery would keep his dad down on the Kenai for the next couple of weeks. He didn't have to worry about his hair or the strict curfew his old man enforced. Anchorage, Pete Quinn said, was a different town after midnight, when the meatheads came out in force. That was colorful as his old man's language ever got. *Meatheads*. Oh, he had a temper, and was known to have caved in a skull or two over the years, especially if anyone disrespected his wife or boys, but that temper manifested itself through his fists, not his words.

Bo's mother taught summer school, so she was always exhausted and gone to bed early. Bo's older brother wanted to get into the Air Force Academy and took his studies much too seriously. He'd been in his room reviewing his brains out when Bo slipped out the back door and rolled the motorcycle down the street nearly a full block before starting it.

Bo had made a clean getaway and was free to stay out all night—which was exactly what he planned to do.

Jace said he knew about a poker game at an apartment near the Lucky Wishbone. Bo was pretty good at poker, winning more than he lost in hunting camp with his brother and old man. There'd be some beer at this game, and probably some weed, but Bo thought he'd stick with the beer. His old man drank a beer now and then, so he couldn't say much if his son decided to imbibe. Getting high, well, that would be a bridge too far in the mind of Pete Quinn.

"Quinn!" Jace snapped him out of his thoughts. "Pull your head out of your ass. You even hear what I said?"

Bo shook his head, flustered at having let the leader of his gang down. "Sorry. What?"

"I said you go in first," Jace nodded to the apartments at the end of the alley. "You got a trustworthy face. They'll open the door for you. Big Ray knows me and Beef, so we can't come in until the door's open."

"What do you mean?" Bo said. "If they won't even let you in the door how do you expect to get in on the game?"

The others laughed. Jace pulled out a small silver pistol. It looked cheap, but Bo knew guns and this one was plenty real. "You idiot," he said. "We didn't come to get in on the game. We came here to rob it."

Bo gritted his teeth. He didn't want to look stupid in front of his friends, but he didn't want to commit a felony either.

"You said Ray knows you," Bo said. "How do you expect to get away with this if he knows who you are?"

"That's the beauty of it," Chris said, backing Jace's play. "It's an illegal poker game. APD knows about it, but it floats from place to place so they haven't been able to bust it. No way Ray's going to report it."

"Besides," Beef said. "We'll be wearing masks."

Bo's mouth fell open at that. "You said I had a trustworthy face. That means Ray will know who I am."

Austin looked at Bo and gave him a half grin. "Don't piss yourself, kid. You're young. You never been in trouble before. Even if you did get popped for this, I doubt you'd do more than a couple hours at McLaughlin."

Bo set his jaw and shook his head again. He'd thought smoking a little weed was a bridge too far. It was obvious all the other boys but him had been privy to the plan.

"I'm not comfortable with this," he said.

Jace sneered. "So? None of us gives a shit if you're comfortable. You're either with us or you're against us."

"I'm not doing it."

Jace brandished the little pistol. "Oh," he said. "You're doin' it all right."

A new voice from the shadows behind the group caused them all to look up. Bo recognized it immediately and turned to find his brother sitting astride his Harley Davidson Sportster. He wore a half helmet, jeans, and a leather jacket, zipped up against the chilly Alaska evening. "What the hell?" Jace said, holding the pistol. Every boy knew that Bo's seventeen-year-old brother was the Golden Glove boxing champion in Alaska.

"Jericho?" Bo said. "What are you doing here?"

The older Quinn sat quietly, considering each boy through narrow eyes, as if they were pieces of meat. That was the thing about Jericho. He was a good enough big brother, but he could scare the piss out of you with a look. Dark, like their mother, he had the intensity of their dad.

"Come on," Jericho said at length.

Bo nodded to the Sportster. "How'd you sneak up on us with those hellacious pipes?"

Jericho shrugged. "Guess you're not the only one who can coast a bike. Now come on."

"Bo's with us tonight," Jace said. He tipped his head back and forth, motioning for the others to spread out. Beef rolled toward Jericho while Austin and Chris duck walked their motorcycles to either side, blocking him between the bikes and the back wall of The Lucky Wishbone.

Jericho ignored them, looking instead at Bo. "I said come on."

Jace chuckled. "You let your brother tell you what to do?"

Bo's neck burned. He didn't want to rob the poker game, but he didn't jump just because his big brother said to either.

"I've got this," he snapped.

"I can see that," Jericho said. "Now start your bike and ride out of here with me. Mom's gonna be worried."

"You just don't get it, do you, asshole?" Jace said. He gave an almost imperceptible nod to Beef. "Bo's made his choice. He's not going anywhere. His mommy will be fine."

Jericho took a long breath, staring directly at Jace.

"Let's go," he said again.

The Harley roared to life.

Beef rolled forward, further closing the distance. "You should get outta here before I drag you off your bike and shove that helmet up your—

Jericho didn't go much for threats. He never had. Bo shook his head and watched as his brother popped the clutch, holding the front brake to throw up a cloud of white smoke from the spinning rear tire. The wheel came around fast, slamming into a startled Beef and catching the big

Samoan's leg between the rear sprocket and the engine of his own bike. The snapping bone was audible even over the *brap* of the Harley.

Both Chris and Austin bailed off their bikes, rushing Jericho from both sides.

"You son of a bitch!" Jace screamed, riding his motorcycle straight at Bo, colliding with the front tire.

Bo scrambled off in time to keep from getting run over. Seething with anger, he peeled off his helmet and swung it like a club, catching Jace in the side of the head and dropping him like a tree.

"That's for calling my brother an asshole," he said, spinning to help Jericho.

Chris and Austin were already flat on the pavement, noses smeared across their faces. Beef leaned against his bike clutching the injured leg.

The big kid spoke through clenched teeth. "You gonna call me an ambulance or something?"

"Nope," Jericho said. He didn't explain himself, but it was apparent that he thought the boys should have anticipated that things were bound to get a little bloody.

He swung a leg back over his Harley and looked at Bo. "Are you okay?"

Bo nodded. "I thought we were just going to play some cards," he said. "I wasn't gonna rob anybody."

"I know that," Jericho said.

Bo strapped his helmet back on.

"Are you gonna tell Mom?"

"Nope," Jericho said. "Not unless she catches us coming in. I won't lie for you."

"I didn't really need any help," Bo said after he'd climbed

back on his own bike. "I'm a better rider than any of those guys. I could have just run away."

Jericho shook his head. "Running away from these meat-heads is something you should have done a long time ago," he said, sounding an awful lot like their old man.

CHAPTER 3

Bo awoke with something sharp digging into the point of his hip. He couldn't move his arms, and for a terrifying moment, he thought he might be paralyzed. Scenes from the kidnapping came flooding back into his mind—overturned motorcycles, Steven's roar as he ran to check on Eva, and then the staggering blow to the back of his helmet. Alma's shouts of warning echoed in his ears with Matt's childlike screams.

Searing pain now seeped into his neck. His eyes felt as though they were filled with hot sand. He blinked to clear his vision, finding the toe of a leather hiking boot a few inches from his face. A small man with the build of a jockey, dressed in designer jeans and a blue V-neck sweater spoke to him in hoarse, whispered Spanish—as if he'd been hit in the throat. The man was young, a boy really, and looked like a student from some Ivy League school. Foreign languages were his brother's thing, but Bo had picked up a lot over the course of this trip. Still in a fog, he had no idea what was being said. The words came again, more pointed this time. Beside Ivy League's seat, leaning against the wall of the van, was an aluminum baseball bat.

Alma's trembling voice followed. "He wants you to sit up," she said.

Bo groaned, drawing his legs around so he could get his knees under him. His hands were cuffed tightly behind him, and he could hardly feel them. They were no help at all. "Kind of stuck here," he grunted, feeling a wave of nausea wash over him as he spoke. He gagged, nearly passing out again, and then felt rough hands grab him by the armored shoulders of his motorcycle jacket, hauling him upright.

He blinked again, fighting the grinding pain in his neck as he turned to get a better look at his situation. He breathed a sigh of measured relief when he saw everyone in his group was still alive. They were all in the back of what appeared to be a panel van with seats running along both sides. This was the one that had pulled in behind them after they'd left the hotel. Three men sat with them in the back of the van. Alma sat across from Bo, next to Ivy League. Her cuffs wrenched her elbows backward, giving her a defiant pose, though the terrified look on her face said she was anything but. Her left eye was red and swollen. Bo knew her well enough to know she would be the type to have put up a fight. His chest convulsed at the thought of someone harming her and he resolved to find out exactly which one of these guys had done it. Hell, it didn't matter. They were all complicit in this, and if he had anything to say about it, they would all pay.

I wish you'd get here soon, Jericho, he thought, forcing his fevered brain to do the math about how long it would take to travel from DC to Buenos Aires. He nearly cried when he looked at the faces of the men who'd taken them and realized it was just too far away. Jericho would never be able to get here in time. His head lolled, feeling much too heavy to keep upright on his neck.

A fat man in a tight t-shirt slumped to Alma's left, gripping his leg with a white-knuckled hand. Like Ivy League, this one was young, and could have easily been in his second year of college or technical school. There was something about them both that was off—if there was anything average about kidnappers, none of these fit the description. Their clothing was on the expensive end of stylish. Cable-like tendons flexed on the side of his neck. A string of invective flew from his mouth with a spray of saliva. He was obviously in pain.

Bo squinted. Nausea still rolled through his gut, but he was beginning to get a handle on it. He didn't have to speak Spanish to understand that the curses from this one were aimed at him. Bo had broken this one's leg with his motorcycle during the initial assault, and the injured man now wanted his pound of flesh.

A third kidnapper used a mobile phone to snap photographs of Steven and Matt where they were seated along the van's windowless wall on either side of Bo. This one was much older than the other two, with a thick silver mustache under a hawkish nose. Bo thought he heard Ivy League call him Bruno. He made a mental note of the name, wondering if his aching brain would be able to hang on to even that tiny fragment of information.

Without windows, it was impossible to pinpoint their location. Bo had been to Buenos Aires before, but didn't know it well, so it wouldn't likely have mattered. Wherever they were, the road was far from smooth. Ivy League smiled passively as he watched Alma try to maintain her balance. Bo had seen that look before. This guy was enjoying her predicament, hoping she'd fall. If she didn't, he'd push her soon enough. His youthful face held a twisted glee when he looked at either of the women, like they were wrapped presents that he could not wait to open. None of the prisoners were human to him—which, Bo knew, made him all the more dangerous.

You could do whatever you wanted to a thing.

Steven and Eva now sat across from each other on either side of the van. Their separation only added to the torture. Eva's shoulders shuddered in uncontrolled sobs. Steven gazed at nothing, slackjawed, his eyes unfocused as if he'd been drugged. Dried blood crusted his nostrils. The guy with the silver mustache didn't seem to care and took all their photos anyway. Matt used a shoulder to wipe a string of drool from the corner of his mouth, as if he wanted to be presentable in his proof-of-life photo. Alma shook her head in shame and disgust.

Matt looked sideways to shoot a daggered glance at Bo as soon as Bruno took the photo.

"You had one job," he said, his voice tinny, sounding like it might shatter into a thousand pieces at any moment. "You were supposed to keep this from happening."

Bo could have argued, but he didn't. This was his fault. His mom always said that no matter how thin you sliced a cheese, there were always two sides. But that wasn't true. Sometimes there was just cheese on one side . . . and nothing but shit on the other. Matt was right. Bo was the one charged with their safety, and here they were—smack in the most dangerous situation imaginable. He should have taken a less direct route out of town as soon as he'd discovered Matt's leak to social media.

Everyone else seemed to have sense enough not to engage, but Matt turned his attention to the kidnappers. "Where are you taking us?"

They ignored him, one of them in pain, the other two indifferent faces swaying with the moving van.

The one with the broken leg locked in on Bo, still seething.

"We are guests in your country." Matt pressed, as if appealing to the better nature of the kidnappers. "You have no right to hold us captive."

Ivy League lifted the tail of his sweater, revealing the grip of a black Taurus pistol. "This gives me the all the rights I need," he said in accented English.

Bo tried to catch Matt's eye, shaking his head to get him to shut up before he got himself—or someone else hurt. Matt would have none of it.

"Which one of you is in charge?"

Ivy League nodded toward the front, on the other side of a metal partition.

"My father has money," Matt said. Alma threw back her head, exasperated at the stupidity, but Matt wasn't finished. "He will make it worth your while to let me go."

It was not lost on Bo, or, from the look on Alma's face, on her either, that Matt made no mention of freeing anyone else in the group.

"A lot of money do you think?" Ivy League asked.

Matt gave an emphatic nod. "He's rich, if you want to know the truth."

"Oh my talkative friend," Ivy League said. "But I already know the truth. Do you think we have reason to grab people who have no money?"

Matt slumped in defeat.

"Idiot," Alma said under her breath, adding a few Spanish curses for good measure.

The kidnappers laughed.

Both Steven and Eva hung their heads.

The one with the broken leg scooted forward, his face just inches from Bo. He ponderous gut caused him to grunt. Beads of sweat covered a wide forehead. Shock and adrenaline soured his breath. He'd decided to speak English now, and did so surprisingly well.

"Some of you are worth money," he said. "Others are not. I think you are one that is not. These others stink of wealth, but you . . . I think you are only their guide. Guides have no money to speak of, certainly not enough to pay a ransom."

"You are sorely mistaken," Alma said. "He's not our guide, he's my boyfriend."

Matt's head snapped up at that, but he said nothing.

The fat guy turned to sneer at Alma. "Then you are worthless as well."

Alma shrugged. "We'll see."

Ivy League smiled, turning sideways to give Alma a slow onceover. "Oh, my dear," he said in his otherworldly whisper. "You have worth to me."

The fat one chuckled despite his broken leg. He directed his glare back at Bo. "They have told us we can have anyone who is not worth the ransom."

"Some we will kill," Ivy League said, and then turned to Alma. "Some, we will . . . entertain."

A small metal plate in the front partition slid open. It was immediately filled with a round face. "Stop scaring the merchandise, La Pulga," the man said. "We're not killing anyone."

La Pulga, Bo mused. *The Flea*. That suited this little squirt better than Ivy League.

"Not yet," the fat one in back said, still focused on Bo. "But if I am right, and you are worthless, I will be the one to put a bullet in your eye—after my friend and I show your girlfriend what it means to have a real man."

Bo heaved a deep sigh. "You'll have to hunt a real man, because that ain't you by a long shot."

The fat one lunged across the van. Bo fell forward to meet him, landing with the full weight of his body against the broken leg. It would probably get him beaten to death, but he couldn't remember anything so satisfying.

The fat one recoiled as if he'd been set on fire, yowling and cursing. "*Pelotudo*! I will cut off your head!"

Bruno grabbed Bo and pulled him back across the van, cuffing him hard in the ear and cutting the inside of his cheek against his teeth.

Bo spit a mouthful of blood onto the van floor in contempt. "A real man?" He glared. "I just kicked your ass with my hands cuffed behind my back."

The injured man growled as if to attack again, but La Pulga pushed him back. "Sit down, Toro," he hissed. "He only tries to make us angry.

Be patient. We will have some fun with them this evening." The Flea spoke in English, no doubt so Bo could understand.

Toro, Bo nodded to himself. That made sense. The fat piece of shit looked like a baby bull. Bo had been awake for five minutes and he already knew three of the kidnapper's names, or at least their street names. If he got a chance, Bo would kill The Flea first. He was evil, even more so than Toro. But being evil didn't make you a pro. These guys were all thugs—even if they did wear designer clothes—but their behavior made Bo doubt they'd ever kidnapped anyone before. The Flea bounced with excitement at the opportunities that lay before him. In some ways, their inexperience was a good thing. Common burglars would surely make more mistakes than a group of polished kidnappers. But amateurs sometimes realized they were in over their heads. And if they got bored with whatever torment they had planned and decided to throw in the towel, Bo and everyone with him would end up in some remote pasture, buried under Argentine dirt.

It was obvious they knew who Steven Grey was, but sooner or later, somebody was going to figure out who else they had, and when they did, things were liable to go from bad to bloody very fast.

CHAPTER 4

"Not a chance in hell, Chair Force," Thibodaux said, throwing his small duffel bag in the backseat of Emiko Miyagi's Acura MDX. "We're not letting you go down there all by yourself. We like Bo too, in case you forgot."

Quinn shook his head. "We'll have no support from Palmer on this," he said.

Miyagi looked on passively. She'd changed into a navy blue threebutton polo and jeans that looked tighter than they actually were, hugging her hips while still allowing her freedom of movement in a fight. Both Quinn and Thibodaux wore button-down shirts they could leave untucked and 5.11 khaki slacks, absent the shoot-me-first cargo pockets that identified the wearer as possible law enforcement or, at the very least, a gun guy.

"That is all the more reason for us to accompany you, Quinnsan," Miyagi said. "One of your loved ones is in trouble, so you are in trouble. Would you not do the same for us?"

Quinn sighed and threw his bag into the back with Thibodaux's. Emiko drove so he could continue with his calls.

Both Jericho and Jacques kept go bags at Miyagi's, obviating the need to return to their respective homes if they were suddenly activated. Quinn's decidedly non-tactical looking Haley Strategic FlatPack didn't have much inside, the bulk of the room taken up by a change of clothes—another pair of khakis, a second no-iron button down shirt, underwear, socks, and a Smartwool quarter-zip sweater. In addition to the extra clothing, he had a small trauma kit, a Leatherman Wave multitool, a half-roll of toilet paper, fire-starting rod, two flashlights, a Riot fixed-blade knife, duct tape, cordage, and several pairs of black nitrile gloves.

Flying on Grey's Citation rather than going commercially allowed him to keep the blades in the carry-on bag. Even so, it would be impossible to get firearms into Argentina without some advanced planning. Quinn preferred not to dwell on what couldn't be helped. If Bo had been kidnapped, there were bound to be weapons around when he needed them.

He called back the emergency transponder company, gave his reference number, and was connected with the same dispatcher he'd spoken with before. Buenos Aires City police had found five motorcycles, all still loaded down with gear, in the middle of the residential street, all on their sides. The one with the SOS device—Bo's Harley—had some damage to the front forks, and a substance they believed to be blood on the fender. They were in the middle of interviewing residents in the area, but had no witnesses so far. The police commander on scene suspected it was all a traffic accident and had his men checking nearby hospitals.

Quinn thanked the dispatcher and said he would call back in fifteen minutes for an update.

"Perhaps it was a simple accident," Miyagi said.

"Perhaps," Quinn said. He closed his eyes, trying to picture a set of circumstances where Bo would activate the SOS button, abandon all the motorcycles and gear on the side of the street, and then not answer his cell. Either he and everyone else in the group were so badly injured that they couldn't make telephone calls—or they'd been kidnapped. Jericho knew his brother. He wouldn't go down without a fight. The probability of him surviving a kidnapping where he was in charge of security was slim to none.

Quinn tried to push the odds stacked against his brother out of his mind and called Ronnie Garcia.

She picked up on the second ring.

"Hey you," she said, her voice husky from sleep. An intelligence officer for the CIA, she'd been on assignment in the Philippines for the past three weeks. She should have been coming home, but the job had gone long—as they usually did.

"Sorry," Quinn said. "Didn't mean to wake you."

"It's okay," Garcia said. "It's just after eight here. I have an op tonight so I was just grabbing a short nap. Need my beauty sleep, you know, because I'll be seeing you in a week or two."

Quinn could picture her broad smile, her long black hair across the pillow.

"A couple of weeks, huh?"

He brought her up to speed on the situation with Bo.

"Jericho," she gasped. The bed squeaked on the other end of the line as she sat up. A hint of her Cuban accent emerged when she was excited or nervous. "This is awful. I'll grab a flight out right away."

"No," Quinn said. "Jacques and Emiko are coming with

me. You stay put and finish your op. I just needed to hear your voice."

"But Jericho, I—"

"I'm serious, Ronnie." Quinn cut her off. "We'll be on the ground in thirteen hours. I'm hoping this will all be a good war story by the time you could even make it to us."

"I could help with the Spanish though."

"We'll figure it out," Quinn said, "Jacques speaks Italian. He'll be able to get the gist of everything."

"*E la veritá*," Thibodaux said from the back seat, keeping things light even in the middle of a crisis. "Mi speaka the Italiano."

"Buenos Aires, right?" Garcia said. "You'll be there this evening."

"Correct," Quinn said. He glanced at his Aquaracer. "I'm estimating around ten or eleven tonight Argentina time."

"Okay," she said. "Hear me out before you say no. I have a friend in Buenos Aires who I went to college with in Florida. She speaks fluent English and has enough contacts throughout the government that she can cut through some of the red tape. There are just two problems."

Quinn leaned back against the headrest. "I'll take all the help I can get to help me find Bo. What's the problem though?"

"She's beautiful," Garcia said. "I hate hooking you up with someone as gorgeous as Soledad San Martín."

"I wouldn't worry about that," Quinn said.

"I know you wouldn't. You get to hang out with Soledad."

"Anyway," Quinn said, wanting to change the subject. He worked in the world of espionage, but he wasn't James Bond.

"It will be good to have someone on the inside of Argentine law enforcement."

Garcia's sigh was audible over the line. "That's the other problem," she said. "Soledad isn't law enforcement or intelligence. She's a reporter."

CHAPTER 5

Justino Medina rubbed bloodshot eyes with the palms of his hands and read over the email, checking for at least the hundredth time that he'd not accidentally used his actual email account. The kidnapping made it obvious that he was somewhere in Argentina, but he wanted the message to bounce around the world before it dropped into Riley Grey's inbox. Sending a ransom demand via email to a man who was a billionaire because of his computer expertise was a harrowing task.

Justino had been up most of the night researching Virtual Proxy Networks and various computer programs that would anonymize emails. He thought he had it figured out, but there was only one way to be sure. He'd heard that the police kept a record of people who purchased such programs. He would, were he a policeman. It seemed like the smart thing to do if one wanted to catch kidnappers.

Angelica hovered above him, hand on the computer desk, thick hair brushing against his face. A red silk robe hung open to reveal the swells and valleys where her black nightgown clung to the contours of her body. The odor of her rosewater soap usually intoxicated him, but he could think of nothing now but the two possible outcomes that lay before him—prison or the loss of his toes to Fernando Richter's blade.

Convincing pregnant women to give up their babies for a modest fee was illegal, and, if Justino thought on it for too long, despicably immoral, but it was relatively safe. Angelica was a judge. She could protect them from any fallout from a crime so petty as *belly hunting*. And anyway, it was a service to society. Oh, they might weep and sling snot at the thought of giving up a baby, but in the end, even the women knew it was best for their little bundle of fat to go to a rich couple. What was it to them if the Medinas made a few dollars for their trouble?

Kidnapping was a different story. Justino had never done anything remotely so dangerous. Moving the drugs for Fernando Richter had been a horrible mistake—but the danger lay in the association with a madman, not in the crime itself. Local law enforcement cared little about a few hundred pounds of drugs going downriver, especially if Judge Angelica Medina was involved in the transaction. Money trickled down from her schemes, and so long as the trickling continued, no one in the province of Misiones took much of an interest.

But a kidnapping scheme meant physical violence to take the hostages into custody—*sucking them up*, the army used to call it—and then more brutality to keep them there. Justino had defended enough criminal thugs to know that violence was a stampeding horse. Once running, the beast was nearly impossible to turn.

"There is no turning back once I push *send*," Justino said, imploring his wife to reconsider this reckless plan.

Her beautiful lips trembled as if in anticipation. She'd always been excited at the prospect of danger. "*Mi amor*," she said. "Jelly has five North Americans tied up in the rear of his van. It is far too late to turn back."

Justino took a deep breath in and out through his mouth, attempting to slow his runaway heart. "Read it over once more, then, to make sure I have typed what you wish to say."

Angelica pushed a pair of purple glasses lower on her nose and leaned in closer, one hand squeezing her husband's shoulder, her lips nibbling his ear as she read.

Dear Mr. Grey:
Your son, Steven, now finds himself the unwilling guest of some very dangerous people. We offer our assistance in negotiating his safe return from these monsters.
Please reply to this email immediately.
A one-time fee of three hundred thousand
U. S. dollars . . .

Angelica took a half step back to stare at him. "That cannot be right. You ask only for three hundred thousand?"

Justino gave an emphatic nod. "Two hundred thousand for what we owe Richter, and one hundred thousand to pay for Jelly, La Pulga, the pilot, and the remainder of our expenses."

"Oh, my darling," Angelica sighed. "You think on much too small a scale." She bumped him aside with her hip so she could get to the keyboard, reading as she corrected the email.

. . . A one-time fee of three million U. S. dollars will facilitate the negotiations. Instructions regarding the transfer of these funds will follow.
We humbly await your speedy reply.

Please note, involving the police in any way would
put your son in grave danger during the negotiation
process.
Your most obedient servant,
Magoya

"Magoya" was the Argentine version of John Doe.

Justino put a hand on top of his bald head, feeling an immediate flush of sweat.

"Three million? I think that might be asking too much."

"Nonsense," Angelica said, pressing the *send* key before Justino could prevail. "Riley Grey's empire is worth billions. A few million dollars is pocket change to such a man."

"That kind of money changes people," Justino said.

"Of course it does, my darling." Angelica batted long lashes. "That kind of money changes them into people with larger houses and better cars. It changes them into world travelers and people who own villas in Tuscany."

"But this is our home," Justino said, struggling to keep his voice from cracking. "We would be targets here with so much wealth."

"We will get a new home," Angelica said. "Better than this dump."

"I thought you loved this—"

A heavy rapping at the door nearly sent Justino out of his skin. He sat frozen in his chair. "Do you think . . ."

Angelica rolled her eyes as she pulled her robe closed and tied a knot in the sash. "No, the police have not traced the ransom note back to our computer. I doubt Grey has even had time to open the email. Now turn off the screen while I see who it is."

She strode across the living room on long legs, flinging open the door as if she was certain it was an old friend.

It was not.

Fernando Richter stood on the other side of the metal security gate five feet away, hands clasped at his waist as if in prayer. He wore his customary white shirt with the sleeves rolled halfway up his hairy forearms. His black hair was slicked with pomade and combed straight back over a high forehead. Descending from members of a colony of Germans who'd immigrated to Paraguay after World War II, he was proud of his Aryan heritage—at least the part that had not been diluted by his grandfathers' intermarrying with Guarani Indians. Blue eyes sparkled with the sort of dark mischief of a man who enjoyed watching the pain of others. Richter was not a big man. Justino had him by a good forty pounds, but The German gave off a predatory air that made him seem much larger. His girlfriend, Violeta, stood beside him, the imprint of a pistol under the tail of her tight black t-shirt. Heavy black boots, presumably for kicking puppies and small children that got in her way, added to her height and saw her towering above Richter. He didn't seem to mind. Violeta was attractive enough, in the way that a piece of rich mahogany lumber was attractive. Fit and trim with a bosom Angelica swore was purchased rather than inherited, her shoulder-length hair was the color of dried pampas grass and stood out in stark contrast to deeply tanned skin. She looked like a child's Barbie doll that had been toasted in the oven. Some said she was Richter's brain. That may have been correct, for she was certainly not his soul. Justino suspected neither of them possessed one of those.

Two men Justino recognized but didn't know stood directly behind the gangster.

"How goes it, my friends?" Richter said.

"Our debt is not yet due!" Justino blurted out.

Angelica turned to shoot him a glare.

Violeta chuckled. She licked her lips as if the meat of a terrified man might be appetizing.

Richter raised his hand and smiled. "A contract is a contract," he said. "We are not here to collect."

Angelica cocked her head to one side. It amazed Justino how she could remain so calm under the circumstances.

"How may we help you then, Fernando?" she asked, one hand on the doorframe.

"We are business partners," Richter said. "Are you not going to invite me in?"

Angelica pushed a button beside the door and buzzed open the outer gate. Stepping back, she motioned him in with a flourish. "Of course," she said. "Our home is your home." She pushed the door closed immediately after Richter and Violeta came through, blocking the other two men's path. One of them, a vicious-looking brute with a bald head, stuck out his boot to keep it from closing.

"You are not my business partner," Angelica said, calm as if asking someone for directions. "You will have to remain outside."

Both the men and Violeta looked at Richter for direction.

"It is fine," he said, giving a flick of his hand. He wore a ring on every finger. "Violeta and I will not be long."

Angelica shut the door and turned to Richter. She tightened the sash to her robe. Justino knew she kept a small pistol in the pocket. He'd even made fun of her for it, but was grateful she had the little thing now.

"May I offer you some toast?" she asked. "Some *mate* or coffee?"

Richter flicked his hand again. "We are fine. Please allow me to come right to the point. I understand you have five Norte Americanos as your . . . shall we say, guests."

Angelica took a step backward, mouth open.

"That is our business," she said. "How could you possibly have known?"

Richter shrugged. "Your husband told me."

Angelica could not have been more surprised if Justino had slapped her.

In retrospect, he knew he should have consulted her, but it was done, and anyway, he'd showed some initiative. She was always saying he should do more of that.

"I wanted to let him know we would be on time with our payment," Justino said, eyes downcast, unable to meet his wife's gaze. "I did not think he would come here."

"In any case," Richter said, plowing ahead. "I wish to let you know that it would be my great honor to take over from here. I will assume all the risk and we will call our debt even. The ransom negotiations for these prisoners will prove a lengthy and dangerous process."

Angelica's eyes darkened. "And you will assume the collection of the money as well?"

"Of course," Richter said. "There is great danger in exchanging human beings for payment. You may take my word on that."

"Justino and I will stay the course with our present arrangement," Angelica said. "You will be repaid before the date agreed, with interest." Her hands dropped into the pockets on either side of her robe as if she were cold. Justino knew she was holding the pistol. She opened the door. "Now, if you will excuse us, we still have much to do."

The two men were still waiting outside.

Violeta remained passive, snakelike, her eyes focusing on nothing—and everything. Richter cocked his head to one side, nostrils flaring at the rebuff.

"You are quite sure?" he asked. "This decision is fraught with peril."

"We have taken precautions," Angelica said, stone faced.

Richter shrugged. "Very well. I wish you much luck."

He turned and left without another word.

Angelica turned the bolt on the door as soon as it was shut.

"From now on," she said. "We talk to no one unless we discuss it first. Agreed?"

Justino nodded. "I only thought—"

"I know what you thought, *mi amor*," she said. "I must ask you a question. Did you tell Richter the names of our . . . guests?"

Justino shook his head. "I did not. I only told him they were North Americans and that we would be able to pay our debt on time."

Angelica rubbed a hand across her face, thinking.

"Nothing else? No numbers?"

"No," Justino said.

"That is interesting indeed," Angelica said. "We could have had two college students down for a holiday. But Richter somehow knew there were five of them. And he knows that at least one of them comes from a wealthy enough family to make it worth his time and risk."

Justino rested both palms on the desk, the chill of sudden realization washing over him. "That means one of Jelly's men is working for Richter. Maybe even Jelly himself."

Angelica shook her head, already pushing buttons on her mobile phone. "Not Jelly," she said. "I have known his mother since we were children. He may as well be blood to me." She held the phone to her ear. "I am calling him now . . . Hello, Jelly . . . Listen very carefully. There has been a change of plans. The pilot will arrive shortly to pick you up. Tell him to take you to the camp instead of the *yerba mate* plantation . . . Correct. Do not tell the others. And instruct the pilot not to contact anyone about the change. We will be waiting for you when you land . . . And Jelly . . . be safe, my friend. Si . . . *Chau . . . Un beso*."

Justino worked to keep from rolling his eyes. Angelica had just told her lead kidnapper goodbye by giving him a figurative "kiss."

They were both coming unhinged.

"Does your secretary still come in early?" Angelica asked. Justino nodded.

"Very well," she said. "Get dressed, *mi amor*. Richter will suspect we will change our plans and is surely waiting out front somewhere to follow us."

"Or to murder us," Justino offered.

"Maybe," Angelica shrugged, stripping her robe and pulling the gown up over her head as she spoke. "But I think not. He is too greedy to kill us before we pay him back his money. Even if he takes Grey and his friends, he will still want to be paid."

"But we will have no way to pay him then," Justino said, near tears.

Angelica ignored his whining. "We will slip out the back and borrow your secretary's car to go and meet the plane. Richter spoke of the *prisoners* and the *guests*. I want to know why he thinks more than one of them is worth his trouble."

CHAPTER 6

A woman wearing tan slacks and a crisp white polo shirt welcomed Quinn and the others aboard Riley Grey's spotless Cessna Citation X. She wore little makeup and her dark hair was cut pixie short, giving her a freshly scrubbed look. Quinn had to stoop as he entered the plush but narrow plane. The interior had the new-car-and-coffee smell common to corporate aircraft.

Quinn had thought the woman was one of the pilots but was surprised to find two men already seated in the cockpit. The front four seats were set up in a vis-a-vis configuration with six more identical leather seats behind it, one on each side of the aircraft in three rows. Depressions in the carpet showed that two of the seats had been added recently, probably within the last hour. The big Cajun came in behind Quinn and leaned into the cockpit, then turned to give a thumbs up. "Salt and pepper hair on both," he said. "Just the way I like my pilots—years of experience."

"Mr. Grey sends his regards," the woman said. "I'm Dr. Roselyn Patrick, Mr. Grey's personal physician."

Thibodaux transferred his bag from his right hand to his left and reached to shake hands with the doctor.

"Damn, Doc," he said. "Glad I didn't jump to conclusions and ask you for coffee."

Dr. Patrick smiled. "I don't mind getting you some coffee," she said. "But my medical opinion is that you should try and get some sleep. This is going to be a long flight for someone as big as you. Please, take a seat anywhere, stretch out as best you can."

Miyagi put her bag in an aft facing seat. "Do you normally travel with Mr. Grey?"

"I do," Dr. Patrick said. "He's a very athletic human being—in some very remote parts of the world. He sent me to care for Steven once you retrieve him."

Quinn nodded. That was optimistic—but what else could a father be?

The first officer, who turned out to have a soft-spoken southern drawl, craned around in his seat on the right side of the cockpit and waved to grab everyone's attention.

"Welcome aboard," he said. "Mr. Grey has instructed us not to spare the horses on this trip, but there's no way around it, we're in for a long ride. We'll make our fuel stop in Panama quick, but even at our max cruising speed of Mach .82, we're still looking at a thirteenhour trip. Doctor Patrick will give you a safety briefing and should be able to answer any questions."

Even with the new configuration, there wasn't a bad seat on the plane. Still, Quinn left the forward seats to Thibodaux so he'd have maximum leg room, and took a spot in the back. Out of habit, he sat on the left side of the aircraft, to keep his gun hand free and in the aisle—though he was traveling light on this trip. The last thing he wanted to do was get sideways with Argentine customs by showing up in their country carrying his Kimber.

Quinn looked across the confines of the Citation's cabin

at Thibodaux and Miyagi, who had both settled into their seats to read—or at least stare at a book while they thought. The monstrous, one-eyed Cajun and the enigmatic little Japanese woman had dropped everything to come with him. Between the three of them they had more scars than most people had skin. Their experience and skill made them formidable weapons. But they were going into this blind, to a foreign country, with none of their usual lines of support. Friends. No, more than that. They were family.

Quinn's cellphone buzzed in his pocket the moment he sat down. He'd long since given up on Bo calling him back, but was grateful to hear Ronnie's voice on the other end. He gave her their ETA. She told him her friend Soledad would be there waiting.

"I feel terrible that I can't help," Ronnie said.

Quinn shook his head, despite the fact that he was on the phone. "Don't," he said. "What you're doing there is important."

"Maybe," she said. "But not as important as what you're doing."

"I'm sure it's important to someone," Quinn said. "Anyway, I might need help running interference from the boss, if he catches wind that we're down here." The line clicked, signifying another call. He took the phone away from his ear long enough to see it was Riley Grey.

"I have to go," Quinn said.

"Be safe," she said. "You'll bring him home. I know it."

Quinn was hopeful, but not nearly so optimistic as everyone else. He'd seen too many good people die because they happened to be standing in the wrong spot or crossing the street at the wrong place.

"Quinn," he said, answering the incoming call.

Grey started right in without a greeting, reminding Jericho

of his boss, Winfield Palmer, the national security advisor. He supposed rich and powerful people got in that habit.

"I received a ransom demand of sorts in my inbox fifteen minutes ago."

"Forward it to me." Quinn put the phone on speaker so Jacques and Emiko could hear and then gave Grey his email address.

"It says not to contact the police," Grey added.

"I'm not surprised," Quinn said.

"Should I do what it tells me to? Not call the police, I mean?"

"That's something you'll have to decide for yourself," Quinn said.

"Aren't you the police?"

"In a manner of speaking," Quinn said. "But if we're going to bring your son and my brother back, I may not have the luxury of acting very much like a police officer."

"That is exactly what I wanted to hear," Grey said. "I'd prefer to trust you to do what needs to be done. We'll keep this between us."

Miyagi nodded. Thibodaux gave a thumbs up.

"Very well," Quinn said. "Please tell me if you change your mind. Have you responded to the email?"

"Not yet," Grey said. "I have my best techs combing the file for any metadata or other digital tracks that might lead us back to whoever has Steven. If there is anything there, my guys will find it. I'm surprised kidnappers would send an email to someone like me."

"That is odd," Quinn said. It might mean they were not particularly sophisticated, which was a concern, but he didn't say it out loud. "How much did they ask for?"

"Three million. Instructions for payment to come later."

Thibodaux grimaced and mouthed the amount.

"Stand by a minute," Grey said. "Another email just landed in my inbox."

Quinn checked the time on his Aquaracer while he waited. Argentina was an hour later than DC. With the time difference, that put them wheels down sometime around 11:00 p.m. local, almost fifteen hours from the time Bo had sent up his SOS. Light-years faster than a law enforcement team could have gotten spooled up, but it was an eternity when you had a gun to your head—as Bo and the others surely did.

The FBI and Homeland Security had capable agents already on the ground in Buenos Aires, but they were few in number, and still had to answer to the bureaucracy of their respective agencies. Officially, Quinn would have told anyone else in this present situation to share the ransom demands and every other correspondence with the FBI. They were the experts in kidnap recovery. But a federal law enforcement response to a kidnapping in another country would mean liaison with foreign governments, deconfliction with their law enforcement—who might or might not be compromised—and a lengthy negotiation.

Quinn planned to do whatever it took to bring Bo and the others home.

Negotiation wouldn't even enter the picture.

Grey came back on the line, his voice even more hollow than it had been. "I'm not sure what to think of this."

"Instructions for how you're supposed to make payment?" Quinn asked.

"No," Grey said. "A second demand for ransom, this one asking for five million dollars—from a completely different party."

Quinn felt a knot form in his chest. "A different party?"

"I'm forwarding you the email now," Grey said.

Quinn left the phone on speaker while he opened the email.

Mr. Grey,
Associates of mine have come into the possession of your son and others. It is my belief that these people have reached out to you for payment by this point. The situation here is fluid and your son will very soon find himself under my care. I would urge you to forgo further contact with the first party and conduct negotiations with me only. Five million dollars would aid in my expenses for your son's safe return.
I will be in touch soon.
A Friend.

"What do you make of this?" Grey asked.

Quinn looked at the others. "I hate to say it," he said. "A double cross maybe. Another cartel? In any case, someone smells a payday, so they're planning to grab Steven from whoever planned the original kidnapping."

"Could be it's the same damned group?" Thibodaux mused. "Just makin' us think there's something going on because they decided they didn't ask for enough in the first place."

"That is a possibility," Miyagi said, uncharacteristically agreeing with Jacques out loud.

An exhausted sigh came from the other end of the line. "If there are more people involved, maybe that will leave more of a trail."

"Maybe," Quinn said. *But a trail of what*?

Grey promised to call as soon as he got any more emails and ended the call.

A moment later, the Citation X threw Quinn back into the leather seat as it shot down the runway.

Able to get awfully close to cruising at Mach 1, the Citation X was the fastest business jet on the market—but there weren't a lot of business owners who could afford to pay over twenty million dollars for a plane. Quinn had a fleeting thought that it must be nice to be so rich, until he realized that Riley Grey's wealth came with a price, the price of turning his family into a target. But then, Quinn wasn't rich, not by a long shot, and his line of work had turned his friends and family into literal targets on too many occasions to count.

He read over both emails again. Quinn wanted to believe that this was merely a case of some unsophisticated kidnappers asking for more money. But that wasn't the case. The wording and tone were different in each note, the "voice" of two separate writers. No, Bo and the others were caught in the crossfire between two warring groups, and "*fluid*" didn't even begin to describe the situation.

He leaned back and shut his eyes. "Keep your head down, little brother. I'm on my way."

CHAPTER 7

The smell of chicken shit and sour apples oozed from the Cessna Caravan's cloth seats. The pilot, an ancient man with squinty eyes and skin as dark as a roasted coffee bean, likely made his living flying whatever anyone paid him to fly, be it livestock or live human beings. He'd surely seen many things over his long life, leaving Bo to wonder if that was the reason his eyes seemed locked in a permanent squint.

Bo's hands were still cuffed behind his back so he couldn't get a look at his watch. He estimated they'd been in the air for nearly two hours. Counting the drive to the remote airfield out of Buenos Aires—north, judging from the sun—and the time they'd spent on the ground waiting for the aircraft to show up, something like five hours had elapsed from the time they'd been grabbed.

Steven was holding up okay, though it was clear from the pained expression on his face that he blamed himself for all this. Eva had started off in tears, but had become more and more defiant the longer they were in captivity. Defiance had a place, but not until they knew a little more about their captors. For now, her angry outbursts only incited the men. Those that were scared reacted with more brutality to hide their fear. La Pulga, the little flea with the Ivy League sweater, just looked at her and smiled as if taking notes about what he planned to do.

Not counting the grizzled old pilot, there were twelve passengers on the plane, taking up all the seats in the back and leaving the wounded Toro lying in the aisle with his head on a duffel in the rear cargo area. He'd cut a walking stick from the green limb of a jacaranda tree and used it to threaten the prisoners when they got in his way or came near his broken leg.

Jelly, the apparent leader, sat up front. He was young, like most of the rest, well dressed in a blue and white rugby shirt of Argentina's national team. Larger than Toro, Jelly's bulk was gained from his time in the gym rather than a diet of empanadas and sweets.

Bo felt his ears pop as the pilot began to descend. Bo recognized the confluence of the Iguazú and Paraná rivers that formed the borders of Argentina, Paraguay, and Brazil. He watched the brown rivers and patchwork of green fields and seemingly impassable jungle as they passed beneath the plane. The deep canyon called Garganta del Diablo, or Devil's Throat, and the frothy white Iguazú Falls came into view as the pilot banked back to the south, staying in Argentina. The sprawling city of Paraguay's Ciudad del Este lay to the left, across the Paraná.

It made sense that Jelly would bring them here. The Triple Frontier had a reputation as a haven for smuggling everything from counterfeit goods to humans. Bo and his group had come down the Pan-American Highway, riding through Quito, Lima, and Antofagasta, before turning east in Valparaíso, Chile to reach Buenos Aires. The original plan was to spend a couple of days poking around BA before riding down to Ushuaia at the southern tip of South America before eventually heading back up to see Iguazú Falls.

Now that they were here, Bo couldn't help but wonder if this aerial view might be the only one he'd ever get. They knew who Steven was, that was obvious from the way they kept him apart from the others and treated him like a golden egg—not exactly good, but valuable. The would be demanding ransom soon, for Steven at least. So far, they didn't seem to know the significance of who else they had. Matt wouldn't shut up about how his dad would be happy to buy his freedom, but for some reason, none of that seemed to impress them, least of all The Flea, who seemed to be in this for something other than money. The captors had made zero attempt at hiding their identities. Maybe that was due to inexperience, but they'd come around to the realization soon that it had been an error. It was difficult to foresee a set of circumstances where the ransom got paid and everyone was released with a handshake.

And now they'd been moved hundreds of miles to the north. Even if Jericho had gotten the SOS, it would take him a full twenty-four hours to get to Argentina—and then he'd be looking in the wrong place.

Ten minutes later, the caravan bounced to a stop on a grass field. The pilot made everyone stay in place while he got out and waddled around to put a support under the tail so the plane didn't squat when everyone moved to the rear door. As soon as this was done, the pilot walked away, disappearing into a small metal building without looking back. Bo imagined that seeing too much in his line of work was a quick way to end up being thrown out of your own plane.

Through the side window, Bo could see a middle-aged woman follow the progress of the airplane. She was tall, and impeccably dressed in crisp white slacks and a matching sleeveless blouse. A midday sun blazed overhead, adding to the oppressive humidity, but this woman did not have a hair out of place. A stooped man in a floppy gaucho beret stood beside the woman, gazing more at her than the plane. A brown Renault Duster was parked in the grass alongside the strip. Beyond the car lay a small brick house nestled among a copse of fir and eucalyptus trees. A dozen head of white-face cattle munched grass in the field behind the house. A windmill turned lazily over two black horses drinking from the water tank. It was a bucolic scene and would have been relaxing had Bo not recently been beaten and bound.

Bruno and The Flea climbed out of the Caravan first and then opened a wide cargo door at the back, allowing Toro to work his way out on the broken leg. It made an easier exit for the bound prisoners as well. Jelly came around from the front to meet them as they hopped down to the ground. Three others with names Bo didn't know came around back. Through it all, Toro—still cringing in pain—leaned against his homemade walking stick. If any of the prisoners so much as looked at him, he reminded them that they no longer existed. He could, he said, do anything he wanted to someone who did not exist.

The woman in the white slacks strode to the back of the Caravan with an air that said she was obviously in charge. The man followed, with an air that said he was not.

She pointed a long finger with perfectly manicured pink nails at Toro, jabbing at the air in front of his chest. He blinked as though looking into a strong wind.

"We will treat the prisoners with respect and dignity so long as they give us no cause to do otherwise." She turned to the group. "Please excuse my friend. His late father was a general during our former military government. Toro is sorry he missed all the mayhem. I think he would have been quite an enthusiastic interrogator." She shrugged. "At the very least, he would have enjoyed himself."

The woman walked down the line of prisoners, stopping one by one to study their faces individually. Even Matt was smart enough not to speak. Once she'd satisfied her curiosity, the woman flicked her fingers, motioning for Jelly to follow her toward the nose of the aircraft.

They spoke in hushed tones, shooting periodic glances at the rest of the group, paying more attention to her own men than the prisoners. Her companion wearing the gaucho hat retreated back to the Renault and stood there, looking like he'd eaten something that didn't quite agree with him.

At length, the woman turned on her heels and marched directly back to silver haired Bruno. Standing in front of him, she put her hands in the pockets of her slacks, which, Bo had to admit, looked out of place for such a smartly dressed woman. They were nearly the same height, but the woman's aggressive bearing made her seem taller.

Alma had maneuvered herself to stand next to Bo when they'd climbed out of the plane. All eyes were on the conversation, so no one stopped her when she gave a whispered translation as the woman began to speak in Spanish.

The woman toed at the grass looking down as she spoke. "I understand you took photographs of the prisoners."

"Si, su señoria," Bruno said, shuffling in place. He was nervous about something. Not a good sign.

Alma leaned sideways toward Bo, to make sure the others couldn't hear her. "Weird," she whispered. "But that guy just called her 'your honor' . . . like she's a judge."

Bo added the name to his mental list. If a judge was involved, then there was a chance law enforcement was involved as well.

Alma continued with her translation.

"Were you certain that the GPS location services were disabled?" the judge asked.

Bruno nodded, looking relieved. "I did, *su señoria*."

The woman cocked her head. "I am curious that you did not send the photos to me. Can you explain yourself?"

Bruno shrugged, gesturing with open hands. "I knew you would meet us here and see the prisoners yourself."

The woman's gaze narrowed. "Then why take any photos at all?"

"Proof of life."

"Very well," the woman nodding smugly. "That makes sense." She turned as if to walk away, hands still in her pockets, but then wheeled.

"Did you happen to text these photographs to anyone else?"

The man paused, then shook his head.

"Suppose I were to have a look at your mobile phone?"

"Su señoria . . ."

Two sharp cracks pierced the still morning air. A small silver pistol had suddenly appeared in the judge's hand.

Bruno's hand clawed at the center his torso, over his diaphragm. He dropped to his knees, eyes wide. Obscene croaking noises escaped his open mouth.

Jelly stepped in quickly and grabbed a black revolver from Bruno's waistband as he pitched forward, writhing in the gravel beside the Caravan's tire.

La Pulga walked up and stooped to get a better look at the dying man. Cheeks flushed, The Flea didn't appear to be interested in his friend, but in the process of death itself.

The man in the gaucho hat leaned against the Renault for support, seeming to grow smaller, fading away by the moment.

The judge began to speak again.

"Sorry," Alma gasped, coming out of her stupor and catching back up with her translation. "The judge just told Jelly to get Bruno's phone. She wants him to collect everyone's phone as well. Looks like that one called Bruno was planning a double cross, working for someone named Richter. The judge doesn't want anyone to contact—"

Toro's walking stick whooshed through the air, cracking against Alma's back. "No talking in line," he snapped. With her hands cuffed, and no way to catch herself, she pitched face first into the gravel.

Bo roared at the assault. Without thinking, he launched himself sideways, directly into Toro's broken leg. Toro screamed in pain, hopping sideways and lashing out with the stick, catching Bo across the jaw. Bo rolled onto his stomach, curling into a ball to try and protect his head as Toro continued to batter him with the heavy stick.

Alma threw herself on top of Bo, screaming, pleading for Toro to stop.

The rest of the thugs converged on the prisoners to keep them under control.

"That is enough!" the judge barked.

Toro hunched over Alma, panting, his walking stick in the air, smiling even amid his pain. The judge had been right. He would have enjoyed doling out torture.

The judge pointed a finger at him. "I told you to treat the prisoners with respect."

"Si, *su señoria*," Toro said.

The woman turned to speak to Jelly again.

Bo waited for Alma to roll off him, and then turned gingerly onto his side. He took a couple of deep breaths and willed the world to stop spinning. Coughing, he spit out a front tooth along with a clot of fresh blood.

"How about we don't do that again," he said.

Alma moved her neck back and forth. "No promises."

She was a tough one.

Matt stayed put as if welded in place, looking away.

Bo drew his legs under him, and wallowed to his feet. He was unwilling to stay down any longer than he had to, but it took him a while without the use of his arms. Alma stepped closer so he could lean his shoulder against her thigh. Not just tough, but smart as well. Sickeningly dizzy, he had to use her for support even after he was standing. The earlier blow across his helmet had rattled his brain. Toro's beating had been icing on the cake.

"Ha!" Toro chuckled. "I gave you a good hit. Soon you will have no teeth at all—"

The judge spun where she stood and shot Toro twice in the face before he knew what was happening.

"Pelotudo!" she spat.

Beside the Renault, the pale man muttered to himself in Spanish. He was obviously not cut out for this much violence.

The rest of the men stared down at their two dead comrades. Even La Pulga had been caught off guard.

Bo couldn't bring himself to care. He spat out another mouthful of blood and then ran his tongue over the jagged remains of his tooth.

An overwhelming dread washed over him at the pain he knew he'd be in once the adrenaline wore off.

The judge walked over and prodded the dying Toro with the toe of her shoe, pistol still in hand. Smoke curled from the end of the barrel.

"I will have someone find clove oil for your tooth," she said. "It is the best I can offer."

Bo nodded. He wasn't about to say thank you to the woman responsible for his kidnapping.

The judge licked her lips, studying Bo. "You are in charge of this group?"

"Yes," he said, keeping his tongue over the broken tooth to protect it from the air.

"Good," she said. "With any luck, we will soon put all of this behind us. It will be nothing but an unpleasant memory and a good story."

"For those left alive at the end," Bo said.

"You will still be alive if you behave," she said.

Bo kept his eyes locked on her. "I'm not talking about us."

A smile spread over the judge's face. "I am no stranger to threats, Mr. . . ."

"Quinn," The Flea said. He had the passports.

"Mr. Quinn," the judge continued. "I meant what I said about treating all of you with respect. So long as you do nothing to deserve otherwise. But do not for an instant take that to mean I lack the needed resolve." She looked down at Toro's lifeless body and then back at Bo. "I once had a dog that killed my chickens. I was very fond of this dog, but I still shot him." She leaned in close to make her point. "Even so, the dog's death did not save the chickens when it came time for me to make a stew."

CHAPTER 8

Riley Grey's Citation X was set up with a satellite phone, so Quinn was able to touch bases with Ronnie Garcia somewhere over the Gulf of Mexico.

Her voice was a comfort amid the chaos going on in his brain.

"I've confirmed with Soledad," she said. "She's all set to meet you. She's already talked to her contacts with the Buenos Aires police as well as the federal Gendarmería, to be on the safe side. The Gendarmería Captain in charge of the precinct where Bo and the others went missing admits that it was likely a kidnapping, but says they have no suspects or witnesses at this point. According to Soledad, they do appear to be working the case, so that's good. She's put out feelers at local hospitals and clinics, but so far she's not heard anything."

"I know it's going to be late," Quinn said, "but I'd like to go visit the scene as soon as we arrive."

"I told her you would," Garcia said.

"Thanks," Quinn said. "I really appreciate this."

"Wish I was there with you," Ronnie said.

"Me too," Quinn said.

Quinn had never been one for long telephone conversations, so he thanked Garcia again and said goodbye.

Quinn called his parents next, checking in on the off chance that Bo had called home. His mother answered, sounding out of breath. She said she'd been shoveling the remains of a March snow in the driveway. Quinn couldn't imagine his dad allowing that unless he was gone or incapacitated. His mother confirmed his suspicion and said he was away at a boat show.

Rather than worry her, Jericho decided not to mention Bo. There was nothing to tell anyway. His mother had a particular soft spot for Bo. He'd broken her heart many times over the years. But he was her youngest, and, sickly as an infant, he'd needed her the most.

Quinn said he'd call back soon to catch up, and ended the call. His mother was a tough woman—she had to be with sons like Jericho and Bo. She'd cried buckets of tears over her two boys—and she would, no doubt, cry many more for one reason or another.

Across the aisle, Thibodaux looked up from his book. "You doing okay, Chair Force?"

"I'm fine," Quinn said, though he was far from it. He held up the satellite phone. "You need to call Camille?"

"Talked to her before we left," the Cajun said. "She'd think I was tryin' to get her to let me buy a new gun or somethin' if I called her twice in a four-hour period."

Miyagi removed her earbuds and gave Quinn a quiet smile.

"I appreciate you both coming," Quinn said.

"*Arrête toi!*" Thibodaux said, telling him to stop. "You got the weight of the world pressin' down on you, *ami*. You need us to take care of the goats while you see to saving your brother."

Miyagi raised an eyebrow and shook her head. She and Quinn both knew there was no way to predict what might come out of Jacques Thibodaux's mouth. It was his way of dealing with—and helping deal with stress.

"My *mémère* loved to tell us about a man who had himself all kinds of misery." Thibodaux's Cajun accent came on stronger when he told a story. Quinn couldn't help but grin, despite the situation. "Well," Thibodaux continued. "This sad man, he took his self to the doctor and he say, 'Doc, I think I'm goin' plum *braque*—crazy. My wife, she givin' me the fits. My kids, they no good rascals. My job, it have me in a rut. Life just ain't no good at all.' Well, the doc, he looks at the man and says, 'You need to buy a goat.' 'A goat?' says the man. 'What would I need a goat for?' 'Just buy the damn goat,' the doc says. Next week, the man, he comes back, and he says things is still awful at the house and at work. The doc shakes his head and tells him to buy another goat. The man, he does what the doc orders, but comes back next week with the same story. 'Buy a third goat,' the doc says. A week later, the man comes back and says that things is worse than ever. The goats, they get into everything and he can't keep them penned up to save his life. 'Sell the goats,' the doc says. Next week the man comes in. 'How's your life now?' the doc asks. 'C'est magnifique!' the man say. 'Now I don't have no goats.'"

"Goats," Miyagi muttered, shaking her head again.

"You focus on savin' your brother," Thibodaux said. "Me and Miyagi-san, we'll take care of the goats."

CHAPTER 9

The judge took the passports and then laid down the law about the treatment of her prisoners, giving a rousing speech on human rights and dignity. She then turned on her heels and took Jelly with her, leaving The Flea in charge.

The medicinal smell of eucalyptus from the tangle of trees overhanging the small brick cottage infused the humid air, mixing with the pungent odor of cattle and horses munching hay in the pens outside. La Pulga allowed the prisoners to drink from the water spigot off the windmill, no doubt to remind them that he was in charge and could give or take away whatever he wished. Bo whispered for the others to dunk their heads in the round metal trough as they took their turns at the tap. The sticky heat was oppressive in their armored riding gear, and the cool water helped bring relief and much-needed focus.

Dripping wet, they were ushered inside.

The interior of the house was dark, with the only light streaming in through small windows and the open door. Thick walls and a tile floor kept it relatively cool. Soot from many fires in the large fireplace stained the red bricks below a rough-hewn timber mantel. The smell of wood smoke and saddle blankets hung in the still air. A number of photographs adorned the stucco walls. Most of them were of polo ponies, but a few showed the judge and the man in the gaucho hat during happier times. Bo nodded to himself. The imperious judge and her milquetoast husband made an unlikely pair of criminal masterminds. The photographs of the couple were what Jericho would have called good intel. But the fact that such evidence had been left around for the prisoners to observe gnawed at Bo's gut.

The remaining decorations were sparse, things normally used around a cattle ranch—an Argentine saddle with a sheepskin cover just inside the heavy front door, a hooked bull goad and several rawhide quirts on the wall, and a braided lariat hanging over the saddle. The place had the feel of a cabin, and should have been cozy, but, considering their captivity, the leather gaucho equipment took on a sinister air.

The room was relatively small, maybe twelve by fifteen, forcing the prisoners to bunch together as they came through the door. With no direction, they milled in place, waiting to be told where to go.

They didn't have long to wait.

The Flea gave a sharp clap of his hands and a gap-toothed man called Tigre grabbed Eva by the hair and hauled her back to the front door.

Steven yelled in protest, starting after her, but got knocked to the floor for his trouble. The two remaining guards pulled pistols and pointed them at the prisoners.

Tigre stopped in the threshold of the door, shoving Eva to her knees. Backlit, she slumped there, hands behind her back, while Tigre held a gun to her head.

Steven cursed. Matt cringed and looked away. Alma offered a whispered prayer in Spanish. Bo stood where he was and glared at La Pulga.

"It occurs to me," The Flea said, his voice breathy and hoarse, "that none of you have been properly searched. Your handcuffs will be removed one at a time and you will take off your clothing so that we may check you for weapons. Cooperate fully, and Eva will remain unharmed."

Bo had known this was coming. He'd been worried they might separate the women, and was actually relieved when La Pulga ordered them all searched as a group. He'd already decided that he would go down fighting rather than submit to watching either of the girls being violated. Alma must have read his mind, because she looked at him and shook her head.

"Just stay alive," she said. "No matter what happens."

"Good advice," La Pulga said. "Now get on with it. Tigre grows tired of not shooting your friend."

Tigre chuckled and cuffed Eva in the head with his free hand. She looked up and tried to spit, but her mouth was too dry, leaving her to sputter impotently and earning a round of derisive laughter from the men.

Bo shrugged off his riding jacket as soon as the cuffs were removed, taking a short moment to massage the circulation back into his hands. The men seemed transfixed by the tattoo of a black octopus on his forearm. The Flea let out a low whistle when he pulled the t-shirt over his head, revealing the scars that mapped his chest and torso. He didn't have near as many as Jericho, but there were enough to know he'd survived some serious contact with people that wanted to kill him. Alma and the others in the group had seen them before, swimming or at the hotel hot tub. It was a good thing, he'd thought, for the man charged with security to have plenty of battle scars.

His arms were yanked behind his back and the handcuffs replaced as soon as he'd removed his boxers.

"Interesting, don't you think?" The Flea observed. "How stripping away a thin layer of cloth can shatter the idea of security."

Bo thought of a dozen threatening comebacks. The image of what he wanted to do to this guy shone bright in his mind's eye. But he willed himself to keep his mouth shut, for Eva's sake.

Alma's cuffs came off next.

"Makes me wish I'd skipped that ice cream yesterday," she whispered a moment later, as she slipped off her own t-shirt, drawing leering murmurs from the men.

Matt fumed, staring daggers. It had not gone unnoticed that Alma had decided to stand beside Bo.

Steven's eyes stayed locked on Eva, rattling the chain on his handcuffs as soon as Alma was undressed. "Let's hurry and get this over with," he said.

Matt snapped at him. "Easy for you to say. Your dad is the reason we're all in this mess."

"Come on," Alma said, visibly shivering, even in the warm air. "We're all scared here."

"Phht," Matt said. "You sure don't look scared."

The Flea clapped his hands again, eyeing Matt. "I seem to remember you saying your father was wealthy as well. You said he would be happy to purchase your freedom. Perhaps you are the reason for all this, and Mr. Grey is just a fortunate coincidence. I wonder," he said, scratching his hairless chin. "Would your wealthy father be willing to pay for the release of your friends as well?"

"My father would," Steven said without pause. "He'd pay for all of them. No doubt."

"That may be true," The Flea said. "But the question is for Matthew."

Matt shrugged "Would he pay for all of them?" He nodded, a little too slowly. "Sure. I guess so."

"We will know soon enough," The Flea said. He smiled, the smile of a child who pulls the legs off live baby birds. "Now, you all behaved very well . . ."

Tigre forced Eva to strip, then stood her naked in front of the fireplace with the rest of the group. Steven looked as though he might cry, but Eva stood beside him, chin up, defiant.

The men went through everyone's clothing piece by piece. La Pulga searched Steven's clothing, and Bo saw him stuff the expensive engagement ring into his pocket. Bo said nothing, thinking this little bit of information might come in handy in the long run. After they'd searched the clothes, the guards led their prisoners individually to the far corner of the room for a more thorough search, in full view of their friends. Quinn wasn't proud of the fact that he'd been to jail before, but the event did give him experience being strip searched. There was a method to it. These guys had no idea what they were doing. Or if they did, their reason behind the search was to intimidate and titillate, not to find contraband. Searching Bo, Steven, and Matt went quickly, each earning a few half-hearted boots and fists to maintain compliance. The process took much longer for the women, with Flea and his men stifling giggles, turning their captives around and around and studying them like inquisitive schoolboys poring over an anatomy textbook.

Bo shuddered to think how bad it would be had the men not feared repercussions from the judge.

At length, The Flea licked his lips and gave a shuddering sigh. He tore his eyes away from Alma long enough to look at his watch. He croaked something in Spanish. Bo recognized the word for judge.

"What are you afraid of?" Bo asked, unable to contain himself. "Are you worried your boss is going to come back and catch you in the middle your fun and games?"

Tigre grabbed Eva and started to drag her toward the doorway. Her defiant attitude vanished and she began to sob, pedaling against the tile with her bare feet, begging not to be taken away from her friends. She surely thought they were taking her away to rape her, but Bo knew men like this would want an audience.

Steven rushed forward, but Tigre kicked him in the chest. Unable to catch himself, he fell across the saddle just inside the door, dragging it and the wooden rack to the floor on top of him.

Bo took a half step. "How about you use a different hostage this time?"

Flea shook his head. "Do you volunteer?"

Bo took another step. "I do."

Flea gave a flick of his hand and one of the men drove a brutal fist into Bo's kidney.

Bo staggered sideways, overwhelmed with nausea and explosive pain. Alma used her body to keep him upright.

"Just stay alive," she whispered again.

"You would not make such good insurance," Flea said. "Apart from Miss Cortez, I am not certain anyone cares enough about you to keep you from getting killed. I would prefer to have a hostage everyone does not want to see shot in the head."

Eva calmed when Tigre placed the muzzle of his gun to her temple.

"Hey," Matt said. "What if I had some information that could make you a lot of money?"

Alma's face fell. "Shut up, Matt."

"I know what I'm doing," Matt said.

"Information?" The Flea said.

Matt gulped. "It's good shit," he said. "Something you won't be able to find out unless I tell you."

"Is that so?" The Flea mused.

"Come on, Matt," Bo said. "You can't bargain with these guys."

"Of course he can," The Flea said. "But first, we should take care of a few things."

"I'm telling you it's good—"

Tigre turned his pistol toward Matt, shutting him up.

The Flea held up an open palm. "Oh, we'll talk. I promise you that. But later, my friend."

One of the men led Bo to the center of the room, while the others were moved to the fireplace and forced to kneel on the hard tile. Bo raised his hands away from the small of his back, but instead of removing the cuffs, one of the men grabbed a handful of hair and yanked his head backward, arching his neck and pulling him to the floor. He landed on his back, hands trapped beneath him, the wind driven from his lungs.

Before he knew what was happening, a rawhide quirt was shoved between his back teeth, making it impossible to close his mouth. Tigre held his pistol on the rest of the group, while the other two tied Bo to one of the heavy timber chairs in the main room. The quirt was lashed in place like a bit and bridle, and then tied to the back of the chair, rendering his head virtually immobile—and the nerves of his broken tooth exposed to the air.

Only after Bo was restrained did The Flea step forward. He held a small plastic cooler in one hand and a pair of channel-lock pliers in the other.

Bo was vaguely aware of Steven shouting, of Eva crying

again, and Alma cursing in Spanish. La Pulga, The Flea, ignored them all, focused entirely on Bo.

He dipped into the plastic cooler with the pliers.

"When I was in school," he said, "my rugby coach told that cold is recommended to treat a variety of injuries."

He leaned in, pressing a small piece of ice against the jagged tooth.

Bo jerked and thrashed but he could barely move his head, let alone escape. Saliva and blood drooled from the corners of his open mouth as he cursed and spat around the rawhide quirt.

The Flea touched the ice to the tooth again and again, lighting up the exposed nerve. Bo arched his back as if he were being shocked.

The Flea loomed above, pliers and ice poised just inches from Bo's cracked lips.

"I should mention," The Flea said. "The judge is busy seeing who is and who is not worth our trouble. She will not return for some time. So, as you can see, I can go about my studies for hours without interruption." He touched the ice to the throbbing nerve again.

"What was it you were saying about fun and games?"

Bo regained consciousness a short time later, his head resting against the warmth of Alma's thigh. The pain in his tooth pulsed through his skull like a flashing white light. His own breath passing over the nerve nearly brought him to tears. Alma brushed the hair out of his eyes and he looked up to see she'd been left with her hands cuffed in the front. Like him, she was dressed in nothing but underwear.

"He told me to give you this," she said, holding up a small bottle of clove oil with both hands.

Bo nodded, turning his head like a baby bird.

She put a couple of drops directly on the tooth.

"More," he said, moving his jaw back and forth.

Alma grimaced, tipping the glass bottle to give him a few more drops. "Swish it around, but don't swallow," she said. "This stuff can make you sick."

Bo nodded, feeling immediate relief. The tooth still throbbed, but the pain was now bearable. He wanted to stay where he was, but couldn't very well spit on Alma's leg, so he wallowed himself into a seated position along the wall with everyone else. Steven and Eva sat together, leaning on each other for physical and emotional support. Matt was halfway across the room by himself, sulking.

All the men were outside enjoying an *asado*, or Argentine barbecue, around a hardwood fire.

Bo spat the clove oil out on the tile, on the side opposite Alma.

"You okay?" she whispered.

"I'm fine," Bo lied. Apart from his tooth, his head was on fire and it was a good bet that his jaw and a few ribs were shattered. Still, he had a job to do, and it helped to focus on that. He motioned at Matt by lifting his chin.

"Come on, bud," he said. "We're all in this together."

Matt sneered. "Some of us are deeper in it than others."

"Seriously," Bo said. "There's a better chance of survival as a group. It's dangerous to separate yourself."

"Dangerous to you," Matt said.

Bo gave up for the time being. Talking hurt his teeth—and he'd never been much of a pleader anyway. He scooted around so he could looked at Alma without turning his neck, and tried to give her a reassuring smile. With the broken tooth and the blood smeared on his face, he was pretty sure he just came off as insane.

"You're probably wondering what I ever saw in him," she whispered.

"Crossed my mind," Bo admitted.

"Honestly," Alma said. "I have no idea. He's handsome, and not so much of an asshole when he's not scared out of his wits."

Bo raised an eyebrow. "Is that so?"

"Okay," Alma conceded. "He's always a little bit of an asshole. Guess I'm just a sucker for a pretty face." She leaned her head against the wall, exposing the curve of her neck. "How do you think this is going to work?"

Bo shrugged. "They will have contacted Steven's father by now."

Steven looked up. "I'm sure he'll pay as soon as they tell him where to send the money. Then maybe this will be over."

"We can hope," Bo said. "The judge is probably building files on each of us this evening."

Matt sneered again, staring directly at Eva. "I wonder how long it's going to be until she figures out who you are."

"Matt!" Steven said through clenched teeth, shooting a glance toward the door and the laughing men outside.

"What?" Matt said. "You know as well as I do that she's our ticket out of here."

CHAPTER 10

Riley Grey's Citation X touched down at Ministro Pistarini International Airport outside Buenos Aires at 10:52 p.m. local time, fifteen hours and six minutes after Bo had sent up his SOS.

Doctor Patrick stayed back with the pilots while they closed out their flight plan, finished up a few reports, and put the airplane to bed for the night while Jericho and the others cleared Argentine immigration and customs. Clearance didn't take long since they'd brought virtually nothing into the country. Their lack of baggage might have raised eyebrows had it not been for the fact that these Norte Americanos arrived in a twenty-million-dollar business jet. There was no explaining the fiats of the rich, some of whom preferred to travel with a platinum credit card instead of cumbersome luggage.

Thibodaux gave a low whistle when he stepped around the corner and into the main terminal.

"Ronnie's friend Soledad," he said. "She happen to be a long cool woman in a black dress?"

"Ha," Miyagi said, stone faced. "The Hollies song . . ."

Quinn gave a slight nod.

"Yep," he said.

They'd arrived in between flights and the terminal was vacant but for a few people sitting at the lounge at the far end of the lobby—and a tall woman with perfectly coiffed blond hair. A black cocktail dress hit her in the middle of her deeply tanned thighs. Her makeup was impeccable, like the on-air television journalist that she was.

"Oh ye yi," Thibodaux sighed. "That's our contact?"

The woman transferred a small clutch purse to her left hand and reached out to greet Quinn.

"I am Soledad San Martín," she said, sounding like a reporter signing off the air. "Mucho gusto. Welcome to Argentina." Her smile faded. "I am very sorry your visit is under such unpleasant circumstances."

Quinn made the necessary introductions and then asked to be taken straight to the scene of the kidnapping.

"Of course," Soledad said, her full lips breaking into a smile again. "My car is in the lot outside. Veronica gave me instructions as to what you would need. I only had a few hours to collect what she described. Hopefully it will be satisfactory."

"What did she ask you to get?" Quinn asked.

Soledad turned as she walked. "It is probably best we discuss it in my car."

Her car turned out to be a small red SUV called a Ford EcoSport. There was no way Thibodaux was going to wedge himself into the backseat so Quinn and Miyagi gave him the front.

Soledad realized the urgency of the situation and spoke as she drove, taking Autopista Luis Dellepiane to head northeast into the city. Her English was accented, but impeccable.

"I have spoken about the kidnapping to my contact with the Gendarmería four times in as many hours. They are a national force and work in concert with the Buenos Aires Police. So far, there are still no witnesses."

"Thank you for trying," Quinn said. "You mentioned something about Garcia's instructions."

"Of course." Soledad's brown eyes were perfectly framed in the rearview mirror. "You will find a small tote in the space behind you—where you put your other bags. I could only find one pistol, but perhaps one of my contacts will locate another by tomorrow. Knives, however, are a much easier item to obtain in this country."

Quinn reached behind him and pulled a leather bag over the seat and into his lap between him and Miyagi. He opened it to find a single Taurus G2 pistol, one spare 12-round magazine, and a box of nine-millimeter ammunition. He passed the gun, along with the extra mag and ammo to Miyagi, who handed everything up to Thibodaux.

"For the goats," Miyagi said.

Soledad shot a backward glance. "Goats?"

"Inside joke, chère," Thibodaux said.

At the bottom of the leather bag Quinn found three large sheath knives. Quinn gave one to Miyagi, who drew the foot-long blade from the sheath a few inches. She tested the edge with her thumb and nodded in approval. Quinn took out a similar knife and studied the thick carbon steel blade under the glow of passing streetlights. The heft of it in his hand brought a certain comfort.

"Thank you," he said.

"De nada," Soledad said. "Veronica described you as a man with the soul of a gaucho. These knives are known as *facónes*, a slightly shorter version of the long fighting blades from early in the last century. It is said the Argentine gaucho used his knife for everything from opening a cow to closing a discussion."

"I'm sure these will come in handy." Quinn returned the *facón* to its sheath, thinking about the people who held his brother captive.

Soledad's eyes narrowed in the mirror, growing more serious. "Veronica has never told me what she does for her job. I know at one time, she worked for your CIA in a uniformed capacity. She speaks easily of guns and knives, so I suppose I could guess if I tried very hard."

"I don't want to put you in a bad spot," Quinn said. "If you could just show us where the kidnapping took place, we'll be fine on our own from there."

"Do you speak Spanish?" Soledad asked. Quinn shook his head.

"Then you will need my help," she said. "And I want to give it. I am several years older than Veronica. I was working on my masters while she just beginning her university studies. She probably did not tell you, but my father was taken off the street much like your brother. Only he was not taken for a ransom. No, he was kidnapped for the high crime of writing an article on unionization in the college newspaper. My mother was abducted and tortured for the egregious sin of being married to him. She was tortured and raped and then tortured some more before being drugged and thrown from an airplane into the Rio de la Plata. My father died of a heart attack shortly after, at the age of twenty-six."

"I'm sorry, chère," Thibodaux said, his voice hushed.

"I would have been adopted out to military family—or killed to make certain the subversive bloodline was stopped—but I had gone to visit my grandparents in Cordoba. The police were looking for them as well, and they sent me to live with other relatives the night before they were kidnapped. I was four years old and I never saw any of them again." She shivered, and then shook off the emotion. "I tell you this not for sympathy, but to explain that I am no talking head on the television. Were it not for the military junta, I would have grown up to be the daughter of a college professor and a beauty queen, but those monsters bathed me in the blood of my parents and turned me into a revolutionary. I would have done anything to have saved my family if I had been able. How could I not help you do the same to save yours?"

Traffic was light and it took less than a half hour to reach the upscale Belgrano neighborhood. Quinn felt a familiar tightening in his gut as Soledad turned onto the quiet side street where the attack had occurred. Large brick houses fronted by rosewood trees lined the quiet avenue. Spiked iron fences and high walls topped with razor wire cordoned off each home.

"These places are like mini forts," Thibodaux said, face to the side window.

"Sadly," Soledad said, "Such measures are necessary to guard against robbery and other crimes. You have gated communities in the States. Outside of Buenos Aires, we have communities that are surrounded by electric fences and moats."

"Is it really so bad?" Miyagi asked.

Soledad gave a solemn nod. "I supposed it depends on one's circumstance. Many Argentines of this generation have never been affected by violent crime. They would tell you this is a safe place to go jogging at night. Others, they have had a much darker experience. They are the ones who build the fences. The only house on the block with no wall would make an awfully tempting target—so, everyone builds walls."

Soledad parked under a street lamp, next to an ivy-covered wall with wrought iron spikes along the top, and got out of the car.

"Your brother's motorcycle was found here, in the middle of the street. The other motorcycles were all around his. Your brother's bike had damage to the front fender, and the bike ridden by . . ." Soledad consulted a long reporter's notebook. ". . . the bike ridden by Eva Turcott had damage to the back tire. All the other motorcycles were simply lying on their sides."

"Someone ran into the back of her bike," Miyagi mused.

Soledad crossed her hands in front of her, clutching the notebook.

"The police suspect that was the case, and that your brother ran into a lead vehicle when it stopped suddenly in front of him."

Quinn shook his head, walking the area, studying the street. "Maybe," he said. "But Bo's not likely to have run into anything unless he intended to." He pointed at the pavement where Bo's bike had gone down. "See this dark patch of rubber? I'm thinking he spun his back tire here, attempting to drift his back wheel. It's something we used to do as kids. There's a good chance he ran into one of the bad guys and that's what damaged his bike."

Thibodaux walked to the middle of the dark street and did a slow three hundred and sixty degree turn. "Tidy spot for an ambush," he said. "Especially that early in the morning. All these walls and fences keep everyone cordoned off nicely from the outside world."

"That looks like a guard shack." Quinn said, nodding to

what looked like a white phone booth on the corner less than fifty feet away.

"It is," Soledad said.

"Is it not staffed at night?" Miyagi asked.

"Sometimes yes," Soledad said. "Sometimes no."

Quinn went to get a better look. Roughly four feet by four feet, it was vacant and secured with a heavy padlock. He could see a ceramic mug and some girlie magazines on the desk, as well as a couple of unopened bottles of water. "Someone's been here recently," he said. "Do you think it would have been staffed early this morning?"

"I can check with the company," Soledad said. She scribbled the telephone number stenciled on the side of the shack into her notebook. "The police may have already—"

Quinn held up his hand, motioning down the street toward an elderly gentleman out walking in the dark with his beagle.

Thibodaux, ever aware of his intimidating size, moved away to give the man plenty of space.

"Could you ask him if he lives around here?" Quinn asked.

Soledad's smile was visible in the darkness. "Of course," she said. "Just leave it to me."

The beagle growled when he saw the group, but the elderly man tipped his hat as he went by.

Quinn could not understand much of what she said, but Soledad introduced herself and then chatted briefly with the man. He became animated and pointed to the guard shack, rattling off what appeared to be directions. Soledad pulled a business card from a clip on her notebook, wrote something on it, and then gave it to the man. He held it briefly to his heart, and then bowed before walking away.

"Did you give him your contact number?" Quinn asked.

Soledad chuckled. "That is already on the card," she said. "It appears that he is a big fan of my news program. He wished for my autograph. In any case, he did not see anything this morning, but he did hear the sound of yelling and a woman's screams. By the time he came to his gate only the motorcycles remained. He said the security guard was in his booth during the kidnapping, but that he left before the police arrived."

"Does he know the guard's name?" Miyagi asked.

"He does," Soledad said. "His nickname at least. The guard goes by the name Viscacha. It's a little animal somewhat like a rabbit or a large packrat. Their meat is actually quite tasty. According to Señor Gomez, this fellow has a pinched face with big ears that resembles one of these creatures."

Quinn tapped his thigh, gazing into the darkness, thinking. "Could your contact get us his address? I don't have time to wait until he comes back on duty."

"We are fortunate there," Soledad said. "Señor Gomez said that Viscacha works at Liniers tomorrow."

"Liniers?" Thibodaux asked.

"A cattle market in Buenos Aires," Soledad said. "More than 40,000 animals are sold here each week to restaurants and supermarkets. Tomorrow is a big sale day." She looked at her watch. "Cattle lorries will begin to arrive in a few hours. Viscacha works the chutes so he will get to work around four or five in the morning."

"How about your contacts?" Quinn pushed. "Maybe they can get us his home address so we don't have to wait."

"Señor Quinn," Soledad said, her voice soft but resolute. "I understand your desire to move forward and rescue your brother. But my contacts would not remain my contacts for long if I telephoned them at one o'clock in the morning and asked them to identify a man whom I only know by the nickname of a small animal."

"I'll give you that," Quinn said, feeling the urge to hit something. He turned to head toward Soledad's car. "Let's go have a look at this auction place then."

"Viscacha will not be there for at least four hours," Soledad said.

"We are less than forty minutes away. I suggest you take a moment to eat something in the event that we do not have a chance to do so later."

Quinn hesitated. Bo was out there somewhere, waiting. Stopping for the trivial human appetites like food and sleep seemed unthinkable.

"She's right, chère," Thibodaux said. "We need to be firing on all cylinders when the time comes.

Quinn sighed. "True," he said. "But I want to get to this Liniers place early enough that we can get the lay of the land."

"Of course," Soledad said, starting up her car. "I know a bar that still serves a wonderful *milanesa* at this time of night. It's like a beef schnitzel. The owner is a former friend of my father's so he can be trusted. He is one of the people I have looking for another pistol."

"That would be good," Thibodaux said, patting the Taurus in his jacket pocket. "But if we can't find one, it shouldn't be too much of a problem to get another when the time comes."

CHAPTER 11

Tigre and the others found the judge's stash of wine, and, for a time, bottles clinked and the wood fire snapped amid the bawdy songs and filthy jokes. The men laughed and farted, raising their voices when they got to the most explicit punchlines so the women inside could hear what was in store for them. Alcohol and the post adrenaline crash from a day of kidnapping and watching two of their compatriots be shot to death, eventually pushed them into deep snoring sleep.

Bo and Alma sat awake in the darkness of the little house, huddled as close as possible against the chill. The cold tile floor sent a sickening ache through the bones in Bo's hips, but the throbbing pain in his tooth made everything else feel insignificant. Alma, whose hands were cuffed in front of her, did her best to tend to him, administering a few precious drops of clove oil every few minutes. The cold, or maybe it was the nerves, caused her to shiver uncontrollably and she had to brace her body against his to keep from spilling the entire bottle every time.

Steven and Eva leaned together, backs to the wall, in and out of fitful sleep. Matt's head lolled to his chest, mouth open, drooling.

"I'm not worth any ransom," Alma blinked back tears. "My father can't even afford to replace his old pickup truck."

"Shhh," Bo said, snuggling closer, fighting the urge to curse at his shackled hands. "We'll figure something out before then."

"Maybe things always work out happily ever after in your world," Alma snapped. "But I have seen too many times they do not."

"Me too," Bo whispered.

"I'm sorry," Alma said. "It is stupid to attack the only friend I have. You must have led a very dangerous life."

"Not really," he said.

"Well," Alma said. "Your 'not really' gave you some cruel scars."

Bo forced a smile. "They're worse than they look."

"Perhaps," she said, sounding far away. "My youth was dull. The most adventure I ever had in Valparaíso was sneaking out at night to go dancing." She sniffed, wiping away a tear. "Dull does not sound so bad at the moment."

"Help is on the way," Bo said. "My brother's not the type to wait around to make a plan. In the meantime, we need to look around for something to get out of these cuffs—a paperclip, something like that."

Alma sighed. "I can appreciate your optimism, but does this look like the kind of place where we could find a paperclip?"

"A hairpin, then," Bo said, refusing to let Alma slide into complete despair. "You've seen the judge. I imagine her to be a slave to fashion, even out here among the cattle."

"Perhaps," she said. "But even if you're able to pick the locks, what then? We are half naked in the middle of nowhere."

"To be honest," Bo said, "I wouldn't mind a few minutes alone with The Flea."

"I am not afraid to die," Alma said. "But the thought of dying among these animals—"

The scrape of a shoe on tile caused her to stop and turn toward the door.

Bo sat up straighter, peering into the darkness.

"How are we doing?" It was The Flea's croaky voice. Rather than wait for an answer, he strode across the room and planted a boot in Bo's side, driving the wind from his lungs and cracking at least two ribs.

Bo rolled with the blow, doubling up for the next kick—because guys like The Flea were never content kicking you only once. He coughed and groaned, but refused to cry out.

La Pulga stopped once he judged Bo to be sufficiently tenderized, leaning against the wall on one hand. Panting from his efforts, he looked down at Alma and grinned.

"Are you cold, little one?" he asked, as if he genuinely cared. He squatted down beside her, speaking English, as if he wanted Bo to understand every word. "I know what would make you warm." His put a hand on her thigh, just above her knee. "Your passport says you are from Chile, so you might not be familiar with the interrogation methods formerly used by our military here in this country."

"Hey!" Bo grunted. He tried to pull himself into a seated position, but earned another swift kick from The Flea.

"Now," La Pulga said, settling down beside Alma again. "I was telling you about the military methods. I think your country used the *parrilla* to warm prisoners up on old bedsprings with a bit of electric current. I suppose it was effective enough, but somewhat . . . handsoff if you ask me. I prefer the more personal touch of the cattle prod." His hand began to inch upward inside Alma's bare thigh. "They say it smells like bacon cooking . . . Such a shame to burn this precious flesh." His voice grew huskier with every word. "But some measures are necessary—"

Alma drew her knees together, trapping The Flea's hand long enough to launch herself forward and drive her forehead into his nose. He recoiled, doubled his fist to hit her, but Bo wheeled on his hips and reared back with both feet, planting them into the man's unprotected groin. The Flea fell backward, out of Bo's reach, but Alma got down, pummeling him in the neck and head with her powerful legs. Bo rolled quickly, intent on getting a leg wrapped around the man's neck and choking the life out of him.

Unfortunately, Jelly came in and grabbed him by the shoulders, dragging him back across the tile to the wall. The muscular kidnapper gave him a half-hearted swat to the side of the head, but it was apparent he probably wanted to kick La Pulga as well, so there was no force in it.

The Flea clamored to his feet, one hand to his bleeding nose, the other clutching his groin.

Jelly raised both hands and rattled off a string of what sounded like accusatory Spanish. The Flea gave an insolent shrug, and then muttered a few halfhearted words. Jelly stood for a long moment with his arms crossed, as if considering what to do. At length, he shook his head and went out to rouse the sleeping men.

Alone again with his victims, The Flea licked the blood from his upper lip, and squatted down beside Alma again, staying just out of her reach.

"Do not worry, my sweet," he said, congested from his broken nose. "This place has no electricity, but we will soon be someplace with more . . . how do you say it? Creature comforts. Anticipation is half the fun. No?"

He ventured forward to pat her on the knee again, and then stood before she could react. Bo jumped forward, rattling his handcuffs, causing him to recoil for fear of another attack.

La Pulga stopped cold, a crooked smile spreading over his face.

"You find yourself amusing?" he said. "Let us see how amusing you are when Jelly is not here to protect you."

He went out the front door, leaving the prisoners alone again.

They were all awake now, staring at Bo and Alma.

Matt's glare was enough to cut through the shadows. "You're going to get us all killed," he said.

"It's not their fault." Steven leaned his head back to stare at the ceiling. "I really thought my dad would get something rolling by now."

Matt turned his glare toward Eva. "What about your dad?" He asked. "He got enough firepower—"

"Shut up!" Steven snapped. "So help me, Matt, I'll kill you myself if you don't—"

"If I don't what?" Matt said. "Lay back and die like a good friend? I'm going to do whatever it takes to stay alive. You can take that to the bank."

Eva sighed. "They'll find out soon enough," she said. "Maybe I can save the rest of you."

"That's not the way these guys think," Bo said. "We keep quiet and let them find out on their own. That gives people time to mount a rescue operation."

"We'll see," Matt said. "But I'm not waiting to get shot in the head."

Bo turned to Alma. Matt was going to do what he was going to do. He leaned closer. "What did Jelly say when he came in?"

"He yelled at La Pulga for taking liberties," Alma said. "And reminded him of the judge's order. Then he said the judge is working out the money details and that she's not coming back until sometime tomorrow morning. She's supposed to be bringing an ice chest and enough food for a couple of days."

"A couple of days?"

"That's what Jelly said."

Bo sighed, thinking. "La Pulga seems to think we'll be at a place with electricity soon."

Alma shivered. "You think they're moving us?"

"I do," Bo said. "And I don't think Jelly knows."

Angelica Medina pushed away from her the laptop and tapped long manicured fingernails on the polished wood beside her keyboard. Her red silk dressing gown flowed down either side of the squeaky office chair where she'd slipped it off her shoulders. The hotel room across the Tancredo Neves Bridge over the Iguazú River in Brazil was cramped and hot but Richter surely had people watching their home in Argentina. Angelica said it did not matter. They could log into their cloaked accounts from anywhere. According to her, the move to a different network would only make them more secure.

The kidnappings had been planned on a whim and she was still in the process of working out the method for Grey to pay the ransom. Justino was not stupid. He understood finance and banking—even the illicit kind. He and Angelica often used offshore banks to hold their proceeds from the illegal adoptions they arranged. The government was hot and cold regarding investigation and prosecution, but a sitting judicial officer could not afford to be found with an overly healthy bank account in the event some enthusiastic prosecutor decided to go snooping. As an attorney, Justino had set up the offshore accounts. But when Angelica started talking about ransoms of Bitcoin and other cryptocurrency, it all went over his head.

The killings at the camp had rattled Justino. Angelica had handed down harsh sentences, but she'd never killed anyone, so far as he knew. He didn't know what to say to her, so he said nothing, sitting across the room instead, watching and waiting to be told what to do.

A small fan at the corner of the desk oscillated back and forth, caressing her bare shoulders and jostling her hair with every pass. Had Justino not been so terrified, it would have been sexy.

Angelica stared at the monitor for a long moment, then closed her eyes, canting her head in thought. Justino knew this look, and it made the back of his head throb. Defendants in Judge Medina's courtroom all knew they were doomed if she closed her eyes and turned her head just so.

"What?" Justino said from his spot on the uncomfortable hotel couch. "What have you found?"

Angelica rose from her chair, her head still canted, one eye half closed. Justino started to speak again but she held up her hand to shush him.

She shrugged the dressing gown back over her shoulders. Justino couldn't help but notice her fingers trembled as she knotted the cord. He'd never seen her kill someone before, certainly not people in her own employ. It made sense that she would be a little shaky after that.

"I am merely exhausted," she said. "We should get some rest before returning to the camp."

"But you found something?" Justino pressed. "Is it a problem with the ransom?"

Angelica sighed, a flicker of uncertainty in her eyes. "Eva Turcott is a problem," she said. "I'd hoped to keep everyone alive for a few days in case we needed them, but I think we need to go ahead and have Jelly take care of her."

Justino's mouth fell open. He'd hoped there would be some way out of this madness, some way that didn't leave a half dozen unmarked graves in the back of his cattle pasture. "Why so soon?"

"Eva is not who we thought she was," Angelica said. She picked up her mobile from the desk. "The sooner Jelly makes her disappear the better."

CHAPTER 12

Soledad had Jericho and the others fed and watered and back en route to the cattle market by two-thirty in the morning. There'd been plenty of coffee and milanesa, but Quinn could only pick at his food. Soledad convinced him to eat a few bites and take a to go mug of yerba mate, which tasted to Quinn like hay and hot water, but at least it woke him up.

They arrived in the rundown Mataderos neighborhood of Buenos Aires a half hour later, parking among rusty livestock trailers and junked pickups behind the block and stucco colonial building that housed the banks that financed the various cattle sales. The business side of the operation had yet to open at the early hour, but the whistle of gauchos and the lowing of cattle drifted through the warm darkness. *Mataderos* meant slaughterhouse—a convenient term for Quinn's mood.

Thibodaux took a deep breath. "Smells like money."

Miyagi shot him a sideways glance.

Soledad smiled. "Money indeed," she said. "We Argentines each consume, on average, a hundred and fifty pounds of beef per year." She pointed beyond a two-story office building to the right. "My contact will be inside. This man,

Viscacha, will probably be out working the lanes, sorting the cattle as they are dropped off at the far end of the facility. I will go into the office and tell them I am doing research for a news story, ask permission to look around."

She had changed into a fashionable white cotton blouse, form-fitting jeans, and only slightly more sensible flats, explaining that while they were skilled in the use of guns and knives, she was quite comfortable using the weapons God had given her.

She returned from the office a few minutes later with something long and white in her hand.

"Free calendars," she said, holding up the roll of cardboard. "People are always giving me things." She pointed behind her with the calendars. "This place is very large, but we have permission to walk the catwalks to look around. I told the office manager that I might want to chat with a few of the gauchos, and that I was looking for someone with a unique look for the camera—not handsome. He said there is one named Rudolfo who looks like a viscacha. He's calling him on the radio now. We can meet him up on the catwalks."

"Outstanding," Quinn said, tapping the hilt of the gaucho knife under the tail of his shirt.

Acres of cattle, separated into holding pens of the same color and grade, ran along broad driving lanes below the metal catwalks. Buyers would be able to look down from ten or fifteen feet above and bid on the cattle as the auctioneer moved from lot to lot. The pens were already filling to capacity with animals bunched tightly in each one. Men in gaucho berets sat on sheepskin saddle pads, riding up and down the lanes on thick-necked Criollo horses. Some worked livestock, others were buyers who'd arrived early to survey the product without being rushed. Cowboys on foot moved up and down the alleys, driving small herds of newly unloaded animals, sorting them with long poles with plastic bags fastened to the ends.

Torture had given the cattle prod a bad reputation in Argentina.

Soledad walked out in front of the group, with Quinn and Thibodaux—and their much more imposing looks—bringing up the rear. Miyagi remained in the shadows, disappearing as only she knew how to disappear. Her job was not to look for Viscacha, but to watch for incoming threats—the "goats" from Thibodaux's story.

Even the best plans had a way of evaporating at the slightest change of wind, and this one was not even really a plan. Unfortunately, Viscacha was in the middle of a smoke break instead of where his boss thought him to be. Instead of meeting them head-on, he climbed up the catwalk from behind them. He'd been told over the radio that Soledad San Martín wanted to talk to him, but when he caught sight of the mountainous Cajun and an extremely serious Jericho Quinn, he jumped the pipe railing of the catwalk and ran into the darkness.

"Watch him!" Quinn hissed to Jacques as he vaulted over the side, and straight into a pen full of milling black cattle.

Quinn pushed his way through the frightened cows, feeling the heat and humidity that surrounded their bodies. They were packed too tightly to stampede or do much of anything but bawl and take a few terrified steps from one side of the pen to the other.

Viscacha hopped the wooden corral as if pursued by the devil, never once looking back. Quinn could hear Thibodaux running above. Maybe Miyagi was somewhere she could get ahead.

Viscacha cut back under the catwalk, making it impossible

for Thibodaux to follow without going halfway around the yard or coming off the catwalk altogether. He didn't slow down when he reached the alley, darting in front of a herd of oncoming cattle. Quinn pulled up short, narrowly avoiding being trampled. The cowboy at the back waved his stick and shouted something in Spanish but Quinn ran past as soon as the bulk of the cattle went past, waving his hands to cause the last few animals to shy and stop in their tracks.

He wasn't about to let the only clue he had slip away.

Running again, Quinn bowed his head and dug in to pick up speed. In front of him, Viscacha ducked around a small outbuilding at the back of the yard.

In different circumstances, Quinn might have slowed down, made a more cautious approach. This guy could very well have a weapon.

Quinn swung wide instead, minimizing a possible ambush from running straight around a blind corner. He nearly tripped over the prone body of the man he'd been chasing. A large figure towered over him in the shadows. At first he thought it was Thibodaux, but he wasn't quite that large— and the big Cajun was behind him.

Quinn was surprised by little in the world, but took a half step back when the man stepped out of the shadows with both hands raised.

"Dad?"

"What'd you think I would do?" Pete Quinn said once they'd secured an unconscious Viscacha and stowed him in the trunk of the elder Quinn's rental car.

Both Miyagi and Thibodaux seemed amused at Jericho's sudden loss of composure. Neither had ever seen him this off kilter, but the appearance of his father had caught him on the back foot.

"I honestly don't know," Jericho said. "Maybe call me and let me handle it."

"Does that sound like something anyone in this family would do? Put yourself in my position."

"How did you know to come here and look for Viscacha?"

"Your brother had me down as an emergency contact," Pete Quinn said. "I was at the boat show in LA and hopped the first flight to Buenos Aires. I rented a car and went to the spot where Bo was taken. There's a little guard shack there. I assumed whoever was in it at the time of the kidnapping probably saw something. There was a calendar inside for this cattle auction with today's date circled. I figured I'd come here and see what I could find out. It was slim, I know, but my gut said it was worth looking into and I ended up running into this meathead." He looked at Thibodaux with a narrow eye. "And anyway, what's a viscacha?"

Soledad stepped forward, extending her hand. "Your gut was correct," she said, introducing herself. "I see where Jericho gets his instinct and his good looks."

Pete Quinn gave a shrug. "Not sure about the intellect, but he got his looks from my wife."

Jericho couldn't help but smile inside. Pete Quinn never missed the opportunity to mention his bride when speaking to a beautiful woman.

A pounding from the trunk of the rental car brought everyone back to the matter at hand.

"You were right," Jericho said, as Thibodaux hauled out the mortified Rudolfo.

Soledad had found a photograph of a viscacha on the Internet, and it was easy to see where this guy got his nickname. Big ears stuck out on either side of equally large eyes. His nose was screwed up as if preparing for a sneeze that never came. The split top lip that Quinn's father had given him only added to the look of a terrified rodent.

Surrounded by a beautiful journalist and four extremely stern foreigners, Viscacha began talking with little prompting. He quickly identified a photograph of Bo from Pete's cellphone, admitting that he'd seen him along with four others taken from their motorcycles early the morning before. Bo was, according to Viscacha, alive when last he saw him, though badly stunned from a blow to the back of his helmet. "I only saw his face because the kidnappers took his helmet off to make sure he was still alive."

Viscacha shied away from giving names at first, but, caught between the elder Quinn and Thibodaux, made the wise choice to tell everything.

Soledad translated.

"I did not know all the men involved," Viscacha said, nearly in tears. "They were wearing masks, but am sure I recognized two of them. The one who hit the blonde man is very small, almost like a child. He is called La Pulga. The other one is called Jelly. I could tell by his great size and the fact that he was with The Flea. Both men work for a judge in Misiones. I only know because my sister wanted to adopt a baby and the judge sold her one. It cost ten thousand U. S. dollars, but my sister did not care. She just wanted a baby. I went with my sister to pick the child up and the men called La Pulga and Jelly were there, to make sure my sister paid her money, I think. You do not forget men like that."

"This judge," Jericho said. "What's his name?"

Viscacha gave an emphatic shake of his head, speaking in heavily accented English now. "The judge is not a man, señor. Her name is Angelica Medina. She is quite beautiful for an older woman."

Soledad and Miyagi, who were both in their forties, rolled their eyes.

Jericho snapped his fingers in front of Viscacha's face to bring him back on track. "Let's say Judge Medina kidnapped someone. Where would she take them?"

Viscacha sighed, weighing his options. A look from Pete Quinn let him know he didn't have any. "One of two places. I did a little research when I found out where my sister was getting her baby. Judge Medina is a known to be a *busca panzas*—one who looks for pregnant bellies—to help women like my sister who cannot have children of their own. There is a good chance your friends will be at one of two places, a yerba mate plantation east of Iguazú Falls or a cattle farm that is so close to the Paraná River it is almost in Paraguay."

"Draw me a map," Jericho said.

"It will not be exact," Viscacha said. "But I know the general area. The locations are a matter of public record. I found them myself on the Internet."

Soledad gave a slight nod, letting the others know this was correct.

"There is one more thing," Viscacha said. "Judge Medina is married, and I cannot be certain of this, but from the whispered conversations she had with Jelly, I believe the two are lovers."

CHAPTER 13

Hours of pain and worry eventually pushed Bo into a dreamless sleep. The warmth of Alma's skin against his kept him there for over an hour. Both awoke to the sound of Steven's frenzied cries as Jelly and one of the other men dragged Eva across the tile floor by her arms. It was dark in the little house, but the fire was going again outside and Bo could see in the flickering light through the open front door that she was awake, and fully conscious of the fact that she was being dragged to her death.

Steven tried to follow but Jelly just shoved him back down. The other guard gave him a boot to the ribs to keep him there.

"I love you," Eva said.

Steven continued to scream until she was out the door. And then he turned his attention to Matt, still slumped by himself on the other side of the room.

"This is your doing!" Steven hissed, spittle flying. His eyes blazed in the darkness. "You cowardly piece of shit! You got her killed. You! Do you understand?" His head sank to his knees. "Oh, Eva . . ."

"I didn't even tell them," Matt said, dumbfounded.

"But you told them she was worth a lot of money," Alma

said, refusing to let him off the hook. "And you would have told La Pulga everything if he'd let you."

Matt began to hyperventilate. "I just . . . I just don't want to die."

Bo sighed. "We're all going to die," he said. "But the rest of us get to die with some dignity."

Steven's head snapped up. He spoke through clenched teeth. "I'll kill you. If it's the last thing I do—"

Eva's screams stopped him cold. They all turned to look toward the door.

A single gunshot cracked outside. Bo's heart sank. Everyone bowed their heads and Alma began to pray in Spanish.

And then, Eva screamed again, this time with more gusto. Men shouted and more gunshots followed on the heels of the first.

Bo recognized the sound of a gunfight when he heard it. The flat crack of pistol fire and the louder, reverberating booms of a rifle. Rounds snapped against the bricks outside. Men spoke in hushed tones, firing back, and then yelling something Bo couldn't understand.

The shooting stopped and La Pulga appeared a moment later, backlit in the doorway. Tigre, the guard with the gap in his front teeth, stood beside him leading Eva by the arm. He shoved her inside.

Steven fell back against the wall in shock.

"Get dressed," La Pulga said, sneering triumphantly. He pulled his pistol and pointed it at Alma. "Tigre will remove your handcuffs. I have no time for games. If you try anything I will kill you all."

A man with his hair greased back like a wood duck came behind Tigre. Someone outside had built up the fire and it was easier to see.

"There will be no need for that, La Pulga," the man said,

blue eyes shifting around the room, dwelling on Alma's long legs. He nodded, like someone who'd found what they were looking for in a supermarket, and then gave a little smile. "We are going to a new, more comfortable home," he said, clapping his hands, each finger wearing a ring.

A slender woman wearing tall leather boots came in next. She was deeply tanned with flaxen hair that appeared to glow in the firelight. She whispered something into the man's ear. He was obviously the boss.

"Excellent," the man said. "Violeta tells me my plane will be here momentarily. Please, Tigre, unhook them so they can put their clothing back on. There is a time to take away someone's clothes—and that time has not yet come. We are not savages."

The prisoners huddled together as they climbed back into their clammy riding gear.

Bo leaned in closer to Eva. "What happened out there?"

"Jelly led me away from the fire," she said. "He said he was sorry he had to shoot me but the judge said it was 'a necessity.' I never saw anybody with such cold eyes. He had his gun up and everything, about to do it, but La Pulga shot him instead. Then a bunch of other men came out of the trees with rifles. The two guys around the fire tried to shoot it out, but they were drunk and only had handguns. La Pulga and Tigre are the only ones left."

"The judge?" Bo asked.

The man with the slick hair laughed at that. "I thought she would be here by now," he said. "She owes me a great deal of money and I thought I might collect before . . . well, you know."

The drone of an aircraft engine overhead came in through the door. It had landed by the time Tigre had replaced the cuffs, this time with everyone's hands behind their backs.

A thickset man with a gleaming bald head peeked in from outside.

"We are ready to go, Señor Richter."

"Outstanding," Richter said, motioning toward the door with a flourish. "Please, after you."

"You know we're worth a lot of money," Matt said, unable to help himself. "My father can make it worth your while. And you already know who Eva is, or you wouldn't have had your men—"

"I know much, Mr. King," Richter said. "I think it's best you keep quiet."

"Okay," Matt said. "I just wanted to make sure you're aware of the entire situation since you're a new player."

"I am," Richter said, rolling his eyes, clearly annoyed.

Bo smiled, trying his best to look as unthreatening as possible. "Come on, Matt," he said. "Let's just get to the plane."

"You get to the plane," Matt said. "I'm trying to let Mr. Richter here know we're worth a hell of a lot more alive than dead." He scoffed. "Well, most of us."

Alma glared. "Matt!"

"What?" Matt said. "Mr. Richter is a smart man. He said he already knows—"

Richter's voice was measured, but deadly quiet. "I also said to keep quiet."

Dense as he was, even Matt understood the implication if he continued to speak.

Richter's plane turned out to be another Cessna Caravan, this one painted white and red and considerably newer than the one they'd arrived in. It only had seats for eight, not including the cockpit, so several of Richter's men left the way they'd come, in cars parked somewhere beyond the trees. Only Richter, his tan female companion, and the bald muscle rode in the plane with the prisoners.

It wasn't until they were on board that Bo realized that the cargo door where they'd entered had been removed, the space secured only with a cargo net of nylon webbing. Richter and the bald man took seats in the back, next to the open hatch, while the woman sat up front in the right seat of the cockpit. The seat directly across from Richter remained vacant until the pilots began their takeoff roll.

Richter motioned for Matt to join him with a flick of his ringed fingers.

"Now we can talk," he shouted over the wind and engine noise.

Matt shrugged, then wallowed up out of his seat, bending at the waist to make his way down the aisle. Hands cuffed behind him, he had to brace his hips against the seats for support as he went.

Bo caught a telltale glance between Richter and the woman up front about the time Matt reached the rear of the airplane. The woman turned and nodded to the pilot, who dipped the plane slightly to the left, causing Matt to lose his balance and stumble. The bald man helped him along, pushing him toward the webbing, which parted the moment Matt leaned against it. He was gone in an instant, disappearing into the darkness before he even had time to scream.

The plane leveled off, heading northwest and the bald man secured the webbing over the hatch.

Richter rose from his seat and came forward, stopping next to Bo. He nodded toward the hatch. "I call that a win for all of us," he said. "That was originally going to be you, Mr. Quinn. Matt was certainly worth more money. I simply liked you more than I liked him."

CHAPTER 14

Soledad used her pull as a reporter to rent a Piper Navajo—no small feat in the wee hours of the dark morning in a country where most adults ate dinner at nine p.m. and stayed up late. The plane was just large enough to carry everyone. If and when they located Bo, they would have to work out some other form of egress. First things first, Quinn thought, climbing into the low-wing airplane.

Pete Quinn sat with his head leaning against the window, lost in his own thoughts. Jericho's daughter, Mattie, was eight, but would forever be the five-year-old girl with dark pigtails and puffy-sleeved dresses in his mind, no matter old she was. To Pete his sons were men. He'd certainly raised them to be. But in his heart, they would surely always be boys.

And now one of them was out there, hurt and needing help.

Jericho sat up front, Viscacha's hand-drawn map on his knee directing the pilot. He'd thought about bringing the big-eared man along with them, if only to keep him from warning Judge Medina. In the end, Quinn decided to leave the talkative man with Soledad's friend where they'd had their supper. The last time he saw Viscacha, he was drinking beer and eating a milanesa, thankful to be alive after being locked in Pete's trunk.

The Piper Navajo made short work of the trip north, arriving as the sun was just starting to come up. The pilot stayed low, skimming the treetops over the yerba mate plantation first. The few outbuildings were quiet and there were no visible vehicles in the large gravel lot at the end of the road that cut through the trees.

"Shall I land, Señor?" the pilot asked.

Quinn pressed his face to the window, then turned toward the back of the airplane.

"What do you think, Dad? No movement. Do we land or check the other location?"

"We can always come back," the elder Quinn said. "I say we check out the cattle operation."

Quinn gave him a thumbs up, and advised the pilot, who banked back to the right.

The Medinas' cattle ranch was an hour's drive by car through winding jungle roads, but it was less than ten minutes by airplane. Quinn saw the glow of the fire outside the dark building when they were still a half mile out.

"Heads up," he said. "Soledad, you should stick with the plane. If things go bad you and the pilot can go for help."

She nodded.

Quinn saw the bodies as the pilot came around in a low pass. Two lay face down beside the house, on either side of the fire. Someone, it looked like a woman, knelt beside a third body some hundred feet from the house, at base of a windmill and water tank. It was difficult to tell, but none of the bodies looked the right size and shape to be Bo. It was some consolation, though a small one with so many dead just lying around.

"You have the pistol ready?" Quinn asked, looking back at Jacques.

"Affirmative," Thibodaux said.

Miyagi spoke while looking out the window, working out her strategy. She held the long gaucho knife by the sheath. "I will circle behind the plane and approach from the south."

"You're with me, Dad," Jericho said.

"Oh," Pete Quinn said. "You are right about that."

Justino Medina was behind the wheel of his car, too stunned to weep. Angelica had abandoned him as soon as they arrived, flinging open her door and falling over Jelly's dead body as if . . . There was no "as if" about it. It was so clear to him now, all of it. Justino knew she had never planned to spend the ransom money with him. He wondered if the ransom note would eventually lead back to him, leaving her with the money and him rotting in prison. It was all for Jelly, a man fifteen years younger than her. The poor bastard was dead now. Justino felt sorry for him. Lucky for Jelly, he was dead. Richter had certainly been the one to kill him. Or that little piece of shit La Pulga. The fire still burned in front of the Medinas' little house—a place that held at least a few happy memories. Justino would be dead too had they arrived a few minutes earlier.

He did not even move when the plane landed and shadowed men got out, running toward the house. If The German was coming back to clean up loose ends, that was just fine with Justino. At least he would not have to sit here and watch his wife wail over the body of her handsome young lover.

Justino hunched forward, wiping away his tears with his shirtsleeve and peering through the windshield. It wasn't Richter, but someone else, three men, one older, one lean and predatory, the other huge, all moving quickly toward the house. Angelica had yet to see them.

Justino glanced to his right at her purse. In her haste to be with Jelly she'd left her pistol. Perhaps if he took it to her, she might forgive him for being so dull, and things would return to the way they had been with her serving *sándwiches de miga* for tea and pretending that she loved only him—before they became entangled with The German.

The men from the airplane were almost to the house now, trotting.

Justino reached into his wife's open purse and snatched up the pistol. He had no plan other than to take it to her so she would see him for the devoted husband that he was.

A small Asian woman materialized from the shadows as he got out of the car. Not a fighter at heart, he held up both hands to ward her off. He forgot that he was even holding the pistol. The cruel Asian woman reminded him by cutting off his hand.

He stared down at the pulsing stump, astonished that he felt no pain. He did not see the men as they reached his wife.

Jericho came to a stop twenty feet from the weeping woman. He recognized her as Judge Medina from a photograph Soledad had found on the Misiones Court homepage. Quinn could see both her hands, but a black pistol lay in the dead man's fist, forgotten there by whoever had killed him.

Quinn whistled to get the woman's attention.

"Hey!"

She looked up momentarily, and then bent back over the dead man. His forehead had been shot away, but that didn't keep her from cradling his face in her hands.

"I'm looking for some friends of mine," Quinn said.

"They are gone," the judge sobbed, without looking up this time.

Pete Quinn shot a glance at Jericho. "Gone where?"

"The German took them," the woman said, breaking down. "He or that traitor La Pulga will kill them soon, just like he killed my Jelly."

"Where?" Jericho said. "Where has he taken them?"

The judge began to mutter under her breath, swaying maniacally over the dead man. "It would have been so perfect," she said.

Pete Quinn lowered his voice. "One of them is my son, ma'am," he said.

Now she looked up.

"Are you Grey?"

Pete shook his head. "Quinn."

"Bo's father?" She began to cackle. "The most worthless one of all? You and your son may go to hell!"

She lunged for the gun in Jelly's fist, earning her a center mass double tap from Thibodaux's pistol. She pitched forward across her lover's body.

Miyagi called out from the house. "We are clear!" She trotted up to him a moment later.

Quinn scooped up the Beretta look-alike, press-checked to see there was a round in the chamber, put it on safe and then stuffed it in his waistband. He clenched his teeth at the cows in long morning shadows.

"Let's get back to the plane and see if Soledad knows who The German is," he said.

"I have someone who can help," Miyagi said, hooking a thumb over her shoulder toward the house. "If he hasn't bled to death or died from his own stupidity."

"Who is it?" Thibodaux asked as they walked toward the house.

"I believe it's the judge's husband," Miyagi said. She nodded toward a slumped figure with a piece of cloth wrapped around the stump of his wrist. "He was crying when I found him."

"Well," Thibodaux whispered. "You sure as hell know how to console a guy."

A broken man, Justino Medina proved to be a wealth of knowledge, providing an address to a warehouse on the outskirts of Ciudad del Este in Paraguay where Fernando Richter, a.k. A. The German, had his office and did most of his business. Richter, Medina explained, was a remnant of a society of would-be Aryans who'd immigrated to Paraguay after World War II. The man genuinely believed himself and his blond consort, Violeta, to be the smartest two people in Paraguay, and certainly in the Triple Frontier. He ran guns and drugs and human cargo, and he had police from all three countries in his pocket.

"It was my wife's crazy idea," Justino said, sniffing. "I love her completely, so I went along." He began to sob in earnest. "And then I find out about Jelly . . . I have nothing more to hide."

He gave a full confession regarding his part in the kidnapping, naming everyone involved. He even let Soledad record the conversation on her phone.

Thibodaux shot a look at Miyagi.

"This poor bastard's eatin' the spaghetti."

She raised a brow. "Indeed."

CHAPTER 15

Bo figured he had maybe an hour to live, less than that if The Flea kept it up.

After dropping Matt King out of his airplane somewhere over the remote jungles of Brazil, Richter had taken them into Paraguay, landing on a small strip along the meandering Monday River. Two black SUVs, which judging from their radios and grill lights did double duty as police vehicles, pulled alongside the plane when it came to a stop. Bo and the others were stuffed inside the back of one of the SUVs, still handcuffed, and the motorcade headed to the northeast toward the sprawling warrens of Ciudad del Este.

The Flea sat in the front passenger seat, turning every so often to leer back at the prisoners, paying special attention to Alma.

"Your friend is jaguar bait by now," he said. "We could have dropped him into the Paraná or the Iguazú, then he would be fish bait." The little man laughed. "But there is too great a danger that some passing tour boat or barge might have found his decomposing body before the fish ate him up. The jaguars will make a fast meal of him."

Alma shivered and turned to look out the window, which only served to urge him on.

"I wonder if he was alive when he reached the trees." La Pulga shrugged. "He seemed a man of delicate constitution. I think it more likely he had a heart attack as soon as the wind hit his face."

Alma threw her head back and screamed, "Would you just be quiet?"

"Interesting," he said. "If you were so fond of him, then why do you take up with your guide?"

Bo leaned forward. "Hey, Flea! Want me to look around for a phonebook back here so you can see over the dashboard?"

La Pulga darkened. "You are so amusing," he said. "Yes, I am short. You are probably not aware of this, but Richter is famous for several things, chiefly, removing the feet and hands of people who owe him money. There are a wide variety of instruments and tools at his warehouse that I am anxious to try." He turned to study Bo up and down before a wide smile spread across his face. "I think that you and I will be the same height very soon. In fact, I may even be a little taller than you when we are finished."

Richter's SUV peeled off as soon as they reached his two-story warehouse in the outskirts of Ciudad del Este. He and the brown woman went into the front of the building with the bald goon, leaving La Pulga and Tigre to see to the prisoners along with two other men that Bo did not recognize, both with jaguar tattoos on their forearms and each carrying a short-barreled SMG on a single point sling around his neck. Tigre and The Flea tromped up the metal stairs in front of prisoners, while the two jaguar boys brought up the rear.

Tigre took a key from the pocket of his jeans and opened a large padlock on the metal door at the top of the stairs. Bo's heart sank when he walked in the room and saw clear plastic sheeting fastened to the floor with black gaffer's tape. There were metal rings affixed to the far wall and a couple of five gallon buckets to use as makeshift toilets. Kidnapping and human trafficking was nothing new to Fernando Richter.

Just as La Pulga had promised, a variety of bone saws, machetes, tinsnips, and hoof nippers hung on a peg board beyond the plastic sheeting.

Tigre and the Jaguar boys secured everyone's cuffs to the individual metal rings on the far side of the room while La Pulga went to a desk beside the pegboard. He'd obviously been here before and knew his way around.

He shuffled through the desk a moment, then came back with a narrow metal cylinder the size of a long flashlight. A thick copper wire protruded from the sides of the tube three quarters of the way up, coiling around the last six inches of the device. La Pulga's thumb rested over a red button in the center of a rubber handle.

"The inventor of this little machine called it *The Cat*," he said. "A strange turn of events. Don't you think? The Flea, wielding The Cat." He chuckled at his joke and ran the copper coil along Alma's thigh, pushing the button.

She screamed, throwing herself backward at the sudden shock.

Bo lunged, flailing with his free hand and narrowly missing a handful of La Pulga's sweater.

Instead of retreating, The Flea turned The Cat on Bo, driving the coil into his chest. Pinned against the wall with nowhere to go, Bo jumped and twitched like a piece of frying fish. He slumped against his cuffs when La Pulga released the button, exhausted, stifling a whimper. His tooth was on fire again, and to make matters worse, he was sure he'd just cracked a couple more.

Eva and Alma both screamed.

Steven stood, holding up his free hand. "Just stop it! My father will pay double, but we all have to leave here alive."

"That is funny," La Pulga said. "Your father has already agreed to Richter's terms. Eva's family may be a bit more problematic, but nothing he cannot handle." He turned to Alma, giving her a quick jolt with the coil. "I will get back to you in a moment, my darling. First things first, though. Mr. Quinn and I have a little appointment."

Bo raised his head and gave a weary chuckle. "I thought Richter liked me . . ."

"He liked you better than Matt," La Pulga said, nodding for Tigre to unhook Bo from the ring. "Not enough to keep you alive."

Soledad borrowed a minivan to drive Jericho and the others across the Tancredo Neves Bridge into Brazil, and then the Friendship Bridge from Brazil into Paraguay. Legally, the Americans should have had a visa to enter each country, but Soledad explained that no one would stop them unless they did something stupid to draw attention to themselves.

"Like launching a raid on a known drug lord and smuggler?" Thibodaux said.

"Exactly that sort of thing," Soledad said.

They reached Richter's warehouse outside Ciudad del Este an hour and a half after leaving the Medinas' cattle ranch. They watched as a slender woman in high leather boots stepped outside to retrieve something from one of three black Suburbans parked alongside the concrete building.

"Yuck," Thibodaux said. "She looks like she's spent too long in the roaster."

"That must be Violeta," Pete Quinn said. "Richter's girlfriend that Justino told us about. Dark skin, bleached blond hair."

Soledad gave a low whistle. "She has the body of a twenty-year-old."

Thibodaux harrumphed. "She better give it back," he said, "'cause she's wrinklin' it."

Violeta took a moment to scan the area outside the warehouse, missed the minivan completely, and then disappeared back inside.

"How do you plan to do this?" Soledad asked from behind the wheel.

"Richter's not expecting us," Jericho said. "I think I'll walk up and knock on the front door."

"There appears to be a side entrance," Miyagi said. "I suggest Jacques and I approach from there, while you make your more direct approach."

"Where do I go?" Pete Quinn asked.

"You're with me, Dad," Jericho said. "Soledad, thank you."

"I will be here when you come out," she said.

A sign above the entrance in bold red and black lettering said FERNANDO RICHTER SHIPPING CO.

"We're at the right place," Jericho said under his breath. "Makes things easier."

"Okay, son," Pete Quinn said. "This is new to me. When you say knock on the front door, you mean—"

Jericho flung open the metal door and shot the two men with guns on the inside, twice each, center mass.

"Knock, knock," he said. "Just like that."

Pete Quinn raised his eyebrows and gave his son a nod. "That's kinda what I envisioned." He scooped up one of the dead men's SMGs.

"You know how to use that?" Jericho asked.

"I do," the elder Quinn said.

Three more of Richter's thugs came down a long hallway, firing as they approached. Quinn took out the leader with two shots from the Beretta and chased another back around the corner, winging him, but failing to deliver a killing shot.

Pete sent half the thirty-round magazine from his SMG downrange with one pull of the trigger. Fortunately, some of the rounds dropped one of Richter's men.

"Take it easy with that, Dad," Jericho said. "Short bursts."

The second shooter poked his head out again down the hall. Pete dropped him, but spent the last fifteen rounds of his magazine doing it.

"Short bursts," he said. "Got it."

Bullets snapped off the wall behind them sending both men jumping for cover. Quinn brought up the Beretta in time to see Violeta slump forward, Miyagi's blade in and then out of her dark brown throat.

"Goats," Miyagi said, slipping back into the shadows.

"Why does she say that?" Pete asked.

"Long story," Jericho said.

Thibodaux's hushed voice came from the same alcove where Miyagi had disappeared. "It's me, Chair Force. Don't shoot."

"We're good," Quinn said.

"Richter's through there," the Cajun said. He held up three fingers, his good eye and the Taurus trained down the hall. "Three more goats, but Emiko and I got 'em. You take care of Richter."

Jericho was already moving toward the office. Quinn flung open the door and handed it to his dad, cutting the pie until the man inside came into view. As he suspected, one more of Richter's men stood inside guarding the boss. This one was a bald thug wearing a black muscle-mapping shirt. Quinn got off the last round from his Beretta, rushing the shot and catching the big man in the shoulder, missing his vitals. Surprised at being hit, the man lowered his SMG and took a step back. Richter stood in the middle of the office, both hands flat on top of a wooden desk as he rose from his chair.

Pete sprang past Jericho, throwing himself at the bald thug, plowing into him and pummeling him with his fists. Jericho had seen the aftermath of a few of his dad's fights. The bald guy didn't stand a chance.

On his feet now, Richter reached for a metal box. His pistol empty, Quinn drew the long gaucho blade from the sheath on his belt and pegged the man's hand to the top of the wooden desk, the razorsharp edge facing outward.

Richter squealed in pain, the metal from his many rings clicking against the wooden desktop. He grabbed the wrist of his injured hand and stared down at the blade.

Quinn heard a roar behind him and turned to see his father punch Richter square on the chin. The force of his blow sent the man flying backward, slicing his hand down the centerline and leaving the blade behind, still impaled in the wood.

"Where's my son?" Pete Quinn said, the bald man's SMG in his hand now as he loomed over the screaming drug lord. Richter pointed upward, at the ceiling.

"Behind you, Quinn-san," Miyagi said. She surveyed the wounded Richter and the unconscious bald man. "I'll take care of them," she said.

"Jacques?" Jericho asked.

"Out back," Miyagi said. "Tending to two other goats."

Jericho took the pistol from the box on Richter's desk, presschecked it to make sure it was loaded, and then motioned upstairs with the muzzle.

"Let's go get Bo."

They cleared the stairs to the second floor in four steps, taking up positions on either side of the door.

"They've heard us coming," the elder Quinn said.

Jericho nodded, the pistol at high ready. "No doubt."

A scream came from inside the room that made Quinn's bones ache. There was no doubt it was Bo.

Jericho looked at his father.

"You ready?"

Pete Quinn answered by putting his foot to the door, hooking around the threshold with the short barreled SMG as if he'd grown up kicking doors. Jericho followed him in, bringing the interior of the room into view over the top of his front sight. A gap-toothed thug stood to the right of three badly beaten prisoners—two women and one man—a pistol in his hand. Quinn dropped him with two shots, wheeling immediately to the left. Bo lay on the floor, chained to a metal ring by one hand, while a small man, not much larger than a boy, stood over him with what looked like a cattle prod.

Pete Quinn emptied the magazine of his SMG into The Flea's chest, causing him to jump and twitch in place, dancing like a marionette.

"Short bursts," Pete Quinn said, dropping the empty gun and running to his boy.

Bo raised his head, staring dumbfounded.

"Dad?"

Pete fell beside his son, cradling his head in his lap.

Jericho watched the door until Thibodaux appeared there a few moments later. "We're clear," the Cajun said.

"This one has the keys," a young man who had to be Steven Grey said, pointing toward the dead gap-toothed thug.

The blond woman beside him closed her eyes, fighting

back tears. The taller one with auburn hair didn't even fight it.

Quinn unchained Steven, then gave him the key so he could release the rest while he went to check on Bo.

"What the hell, Dad?" Bo said, wincing as he sat up on one elbow. His right front tooth was nothing but a jagged shard and had to be terribly painful.

"How bad are you hurt?" Pete Quinn asked.

"Honestly, it would probably take me less time to tell you what's not hurt."

Pete closed his eyes and shook his head. "I have to call your mother and tell her you're all right."

"I say again, Dad. What the hell?"

"What do you mean?"

"I mean," Bo groaned. "What are you doing here?"

"You sent an SOS. What did you expect me to do?"

Bo shook his head, looking incredulous. "I don't know. Call Jericho . . ."

"Well." Jericho sighed. "I for one am glad he came along, baby brother. Turns out our old man's pretty good at taking care of meatheads."

EPILOGUE

Leaving Paraguay without a visa and entry stamp after a prolonged gun battle would have been much more difficult had it not been for Riley Grey's anonymous donation of ten brand-new Chevrolet Suburbans. Had immigration officials known that the vehicles were from Grey, they might have held out for twenty.

Soledad said goodbye at the base of the aircraft, vowing to visit the US again one day soon to see her old friend Veronica. She kissed everyone including Miyagi goodbye, catching the Japanese woman off guard.

On board, Doctor Patrick started Bo on fluids and he was asleep by the time the pilots began their takeoff roll. Steven and Eva held hands across the aisle. Alma Cortez sat facing Bo, watching Dr. Patrick take care of him. She'd asked permission to accompany him back to the States, to make sure he was settled.

"He saved our lives on this trip," she said. "Many times when we did not even know he was doing it."

Dr. Patrick brought a cellphone back from the galley and handed it to Eva Turcott. Eva punched in a number, then put the call on speaker so Steven could hear.

". . . United States Drug Enforcement Administration,"

the female voice said. "Office of the Director." A moment later a male voice came on the line. "Director Turcott."

Eva grinned. "Daddy?"

"Eva?"

"I know it's been a long time, Dad." She sniffed. "But I have someone here who wants to talk to you . . ."

Pete Quinn leaned back in his seat.

"We best not tell your mother about what went on here," he said.

"No doubt," Jericho chuckled. "You got some moves, old man."

"An aching back and two delinquent sons is what I got," Pete said. He took a deep breath and looked at Jericho with a jaundiced eye.

"Tell me again what it is you do for a living."

Connect with U s

Visit us online at
KensingtonBooks.com
to read more from your favorite authors, see books
by series, view reading group guides, and more.

Join us on social media

for sneak peeks, chances to win books and prize packs,
and to share your thoughts with other readers.

facebook.com/kensingtonpublishing
twitter.com/kensingtonbooks

Tell us what you think!

To share your thoughts, submit a review,
or sign up for our eNewsletters, please visit:
KensingtonBooks.com/TellUs.